Six Months with Buddha

www.mascotbooks.com

Six Months with Buddha: A Novel of Buddhist Wisdom

For more information, please contact:
Mascot Books, an imprint of Amplify Publishing Group
620 Herndon Parkway, Suite 320
Herndon, VA 20170
info@mascotbooks.com

Library of Congress Control Number: 2022903859

CPSIA Code: PRV0422A

ISBN-13: 978-1-64543-873-1

Printed in the United States

I dedicate this book
To the Buddha, who is
Majestic like the Himalayas,
Pure like the lotus freshly bloomed in the morning,
Noblest of all, including gods and devas, and
One who attained the mind of pure essence like space.

SIX MONTHS *with* BUDDHA

A NOVEL OF BUDDHIST WISDOM

Jeong-bin Kim

TRANSLATED FROM KOREAN BY OOGHEE JIN

MASCOT
BOOKS

Contents

NOTES FROM THE AUTHOR

1. Because the stories in this book take place in the time of the Buddha, the names of people and villages are mostly rendered in Pali (Pāli), with diacritical marks deleted for the enhanced readability of the general public not familiar with the Pali language.

2. A few exceptions to this principle are applied to some words for which most people already know the Sanskrit term. They are: arhat, arhatship, nirvana, and parinirvana. However, in the case of the term sutra, the names of sutras are rendered using the term sutta, as in the example of the Culamalunkyaputta Sutta.

3. The Buddha refers to Shakyamuni Buddha.

4. Beings who inhabit the various levels of the Buddhist heavens are referred to as either heavenly beings or devas.

THE
Relationships
OF THE
Major Characters

PRESENT LIFE (0)

RAJA
HEAVENLY MAN, SIRIMA'S HUSBAND

SIRIMA
HEAVENLY WOMAN, RAJA'S WIFE

The two descend to the earth from the Tavatimsa
Heaven, become special disciples of the Buddha, and
for six months they learn Buddhadhamma while
witnessing many events

PREVIOUS LIFE (-1)

RAJA
YOUTH TRUTH-SEEKER

Travels to meet the Buddha

SANU
MALE DISCIPLE OF THE BUDDHA

Arouses lust for Sirima, the
courtesan (different from Sirima,
the heavenly being)

THE LIFE BEFORE THE
PERVIOUS ONE (-2)

YASOJA
DAUGHTER OF KULA & PUNNA

Raped by her father, Kula

THE BUDDHA

Makes a six-month journey to predict Binggisa's future attainment of Buddhahood

UPPALAVANNA

THE BUDDHA'S BHIKKHUNI DISCIPLE, TEACHER OF AYUTHA

SARIPUTTA

THE BUDDHA'S BHIKKHU DISCIPLE, TEACHER OF BHADDIYA

Makes a journey with Bhaddiya, and joins the Buddha

PRESENT LIFE (0)

AYUTHA

BHADDIYA'S WIFE, THE QUEEN CONSORT

Falls in love with Binggisa, and thus, betrays Bhaddiya
→Disciple of Uppala-vanna
→Enlightenment (3rd stage), walks the path of bodhisattva
→Reborn in a heaven (next life = 1)
→Reconciliation with Bhaddiya
→Enlightenment (last stage)
→Parinirvana (death)

BHADDIYA

AYUTHA'S HUSBAND, THE KING

Becomes a bhikkhu after being betrayed by the two
→Disciple of the Buddha & Sariputta
→Enlightenment (last stage = arhat)
→Travels with Sariputta
→Reconciliation with Ayutha
→Reconciliation with Binggisa

BINGGISA

ART TEACHER OF BHADDIYA & AYUTHA

Falls in love with Ayutha, and thus, betrays Bhaddiya
→Returns to the Huruva Order, his childhood faith
→Becomes a powerful Huruva missionary
→Conversion after the religious war
→Continues Ayutha's bodhisattva deeds
→The Buddha's prediction of Binggisa's future attainment of Buddhahood
→Reconciliation with Bhaddiya

ASATHA

JATU'S WIFE

→Loves Jatu
→Pities Dhammadinna
= Works as karma for the next life (0)

JATU

ASATHA'S HUSBAND, GENERAL

→Loves Asatha
→Dies without knowing the sacrifice of Dhammadinna

DHAMMADINNA

OFFICER UNDER JATU

→Sacrifices himself for Jatu & Asatha
→Loves Asatha
= Works as karma for the next life (0)

PREVIOUS LIFE (-1)

FOREWORD

L oftiness and beauty have been the two beams of light that have guided me.

Loftiness as demonstrated by Confucius who soars as high as the mountains, by the Buddha who is as magnificent as the Himalayas, by Jesus Christ who is as pure as the ripples on the Sea of Galilee or a lily swaying in the breeze, and by Socrates whose far-sighted vision is tempered by humor.

And beauty? Should I enumerate each and every one? I can't, because all things in the world are beautiful. Into each new apple-hued morning I awoke between youth and middle age, I filled with positive thoughts, and they were beautiful; even now as an elderly man, life is full of beauty.

Of course, the river of life sometimes becomes muddy, and at other times it slices harshly into my bones and flesh. Fortunately, I was always guided by lofty thoughts that made the muddy water clear again, and with beauty which soothed my aching bones and flesh. Heaven is only as far away as you think it is. I am in the heaven of "here and now" several times a day.

Like Ernest, the protagonist in Nathaniel Hawthorne's *The Great Stone Face*, I have looked up to the sublime world all my life and dreamed of beautiful rainbows. In the end, Ernest becomes a virtuous man, whose face resembles a rock formation all the locals call the "Great Stone Face." But what about me? In this respect, I feel ashamed that I cannot measure up to the saints, sages, and literary giants.

Nevertheless, man is supposed to dream. As such, I have dreamed long of creating my own work integrating loftiness and beauty, and at last it has come to pass. From the seeds of my dreams, leaves and flowers have sprouted, and the fruit titled *Six Months with Buddha* has appeared.

It is not mine to judge what kind of fragrance will come from my stories-dreams-flowers, or what taste it will have. Regardless, I have been sufficiently rewarded from the process of writing itself. To create something is to give something to the world that did not exist before. To an author and artist, that is sufficient satisfaction.

March 1, 2022
Jeong-bin Kim
from Goyang-si, Gyeonggi-do,
Republic of Korea (South Korea)

PROLOGUE
Binggisa the Minstrel

It was when Shakyamuni Buddha (a sage from the Shakya Clan, also referred to as the Sun Clan) was in this world that a man was walking in an isolated desert. Behind him were steep peaks of the snow-capped Hindu Kush Mountains and the blue sky far in the distance overlooking this marvelous masterpiece of nature. He was around thirty years old. Upon a closer look, however, he appeared almost seventy. His face eluded an estimation of age.

After a while, a shepherd with a red and black turban appeared from behind the man along with several black and white goats; all of them caught up with the slow-footed man. A dry draft blew from the northwest and flipped the shepherd's turban off his head. Grumbling to himself, the shepherd ran after the turban, picked it up, and put it back on his head.

The man wore a turban too; it was in the shape of a coiled cobra. Although his turban had not been carried away by the wind, it was not in good shape. Covered thick with sand dust, it was hard to believe the turban was made of fabric—he had walked the desert for several days; the sand had covered it completely.

Looking exhausted, he plopped down onto the ground with a thud. While he was immersed in thought, the shepherd disappeared over the sand dune, which made the man the only human being in the vast space.

Not far away from him, the man discovered a small prickly pear. He slowly walked toward it and squatted to inspect it. He pulled out a water bottle from his waist belt and opened it, dug the soil around the prickly pear so the water could collect easily, then poured water from his bottle. The arid desert soil soaked the water up in a flash.

His insteps, revealed from his worn-out shoes, were cracked like the soil from a rice paddy in a drought spell. The skin on his face was dried up like the handful of thickets lying low around him. However, he had at least one moist spot—his left eye. The eye had lost its vision and was covered with a white patch. His pupil was radiating a mysterious energy.

That energy was distant and pure at the same time. It was as beautiful as it was distant, and sad as it was pure. In that way, the energy was like the snow-capped, steep peaks of the Hindu Kush, which the desert chose as its backdrop. Or it was the white clouds of the sky above the steep peaks.

He poured the rest of the water remaining in the bottle onto the prickly pear. As if to repay his kindness, the cactus grew straight up to his height. He raised himself from the squatted posture.

"Oh!" The exclamation slipped from his mouth.

Soon, an impromptu poem was uttered from his lips.

> Your prickling thorns
> Return to my eyes
> As a sigh of a handful of sands.

> Reckless love,
> Tears shed by stray passion,
> Daughters of sorrow.

> Fate! Stab ruthlessly!

Beyond the grove of swords,
Rising up on the tune of lute,

I walk on the desert
Yearning for the flower of obscure dreams.

Upon reciting the poem, he began to sing an impromptu song using the poem as the lyrics. His singing voice traveled far to reach the Hindu Kush, which looked like starched white cotton clothes crumpled in angled lines, which then returned in elegant purity like echoes that rang the valley dense with needle-leaf trees.

The man's attention turned to the prickly pear again. On a stem of the prickly pear, a tiny yellow flower bud had sprouted. He gazed at the flower bud and gently closed his right eye.

The flower bud grew, little by little, in his inner eye, beyond his physical eye, and soon became a full-grown flower about the size of a baby fist. Then, the yellow flower from the prickly pear embodied his ardent heart. The flower began to transform into a beautiful woman.

The woman, who came into his mind, had light brown eyes and translucent complexion like ice; she had the grace that belied her being a human. She never turned her eyes to any of those men who looked at her with admiration, but only dreamed of an ideal of distant stars. Thus, she had a lofty elegance that would not allow any man to claim her as his, no matter how high a stature he had.

"Oh, Ayutha!" The man cried. "Ayutha! Where are you now?"

However, despite the man's desperate call, the woman did not answer. She only gazed at him softly with remorseful, teary eyes.

"I want to see you, to death! And I'd like to apologize to you with all my life." The man's voice was sad and earnest. "Oh, Ayutha! I beg you to tell me where you are."

With eyes closed, the man extended his hands toward the woman in vain. Then the woman's figure became hazy and was soon buried under the fog that rushed in like a flood.

The fog, which had been white, began to turn pale pink. From the corner of this pale pink fog, a yellow-brown mass of light formed and grew in size. The pale pink fog and yellow-brown mass of light intertwined. They looked like a man and a woman dancing in each other's arms or a couple making an impassioned physical love.

Then the two colors faded away. From the thick mass of white fog, what seemed like a human figure arose, which soon took a distinct form. He was Sakka, the king of the Tavatimsa Heaven,[1] who was wearing a jeweled crown and a jewel garland.

The moment the figure became visible as Sakka, the man opened his eye and found that Sakka was standing stately in front of him. The remorseful attitude the man had a while ago quickly dissipated. In a dignified manner like that of an elephant, the man straightened up his shoulders and stuck out his chest.

Sakka approached the man and said with his palms joined together, "Honorable practitioner! Greetings!"

"Who are you that appeared in such dignified manner before me?" the man asked.

"I am Sakka, the king of the Tavatimsa Heaven."

"That is what I thought. But deva! What brought you to appear before me?"

"Practitioner Binggisa!" Sakka continued. "There is a throne made of ruby in my Vejayanta Palace. The throne becomes hot if there is a practitioner I must help.

"A few minutes ago, I was sitting on the throne, conversing with a heavenly being. I felt the seat turning hot, and I looked down at the world with my heavenly eyes. I discovered that you were searching for Ayutha, and your mind was exhausted. I came down to you right away to give you a hand."

"You are right," Binggisa admitted. "For three years, I have

---

1 Buddhism classifies the physical world into the Desire Realm, the Form Realm, and the Formless Realm. The Tavatimsa Heaven, where one enjoys pleasure, is the second heaven of the Desire Realm. Sakka is the head of the Sudamma Council, a community of thirty-three heavenly kings, including himself. Sakka is an ardent guardian of Buddhism.

searched all over the continent, the area of human existence, looking for my dear old friend. But I had no idea of her whereabouts until now—she is the quintessence of my poems, the soul of my music, the corolla of my mind, and the gorge of my remorse. My footsteps have lingered, passed, crossed, and wandered countless villages and cities, brooks and rivers, and hills and mountains, but still I haven't found her.

"Heavenly king! I implore you to help me. With your divine power you could easily discover if my woman is still alive who constantly haunts me before my undamaged eye, who is stuck as a corn in my other eye—which cannot receive light—who was the beginning and should be the end of all procedures wherein a yearning bears estrangement, the estrangement bears ignorance, the ignorance bears evil deeds, and the evil deeds bear repentance.

"If she is alive, you would know where she is and what she is doing. Dear heavenly king! Please inform me about her."

"Oh!" Sakka, who was well aware of their painful past affairs, moaned in a low voice. Binggisa also closed his mouth and kept silent while recollecting the deeds he committed with Ayutha.

After a moment Binggisa said, "Heavenly king! My past actions to stab the heart-eye of King Bhaddiya,[2] and my actions to steal the body and heart of Ayutha, who was the most cherished woman as well as the dearest friend to the king, should return to me deservedly as a stabbing to my body-eye, and as sands of lamentation to be sprinkled to my mind-eye. I was not aware before, but now I know clearly.

"Oh, how beautiful a darkness it was! And how the darkness continued to exist as serious evil, sacred evil, and sublime evil! Heavenly king, the greatest evil of the world is the one committed by the holy mind or religious conviction, and I am one of those sentient beings suffering from afflictions, who accrued heavy negative karma by killing tens of thousands people.

---

2 Bhaddiya Kaligodhaputta: The Buddha's younger cousin who was the son of Kalighoda, Buddha's uncle. Bhaddiya later became a bhikkhu. Some sutras record him as a king while he was in the secular world. In this book, some descriptions of Bhaddiya correspond to these sutras, while others don't.

11

"That pushed me to think of meeting Ayutha to escape from the dark and damp muddy field of karma. Now, by adding the morning glow of the rising sun to my karmic ties of beautiful darkness with her, I want to let go of the darkness and leave only the rosy beauty behind. Then I want to visit King Bhaddiya with her, and wash the pain embedded in his heart like countless cactus thorns with our tears of repentance.

"Oh . . . And I must go further from there. I mean where tears of repentance well up should also be where bright splendor begins to bloom. Heavenly king! At that time, I decided to dedicate my life to countless people suffering from broken hearts, until they are filled with love, compassion, joy, and fruitfulness like a full lake, until their hearts flow like rivers, blow like winds, and become boundless like vast space."

As he poured out his pledges, Binggisa's face gradually changed. Desperate remorse began to dissipate from his face like ice thawed in spring breeze, and his eyes began to take an atmosphere of affirmation, which eventually integrated with his firm determination, and filled his whole body with strong and vibrant energy.

Filled with admiration, Sakka broke into a bright smile all over his face and said politely, "I am happy to give you this news, honorable practitioner! Ayutha is alive. I hope you do not exhaust in the middle and continue your journey in search of her."

"If she is alive, dear heavenly king, where is she?" asked Binggisa.

"According to the law of Heaven, I am prohibited to tell you that," said Sakka.

Binggisa nodded his head. "Great! That is enough for me—the news that she is still alive."

Saying that with an upbeat voice, Binggisa expressed his gratitude to the heavenly king by joining his palms in front of his chest.

Looking at Binggisa, who regained his vibrant energy, Sakka said, "Well, I wish you a pleasant and peaceful journey! I wish you to meet her and end your karmic ties in nobility! I wish your great vows to be realized!"

Listening to these blessings from the king of the Tavatimsa Heaven, Binggisa closed his single remaining eye. After a moment, Binggisa opened his eye and said ferociously, "Oh, King Sakka! I will arouse my good intentions again and continue my journey in search of her. I will definitely find her! And then I will transform my past karmic associations with her, which had been thickly covered with the cactus thorns of hers and mine into those full of flowers and fragrance."

"Sadhu! Sadhu! Sadhu!"[3] Sakka said with an admiration for Binggisa's determination.

"Sadhu! Sadhu! Sadhu!" Binggisa answered.

Soon Sakka began to rise up into the air toward the heaven he ruled. Binggisa resumed his journey and walked the desert with energetic strides.

---

3 A Pali term meaning "Excellent!" or "How good!" that is often used to praise the Buddha, the Buddhadhamma, good deeds, and one who performed good deeds.

CHAPTER 1
Raja and Sirima, Residents of Tavatimsa Heaven

Five years have passed since then, and a heavenly man named Raja was born on the Tavatimsa Heaven, the heaven of pleasure. When a sentient being receives a life of a human being, they are born through the womb of the mother. However, when a sentient being receives a life of a heavenly being, they are not born through the womb, but they appear suddenly on the body of the mother or on the bed used by the parents, in the shape of a twenty-year-old man for a man and a sixteen-year-old woman for a woman. And when a heavenly being is born, luxurious houses and various other objects of pleasure—befitting his or her virtues—appear at the same time.

As Raja was born on the Tavatimsa Heaven, his parents brought him to Vejayanta Palace of King Sakka of the Tavatimsa Heaven. His parents conversed on diverse topics with the Great Deva Mita who was in charge of the education of heavenly beings newly born on the Tavatimsa Heaven. However, as the heavenly beings are made to know the laws of the heaven by themselves, without having to go through education, there was not much to do for Mita.

Save a small number of heavenly beings who are exceptional, for each heavenly being born on the Tavatimsa Heaven a suitable spouse is supposed to be born as well. Being aware of this, Raja's parents were curious about which heavenly woman was born as his spouse. Their curiosity didn't last long. When his parents were conversing with Mita, the heavenly woman Sirima, born as Raja's spouse, came there guided by her parents.

"Oh!" The moment Raja saw her, giving a shy smile at him, a sound of exclamation came out unnoticed from his mouth.

Not only from Raja's mouth came the sounds of exclamation. For Mita as well as Raja's parents—who lived in the Tavatimsa Heaven and taught numerous heavenly men and women for seventy thousand years or more by the measure of time of the human world—the beauty of Sirima was surprisingly outstanding. The moment Raja first saw Sirima, he fell deeply for her. Sirima also fell in love with Raja at first sight.

Missing and yearning more and more even when they are seeing each other before their eyes—the first encountered couple of heavenly man and woman watched each other with profound affection aroused in their hearts, at the sight of which their parents smiled. However, for the heavenly parents who thought of neither giving birth nor troubling themselves of raising children, their attachment to their children was not so deep.

After a while, when Mita was pairing up the couple by putting rings made of blue jade and white jade on the fingers of Raja and Sirima respectively, the parents of the bride and groom watched the wedding with a neutral expression that things were just moving on the path that they were supposed to.

Mita declared Raja and Sirima a husband and wife, and briefly explained to the two heavenly beings how the heavenly world—consisting of twenty-six levels—operated, the essence of which being that the entire heavenly world reflected the minds of their inhabitants.

Therefore, on the Tavatimsa Heaven, many things were realized by simply making up one's mind. Having said that, Mita told Raja and Sirima to close their eyes, concentrate, and bring to the mind fifty maids who would attend to each of them. The moment Raja did so, fifty heavenly maids suddenly appeared beside Raja. Sirima too had fifty maids manifest by the same method.

After a while, the two heavenly beings returned to Raja's abode after saying goodbye to their parents. Upon arrival at the abode, the heavenly maids who had escorted the two heavenly beings changed the clothes of the couple to ones that were much thinner and lighter than the ones they had been wearing; they also hung necklaces decorated with dozens of gemstones around their necks.

Then, they served the two heavenly beings some fragrant food of the Tavatimsa Heaven. Consisting of the essence of nutrients, the heavenly food was light as air. As such, the two heavenly beings did not eat it with their mouth but whiffed it through their nose.

Raja and Sirima took enough heavenly foods and felt relaxed. Then, curiosity arose in Raja regarding the Rapture Grove, which he had heard about from Mita a while ago. He thought, *Is there such a place indeed? A more pleasurable place than the Tavatimsa Heaven, where it appears that there could be no more pleasures beyond the pleasures enjoyable there?*

Sirima soon noticed Raja's thought. The two heavenly beings exchanged a glance, which could only be understood between lovers. After a while, Raja and Sirima, surrounded by their maids, went out for a walk to the Rapture Grove.

Upon entering the Rapture Grove, they submerged into a vague ecstatic state. While hundreds of thousands of birds with red and yellow wings were flying in the sky where double rainbows were rising in pairs, a distant peal of a bell was heard in waves, making a *woowoong, woowoong* sound. "Right, that sound is from a temple bell rung for the sentient beings in hells to forget their pains for a moment," Raja murmured quietly.

Heavenly winds were blowing through the mango trees with their branches drooping down and through the sandalwood emitting delicate fragrance. Again, a draft of wind blew and with the draft came the fragrance of the lotus and the jasmine tickling the tip of the nose.

Sirima cast a glance back at Raja and danced away into the forest. As Raja ran after her, the hide-and-seek began. However, not long after, Sirima stopped running and, gladly, became the prisoner of Raja. With a look as if to say, "I am all yours, from head to toe." Sirima knelt down and looked up at Raja.

Raja too knelt down before her, the unbelievably endearing woman, and embraced her tight in his arms. However, he soon freed his arms, broke her away from him, and looked down at Sirima with a playful look. Then, he shook his head twice as a sign of refusal to Sirima, who was looking up at him with an expression entreating him to hug her again, and then he ran deeper into the forest.

Sirima and the one hundred maids followed him, but Raja evaded them, moving fast from tree to tree. The high-pitched voices unique to women filled his ears with a chortling sound, but they were not able to catch him.

Raja moved deeper and deeper into the center of the Rapture Grove, where the tagara flowers, with a color as gloriously crimson as blood, were in full bloom. The place was filled with layers of fragrance, as if the flowers had been brought by thousands of wagons and poured in.

Smelling the fragrance of the hundreds of thousands of tagara flowers, Raja's eyes were slowly closed. Like sticky honey water, his body became languid, and a memory of his previous life flashed unexpectedly in his head. The memory lasted only for a moment, but it felt very long as well. Like this, it appeared that in heavenly time, a long time seemed to remain for a moment but a dozens of years passed by within a second.

After a while, Sirima found Raja. She approached him and said while smiling,

"My dear king, here you are!" she exclaimed.

"I . . . For a moment . . ." said Raja, "I was recalling my previous life."

"Oh, really," said Sirima as she watched Raja quietly with eyes that aroused the protective instinct of a man. "Then, my dear husband, please tell me where you were born and what kind of life you lived in your previous life."

"I will do so," said Raja. "That would be good. Because to love each other means that we know more about each other, or that there are no or little secrets between us. So you also, after hearing my story, tell me about your previous life."

With Raja's remarks, a shade of sorrow—no, it is not sufficient to call it a sorrow—a shade of remorse, as a result of buildup of sorrow after sorrow, slid across Sirima's eyes. To suppress her emotion, she closed her lips tightly.

There was a silence for a while. Raja stared at his wife softly, and by then, realized the reason why his mind was leaning so irresistibly toward Sirima. That was it. It was regret from the previous life that existed in himself too, but was more deeply planted in Sirima. It was a sigh. It was a moan. It was a crying and a remorse in the end.

"My dear husband, as you may know . . ." said Sirima after a long while. "This place is not appropriate for me to tell my previous life. The Rapture Grove is a difficult place to recall painful thoughts or memories, and my previous life was not necessarily a happy one. So let us leave this place, and go back to our palace to talk."

"So we will do, my dear," said Raja and grasped Sirima's hands.

The two heavenly beings left the Rapture Grove and returned to their place. Their country named Raja–Sirima Heaven was on a square land with each side as big as one-tenth of a yojana (about seven miles). In the middle of their territory stood two large palaces side by side; they were indescribably splendid—built in white and red colors and decorated with various kinds of beautiful jewels.

Among the two palaces, the one prevailingly white was for Raja and the one prevailingly red was for Sirima. Though the two palaces were separated by some distance, they did not feel any difficulties in coming and going between the palaces. According to the laws of the heaven, one just needed to make up his or her mind to move from here to there, then it would happen instantly without any time gap.

The heavenly couple went to Sirima's red palace and sat facing each other on two chairs, which were made of amber and decorated with emeralds. Raja thought that the maids need not stay around while he and his wife talked. Therefore, as soon as he looked at the maids with that thought, the maids who attended them disappeared the way smoke vanished.

Sirima said to Raja, "Now, my dear husband, please tell me where, and what kind of life you lived in your previous life."

As he spoke, Sirima watched Raja with her pure, clear eyes.

CHAPTER 2
Raja in His Previous Life

I n his previous life, Raja was the only son of a commoner. Although born a commoner, he had led a life of relative affluence since infancy. However, the year he turned six, the Hori, the tribe to which Raja belonged, was annihilated by their arch enemy, the Muriya.

Luckily, Raja's family survived when Raja's father took his wife, Raja, and his mother to safety, deep into a small village in the woods. Afterward, Raja's father worked hard to accrue wealth.

But misfortune found Raja once again. The year he turned sixteen, his grandmother passed away, and his mother died three nights later. But tragedy did not stop there. Three months later, Raja's father also died after developing a high fever.

As a great fear took over him, Raja asked himself: *Why must those who are born also face death?*

Since I came to this village with my family at the young age of six, I have assisted my father in herding our sheep. After a few years of this, I came to notice a difference between these sheep and myself. Sheep always look downward but never up. They occasionally raise their heads to look straight ahead, because that is the only way to spot other sheep, wolves, or their master. But they never look upward or behind. Then, what about me? Am I not just like the sheep herd, only following my father's orders? Raja thought.

Before his family all died, Raja had once looked up toward the sky while pondering these thoughts. There was his father, who was looking down at him and the whole herd of the sheep.

That's all I am! Just a sheep of my father! If sheep are on the grass, I am above sheep, and my father is above me, then perhaps someone or something exists who is much higher than my father, Raja thought.

With this question in mind, he thought even more deeply. Raja realized that numerous leaders from the village were above his father. And above them, the village headman. And above him was an elderly man named Suru, the wisest man in the village.

When the questions on death arose, Raja first sought out the village leaders to ask their opinions about death, but they couldn't answer him. They all thought he was just asking silly questions in the shock from losing all his family in such short time. No one bothered to take this young sixteen-year-old's questions seriously.

Raja then went to the village head to ask him about death. Even this man, who prided himself on knowing so many things, did not have an answer for Raja. He knew much about how to dispose of a corpse and other such matters, but that was not what Raja was after. Raja wanted to know about the meaning of death for himself, not for somebody else. He had a sense that death was approaching him closer by the hour, and this urgency to understand death stirred him most deeply.

Finally, Raja went to see the elder Suru, but he first had to receive permission from Suru's family. Suru's family would not allow Raja any time to see Suru. Raja pleaded and even offered them nineteen of his twenty sheep just to meet with Suru. Pretending they could no longer resist his plea, though secretly elated by his offer, the family escorted Raja into the elder's room.

Raja was astounded at the scene before him. Suru already seemed to be at death's door, and his countenance was truly appalling. Suru was lying in bed and drooling with his mouth half open. He was flailing his arms in an apparent vain effort to fight off some illusion, or so it appeared to Raja. However, Suru's arms soon went limp and fell.

On the face of this poor old man were ugly liver spots and innumerable deep wrinkles. At some time in the past, his eyes probably shone brightly with the vigor of youth, but they were now filled with a sticky yellow muck and half-closed. The old man stared vacantly into nothingness. Tears streamed down Suru's face, and in the next instant, the elder breathed his last breath. His eyes suddenly opened wide as though in surprise and then rolled back into his head; he was gone.

Raja had to return home empty handed, but he felt no resentment, even when Suru's son followed him home to collect the promised nineteen sheep. Instead, Raja felt thankful because the incident had brought him a deeper understanding of death and given him greater motivation to strive further to understand the meaning of life. With the three hundred rupees he got from selling his last sheep, and with the last of his inheritance, Raja left the village that very night.

With no particular destination in mind, Raja simply kept on walking. He scrounged whatever food he could find and stopped to rest wherever he wanted. Raja paid little attention to his ragged clothes, his rain-soaked body, or his physical exhaustion. He did his best to stay mentally alert.

He went wherever his feet took him and stopped every chance he got to ask the question to anyone who would listen.

"Do you know anything about death?"

Most people simply shook their heads, but that didn't stop Raja from asking further. "Then, do you know anyone who can tell me the meaning of life?"

But no one could answer Raja's desperate questions. Then one day, a little girl told Raja that the Buddha was staying in the neighboring town of Yaku.

"The Buddha always speaks of death, but he also speaks of life," she said.

The girl poured Raja a glass of milk. Savoring the milk, Raja gave her his last seven paise and hurried toward Yaku.

After some time, Raja went around a bend in the mountain road and saw a man walking ahead of him who was swaying side to side as though he was about to collapse.

Raja caught up to him and asked, "Dear sir, do you need my help?"

When the old man stopped and stared back at him, Raja was deeply stirred by the pureness in his eyes. The old man said, "Young man, you have very kind eyes."

"That's exactly what I was thinking about you. Sir, your eyes sparkle like a snow-capped mountain or the clear sky that stretches far beyond such a mountain."

"A snow-capped mountain!" With that exclamation the old man asked with deep emotion, "Have you actually seen a snow-capped mountain?"

"Sir, I have glimpsed a few here and there while I was traveling, but I have not yet seen the entire mountain. Just glimpsing a part of such a mountain gives me a great sense of inspiration that I can't describe with words," shared Raja.

"I see," the old man responded. "So, you have seen such mountains. But dear boy, the great mountain I am searching for is of a different kind."

Saying that, the old man gave a serene smile.

Raja then asked, "What is this great mountain of a different kind you are referring to?"

"Will you try and guess? I am looking for he who is much loftier, purer, and nobler than even the greatest snow-capped mountain," said the old man.

"That means," continued Raja, "the great snow-capped mountain you search for is most definitely the Buddha!"

"That's right! You are absolutely right!" said the old man with a beaming smile. He then pointed toward a patch of grass. Raja supported him as they both walked down to sit on the grass.

After catching his breath, the old man said, "My name is Chuchu. What is yours?"

"I am Raja."

"Raja, where are you headed?"

"I am also on my way to Yaku to see the Buddha. There is no doubt that seeing the Buddha will be a great honor, but what made you embark on this pilgrimage with such a frail body?"

"Boy, you speak as if people in poor health can't seek the path of truth." The old man was gasping for breath, but after a moment, he continued speaking, slowly this time with pauses in between.

"Hey little boy, my young friend with such pure eyes, I may be old as you say . . . and death may fall upon me soon enough . . . but . . . you must understand . . . my journey . . ." He was barely catching his breath. ". . . is much easier than the journey through the eternal cycle of birth, death, and rebirth, that is, samsara."[4]

Genuine regret could be felt in the old man's words and in his facial expression, as though he was carrying the burden of hundreds of past lives all at once, and it deeply affected Raja. Soon, Raja found himself removing the old man's sandals, and then also massaging his feet. Perhaps simply from exhaustion or from the relaxing massage, the old man, Chuchu, calmly dozed off on the very spot where he sat.

Staring down at the old man, who even gasped for air in his sleep, Raja sensed that he didn't have much longer to live.

Raja thought, I may have other opportunities to meet the Buddha, but this old man may not. That is even more of a reason why I should help him get to Yaku.

Raja waited until the old man woke up, and then they walked toward Yaku together, Raja carrying the old man on his back. It was

---

4 Samsara: The endless karmic cycle of existence where sentient beings die and then are reborn into either wholesome or unwholesome spheres of existence, according to their past actions. Sentient beings are either reborn into one of the four spheres of suffering (hell, hungry ghosts, animals, or asuras) or one of the two spheres of happiness (as humans or devas).

hard, and Raja collapsed after passing over a hill. However, Raja refused to give up. Having rested for a moment, Raja mustered all his energy and continued on. By the time they passed through another hill, the old man became unconscious, and again, Raja laid him down and massaged his feet for some time.

When the old man came around, Raja picked him up again and continued on. Raja was feeling more and more exhausted. His legs staggered beneath him. Several times he felt his consciousness was slipping away. And, next moment, he felt something plop.

When Raja regained consciousness, he found himself lying at the bottom of a cliff with the old man beside him. *Is this how it will end?* he wondered. Fear engulfed him, but he could not even lift a finger.

Excruciating pain rushed in and every bone ached. In spite of the pain, Raja felt extremely lucky to still inhabit his body. The truth of the matter is that having a body was the reason for his happiness as well as for his suffering.

Then, what about the heart? Surely the heart is the same. The heart is responsible for desire, and desire ultimately leads to frustration, regret, and loneliness. But then a voice came to him from deep within:

"But that may not be totally true. There may be a path where life doesn't lead to frustration, regret, and loneliness."

And, right at that moment, strangely enough, his pain disappeared like a receding tide. *How strange!* he thought.

That's right. Raja thought. That's what heart does. It can transform pain into something that is not pain.

With this thought in mind, Raja stared into the empty space that stretched out before him. That's when he saw it, a magnificent peak covered with snow, sparkling in peaceful tranquility—a massive glistening peak that seemed to stretch into infinity.

Oh, a snow-capped mountain! Raja fixed his piercing gaze on that which is supreme, the loftiest, the most noble, and the most majestic of all. Raja then pondered once again.

There was grass. There were sheep. There was myself. There was my father. There were the village elders. There was the village head. And there was the old man Suru.

From his father up to the old man Suru, Raja saw no difference. They may be at higher level than sheep, but none of them could answer his questions about life and death. Thus, ultimately, there were no essential differences between them.

But then there was the elder Chuchu, who seemed to stand apart from them all. He had a higher vision. Much higher! Chuchu sought the most noble, the most sacred, and the most majestic. Chuchu had a mind that sought the Truth.

Then, Chuchu must be a bird, unlike the men, from his father up to the old man Suru, who were like animals, bound to the ground. Chuchu was a fantastic soaring eagle that flew as high as he could. How high could Chuchu fly? Nobody knew. However, one thing was certain. Even birds had different levels or dimensions.

Small sparrows are usually found near houses, whereas some wild birds only live in the forest. Then there are eagles who soar to great heights, the most majestic of all birds.

Oh, how I wish to be an eagle that can pierce the clouds and fly up toward the end of the universe!

Raja's pain rushed in again, blinding his body and mind. But in spite of his plight, Raja desperately tried to regain his clear consciousness and shouted as such in his mind with great yearning. That was when Raja heard a sound close to his ear. Was he imagining it? But surely he had heard a man's voice.

"Sleep . . . less . . ." It was Chuchu, speaking through a haze, as if in a dream. Even in his broken state, Chuchu was subconsciously reciting a verse from memory.

This is surely a verse of the Buddha! Raja thought. Raja recognized it right away. Though it was difficult in such extreme pain, Raja made out Chuchu's words:

Long is the night for the sleepless;

Long is one yojana[5] for the weary traveler;

Long is samsara for the deluded,

Who know not the true Dhamma."

Suddenly, Raja felt as light as a feather and thought, *That's right. Everyone dies, including myself.*

With this thought in mind, Raja welcomed death without any trace of hatred.

And then, in an instant, Raja died and was reborn in the Tavatimsa Heaven.

---

5 Yojana: an ancient Vedic measure of distance equal to about 1 mile.

CHAPTER 3

Sirima in Her Previous Life
and Her Life before the
Previous One

hile Raja was telling about his previous life, Sirima was immersed in his story, rejoicing at times and sighing at other times as the story evolved. Raja said lastly that at the moment of death his mind was very light, and that this could be the reason why he was reborn in the Tavatimsa Heaven. After hearing all this, Sirima rejoiced once again with her eyes gleaming with overflowing charms.

"Looking at your eyes that watch me," Raja continued, "my heart beats wildly."

With a flushed face, looking straight into Raja's eyes, Sirima said, "Isn't it strange enough? We met not long ago, but I don't know why my heart is leaning toward you like this. Well may I ask a favor to my dear?"

"Whatever you wish," Raja replied, accepting Sirima's request.

"Please give me a hug. Yeah? Now, right this instant!" with a yearning look in her eyes like a deer's.

"That's what I wanted to hear," said Raja.

Raja held her tightly in his arms. Sirima panted for breath in the arms of her lover, like a small chickling.

After a while, Raja freed his arms that had been embracing his wife and scanned her face slowly. For Raja, the face of Sirima looked cuter, more beautiful, and much lovelier than any other woman in the human world.

However, at the next moment, Raja noticed that Sirima was more than a sweet and lovely woman. In Sirima's beauty, there was a subtle and delicate sensation that could be felt from a very thin flower petal, which could likely be injured even by the slight touch; Raja saw this suddenly.

What would I do . . . What would I do . . . What would I do with this mind of mine that wants to surrender whatever in my possession for her, and seems ready to do whatever in my means to protect her from being hurt? With such thoughts, a dim light of sorrow seeped into Raja's love for his wife.

Staring at such Raja, Sirima said, "My dear husband, now let me tell you about my previous life."

In the previous life, Sirima was born as the only son of a brahmin living in Rajagaha, the capital city of the Magadha Kingdom, and his name was Sanu in that life.

When he was young, Sanu was greatly inspired to hear the discourses of the Buddha. He thus cleared up his secular affairs, left home, and became a Buddhist monk. However, the Buddha, who was unable to teach so many disciples personally, sent him to Elder Moggallana, who was recognized as one of the two foremost disciples of the Buddha, together with Elder Sariputta.

But the progress in the practice cannot be guaranteed solely by the fact that one is taught by a great teacher. Though the Buddha once taught, "Good spiritual friends are 'the whole' of the path to the Truth," the whole that can be given by spiritual friends is no more than assisting of others, thus it cannot be said the whole in the sense that the practitioner helps himself or herself.

In other words, consummating the practice is not through others but through oneself. Being well aware of this, Sanu threw his heart and soul into the practice. He strived and strived. As a result, he was able to attain a little progress in his practice.

However, the progress soon stalled. Though he could make a little progress, he could not attain enlightenment, which was the ultimate goal of the practice. So, he mustered up his strength and strived once again. He was a born a sleepyhead, but whenever sleep came upon him, he poked his arms and legs with a sharp stick, and after some time, his body was covered with scars and wounds. Nevertheless, no further progress in the practice was attained.

Then, his mind began to be weakened slowly. Utterance of sighs, feelings of emptiness and helplessness, and tears. *Is my limit up to here only?* Thought Sanu. At last, his passion for the practice started to fail slowly.

And slowly, laziness sprang up and began to grow in his mind. After some time, the laziness changed into a sense of shame in himself. The thought of unworthiness swelled up day by day. Eventually he completely stopped his practice and only consumed in the bread of idleness.

He was lost deep in thought. *Why did I leave the family and wealth that others cherish so dearly to become a monk? And why did I get my head shaved, removing all the hair secular people would grow, and wear these yellow monastic robes that ordinary people would not like to wear?*

He pondered again.

Alright, let's forget what already happened in the past. But why do I, who has failed to achieve the goal of enlightenment and thinks that it is not likely to be achieved even in the future, still believe that I must not return to my secular home?

Sanu could not understand those two minds that co-existed within; one that wished to return to his secular home, and the other not to do so. However, he thought he would leave the understanding of the minds for the future, and for now, he should give the practice one more try.

He again stoked the passion for the practice. For months, he practiced vigorously thinking that he might as well die while practicing. Nonetheless, there was still no further progress made in the practice.

So, Sanu cried, crouching at a corner of the temple that was not visible by others. After tears were shed, his mind was refreshed.

It was at that moment that a powerful and strange force shrouded Sanu, who sat absent-mindedly. The force was as soft as the wind, but at the same time it was irresistibly powerful.

Sanu noticed instantly that the force came from his teacher. Sanu, thanks to the supernatural power of Elder Moggallana, who was known as the best in sagely powers,[6] had a glimpse of the most important period in his previous life, within a very short time of three to four blinks of an eye.

"Oh!" Burning tears began to flow from his eyes.

In his previous life, Sanu was born as Yasoja, the only daughter of Kula, who was a man of gigantic frame and exceptionally strong, and his wife Punna, an outstanding beauty.

When Yasoja was young, she was so beautiful that any adults couldn't resist from approaching and looking happily at her childish smile and black eyes, or kissing her on her chubby cheeks.

Naturally, the love her parents felt for her had to be very deep. Particularly, Kula's love for his daughter was even stronger than his wife's. To express his love, he often rubbed his shaggy-bearded face wildly against his daughter's. Though, Yasoja, crying uncontrollably, turned her face, he didn't mind and continued his shower of love.

However, with time, Kula changed. Since he became an executioner who punished the felons of the state, he became violent. What's even worse was that he was drenched in alcohol almost every day.

---

6 Sagely powers (abhinna): Five sagely and miraculous powers obtained through practice. Namely, the power of divine vision, with which one can see things in distant places; the power of divine hearing, with which one can hear sounds in distant places; the power of reading the minds of others; the power of knowing the previous and future lifetimes; the power of unimpeded bodily action (with which one can fly in the sky, walk underground, and walk on water).

At times he came back home after drinking more alcohol than usual, and this meant that he had terminated the life of a person that day. On such days, he'd shout, "Yes, I am a filthy guy. I, Kula, yes, I am a dirty bastard! Dirtier than the guys whose breaths I stopped!" He then stared with bloodshot eyes at his wife, and said, "What? Do you also hate me, who lives with the money earned by stopping someone else's breath?"

Whenever this man—who was taller than others by about four heads and whose arms were as bulky as logs—shouted in a raucous voice, as if scratching his uvula harshly, and threw household goods and broke them, Punna crouched at a corner with Yasoja in her arms and shook uncontrollably from fright.

But what else could be done? When her husband, who had been creating havoc, entered the room and collapsed to sleep like a thrown mud lump, Punna put a blanket over his body, then walked to the kitchen. She boiled the piece of pork, which her husband had earned as the price for the execution, added one or two spices and drank it with her daughter; the soup mixed with tear drops that fell in.

Like that, Yasoja grew up to sixteen years old. She became more beautiful as she grew. As a result, there were many who wanted to take Yasoja as their daughter-in-law, and among them Kula accepted the proposal from the Devani family.

With no regard to her intention, she was going to be married to a stranger in a village she had never been to. She felt somewhat relieved, yet she was scared at the same time. That was because expectations grew in her that she could escape from the violence of her father.

The wedding date between Yasoja and the third son of the Devani family was set. Having heard the news—and learning that not only was the family rich but the bridegroom was also very handsome—Yasoja's mind swelled in expectation. The day she heard the news, she could not sleep because of her racing heart.

Deep in the night, Yasoja drifted into a light sleep. How long was she asleep? She woke up from sleep when she suddenly felt something heavy on her body. In the next moment, she was frightened, and she tried to raise herself up. However, a human hand appearing as big as the foot of an elephant instantly gagged her mouth. The owner of the man's hand was her father, Kula.

The other hand of Kula moved to the lower part of Yasoja's body. The lower part of her body became helplessly naked, and moments later the upper part of her body too was entirely exposed. At first, she struggled hard to free herself but soon fainted with a feeling of being suffocated to death.

Sometime after, she returned to herself and realized she was being raped by her father. Her lips were bitten violently, her breasts kneaded painfully, but the biggest pain was from the symbol of a man penetrating the private parts that were not ready to accept it. It was a warrior. A spear and a sword.

This way, the blossom of a pure virgin was helplessly stabbed, cut, and torn. *Ouch! Ouch!* The sound was forced out of her mouth. No, the sound didn't come. *What if mother will be awakened from sleep?* Yasoja shut her eyes, closed her lips tight, and confined the sound within her throat.

Though numbed by the tragedy, she turned her head to look at her mother lying next to her. Mother was asleep. No, she pretended to be asleep. Yes, Punna was not asleep. Yasoja heard the painful groan that escaped the mouth of her mother when she tried to suppress and endure the grief.

Yasoja knew it—her mother was awake, and she was accepting the whole situation, pretending that she was not aware. Thus, Yasoja's mind, which had already tumbled down, collapsed once more again.

Though her purity was being violently trampled by her father, her blame was directed to her mother, not to her father. She shouted in her mind, *Mother, until when will you live like this? Please, try to resist at least once! Just once, if not more!*

However, she was no different from her mother, in that they could not resist the violence.

After a while, catching his breath, Kula withdrew from Yasoja's body. He muttered something to himself and put on his clothes slowly piece by piece. Then he said, "You are too beautiful to give away to another guy."

After that day, the three people lived as if nothing had happened. Kula did not apologize, Punna pretended not to know, and Yasoja did not blame anyone.

However, their minds could never be the same again. The mind of young Yasoja, who had no one to turn to, turned dark and blue, and the mind of Punna, which had already been bruised from being exposed to the atrocities of her husband for a long time, festered.

However, Kula did not bother with the pains of the two women whom he must take care of, and he pushed them further into a deeper swamp.

One night, Kula, who returned home late sodden with drink, smirked at his wife.

"Hey, you love this, don't you?"

Kula extended his palm, which held six paise of silver coins. "This . . . don't you like it?" Kula snatched Punna, who was small in stature, with his other hand, then he pushed his face close in front of Punna and said, "Now, open your mouth! I will let you eat the most delicious one in the world!"

"Dear, why are you doing this to me?" asked Punna. Feeling the evil spirits from the man, Punna shivered. "Please, forgive me!"

"Aha, forgiveness!" A wicked light sparked in Kula's eyes. "Forgiveness for what! I am now giving you a big prize. Come on, open your mouth wide!"

Punna had no choice but to open her mouth. Kula popped the coins in and said, "Eat! Eat and find out how delicious they are!" He gagged her mouth with his hand. "This is the money you love so much. You should chew and swallow them and don't you dare leave a single piece behind!"

Kula shoved her down onto the floor. Then he stamped on her with his two feet and shouted at the top of his lungs. "Dirty bastards! Dirty world! Yes, being alive is a dirty thing! Dirty and cheap!" He pushed his head in front of Punna and said in a loud voice, "Do you know how difficult I am? Do you know how dirty and cheap the things I am doing outside of the house are to make a living?"

Saying this, Kula kept on beating Punna ferociously.

"Dear, please spare my life!" she cried. But Kula did not stop his savagery, while Punna just repeated, "Please! Please!" Yasoja, squatting at the corner of the room, just watched what was happening between her parents.

Yasoja was very scared of the viciousness of her father, who was like a demon straight out of hell, who could make no distinction between good and bad, nor front and back.

At that moment, though reason unclear, a spell of quiet peacefulness settled in her mind. From that peacefulness, arose a courage that surpassed the fear. She stood up, approached Kula, and threw herself in front of her father.

Kula's face lit up with surprise, and he stopped stomping on his wife. Yasoja quickly went to her mother and embraced her firmly in her arms.

Kula pulled Punna away from Yasoja's arms, then opened the door widely and threw her outside.

"You stay there. I now have something to do with this girl!" he said, pointing to Yasoja.

Horror raided against Yasoja's mind. Sure enough, Kula approached his sixteen-year-old daughter and said in an indifferent and casual tone, "What do you think? Won't it be rather good to empty your mind and accept it obediently?"

Yasoja knew what the beast before her eyes wanted. Recalling the pains of the past, she trembled from shame and fear. However, after a while, a streak of quiet peacefulness visited her again and said this.

It's a fate . . . What else could I do, if this is the fate, I have to accept it.

"Yeah, alright" said Yasoja calmly. "I will let you do it if you so wish. But please don't treat me too harshly."

Slowly Yasoja shed her sari, and with a nonchalant expression she lay down on the floor on her back; a beast started to violate her, exhaling heavily.

After her father had left, Yasoja remained lying down, struck dumb by the violence. However, when it came to pain and shame, Punna was suffering more deeply than Yasoja.

Punna entered the room and put the clothes back on her daughter. Meanwhile, the two did not exchange any words.

Leaving herself under mother's care, Yasoja thought.

Oh, human beings are filthy; human beings are cruel, so there will be nothing but pain that comes between human beings!

Kula's brutality toward his wife and daughter continued. Then, one day Yasoja realized that a new life had settled in her womb.

Yasoja could not help but be gripped with panic. It was possible that the people in the Devani family, who were waiting for her after fixing the wedding date, might consider her pregnancy as an offense and give her a group beating. Private punishment of this kind was being tolerated by law.

What should I do, what should I do . . . she thought.

While she was in deep trouble worrying about the consequences, her parents noticed her pregnancy.

One day, Kula returned home and called Punna and Yasoja to sit.

"Pregnancy is not allowed!" he said. "So, boil this and have Yasoja drink it! Then the baby will be aborted." He threw a maddava mushroom to Punna.

"Isn't this maddava? This may kill our girl!" Punna protested.

"She will be killed anyway if her pregnancy becomes known," the man said in a grim voice. "Anyhow, you have her drink this today. If the baby will not be aborted in three days, then I will have to kick Yasoja's stomach. If it will still not work, I cannot guarantee how the lives of you two will become!" Having said this, Kula rose and left the room.

Being put in a situation like a bolt from the blue, Punna and Yasoja embraced each other and cried. But the only choice left to them was to follow the will of the husband cum father cum demon.

Punna offered the maddava soup to Yasoja. She took the bowl from her mother without protest and drank it at one gulp. While drinking the soup, Yasoja thought, *Mother, I will drink it. I don't care if I die. I am already dead, I died at that time when my father raped me . . .*

After drinking the maddava soup, Yasoja walked slowly out of the house to kill her body for good. Punna asked where she was going, but Yasoja did not respond. Her steps headed for the mountain, and after some time she was standing on a high cliff.

"Oh, I will never again receive the body of a human being! I would rather be born in hell or born as an animal. Oh I will never receive a life of a human being!"

Pledging as such, Yasoja threw herself off the cliff.

CHAPTER 4
Sirima in Her Previous Life

B
ut to despise life in reality means to desire life.[7] She could not rid herself of the karma that longed for a better, happier life. Thus, despite her wish, she was pushed onto her next life and reborn as Sanu.

Yes, that was it, Sanu thought. *That was how I came to be a monk, even if it meant I had to give up my family and wealth. This is the reason why I didn't return to the secular life, despite not making any progress with my practice . . .*

Thus, Sanu got himself up again, in order not to repeat the dreadful pain of his past life.

Such suffering must have not been limited to his previous life. The Buddha taught that tears shed by sentient beings during their endless reincarnations through eternity could sum up to oceans of water. The Buddha also said the only way to put an end to seas

---

7 The desire for existence (bhava-tanha) and desire for nonexistence (vibhava-tanha) are flip sides of the same coin. In other words, the desire to not want to exist or the mind that wishes to take its own life occur because life doesn't turn out the way one wishes. The thought of suicide subsides when life turns out well. Buddhism suggests that the only path to transcend both desires is enlightenment. That means the enlightened neither have the mind that wishes to exist nor the mind that wishes not to exist.

of suffering (samsara) is through practice—practice to reach the state of spiritual awakening where one would never be born again.

But even with the firm resolve to concentrate on his spiritual practice, Sanu could not make any further progress. In fact, his practice began to regress. What caused the regression this time was what his father Kula had in the past life, which pushed Sanu to devastation—lust and desire for the opposite sex.

The object of Sanu's desire was toward a courtesan named Sirima. At the time, courtesans were highly regarded in society. These courtesans only received men of affection. In these circumstances, brahmins and children of other noble families felt proud to win the hearts of famous courtesans.

The popularity of Sirima the courtesan was incredible. In Suruva, a city close to the Silavanna temple where Sanu practiced, many youths and even elderly with their grey hairs and wrinkles, wished to spend a night with Sirima.

With such fierce competition, public biddings were held to spend a night with Sirima. In the first month, the price of spending a night with her was only one hundred rupees. But the price rose to two hundred rupees in the second month, then three hundred in the following month.

Sirima the courtesan and her brother Jivaka, a renowned doctor during the time of the Buddha, were devout Buddhists. Every day, Sirima offered food to eight bhikkhus who were on their alms round[8] and her food was exceptionally delightful.

One day, a bhikkhu proudly boasted to another bhikkhu that he had been receiving alms every day from Sirima the courtesan, a woman not only of unsurpassed beauty but with remarkable culinary skills. Coincidently, the bhikkhu who heard this boastful monk was no other than Bhikkhu Sanu.

---

8 During the Buddha's time and in the Theravada Buddhist countries in Southeast Asia at present, monastics go out to village to receive donated food. This sustains them for a day. This going out for begging is called an "alms round."

On hearing the stories of Sirima, Sanu fell in love with her before even seeing her. After a sleepless night in lusting after Sirima, Sanu went to her house with other bhikkhus to receive alms the next day.

However, Sirima had been suffering from a mysterious illness. She was unable to offer alms due to the illness that even her brother, a renowned doctor, could not cure.

At first, Sirima wished for her maids to offer alms in her place, but she changed her mind when the bhikkhus arrived. Although she felt ill, she decided in the last minute that she should not welcome the bhikkhus lying down. Sirima got herself up with the help of her maids and went out to offer alms.

To Sanu, who was already head over heels in love, Sirima looked as beautiful as a goddess. He wondered if she looked that beautiful with an illness, then how beautiful would she be if she was healthy and beautifully adorned. Such imagination encouraged Sanu to develop even stronger desire for Sirima.

Upon returning to his temple, Sanu thought again and again about the woman of beautiful figure and exceptionally elegant lashes he had seen that day. His heart bubbled up like soap suds and burned up fiercely with desire.

Sanu dreamed about the woman, tainted with lust. In fact, he dreamed of Sirima whether he was asleep or awake. Then suddenly, Sirima appeared in front of his eyes. He stumbled toward this fantasy and spoke to her with a trembling voice of the most delicate string of a sitar.

> You are young and beautiful.
> Let us delight in the flowering grove.
> Aren't the towering trees and their pollen
> Exuding sweet fragrance from all around?
> The beginning of spring is the season for youth.
> Let us delight in the flowering grove.

Your eyes are like those of a fawn.
Looking at your eyes like gold without a speck,
My sensual delight grows all the more.
Dear lady with pure and graceful eyes!
You are like daffodils, my sweet lady!

You are a celestial being in the Chattarata garden,
Or you are like a nymph in mountains.
Oh lady with such slender waist!
Lady with bosom like elegant lotus!
There is no one as beautiful as you!

Chasing after the illusion of Sirima and muttering these words for three days, Sanu occupied himself with obsession to win her over. But the Buddha has set "no sexual misconduct with women" as the first and the foremost important of the four main precepts for bhikkhus. In fact, the bhikkhus must not even allow their sleeves to brush past a woman, thus Sanu fell into dilemma on whether he should disrobe and return to lay life.

Sanu was not the only bhikkhu lusting after Sirima. When Elder Moggallana discovered the situation, he gathered all the bhikkhus infatuated with Sirima and said, "About women, exactly which part of them do you love?" He taught the dangers of lusting after women.

Although the hearts of the other bhikkhus were somewhat settled, the great passion they felt toward Sirima was not subdued completely. Fortunately, the elder's teaching temporarily postponed Sanu's thought to give up his life as a bhikkhu.

A few days later, Sirima died from her illness. The city mayor, who was a devout Buddhist, went and reported her death to Elder Moggallana, who already arranged with the mayor to be informed in case of Sirima's death.

Elder Moggallana asked the mayor to request Jivaka, Sirima's brother, to not bury Sirima's body and to have it protected from crows and vultures.

The mayor asked, "Dear elder, what else do you wish for me to do?"

"You can announce that Sirima is available to anyone who wishes to have her for a night," he said.

"But elder . . ." said the mayor. "Who would want to spend a night with a woman's corpse?"

"Make an announcement that anyone who spends a night with Sirima the courtesan will be rewarded with one thousand rupees," said Moggallana.

The mayor followed the elder's proposal and announced it to the public. But no one dared to come forward to spend a night with Sirima.

On the next day, the mayor came and told the elder that no one wished to spend a night with Sirima's corpse. The elder then said, "From this day forward, the reward will be increased each day. So, a thousand rupees will be two thousand on the second day, and three thousand on the third day."

The mayor returned and made this announcement, but no one came forward to take the reward. The reward multiplied, day by day, up to ten thousand rupees. Still, no one wanted it at any price.

Around that time, Sirima's once beautiful body had deteriorated to an unrecognizable state. Her body was bloated like soft jelly, odor and pus came out from her, and ants and maggots swarmed to take her flesh, which made the place she lay look like a den of evil.

Elder Moggallana then gathered all the bhikkhus who gave their hearts to Sirima and headed toward the spot where Sirima's body was laid.

When the bhikkhus encircled the corpse, the elder said, "Dear bhikkhus, this corpse once belonged to Sirima. When she was alive, people would not hesitate to pay large sums for even a single night with her. Now, if anyone spends a night with her, they can earn ten thousand rupees. But look now! Nobody is willing to take the corpse. That is the nature of physical body, and that is the nature of death. So, the Buddha taught, 'Do not cling to the body, but practice to reach the state where you can end death[9].'"

---

9 The arhat (arahant), who has reached the stage of the final awakening, is often referred to as the "slayer of enemy." Here the enemy is referred to as "all defilements that represent death."

Then Elder Moggallana recited the following verse.

> Look at this dressed up body,
> A mass of sores, dirt, and dead skin.
> Linked together with a chain of bones,
> It is the jacket for sickness,
> A subject of many thoughts (of sensual desire).
> Indeed, that body is neither permanent nor stable.
>
> The dove-grey bones of a woman, once so beautiful,
> Now look like gourds that fall and roll in autumn wind.
> What beauty is left in them?
> What pleasure is there in being attached to them?
> The body is like a bubble or a haze.
> Break all flowers of Mara,
> That stem from this body.
> Then, even the king of death cannot win.

When the great master offered these teachings and verses, Sanu came forth, bowed, and said, "From this day on forward, I will stay and observe Sirima's decaying body."

"Alright, go right ahead," he said.

Through these processes, Sanu came to observe Sirima's decaying body for a month as a practice. To a certain degree, Sanu managed to pacify his lust toward the opposite sex. However, he could not rid himself of lust and desire, as resilient and persistent as bamboo roots.

Sanu returned to his temple and carried on with his practice. But again he could not make that crucial advancement. When Sanu was not making further improvements, Elder Moggallana sent Sanu to Veluvana Monastery where the Buddha resided.

Problems began on the third day of Sanu's arrival to the temple, where boils began to appear on his body. These boils suddenly emerged and increased in numbers and size. They spread throughout his entire body, turning soft and rupturing repeatedly. Finally, Sanu's upper and lower robes were covered in pus and blood.

Sanu's illness spread and worsened to the extent that he could hardly move his body. But he writhed and endured the pain that carved through each part of his flesh and every joint of his body.

When Sanu became sick, other bhikkhus took care of him. But Sanu came to realize that the stench that came from the dried up pus, which mudded onto his entire robe, made it impossible for Sanu to stay with other bhikkhus. Thus, when his friends fell asleep, Sanu rolled his body like a log to get out of bed and move to a nearby barn.

In the early morning hours, the Buddha entered into the samadhi of great compassion, like he always did, to perceive which sentient being should receive his teaching to benefit from the Dhamma. The person who caught the Buddha's heavenly vision was Sanu. The Buddha came out from the Hall of Fragrance[10,11] toward the barn where Sanu was.

The Buddha drew a bucket of water from the well to boil. The Buddha's three disciples then came and asked the purpose of boiling the water. When they discovered that water was for washing Sanu's body, they all said with one voice, "O Lord, we shall also help you," and they assisted the Buddha.

When the water was warm, the Buddha evenly sprinkled it all over Sanu's robes. A few moments later, when the robe that clung to Sanu's body came apart, the Buddha carefully washed Sanu's

---

10 Buddhism believes the universe contains other highly evolved sentient beings similar to that of human. Moreover, Buddha can exist in the past, present, and future. The word Tathagata refers to all Buddhas. In this literary piece, the writer describes the Buddha, who refers himself as the one who gained the perfect enlightenment. When required, the writer describes in the first person narrative where the Buddha humbly refer himself as "I" when conversing with ordinary sentient beings.

11 Hall of Fragrance (gandhakuti) is a structure made of sandalwood in Jetavana Monastery, where Buddha resided. This name was given since the hall was always filled with beautiful fragrance as myriad devotees offered flowers and incense.

body with two bhikkhus while the other remaining monk washed the robe filled with blood and pus and hung it to dry.

Finally, having received bath and changed robes, Sanu was able to lie down comfortably feeling refreshed both in body and mind.

"Sanu," asked the Buddha. "Are you feeling any better?"

"Lord, it feels more bearable now."

"Then Sanu, please listen carefully to what I have to say," said the Buddha.

"Yes, Blessed One."

The Buddha explained to Sanu the finiteness of life, the pain and suffering that follow, and the path that could free him from them all.

In the meantime, numerous monks within the temple gathered into the barn with the news that the great master was teaching Sanu. However, Sanu did not pay attention to the bhikkhus who gathered. All that he could think was, *Such is the suffering of life,* and *How could the Buddha be so compassionate?* Sanu kept thinking, *I will always remember this pain for the rest of my life and all my future lives to come.* He also thought, *I am determined to attain enlightenment, if not in this life then in my next life, and if not in the next life then in the life after the next.*

After the Buddha finished his discourse he said to Sanu, "Sanu, remember the lustful feelings you had toward Sirima, the courtesan not too far ago?"

"Yes, Blessed One."

"Sanu, then think again on how you observed the deteriorating body of Sirima, the courtesan," said the Buddha.

"Yes, Blessed One."

"What have you gained by observing Sirima's corpse?"

"In that moment, I benefited from non-attachment to the body and less lust toward the opposite sex," said Sanu.

"You no longer have any attachment toward the body and passion toward women?" he asked.

"Not entirely, my Lord. Sentient beings have so much attachment toward the physical body and desire for the opposite sex, which is much too strong, deep-seated, resilient, and persistent."

"That's right," said the Buddha. "Sanu, although you may not completely rid yourself of all attachments, you did manage to lessen your attachment toward physical body and lust toward women. Although you will not be born in the Heavenly Realm of the meditative absorption,[12] you may be at least born in the heavenly sphere of the Desire Realm with the merit of your practice.

"Sanu, although you can be happy in the heavenly sphere of the Desire Realm, you cannot ultimately relieve the suffering and agony of life. Thus even if you are born in the heavenly sphere of the Desire Realm, you must not remain content with its finite happiness, but work hard to advance toward nirvana, where you will find true happiness without any conditions," the Buddha shared.

After finishing his discourse, the Buddha read out two verses for Bhikkhu Sanu.

> Before long, this body will be dumped to the ground,
> And the mind too will vanish to somewhere unknown.
> Then this transient body will be
> Of no use like a scrap of rotten wood.
>
> Why the laughter?
> Laugh when the world is ablaze?
> Why this great joy?
> Great joy when the body is dying?

---

12 The Heavenly Realm of meditative absorption (jhana) is where the sentient beings that have attained jhana through meditative practice are reborn, whereas the Desire Realm is where sentient beings are reborn by the merit of performing good deeds without meditative practice.

CHAPTER 5
Followers of the Way
in Heaven

"My life was over in that moment of hearing the Buddha's verse . . ." said Sirima, while gazing at Raja, "Then I was reborn in the Tavatimsa Heaven upon my death in the Human Realm."

"But how did you get the name Sirima, instead of Sanu?"

"My desire toward Sirima may have been subdued, but I could not completely cut off my attachment to her. For that reason, I thought of Sirima at death and perhaps the memory of her became a rebirth-consciousness for me to earn this woman's body with the name Sirima."

"I understand now."

"My dear husband! Although I was given the opportunity to renounce and become a bhikkhu while the Buddha was alive, I could not attain enlightenment because of my attachment to women. Again, I am falling for you deeply with such uncontrollable emotional longing. What a great fool am I?"

As she said this, Sirima's eyes quickly dampened with tears. Raja responded with a smile, "My beloved, you speak as if the feelings of love and longing are same as lustful passion."

"Yes, that's right."

"But aren't feelings of affection toward the opposite sex one of the most important sources of power that motivate people to go on?"

Sirima didn't respond. She simply stared allusively at her husband with sorrowful eyes. Sirima's eyes clearly revealed to Raja that she did not share his views.

Raja then thought, *But why do I arouse such intense affection in seeing Sirima, who believes love is just a hindrance?*

Raja closed his eyes and continued his thought. His karmic tendency from his previous life—to ruminate his thoughts two or three times over—still remained strong even if he was reborn in the Tavatimsa Heaven.

Raja kept on thinking with this particular character.

On the one hand, Sirima has a loving feeling toward me, but on the other hand, she rejects me because she perceives such feeling as a form of lustful passion. And this duality makes her character even more attractive. I would not have fallen in love so deeply if she simply loved me like other ordinary women, without the view that love is a lustful passion to be overcome.

This is a circumstance in which any other ordinary man would have drifted off with their feelings of love and their rational function would have ceased, but Raja continued with his thought.

Oh, how beautiful is she! She is more beautiful than a lake forming soft waves by a brisk of wind, more beautiful than a lake that remains still without waves or breeze. Just as a practitioner who ultimately returns on their path seems more beautiful than a practitioner who always remains on the path and never goes astray, even if their mind has once trembled like flower petals by passing wind, Sirima is more beautiful than ever as she is noble, yet not noble, as she is ignoble, yet doesn't stop searching for the quintessential path, as she is a tiny little chick, but cultivates the dream to become a mother bird, and ultimately an eagle.

With these thoughts, Raja developed greater affection toward his bride. Raja reached out and held her hands. Gently pulling Sirima toward him, Raja embraced Sirima tenderly.

For a moment, Sirima surrendered and remained silently in his arms. But she tore herself free from her husband and gazed up at him with her bright and cheerful eyes, unlike a moment before. With a bright smile she pulled Raja's hands and put his palms together. She also held her palms together in a prayer position and said, "Please be mindful of the Buddha, of the Dhamma, and of the Sangha."

Sirima continued, "Dear husband, your deep contemplation on the meaning of life in your past life brought positive karma. What's more, your reflection on the Three Jewels of Buddhism at the moment of death led you to be reborn in the Tavatimsa Heaven. As such, mindfulness toward the Three Jewels brings such great virtues and merits."

"Yes, I am aware of that too," said Raja, "That is why I take refuge in the Buddha, the Dhamma, and the Sangha. But my heart goes out to you in such great waves of passion."

"Oh, oh, my dear husband! But this is not the time to be consumed by desire!"

But Raja did not yield to Sirima's words. In the next moment, Raja held her in his arms, laying his hands softly on her bosom. Sirima's thunderous heartbeat could be felt under a thin layer of heavenly clothes.

Hearing Sirima gasp for breath, Raja thought, *She wants me too, in spite of what she says.*

With these thoughts, two heavenly beings found themselves on a bed instantly. Their heavenly garments that once covered their bodies slipped away, and two heavenly beings reached the peak of their passion and lust.

Shortly after, their heated passion faded away like a bonfire extinguished by a rain shower. The heavenly couple suddenly felt awkward. Perhaps that may have been the reason Sirima rose from the bed and seated herself in a corner of the room with her back turned. Her heavenly garments found themselves on her beautiful figure again; Raja was clothed again as well.

Raja approached his wife and sat on a chair across from her. He could see her eyes were moist with tears again. The most enchanting and seductive woman, who had been exhilarated by his caress just a moment ago, could no longer be found.

"My dearest, my love, what is the reason for your distress?" Raja asked, but he knew Sirima was crying.

After wiping away Sirima's tears with a handkerchief, Raja stood up quietly. He then respectfully offered a prostration to her. Startled, Sirima quickly lifted Raja from the floor and asked, "Dear husband, why are you bowing down to me?"

"I can't deny my irresistible passion to want to make love to you, but what still remains in me is an aspiration for the pursuit of truth, because in my past life I also searched for the meaning of life. I believe that this has led me to pay humble respect to you, as you received direct teachings from the Buddha in your past life."

"Being a bhikkhu only applies to my past life. In this life, I am simply your wife," said Sirima.

"That may be so, but I think it would be great if you could be my master and my spiritual guide."

"I will gratefully take those words as a compliment," Sirima said with a smile. "In that case, may I dare suggest something as your humble spiritual guide? From this point on, the most important question we must ask ourselves is what kind of life we want to lead from now on."

"Regarding that subject, why don't you, my spiritual master, tell me how we must live?"

"We should practice and cultivate our minds," said Sirima.

"But as you may already know, Tavatimsa Heaven is not the best place to practice."

"Yes, that may be right," Sirima responded, "except for the birth in the Human Realm, the other five modes of existence—Hell, Hungry

Ghost, Asura, Animal, and Heavenly Realms—have unfavorable conditions for practice. That is due to extreme pains in the Hell Realm, excessive hunger in the Hungry Ghost Realm, excessive wars and fights in the Asura Realm, severe ignorance in the Animal Realm, and superfluous blissfulness in the Heavenly Realm."

"That is right. As far as I know, that is the reason why the Buddha manifested in the Human Realm and not in the Heavenly Realm," said Raja.

"Yes. That is the reason why all Buddhas of the past, present, and future attain awakening in the Human Realm, rather than the Heavenly Realm, while edifying sentient beings by their teachings," said Sirima.

"My dear, our Shakyamuni Buddha was an ascetic named Sumedha in his past lifetime, and Dipankara Buddha prophesized that Sumedha would become a future Buddha. Thereafter, the Buddha-to-be dedicated his body and mind to accumulate merits and spent his final life in the Tusita Heaven," she continued.

"He was then born as prince Siddhattha, to a family named Gotama[13] in a clan called the Shakyas. At age twenty-nine, Siddhattha left his home and for the next six years led an ascetic life to attain perfect enlightenment to become a Buddha. To this day, the Buddha teaches countless sentient beings on heaven and earth," she shared.

"However, my dear one, the lifespan of a human varies in different eras. In this particular era, humans live more or less one hundred years. This means that the Buddha will enter parinirvana[14] soon. Thus,

---

13 Gotama is a family name that politically led the Shakya Clan during the time of the Buddha. Shakyamuni Buddha is referred to as "Gotama Buddha" or the Buddha when distinction is required from Buddhas of the past, future, and of other realms.

14 Parinirvana (parinibbana) refers to a death of a supremely enlightened as idealized by Buddhists. A death of an ordinary sentient being and that of a highly enlightened is different because a sentient being is born again after death and continues on a cyclic samsara, advancing toward an unknown with fear. In comparison, death as in parinirvana is that of a great peace, quietude, and serenity. Thus, parinirvana is dying without death, or death that transcends death.

we must not forgo this rare chance. While the Buddha is still alive, we must receive teachings to improve our lives," she concluded.

"I agree with you completely," said Raja. "Sirima, you are more than my wife but a great friend on the path in search of truth. Let us now travel down to the Human Realm swiftly. We will take refuge to the Three Jewels and become the Buddha's disciples."

CHAPTER 6
The Talk by King Sakka
of Tavatimsa Heaven

When the two heavenly beings were about to rise from their seats after the discussion, a dim *doowoo doowoo* sound was heard from afar, which was the sound of the Dhamma conch blown by the King Sakka of the Tavatimsa Heaven. With a gentle smile on his face, Raja said to Sirima, "The King of the Tavatimsa Heaven is blowing the Dhamma conch, which signals that the Dhamma assembly will begin soon."

"Then, what shall we do? Shall we attend the assembly first or go down to the Human Realm straight away?" asked Sirima.

"What do you think?" asked Raja.

"I think we better attend the assembly first and then descend to the earth. I am quite curious about what a Dhamma assembly of the heaven looks like."

By saying this, Sirima laughed softly. Raja nodded in agreement and thought of the way to reach the Sudamma Hall where the assembly will be held. In the next moment, a golden wagon drawn by four white horses suddenly appeared in front of them, with a coachman of heavy build seated at the coach box. The coachman, after helping them mount the wagon, began to drive the wagon fast toward the Dhamma hall.

Upon arriving at the Dhamma hall, Raja and Sirima walked slowly into the hall after letting the coachman go. The interior of the Sudamma Hall was beautifully decorated with hundreds of thousands of red and white lotus flowers, and a Dhamma seat was prepared at the front, over which a big canopy was adorned with various jewels.

By the time the couple arrived, several hundreds of millions of heavenly beings had already gathered, packing the floor and space inside the hall densely. Though an assembly hall of the Human Realm, no matter how big it may be, could not have accommodated as many as hundreds of millions of heavenly beings, the Heavenly Realm exists according to the laws of mind, where myriad heavenly beings could be accommodated in a small space.

The audience of the Dhamma assembly was not limited to these heavenly beings. Hundreds of thousands of sentient beings—who were subjects of the four heavenly kings who were ruled by the King Sakka of the Tavatimsa Heaven—surrounded the heavenly beings of the Tavatimsa Heaven, floating in the air, keeping a little distance from them, and waiting for the Dhamma assembly to begin.

All attendees of the Dhamma assembly were sitting in an orderly manner according to their order of arrival, with heavenly men on the left and the heavenly women on the right. This was due to the rule of the Dhamma assembly that requires men and women to sit separately.

The heavenly kings sitting side by side in the front row, were without their crowns that they normally wore. And, the queen consorts and other heavenly women—who usually decorate their hair, carry accessories, and spray themselves with perfumes—were now in unusually simple and modest outfits. The appearance of Sirima has already changed into that of a practitioner, with a simple hairstyle and clothing.

With a loving look in his eyes, Raja said to his wife, "After the Dhamma assembly is over, we will meet in front of the large stupa." The two devas took their seats, one on the right side and the other on the left side.

The master who would give Buddhist teachings was Sanankumara,[15] a deva from the Brahma Heaven.

While the heavenly beings in the Desire Realm have sensory organs as do men in the Human Realm, the heavenly beings in the Form Realm have only the organs of nose, tongue, and body without any sensory faculties, and there is not even a body for the heavenly beings in the Formless Realm. It is because they have, partly or wholly, transcended the sensual pleasure, and therefore, for the heavenly beings in the Form Realm to present themselves to the sentient beings in the Desire Realm, they have to go through temporal manifestation.[16] Accordingly, Sanankumara, who was from the lowest of the four meditation heavens in the Form Realm, had to manifest in a temporal body for the Dhamma assembly, and on this occasion, his name was changed to Pancasika.

Mystical heavenly music resonated peacefully from above. As this meant that the Dhamma teacher Pancasika would be arriving soon, Sakka flew up to the air to receive him. Moments later, as Pancasika appeared, Sakka greeted him with joined palms, and in response, Pancasika also replied with joined palms.

The King of the Tavatimsa Heaven, Sakka, said to the young Dhamma teacher whose fine skin glowed with luster, "Dear heavenly

---

15 Sanankumara: A deva from the Brahma Heaven who has deep faith in the Buddhadhamma, often requests the Buddha for teachings, or delivers teachings himself in the Tavatimsa Heaven. When he descends to the Tavatimsa Heaven, he temporally manifests in the form of a boy, and his name is changed to Pancasika.

16 The devas in the Formless Realm cannot come down to the Desire Realm, and only the devas in the Form Realm can descend to the Desire Realm. And the bodies of the devas in the Form Realm are bigger as they reside in higher heavens, radiate vast amount of lights, and their constituents are extremely fine. However, the author did not always keep these principles in this work.

being, I would like to offer my greetings. Was your mind at peace in the meantime?"

And the words Sakka uttered, in accordance with the laws of the heaven, were heard clearly even by the heavenly beings farthest away from them, regardless of the distance.

"I have been at peace, but how about you? Did the exiled asuras[17] bother you?" asked Pancasika in a calm and innocent voice.

Sakka replied while laughing, "Those fools are always making trouble. However, we have been fending them off well as usual."

"That is the way it should be. However, Your Highness, as today is the day of the Dhamma assembly, and this is the Dhamma hall, you better not call them fools."

"Oh!" A mischievous smile drifted across Sakka's face who said, "However, they still deserve to be called fools because they are folks of much lesser quality."

"Nevertheless, my dear King of the Tavatimsa Heaven," said Pancasika. "Aren't we the disciples of the Buddha? And hasn't the Buddha taught us the ten kinds of wholesome behavior,[18] which include saying no harsh words to others?"

"Of course. Since this is your request and considering the teaching of the Buddha, I will call the fools the bunch for today. Anyway, I have made some arrangements so the bunch would not disrupt the Dhamma assembly."

Saying this, Sakka made a happy smile, and at hearing his voice and seeing his look, smiles appeared on the faces of all sentient

---

17 Exiled asuras: Heavenly sentient beings exiled from the Tavatimsa Heaven. There are two kinds of asuras: One is asuras who are sentient beings in one of the six realms of rebirth, and the other is asuras exiled from the Tavatimsa Heaven by King Sakka. As these two asuras are distinctively different, the latter is called as "exiled asuras" in this work. For this reason, the exiled asuras often challenge the Heavenly King Sakka to reclaim the Tavatimsa Heaven.

18 Ten kinds of wholesome behavior: Virtuous behaviors of not committing the following: ① to kill life (existence) ② to take things not given ③ to engage in sexual misconduct ④ to lie ⑤ to speak divisively ⑥ to use harsh language ⑦ to speak idly ⑧ to be greedy ⑨ to be angry ⑩ to have wrong views.

beings of the heaven. Sakka, as usual, guided Pancasika to the Dhamma seat.

"By the way, dear Heavenly King," said Pancasika seating himself. "May I suggest that you deliver the Dhamma talk today?"

At such request, Sakka hesitated whether to accept or refuse it, and having noticed this, Pancasika said once again. "As you are well aware of, I am staying in the heaven where they enjoy the joys of meditative absorption."

"Certainly."

"So it seems that my talk does not seem to be well received by beings in your realm. The essence of my talk is centered on the idea that you have to escape from desire and pleasure. By doing this you will have to be reborn in a higher heaven than this one or in the Human Realm. By practicing the Buddhadhamma, you will have to transcend the Desire Realm, the Form Realm, and the Formless Realm. However, I do feel from my past experience that such talks are difficult for you to fully understand. This is the reason why I suggested that Your Highness, who is considered to stand in the middle between myself and the heavenly beings in the Tavatimsa Heaven, deliver the Dhamma talk."

After some thought, while nodding his head Sakka said, "That could be true in a sense. But many heavenly beings in the Tavatimsa Heaven, including myself, are counting the day for the Dhamma assembly to take place, presided by you. Though we have not made big progress in our practice, we are, nevertheless, still happy to wait for the day of your Dhamma talk because through it, we could pull our mind together which could easily degenerate."

Having said this, Sakka asked the hundreds of millions of sentient beings who gathered in the Dhamma hall, "Dear heavenly beings, and other sentient beings! Do you agree with my words?"

"Yes, we do agree!"

All heavenly beings shouted with one voice. The shout made a sound like one thousand thunders crashing at a time, spread throughout every corners of the Tavatimsa Heaven, and soon returned as a long echo with deep resonance.

"However, dear heavenly kings and devas!" said Pancasika, having waited for the echo to die down, to the attendees of the Dhamma assembly. "Most of you, including the Heavenly King Sakka, who frequently visited the Buddha and received his teachings, have not yet attained the first level of the meditative absorption," he said.

"Dear all devas, the meditative absorption is divided into eight levels, and this is the reason why the Heavenly Realm of meditative absorption is also divided into eight levels. Below the Heavenly Realm of meditative absorption, there is the heavenly sphere of the Desire Realm that is divided into six levels, in which those who have not practiced or failed to attain the meditative absorption will be reborn, and the Tavatimsa Heaven, in which you were born, is the second level of this heavenly sphere," he explained.

"Below the heavenly sphere of the Desire Realm, there is the Human Realm, and on further lower levels, there are realms of Hell, Hungry Ghosts, Asuras, and Animals, where those who have committed evil acts in their previous life are reborn and suffer. Like this, the world we are living in is divided into four evil realms where you must not go and two good realms where you must go," he shared.

"Well, dear heavenly beings, the Human Realm, which is one of the two good realms along with the Heavenly Realm, is a very special world. This world is, in a sense, lower than the Heavenly Realm, but in another sense, more important than the Heavenly Realm. It is because, while other worlds are places where they receive the retribution for their good or evil actions carried out in the Human Realm, the Human Realm is the place where they create the causes of karmic retribution through good or evil deeds," he said.

"In other words, in the Human Realm, people may commit actions causing them to go to the lowest bottom of hell, or perform deeds which can transcend the highest level of the heaven of meditative absorption; they may attain enlightenment that transcends the three spheres of existence. However, even in the Heavenly Realm, certain amounts of progress in practice, though not as much as in the Human Realm, can be achieved. In anticipation of this, I often come down to this heaven to teach the Dhamma to you, but my efforts do not bring about as good of results as I intended. I mean very few of you have achieved a notable progress." As Pancasika said this, the faces of all heavenly beings, including Sakka's, flushed from shame.

"Oh, no!" said Pancasika. "I am not telling you this to make you feel ashamed. I understand, I fully understand. I was like that as well. In my previous life when I was a human being, I also tried hard to subdue desire and ignorance, nevertheless I failed on many occasions. Even now I go down personally to the Human Realm, meet the Buddha, and receive his teachings, but I have not yet reached the stage above the first meditative absorption."

After comforting the shameful mind of the heavenly beings, Pancasika continued.

"Nevertheless, when I was a human being, I practiced meditation with all my strength, and as a result I reached a certain level of meditation, and therefore I received the karmic fruits in the heaven of the followers of Brahma. This means, I repeat, the Human Realm is an appropriate place for you to practice.

"The Human Realm is the most favorable place to attempt to make improvements in duration of the extended samsara. Therefore, you have to make an effort to be able to be reborn as a human being in your next life, by way of maintaining your belief well in the Buddhadhamma, while you are in the Heavenly Realm.

"As a matter of fact, since the wealth and honors you enjoy in the Tavatimsa Heaven are incomparably bigger than those enjoyed by the human beings, it may seem to your eyes that the Human Realm is no more than a detestable space full of dirty filth. But as a rapid progress can only be achieved in the Human Realm, you have to remain here maintaining your faith in the Buddhadhamma well, so that you can, without fail, be reborn in the Human Realm in your next life."

"You are right, Your Reverence," King Sakka said. "So I keep on telling myself that I must firmly hold my faith in the Buddhadhamma, so that as a result I will surely be reborn in the Human Realm in my next life. For that purpose, Your Reverence, I have been to the Human Realm recently for a short while in order to strengthen my faith."

"Oh, have you? Then how about Your Highness telling the story to all heavenly beings present here today?" he asked.

Sakka, being requested by Pancasika once again, with a look that says there is no way out, expressed his agreement with a nod. Then the brahma deva Pancasika descended from the Dhamma seat, guided King Sakka toward it and then went to the seat arranged separately for the teacher.

The King of the Tavatimsa Heaven, Sakka, before ascending the Dhamma seat, stood with palms joined together, and recited the Verse of Three Refuges and the Vows for Eight Precepts, together with all other heavenly disciples of the Buddha.

> I take refuge in the one who is the most noble, who is the most treasured, and who has himself attained the perfect awakening (three times).
>
> I take refuge in the Buddha.
> I take refuge in the Dhamma.
> I take refuge in the Sangha.
>
> Again, I take refuge in the Buddha.
> Again, I take refuge in the Dhamma.
> Again, I take refuge in the Sangha.
>
> Thirdly, I take refuge in the Buddha.
> Thirdly, I take refuge in the Dhamma.
> Thirdly, I take refuge in the Sangha.
>
> I undertake the precept to refrain from destroying life.
> I undertake the precept to refrain from taking that which is not given.

I undertake the precept to refrain from sexual misconduct.

I undertake the precept to refrain from incorrect speech.

I undertake the precept to refrain from intoxicants, which may cloud the mind.

I undertake the precept to refrain from adorning the body or enjoying singing or dancing.

I undertake the precept to refrain from lying on a high or luxurious bed.

I undertake the precept to refrain from eating after noon.[19]

Having finished all proper observances, Sakka sat on the Dhamma seat, closed his eyes, and concentrated his mind for a while. In response to this, all heavenly beings closed their eyes and concentrated their minds.

Suddenly, a silence came down as if heavy snowfall had covered the mountains and rivers in all white. Then, the space came to a stop all at once. The chirping of birds from a mango tree standing near the Dhamma hall subsided, and the passing breeze brushing against dainty dresses of goddesses also died away. Time too seemed to have halted.

Accordingly, the place was not the Tavatimsa Heaven anymore, nor inside the Dhamma hall, nor at a specific time. It was a space that was not space, or the mind halted in a certain space or a special time that cannot be called time.

Sakka at last emerged from meditation and opened his eyes. Then, hundreds of millions of gods and goddesses also emerged from meditation and opened their eyes, though it required some time for them to come completely out of the deep stillness that they were in a moment before.

After the lapse of time required for inhaling six to seven breaths, the Dhamma teacher Sakka adjusted his heavenly voice so even the

---

19 Five precepts and eight precepts: Of the precepts in the text, the first five are the precepts that lay Buddhists should observe, and the eight precepts including the latter three precepts are the precepts that must be observed on the days of purification (uposatha days).

sentient beings standing at the rearmost part of the assembly hall could hear him clearly.

(Dhamma talk of the Heavenly King Sakka)

"My dear friends!

"As you know well, in the Tavatimsa Heaven, there are eight heavens each in four cardinal directions and a heaven at the center, so there are thirty-three heavens in all. And I am the king of the central heaven (looking at the heavenly kings), the leader of the thirty-two lesser heavenly kings who are present here, and I frequently hold meetings with them to discuss matters related to the entire Tavatimsa Heaven or on the Buddhadhamma.

"As late as one month ago, I called all the heavenly kings of the Tavatimsa Heaven in one location and gave a discourse on the Dhamma. At that time, the following four questions were posed by the Heavenly King Maruyana.

> What is the foremost of all generosity?
> What is the foremost of all tastes?
> What is the foremost of all delights?
> Why the extinction of desires is deemed most virtuous?

"We had varied talks on this topic. However, as we could not reach a concerted agreement, we visited the Buddha and requested for his teachings, and the Buddha said:

"'Dear heavenly kings, the gift of Dhamma excels all gifts; the taste of the Dhamma excels all tastes; the delight in Dhamma excels all delights; and the extinction of desires vanquishes all sufferings.'

"I was ashamed to hear these words of the Buddha because I was not yet fully enjoying the deep taste and the great joy of the Dhamma.

"Nevertheless, I am working every day to move upward in my enjoyment of the taste and joy of the Dhamma. Then what should we do to upgrade the level of the taste and the joy of the Dhamma?

Basically, we should live in this Tavatimsa Heaven in mindfulness that we won't be distracted. Next, based on this practice, we must be reborn as humans in our next life.

"Then how can we be reborn in the Human Realm? Needless to say again, it is through accruing various merits, including generous giving.

"Dear friends, though we are born in the Tavatimsa Heaven, there is no guarantee that we will be reborn as a human being in our next life. It was the merits in our previous lives that caused us to be reborn here now, but we could have committed lots of evil actions as well in our previous lives.

"This means that, for the virtuous deeds, we are being compensated by the joy in the Tavatimsa Heaven, but that the evil actions in our previous lives may cause us to fall down to the hell in our next lives. I am scared of that. Therefore, even now I make considerable efforts to accrue more merits.

"This is the reason why I frequently descend to the Human Realm. As some of you might be aware of, I go down to the earth and observe the eight precepts on certain days deemed appropriate when there are no Dhamma assemblies in heaven, especially on uposatha days[20], because in the Tavatimsa Heaven the pleasure of the five senses is so strong that, though we can still keep the five precepts, it is extremely difficult for us to observe the eight precepts.

"Of the eight precepts, there is the precept of refraining from eating after noon just as we recited in one voice a while ago.

---

20 Uposatha literally means to cleanse the body and the mind. It is divided into the uposatha for laity and that for monastics. Laity shall, on the 1st, 8th, 15th, and 23rd day of the lunar months, observe the eight precepts, adding three more to the five precepts they usually observe, and keep their body and mind clean and pure close to the level of monastics. All monastics residing at the temple gather on the 1st and the 15th day of the lunar months, recite the 227 precepts, and they examine if there were any faults against the precepts. For those who have light faults, let them confess, repent, and be pardoned, and for those who have heavy faults, give corresponding punishment.

However, as the foods in this Tavatimsa Heaven are so palatable to me, who has particularly strong food cravings and fastidious taste (nasal taste, because the heavenly beings take food by smelling with the nose), it is difficult for me to control the food cravings.

"Not only the food. In the eight precepts, there is a precept of not to enjoy the pleasure of adorning the body or singing, but this is also difficult to keep in the Tavatimsa Heaven, because, the dances and songs of the gandhabbas, who are near us even now, are superb enough to steal our hearts away. For this and other reasons, I go down to the Human Realm on uposatha days and keep my body and mind pure.

"Not long ago, I went down to a forest in the Human Realm where the hermitage of Elder Sariputta was located. However, as it happened, Elder Sariputta was preparing to enter the meditative attainment of cessation[21] for seven days. Oh, the marvelous meditative absorption that transcends death while still alive. The foremost disciple of the Buddha was about to enter this great meditative absorption.

"I hid myself and watched Elder Sariputta from some distance away. As I watched the noble demeanor of a man who had perfected the practice, gentle waves of emotion swelled in my mind. I slowly suppressed the emotion and thought that I could make the merit of giving him an offering when he comes out of the state of cessation.

"As you know well, making offerings is one of the most beautiful acts for a Buddhist who has not attained any meditative absorptions, which may increase their happiness. The act of making offerings is like sowing seeds in the ground. It means that, just like you can get good fruits when you sow in good soil, you can expect good karmic fruits when you make offerings to respectable persons.

---

21 The meditative attainment of cessation (nirodha-samapatti): A special state of meditative absorption (the ninth meditative absorption), which can be reached only by the sages who have attained the third stage of the enlightenment (non-returner) and above and when one reaches this state, he sits upright and does not breathe, so that he looks as if dead outwardly, but it does not mean that his life has expired. When in this meditative absorption, all perceptions (sanna) and feelings (vedana) cease.

"Then who could make a good field of merits?[22] Needless to say again, those who are pure in body and mind have good fields of merits. Then again, who could be with pure body and mind? Naturally, the Buddha is the purest one throughout the entire heaven and earth. The next pure will be arhats who have attained all four stages of enlightenment, and the next will be non-returners who have attained the three stages of enlightenment, and the next will be once-returners who have attained the two stages of enlightenment, and the next will be steam-enterers who have attained the first stage of enlightenment.

"In the next, we can still think of some practitioners who, though they have not yet reached the level of sages, have attained a certain degree of purity of their own. Though to make offerings to these practitioners is, without doubt, a meritorious deed, but in terms of karmic rewards, it cannot compare to offerings to the sages who have attained enlightenment.[23]

"Dear friends, at that time and place was the great arhat, Elder Sariputta, who was, except for the Buddha, the greatest field of merits. Much more, as he was in the attainment of cessation, the enormity of the field of merits was beyond description of words.

"Oh, dear friends, imagine the look of His Holiness who is without defilement and now is in the state of attainment of cessation. The sage in attainment of cessation ceases all signs[24] and feelings. As a result, the sages, who are essentially pure, will become even purer, and accordingly, to make offerings to the sages who have just come out of attainment of cessation will become enormously meritorious deeds.

---

22 Field of merits: Buddhist monks and good practitioners are called fields of merit, in the sense that they are the fields where sentient beings sow the seeds of merit.

23 To make offerings to one whose mind is pure is to shoot a light beam to a mirror. Like the mirror reflects well if it is clear and even, the more the mind-mirror of the recipient of the offerings is clear and even, the more he can return the offerings with more merits

24 Sign (nimita): The image arising in one's mind. It represents abstract objects or concepts in the mind.

"So, I thought that I would make an offering to Elder Sariputta when he emerges from attainment of cessation, and stayed silently near Elder Sariputta. While I was watching, Elder Sariputta, for the seven days when he was in attainment of cessation, did not breathe, nor move his body, and he just sat gracefully.

"Delicate fragrance spread out from Elder Sariputta. The delicate fragrance can only be known to ones who have smelled it, and there is no way for those who never smelled it to know. And any sentient beings who do not understand the profound state of the Dhamma, even though they might stay a whole day with Elder Sariputta, could not have smelled the fragrance.

"After seven days, the sage emerged from attainment of cessation, and thought, *To make an offering to a practitioner who has just come out from attainment of cessation would be a great meritorious deed. Then to whom shall I give this opportunity?* Elder Sariputta further thought, *I would give this opportunity of making an offering to the poorest person I encounter today.*

"I could not fully understand Elder Sariputta's mind, but roughly guessed it with the slight supernatural powers that I have. So I decided to keep hiding myself, follow Elder Sariputta, and at an opportune time I would manifest before him as the most miserable person.

"However, things did not turn out as I intended."

CHAPTER 7
Sariputta, a Leading Disciple of the Buddha

In that moment, Heavenly King Sakka witnessed the following scene:

Elder Sariputta walked slowly into the village and reached the house of a master merchant named Hari, where an elderly woman beggar sat squatting in front of its main gate.

When Sariputta saw the elderly woman, he approached her and asked, "Granny, what are you doing sitting here?"

Although Sariputta spoke to her gently, she responded as if she had been attacked, withdrawing with fear and taking a deep sigh. For a while, Sariputta silently gazed at the old woman of such unusual behavior.

Eventually, the old woman turned her body and raised her head toward Sariputta, and that is when Sariputta realized she was a leper. Her face was covered in sore patches, lacerated with scabs that had formed. Although she revealed herself to be a leper in lifting her head, not a hint of surprise or repulsion could be seen on the elder's face.

With clarity and peacefulness still intact since coming out of meditative attainment of cessation, Sariputta's eyes were clear and pristine like a morning star. With movement as gentle as a breath of a baby in a sound sleep, Sariputta calmly watched the sight of this unfortunate being.

The elderly woman with a voice more hoarse than that of a man, yet still very soft and feeble, then said, "Elder! I am preparing for lunch."

"How and with what do you propose you will make lunch?" he asked.

The elderly woman responded again with a husky voice, as if she had a flu. "Unfortunately, elder, I've caught a hideous illness, and even my family has abandoned me. Since then, I have been wandering towns and streets aimlessly. But who would welcome a wretched person like me that even my family had abandoned? People run off when they see me appear from far. Most people don't even want to look at me, turning their eyes away from me."

She continued while crying.

"Elder! I am waiting in front of this rich family's house in hopes of getting some leftover vegetables and rice water that flows out from their drainage. I will take that as my lunch for today. Soon, the daughter-in-law from that family will prepare a meal for her husband and her parents-in-law, and leftover rice water and vegetable scraps will flow out from their drainage. I will gather and eat that with the food I found near the dumpster of another house."

While the old woman spoke, rice water and vegetable scraps began to flow out of the drainage. She held out her cup and received the water. Then she looked up toward the elder with veneration, and Sariputta was gazing down on the old woman with compassion.

"Elder," said the old woman, "you stand before me, which I know is a great opportunity for me to offer you alms. But unfortunately I have nothing to offer you."

"Granny, you could offer the water you have on your hand. Actually, you should just drink that water, and I will be happy to receive the second batch of water that flows out," the chief disciple of the Buddha said to the ill-fated one.

"Oh, elder!" The old woman got up and cried out in joy. "If I am allowed to offer you rice water, how could I possibly offer you the second batch? Elder, allow me to offer this rice water with utmost sincerity."

That being said, the old woman poured the vegetable scraps and rice water into the elder's bowl. At the moment, her leprous finger from her thumb that barely hung, got detached and fell into the alms bowl along with the rice water.

"Oh my! I am so sorry, elder!" Completely flustered, the old woman was at a loss about what to do. "I ruined this precious opportunity to make offering! Oh, oh, what am I to do? Venerable, quickly throw out what is in your bowl!"

However, the elder looked peaceful as a swan floating on the surface of a lake.

"Granny," said Sariputta, "the Buddha set out a precept that every bhikkhu must accept all alms by their devotees, without any preference. So, it's not up to me to refuse the food you offered with such sincerity. The Buddha, however, didn't mention that we must consume everything that has been offered. This means I may not eat this food, but I will decide on whether I will have it or not once I return back to my monastery."

On hearing this, the elderly woman placed her palms together with gratitude. She then sat herself down in front of the drainage and reached out her bowl to receive the sporadic flow of leftover vegetables and rice water for her to drink. In the meantime, Elder Sariputta returned back to his residence.[25]

After witnessing all this, Sakka stayed hidden and followed Sariputta without revealing himself. Shortly thereafter, the Elder Sariputta went into his small hut, and Sakka floated above the home of this great sage who had overcome all ten hindrances[26] to enlightenment.

---

25 The story of a leper eating from the drainage of a rich man and taking a leprous finger that was dropped into the alms bowl without revulsion is from the original story of Mahakassapa. In this book, the story occurs to Elder Sariputta.

26 Ten hindrances: Ten hindrances to enlightenment that prevent progress of practice: 1) Wrong view in a permanent self. 2) Doubt and extreme skepticism of Dhamma. 3) Attachment to incorrect practice. 4) Attachment to sensory desires. 5) Ill-will or anger. 6) Craving for existence in the form world. 7) Craving for existence in the formless world. 8) Conceit. 9) Restlessness and anxiety. 10) Ignorance. When all ten hindrances are eradicated, the stages of arhat is realized and all practice comes to completion.

It was right then when a stream of eerie dark energy seemed to flash across the sky and Mara appeared in front of Sakka. Already foreseeing what Mara was up to, Sakka roared, "Wait!" while blocking his way.

Mara frowned and asked, "Why are you standing in my way?"

"I know why you are here. Without a doubt you came to tempt Elder Sariputta."

"No!" said Mara with a hint of sneer on his face. "I am here not to entice him, but to show him there is a much better path than the one he is on. But what does my coming here have anything to do with you for you to block my way?"

"I'm standing before you to protect goodness."

"For goodness?" Mara smiled while puckering his lips. "What goodness? What is this goodness that you speak of?"

"Goodness promotes happiness and reduces suffering. The Buddha distinguished the path of goodness in two; goodness based on desire in the mundane realm and goodness that transcends desires in the supra-mundane realm," Sakka said.

Mara said in protest, "I know that too. I also know that the Buddha primarily recognized desire, but he sees desire as something tarnished and filthy that must be avoided ultimately. I have a different opinion, however. What is your take on that? Without petty arguments on this and that, wouldn't you agree that desire itself is something good?

"For example, fulfilling one's desire to sleep when sleepy, fulfilling desire to eat when hungry, fulfilling man's carnal desire toward woman and vice versa in fulfilment of their erotic desires, fulfilling one's desire to take control another when one wants to, and fulfilling one's desire to stand out and show off. Isn't that all about happiness?"

"That is true," Sakka said.

"Then, why does the Buddha speak as if desire is as awful as poison?" asked Mara.

Sakka hesitated, unable to respond. Mara then quickly took the chance to enter the hut of Sariputta.

When Sakka followed him into the hut, Mara had already exposed himself to Elder Sariputta and was saying, "Dear elder, what have you done with the rice water and vegetable scraps? What about the leprous finger that fell in?"

The Buddha's chief disciple responded, "I buried the finger into the ground and drank the rest of rice water with vegetables."

"Then you must be extremely disgusted right now," replied Mara.

"That is not so, Mara."

"I don't believe you. How could you not be revolted by the food where a leprous finger fell in?" Mara asked.

"Mara, to be freed from afflictions with practice is to have your feelings roll off, like a lotus flower rolls off dewdrops. I saw the food I ate as a lotus flower, smelled it as a lotus flower, and tasted it as a lotus flower, and thus rolled it off like a lotus flower rolling off dewdrops. Mara, a learned practitioner must prevent all feelings from entering the mind, thus prevent them from being transformed into suffering."[27]

"Personally, I don't really get it. But that's beside the point. That filthy food you had is not going to be the only food you will have for lunch, is it?" Mara asked.

"Yes, it is."

"But elder, did you not starve while you were in a meditative attainment of cessation for the last seven days? How could you eat food without any nutritional value that won't even satisfy your hunger? Today should be an exception, and why wouldn't you go out and beg for alms again?

"Luckily, a devout Buddhist, Sakka, is present here, and he had been waiting for an opportunity to offer alms to Your Reverence. Why wouldn't you accept more food, not only for yourself but for the sake of Heavenly King Sakka. With your permission, Sakka

---

27 To dodge the second arrow: Just because one is an awakened sage doesn't mean they don't feel any sensory stimulus. While the ill-instructed disciples misunderstand and mishandle the first feeling encountered, thus allowing it to advance to a secondary feeling, the well-instructed disciples correctly understand and handle the first feeling and prevent the secondary feeling or afflictions to arise. Buddha referred to this as "pierced by a first arrow but dodging the second arrow."

will bring finest food from the Tavatimsa Heaven instantly with his supernatural powers," explained Mara.

"Mara, it's already past noon, and I wouldn't be taking any more food today," replied Sariputta.

"What does taking food have to do with the time being past noon?" asked Mara.

"The Blessed One set a precept for bhikkhus not to take any food after noon."

"Dear elder," started Mara while sneering his weary smile, "may I ask you something about the precept you just spoke of?"

"Go ahead and ask."

"Why did the Buddha create such a nuisance as a precept to torment practitioners? He always says 'Dhamma is bliss, Dhamma is joy, and Dhamma is delight,' does he not?" asked Mara.

"The Buddha established precepts to establish foundation of happiness, joy, and delight and how they should be further cultivated."

"But I don't understand what that means. Because it will certainly cause lack of freedom if you set precepts and live within the boundaries. Such lack of freedom neither makes one happy, nor joyous, nor delightful."

"Then what is the freedom that you speak of?" asked Sariputta.

"Freedom is to act just as one pleases," Mara replied.

"Mara, that is not freedom but self-indulgence."

"What's the difference between self-indulgence and freedom?" asked Mara.

"Self-indulgence is acting any way one pleases outside of law, which is an act of surrendering to desire; while freedom is following the law, which is achieved by overcoming desire," said Sariputta.

"The subject of desire again. The very subject the Buddha discusses so often. Just as impressions are left on the ground by wagon wheels, the subject of desire will be left as impressions by the wagon of the Buddha's lips. Then let me ask you. Why does the Blessed One treat desires with such hostility?" asked Mara.

"Dear Mara, you assume a deceitful appearance of requesting

for Dhamma, but in truth you do not wish to hear my discourse at all. From the time when I spoke of lotus flower and water dew as a figure of speech, I saw that you were not ready to hear the teachings that negate desires."

"Does that mean you refuse to teach me? Despite what the Buddha said about Dhamma talk being the highest of all generosity?"

"Mara, Dhamma talk should not be offered to just anyone, but only to those who are ready. This is because when Dhamma talk is offered to those who are not ready, it neither blossoms into flowers nor bears fruits. Thus, wise masters keep noble silence toward such beings and simply go on with what they must do."

Elder Sariputta kept silence after this discourse, and his silence became a mental strength more powerful than that of one hundred elephants, which temporarily led Mara's mind back to goodness away from the path of evil.

Soon, the great sage with none comparable in wisdom throughout heaven and earth except for the Buddha, who the Buddha praised as the "Marshall of Dhamma," spoke again. But this time not in a tone of a general ready to fight against its enemy but of a gentle mother who speaks kindly and lovingly toward her baby.

"Mara, I am aware that you approached the Buddha to entice him in the past, just like you came to entice me today. At that time, the Buddha refused to be lured by you and he recited the following four verses, which I am also going to share with you. Do not think that you are berated, but take this opportunity for you to become virtuous."

With these words, the elder recited the following verses.

> Happy indeed we live
> Free from worries, cares, and possessions
> Feeding on joy and fulfilment, let us live in happiness
> Like the gods of the Heaven of Radiant Sound.[28]

---

28 The heavenly beings in the Heaven of Radiant Sound take joy of meditation as their food.

Happy indeed we live
Free from hatred among those full of hatred
Without aversion among those full of aversion
Let us live in true happiness.

Happy indeed we live
Free from illness among those diseased[29]
Without pain amidst those who feel pain
Let us live in true happiness.

Happy indeed we live
Discarding pleasures among those who seek pleasures
Free from craving amidst those full of craving
Let us live in true happiness.

When these teachings and verses were offered by Elder Sariputta, Mara flinched like the way a soldier would when shot by an arrow. Mara frowned and thought, *I cannot entice this practitioner, as he had transcended all desires.*

Mara turned red with embarrassment, but he quickly left the hut once he turned back to his evil mind.

"Sadhu, Sadhu, Sadhu!"

The Heavenly King Sakka, who had seen the full account of what had happened, appeared before Sariputta and praised the great master. "Venerable elder, you skillfully defeated Mara and brought me such great joy. Although I wasn't given the opportunity to offer alms and gain merits, I attained greater virtue of learning Dhamma, superior than making material offerings."

With these words, the king of Tavatimsa Heaven, Sakka, offered three prostrations to Sariputta with respect and gratitude.

"Heavenly King Sakka," said Sariputta, "Rejoicing in others'

---

29 Refers to the sickness of mind.

happiness is one of four immeasurable minds[30] encouraged by the Buddha. Thus, by rejoicing the way I defeated Mara, you were able to gain another merit over the one you gained in correct understanding of Dhamma. But Sakka, you can gain one more merit over the two you have already gained."

"Dear elder, please tell me. I will perform the meritorious act without any hesitation."

"Share with the other heavenly beings what you have seen and heard. Their devotion will not only increase but they will gain power to plow through and lead a correct path of life," explained Sariputta.

"Great elder, I will certainly do as you have instructed."

After sharing all he had seen so far with the other heavenly beings, Sakka said to the Dhamma assembly, "Dear friends, I experienced what I have just told you a while ago, and Brahma Sanankumara suggested that I disseminate this teaching. Thus, I am openly sharing this with you. My dear ones, I hope you will develop greater devotion toward Dhamma and walk the right path of life, just as I do."

After finishing his speech, Sakka with joyful smile said nothing for a while. And all those heavenly beings from the Tavatimsa Heaven, who were happy with Sakka for his teachings, felt happier in seeing joyful smile of their leader.

Then, saying "Sadhu, Sadhu! Sadhu!" all the Buddhist disciples who had gathered at the assembly praised Sariputta's victory over Mara and Sakka's merit in sharing the Dhamma. Hundreds of thousands of praises echoed throughout the Tavatimsa Heaven. In time, these praises echoed back in multiple folds, just like a shout into a great rock cave.

Dhamma teaching was over and the assembly began to disperse. First, Dhamma master Pancasika and Heavenly King Sakka paid homage at the great stupa and returned to their abode with farewell

---

30 Four Immeasurable Minds: Four minds of metta (wish for all beings to be happy), karuna (wish for all beings to be free from suffering), mudita (rejoice in goodness of others), and Upekkha (remain in equanimity, free from attachment and hatred). Four immeasurable minds are boundless minds that abide in noble mind (brahma vihara).

from heavenly beings. Although the assembly returned separately to their lesser heavens, there was no disorder or confusion despite the hundreds of millions of heavenly beings that went their separate ways at once, which was possible due to their supernatural ability to diminish their body.

CHAPTER 8
Two Heavenly Beings Start Cultivation of the Mind

After closing of the Dhamma assembly, Raja and Sirima met again as promised in front of the large stupa. They proceeded to the large stupa with flowers and incenses they had prepared and offered them politely. Then they sat cross-legged, closed their eyes, and thought about the holy virtues of the Buddha and thereafter they receded.

Sirima told Raja, "Now, let us go down to the Human Realm."

"But," Raja stopped Sirima and said, "wouldn't it be better for us to tell our parents before our departure?"

Sirima shook her head showing a firm determination on her pretty face. "Our parents wouldn't approve of us going down to the Human Realm. So we will tell it only to Great Deva Mita. Then he will take good care of the rest on his own."

After the dialogue, the two heavenly beings visited the Great Deva Mita and told their plan to descend to the Human Realm, however rough and rugged it might be, to learn the Buddhadhamma. Then Mita praised the decision of Raja and Sirima. Nevertheless, the two heavenly beings knew what Mita thought: *Why on earth they want to leave such a good place like the Tavatimsa Heaven? Besides, it is less than a day since they were born.*

After retreating from the abode of Great Deva Mita, Raja and Sirima began to fly down slowly from the top of the Mt. Sumeru, passed the Heaven of the Four-Quarter Kings, arrived in the Human Realm, and went to the Jetavana Monastery in a wide grove just outside the capital city of Savatthi of Kosala Kingdom. When they arrived at the monastery, it was early dawn.

They joined their palms together and stayed for quite a while in the space above the grove that was filled with shrubs. In the dark grove, small cottages were scattered here and there, and in the middle was the Hall of Fragrance where the Buddha resided.

As all bhikkhus were asleep, it was quiet all around. After a while, the bustling noise of people could be heard. This meant the bhikkhus were being awakened from their sleep. They straightened their robes, washed their faces, sat neatly in their cottages, and entered into meditation—each with their own subject of practice. The heart of Sirima, who was watching such movements of the bhikkhus, was filled with emotions and aching at the same time. That was because her pervious life as a bhikkhu acted upon her as a remaining karma.

After some time, bhikkhus came out from meditation and ate the leftovers from yesterday. Afterwards, some bhikkhus walked slowly outside of their cottages in walking meditation, some others recited the Buddhist teachings, and likewise, everyone spent time on their own.

Thinking that this was the right time, they went to Ananda[31] who was the attendant of the Buddha, at the cottage built adjacent to the

---

31 Ananda was from the royal family of the Shakya Kingdom and a first cousin of the Buddha, and he had a beautiful look and a warm heart. He was influenced by the Buddha and left home to be a monastic, together with five other members of the royal family and their barber Upali. For twenty-five years—from the time when the Buddha was fifty-five years old until he entered parinirvana at eighty—he faithfully performed his duty as an attendant to the Buddha. While the Buddha was alive, Ananda attained the realization of the stream-enterer, and after the Buddha's parinirvana, attained the realization of the arhat and attended the council of five hundred arhats, which was organized by Elder Mahakassapa to compile the teachings of the Buddha; he memorized and recited many of the discourses of the Buddha.

Hall of Fragrance as an annex. They revealed themselves and made three prostrations toward the elder.

"Dear heavenly beings, what brought you here?" Ananda, whose face was as immaculate as a sculpture, asked with a soft voice.

The two heavenly beings replied, "We are here in the hope of having an audience with the Buddha."

With a nod Ananda said, "I understand. You two, please continue to conceal yourselves and follow me."

Having said this, Elder Ananda came out of his cottage and proceeded to the Hall of Fragrance. Then the two heavenly beings, with their bodies concealed, followed Elder Ananda.

After making three prostrations to the Buddha, Ananda asked his master. "Blessed One, to whom will you go and receive the offering today?"

The Buddha replied, "Ananda, the Tathagata will go to the Savatthi city and receive the offering from a Brahmin named Subhuti. And, Ananda, as the attendant of the Tathagata, you should know that the Tathagata, for the next six months, plans to go to the port city of Subbaraka of the Assaka kingdom to meet Binggisa. During the time, the Tathagata will receive offerings from the most appropriate sentient beings at each place where the Tathagata will stop over."

Ananda opened his eyes in surprise and asked his master, "Did the Blessed One just mention Binggisa?"

"Yes, I did."

Very surprised Ananda responded, "Isn't the Binggisa the Blessed One just mentioned that troubadour Binggisa who is well known among the bhikkhus for his ill-fated association with Elder Bhaddiya?"

"Right, that's the same Binggisa."

"But Blessed One, at the time when Bhaddiya was the king of the Shakya Kingdom, he seduced the queen consort and committed the sin of adultery. And far from repenting his sin, he accepted a wrong and evil belief and started a religious war that destroyed tens of thousands of lives and properties. Judging from this, going to hell and suffering for a long time in his next life will even be insufficient.

Then, how does the Blessed One, who is the teacher of the Human Realm and the Heavenly Realm, plan to embark on a journey to meet him, which will take as long as six months?"

The Buddha stopped Ananda and said, "Stop it, stop it, how could you understand the profound meaning of the Tathagata traveling to meet him? Ananda, if your wisdom can be compared to a single leaf of this Jeta grove, the wisdom of the Tathagata is like the entire grove. Therefore, though the Tathagata would tell you on that, you will never be able to fully understand the meaning of the Tathagata going to meet Binggisa.

"However, the Tathagata will tell you just this. Ananda, the subtlest in the Human Realm is the mind, and as the mind is limitlessly subtle, even arhats who have achieved a high level of practice cannot fathom its full depth, and only the Tathagata who has attained the unsurpassed perfect enlightenment can, by his wisdom, illuminate and see each and every part of it.

"As the Tathagata sees through this wisdom, though the sin of Binggisa, who you blame, might appear greater than the Mt. Sumeru, dear Ananda, the mind may rise higher by falling lower, and it can be extremely brightened by becoming extremely darkened, and such is the mind of Binggisa. Therefore, Ananda, do not worry about the Tathagata who will go to meet Binggisa, but only mind making preparations for the journey," the Buddha finished.

Once the Buddha said this, Ananda, who had a pure and undefiled nature, said, "So I will do, Blessed One," and accepted the master's instruction.

After calmly watching his disciple accept his words, the Buddha turned his head toward Raja and Sirima who concealed themselves behind Ananda and said, "As now is the right time, dear Raja and Sirima, reveal yourselves before the Tathagata."

Then, Raja and Sirima soon revealed themselves and expressed their respect by making three prostrations. The Buddha asked the two heavenly beings, "What is it that you want from the Tathagata?"

Raja answered, "Omniscient Blessed One, because of the merit of hearing a verse of the Blessed One at the last moment of my previous life, I was born on the Tavatimsa Heaven. And I consider that the Blessed One is well aware that my wife Sirima, who was the bhikkhu Sanu who died immediately after receiving the Blessed One's teachings and was soon reborn on the Tavatimsa Heaven."

The Buddha said, "The Tathagata remembers that which happened some time ago. However, for the time of the Human Realm is different from that of the Heavenly Realm, during the short period of time you spent in the Tavatimsa Heaven, as much time as a year has elapsed in the Human Realm, and during this period, the Tathagata left the Veluvana Monastery where the Tathagata used to reside and came to stay at this Jetavana Monastery."

"Blessed One, we, as husband and wife, wish that rather than staying in the Tavatimsa Heaven to enjoy pleasures, stay in the Human Realm as long as possible to learn the Buddhadhamma more deeply, howsoever big the trouble might be. Therefore, the most noble and ever joyous one, we plead you that you please guide us, foolish ones."

"Excellent! Excellent!" the Buddha praised the two heavenly beings. They were deeply moved by the praise of the Buddha.

Having subdued his excitement, Raja asked the Buddha, "However, the Blessed One, are we, those who are not human beings, also able to achieve the high level of the Buddhadhamma like human beings?"

"Yes, you are. But certain conditions must be met to be able to achieve that goal," the Buddha explained.

"What are the conditions?"

"To achieve the goal, there should be a disciple who has reached the level capable of learning the Buddhadhamma and a master who has attained his goal; the disciple should ask the master for teachings with due courtesy;[32] the master should teach the disciple properly, and the disciple should practice what they have learned."

---

32 The Buddha told bhikkhus to teach the Dhamma only when one asks for it with due courtesy. Because not showing due courtesy means that one does not respect the Dhamma, and not respecting the Dhamma means that one is not expected to practice the Dhamma.

"Blessed One, have we arrived at the level capable of learning the Buddhadhamma?"asked Raja.

"Yes, you have arrived at the level."

"Then, Blessed One, please tell us on the due courtesy with which the disciples should ask the masters for teachings?"

"The best way of asking for teachings is to leave home and become a bhikkhu or bhikkhuni at the Buddhist community of the Tathagata. Once you are on this path, you will receive these and those instructions from the Tathagata or senior bhikkhus (bhikkhunis), and it is because you, with your free will, became a bhikkhu (bhikkhuni) and asked for teachings. But since you are heavenly beings, you cannot adopt this method."

With a sad look on his face, Raja said, "Blessed One, even though we cannot adopt the best method, there should be the next best one, so please tell us what that is."

"The next best method is to become lay disciples of the Tathagata. When you enter this path, you will not receive these and those instructions from the Tathagata. You can receive teachings from the Tathagata only with questions you ask, and the Tathagata will only suggest, but not force, the right path of life."

"Then, Blessed One, please teach us in that way."

"In that case, however, it is difficult for you to make big progress in your practice," said the Buddha.

This remark of the Buddha disappointed Raja and Sirima, who had a high expectation. They breathed a thin sigh, and their foreheads were cast with shadow. The Buddha was immersed in thought for a while, and the two heavenly beings waited anxiously for the Buddha's next words.

At last, the Buddha said to them, "Raja and Sirima, the Tathagata will specially allow you a position, which is not exactly the same but approximate to bhikkhu-bhikkhuni; this is a decision taken in consideration of the relationships you had with the Tathagata in your previous lives.

"Two heavenly beings, you could maintain the present state as heavenly beings and become the special disciples of the Buddha. In this case the Tathagata will give these and those instructions to you and as a result you will be able to learn the Buddhadhamma more efficiently. However, according to the law of the Heavenly Realm, you can be special disciples of the Tathagata for only six months, and you will have to return to the Tavatimsa Heaven after the six months."

Raja and Sirima rejoiced and addressed the Tathagata, "Blessed One, who has no comparison in dealing with humans, we do happily wish that we become special disciples of the Blessed One, so please accept and guide us well!"

The Buddha declared, "Raja and Sirima, truth-seekers of the Heavenly Realm who have renounced the pleasures in the Tavatimsa Heaven and come down to the Human Realm, thickened with filth and defiled with disgrace, where humans must toil! As the Tathagata now accepts you as my special disciples, you shall, for six months, come and receive the Tathagata's guidance, learn well, think well, practice well, and achieve great progress!"

Raja and Sirima thereupon became the special disciples of the Buddha by making three prostrations again to the master.

The Buddha said to the two heavenly beings, "From now on, you will conceal yourselves so that no ordinary humans can see you, and learn and practice the teachings taught by the Tathagata and his disciples."

"Yes, Blessed One."

"Now you go to Bhikkhu Malukha right away, and listen to his conversation of Dhamma exchange shared with Bhikkhu Bhaddiya. And thereafter, you will continue to follow them on their journey, watch the manner in which they practice and a range of things happening around them to learn and practice well."

"Blessed One, we will do so."

Having replied like this, Raja and Sirima expressed their gratitude to the holy master, receded from the place, and with the heavenly eye, looked for the place where Bhikkhu Malukha resided.

They learned that Malukha was at a monastery near Bodhgaya of the Magadha Kingdom and was making preparations to go out to beg for food. The two heavenly beings flew high into the sky and, at heavenly pace, went to the dwelling of Malukha with the blink of an eye.

CHAPTER 9
The Parable
of the Poisoned Arrow

While the two heavenly beings were watching, Bhikkhu Malukha went to the city to beg for food. After some time, he proceeded to a quiet place and ate the food for which he had begged. After the meal, Bhikkhu Malukha went to a nearby creek and washed the bowl. Then he straightened his robe and walked slowly, heading for a place that was not the place he had come from.

After walking a half yojana, Malukha arrived at the cottage of Bhikkhu Bhaddiya seated deep in the forest full of various kinds of shrub. As it happened, Bhaddiya was returning home from a walking meditation at a place not far away.

At the sight of Malukha, Bhaddiya joined his palms saying, "Welcome, brother!" and the two heavenly beings, who were watching them closely, did not feel any conceit from Bhaddiya that could easily be felt from a man who had once been a king.

The two bhikkhus went into the cottage. Malukha, after showing respect by making three prostrations to Bhaddiya who was a senior monk to him, said, "I am here to meet with the elder at the instruction of the Buddha."

Bhaddiya nodded calmly. Malukha started to explain the reason for his visit.

"Dear elder, I renounced the world seven years ago, and for the last two years I have practiced meditation with the subject given by the Blessed One. One day arose in me such questions as *Is the space limited or limitless? Is it limited and limitless at the same time? Is it neither limited nor limitless? Is the time limited or limitless? Is it limited and limitless at the same time? Is it neither limited nor limitless? Why is there space? Why is there time? Why is there death? Why is there life?*[33]

"I thought about the questions intently. However, thoughts were just overlapped and entangled, giving no satisfactory answers to the questions. Therefore, I went to the Blessed One and asked for answers to the questions, but the Blessed One did not say a word. So I tried hard to forget about the questions and concentrate on the subject of meditation. However, not long thereafter, the questions resurfaced in my mind and demanded answers more strongly than before.

"I could not endure the curiosity any further, so I went to the Blessed One once again and asked about the questions, but the Blessed One still did not say anything. I thought there should be reasons for the Blessed One not giving answers, and again I tried hard to forget about the questions and concentrate on the subject of meditation.

"But not long thereafter, questions surfaced again, and this time they became an unbearable delusion and anguish that pushed me into a tremendous suffering. So, I came forward to the Blessed One

---

33 No response (avyakarana): According to Culamalunkyaputta Sutta, Bhikkhu Culamalunkya-putta asked fourteen metaphysical questions to the Buddha, but the Buddha did not answer for the first two rounds of questions. Like this, that the Buddha doesn't answer certain questions is called "no response" (avyakarana), and "response" here means to make conclusive remarks on certain subjects. In this work, the author arbitrarily changed the questioner to Malukha and expanded richly on the dialogue between him and the Buddha and the experiences he went through thereafter.

for the third time and asked about the questions. But the Blessed One still did not utter a word. I was deeply disappointed and said, 'Blessed One, as you have refused to say a word for as many as three times, I think I will leave the Sangha and return to my secular home.'"

(Then it happened.)

The Buddha said to the disciple who was full of thoughts, "Malukha, you, as well as all other monastic disciples of the Tathagata are free to return at any time to the state before renunciation."

At such remarks of the Buddha, Malukha, with a dejected expression, said to the Buddha, "Blessed One, such remarks of the Blessed One make me doubt about the Blessed One as the master and as the father. Having heard such remarks, I am now thinking that *Oh, the Blessed One has abandoned me! The Blessed One is so coldhearted.*"

The Buddha responded, "Malukha, the Tathagata is in fact a cold-hearted master, and it is because he clearly illuminates the truth that to be born as a human being is to be put into a harsh reality that I am not you and you are not I. In relation to this, you should know that by well studying this cold reality there shall arise wisdom, and based on such wisdom, true human relationship will be established."

However, these remarks of the Buddha were not what Malukha had anticipated. Since he was drawn only to the coldheartedness of the two elements the Buddha mentioned, namely the coldheartedness and the truth, he did not pay any attention to the truth.

Malukha said, "If the Blessed One is so coldhearted, I will also address him coldheartedly. Blessed One! Seven years ago, out of respect for the Blessed One, I left home and became a bhikkhu, and this renunciation meant that I left my freedom with the Blessed One and that in response to this, the Blessed One undertook the duty to teach me."

"So I think," said the Buddha.

"But is the Blessed One not neglecting his duty toward me by saying no words to the questions I ask?"

"Malukha, try to recall the time of your renunciation. At that time, did the Tathagata promise that he would teach you on whether the space is limited or limitless or whether the time is limited or limitless?"

"No, he did not."

"Then what did the Tathagata promise to teach you?" asked the Buddha.

"As the Dhamma of the Tathagata is the Four Noble Truths, the Blessed One has implicitly promised to teach me on the Four Noble Truths."

"Then Malukha, what are the Four Noble Truths as you understand them?"

"Blessed One, I understand that the Four Noble Truths are truths comparable to a doctor (the Buddha) treating patients (sentient beings). The Four Noble Truths consist of the truth of suffering, the truth of the arising of suffering, the truth of the cessation of suffering, and the truth of the path to the cessation of suffering, and among these truths *suffering* can be thought of as being analogous to a patient showing symptoms of illness, the *arising of suffering* to a doctor identifying the causes of the illness, the *cessation of suffering* to the health which is the ultimate goal of the treatment, and the *path to the cessation of suffering* to a doctor recommending a treatment for the illness."

"Then Malukha, are the questions you asked to the Tathagata such as 'Is the space limited or limitless?' included in the Four Noble Truths or not?"

"They are included in the Four Noble Truths."

"In what sense do you think that such questions are included in the Four Noble Truths?"

"I think that the truth of suffering points to the eight sufferings, that is, physically the four sufferings of birth, aging, illness, and death, and mentally, the suffering of union with what is displeasing, of separation from what is pleasing, of not getting what one wants, and of losing what one has acquired with difficulty. Is my understanding correct?"

"Yes, it is correct."

"Then, my other questions aside, at least the one question, 'What is death?' should be included in the Four Noble Truths, shouldn't it?"

"But Malukha, the Four Noble Truths deal with all sufferings of life including death. Firstly, from the perspective of *self*, and secondly, with the focus on *how to resolve such sufferings.*"

Then, Malukha asked, "Blessed One, what does it mean that the Four Noble Truths deal with all sufferings from the perspective of self?"

"Malukha, from whom will the physical and mental sufferings which the noble truth of suffering refers to arise?"

"They arise from everybody."

"That is correct but at the same time incorrect, because viewed from the basic dimension, the physical and mental sufferings, which the noble truth of suffering refers to, arise from *me*."

"Blessed One, please explain with examples so that I can fully understand the point."

"For instance, let's assume that death is imminent upon you, and sitting beside your bed is your mother who loves you dearly. In this case can your mother die instead of you?"

"It is not possible, Blessed One."

"Then in the opposite case—namely, suppose there is your mother who you love dearly, and death is impending upon her, then, can you die instead of your mother?"

"That will never be possible."

"Again, in the former example, what would it be if death is substituted with aging and illness? Malukha, can you transfer the aging and illness from your mother to your body, and you age and become ill instead of your mother?"

"That is not possible, Blessed One."

"What about the opposite case? Namely, can your mother transfer your aging and illness to her and age and be ill instead of you?"

"That will never be possible."

"Again, what if death, aging, and illness are replaced with worry and fear—namely, afflictions? In this case, can you move the afflictions from your mother to your mind and suffer the afflictions in her place?"

"That is not possible."

"What about the opposite case? Namely, can your mother transfer the afflictions from you and suffer the afflictions instead of you?"

"That will never be possible, Blessed One."

"How is it so?"

"Blessed One, it is because that I am not my mother, and my mother is my mother and not I."

Having led the dialogue up to this, the Buddha stopped talking and fell silent. Malukha closed his eyes and was immersed in thought for a while.

After some time, Malukha opened his eyes and looked up at the Buddha, then the Buddha said to his disciple, "Malukha, just before, the Tathagata asked you 'from whom the physical and mental sufferings that the Four Noble Truths refer to will arise,' and you answered that 'they arise from everybody.'"

"That is true."

"Then, the Tathagata taught that the physical and mental sufferings arise from *yourself* and from nobody else, and I took the example of you and your mother to facilitate your understanding. Malukha, by now you should have understood that the physical and mental sufferings the Four Noble Truths refer to arise from the self."

"Blessed One, I understand what you have said."

"Then again, Malukha, what is the second truth of the Four Noble Truths?"

"Blessed One, that is the truth of the arising of the suffering."

"That's correct, and Malukha, as you said before, the truth of arising of the suffering is the truth of identifying the causes of the illness to develop the cure for decease."

"Yes, Blessed One."

"And here, the methods of diagnosing the causes of the illness that sentient beings are suffering from—namely all physical and mental sufferings—are divided into *inner ones* and *outer ones*."

"Blessed One, please explain in detail so that I could understand."

"Malukha, you must first know that the eight physical and mental sufferings of the sentient beings are eventually no more than the suffering of 'seeking but being unable to obtain.' In other words, that certain living being is called a sentient being because he is desirous of something, and the fact that he is desirous of something means that his mind is an empty cup that waits to be filled."[34]

The Buddha continued, "In this respect, sentient beings have an empty cup to be filled for their wish to avoid death, for their wish to avoid aging, and for their wish to avoid illness. In addition, sentient beings have an empty cup to be filled for their wish to enjoy sensual pleasures, for their wish to earn favor of others, for their wish to be respected by others, for their wish to rule others, etc. In addition, there are too many empty cups of desire for sentient beings to enumerate them all one by one."

"It is really so, Blessed One."

"Then Malukha, what do the people of the world do to fill so many of these empty cups in their minds?" asked the Buddha.

"They will go to the place where there is water to fill their empty cups from the well often called *society*. And there, they draw water by the name of wealth, opposite sex, fame, power, and so on."

"You are right. But Malukha, at the well you mentioned gathered myriad sentient beings who want to draw water."

"That is right, Blessed One."

"However, the quantity of the water is very much limited compared to the amount of the desire of the sentient beings, so there will be competition among them to draw more water."

"That is so, Blessed One."

"And those who win the competition will draw more water before others."

---

34 The mind desires: The reason why the lowest realm of the three realms is called the Desire Realm is that it is the world where sentient beings who desire something reside. Another name of the Desire Realm is the "saha world," which means "a world that must be endured." In other words, a mind desiring something inevitably gives rise to a situation that must be endured. Therefore, Buddhism first teaches human beings born on the Desire Realm about how to endure desires (ethics training). However, as the desire issue cannot be resolved fundamentally by enduring, it recommends, as the next step, to cease the mind that desires (concentration training), and again presents the way to remove the mind that desires (wisdom training).

"That is so, Blessed One."

"Then he will fill his cup with the water drawn with difficulties."

"That is so, Blessed One."

"Thus, he will be satisfied and feel happy."

"That is so, Blessed One."

"Then can he fill *all* his cups with the water he has drawn or not?"

After a moment's thought Malukha answered, "He will fill part of his cups but cannot fill the whole of his cups. For example, some sentient beings fill the cup of wealth but cannot fill the cup of pretty wife, and some other sentient beings fill the cup of beautiful wife but fail to fill the cup of fame."

"Then Malukha, what do you think? Will the cups that have been filled by sentient beings through myriad hardships be able to maintain the state of satisfaction continuously or not?"

At the question of the master, Malukha was again absorbed in thought. At last, Malukha answered, "Blessed One, filling the cup means that the mind is satisfied, and it is fairly rare for a sentient being to keep on maintaining the state of satisfaction that he has once earned. For example, once a person who wanted to have one thousand rupees gets one thousand rupees, his mind is satisfied. However, not long after, he will take the one thousand rupees for granted, as a result he starts to want two thousand rupees. Like this his state of satisfaction lasts for some time, but then changes into a state of dissatisfaction."

"Then what will he do?"

"He again goes to the well, draws water, and fills his cup, which has grown bigger."

"What will happen next?"

"Oh, Blessed One, though he will fill his cup with difficulty, his cup grows even bigger again."

"Then he has fallen into a state where he is more dissatisfied than before, hasn't he?"

"That is exactly true, Blessed One. When he gets one thousand rupees when he wanted two thousand rupees, he is half satisfied and half dissatisfied. However, when he gets two thousand rupees although he has longed to have five thousand, he will not enjoy even half of the satisfaction though he has more money."

"If that is the desire and satisfaction of sentient beings, how do you think you should resolve this problem?"

"Blessed One, please expound on that for me."

The Buddha said with a smile, "Malukha, to fill the cup of desire, there is a way other than drawing water."

"Blessed One, you just said that there was a way other than drawing water."

"That is correct."

"For I cannot fully understand it, Blessed One, I request you to expound on that for your silly disciple."

"Malukha, you must know that it is to stop the cup from growing bigger, reduce the size of the cup, and eventually eliminate the cup."

Malukha was absorbed in thought for a short while, and having understood the meaning of the words, he rejoiced saying, "Oh, Blessed One, I understand your words. There is another way to fill the cup—reduce the size of the cup."

The Buddha spoke, in a compassionate voice, to his disciple who is often overflowing with thoughts. "That is exactly so. There are two distinctive means to fill the cup of wanting: One is to go to the well, in other words, go to the society and material world and bring back what you want; the other is to come back home to yourself and stop, reduce, and remove the wanting. And the Tathagata preaches that the latter is the more fundamental way to fill the cup, and that based on this, the Four Noble Truths of the Tathagata identify and cure the illnesses of sentient beings.

"Malukha, the Tathagata will call the wanting he has referred to up to now as the desire. To fill the cup by means of drawing water is to recognize the desire, and to fill the cup by means of reducing and removing the cup is to deny the desire.

"Of these two, the Tathagata expounds lay believers to appropriately mix the water-drawing outward path, that is, outer-directed way, with the cup-reducing and cup-removing inward path, namely, the inner-directed way. The Tathagata teaches monastic disciples to concentrate on the inner-directed way, and to cut and kill all sufferings of life by way of removing the cup of desire."[35]

Malukha was deeply moved and said, "Oh, Blessed One! Now I fully understand what it means for the Four Noble Truths to deal with all sufferings of life from the perspective of self."

"Excellent! Excellent!" The Buddha, with a delighted look on his face, praising Malukha.

Malukha asked, "Blessed One, you have expounded till now that the Four Noble Truths deal with all problems of life, including death, from the perspective of self. Now, please teach me on that the Four Noble Truths focus on 'how to resolve the sufferings.'"

The Buddha said, "On that matter, the Tathagata will explain using the relationship between a doctor and a patient. Let's assume that there is a good doctor, and he is about to treat a patient. The objective of the doctor at that time is only one, to treat the patient. Therefore all his efforts are centered on and directed to the objective of curing the patient. However, if there is a doctor who loses his objective and goes 'excessively far' to identify the causes of the illness, can you call him a good doctor?"

"Blessed One, please explain it in further detail so that I could understand."

"As an example, the doctor, being excessively absorbed in identifying the causes of the illness, thought like this: *This patient caught a cold. Therefore, I have to find out and remove the causes of the cold. A cold is a respiratory disease, respiratory disease is a bodily disease, his body was born by his parents, and his father was born by his grandparents. Therefore, I will examine his grandparents and clarify who they really are, and thereafter based on such findings determine who his parents are, and based on that find out what his*

---

35 Both for monastics and laity who pursue enlightenment, wants and needs are all to be extinguished. However, for lay believers, wants are to be extinguished while needs are to be encouraged.

body is like, and based on that find out what his respiratory disease is, and again based on that define what his cold is. Malukha, do you understand this parable?"

"Blessed One, I do understand the parable."

"Malukha, based on the understanding, you recall the questions you asked the Tathagata: 'Is the space limited or limitless? Is it limited and limitless at the same time? Is it neither limited nor unlimited? Why is there space? Why are there time, death, and life?' and you demanded an answer from the Tathagata."

"Yes I did, Blessed One."

"To that, the Tathagata did not answer, and the Tathagata will tell you the reason why the Tathagata did not answer, using another parable. Suppose there is a soldier hit by a poisoned arrow. If there is a close friend nearby, he surely wants to take out the arrow for the soldier."

"I think so, Blessed One."

"But if the soldier tells his friend 'Dear friend, do not remove the arrow. I must find out, before removing the arrow what the shaft is made of, what the arrowhead is made of, and what the arrow feather is made of,' then Malukha, do you think such remarks of the soldier are reasonable?"

"I don't think they are reasonable, Blessed One."

"Then if he tells his friend, 'Dear friend, I must know before you take out the arrow who shot the arrow' and won't release the hands of his friend who wants to treat him, can you call him a wise man?"

"Oh, Blessed One, I cannot call him a wise man."

"Malukha, though the soldier kept on insisting like that, his friend disregarded his remarks and tried to remove the arrow. But the soldier, with all his strength, held his friend's hands firmly and pleaded again, 'Dear friend, I beg you, please do not pull out the arrow for me. I must know who the shooter is before the arrow is pulled out. And I have to know who his father is, who his father's father is, who his father's father's father is, and who his father's father's father's father is. Furthermore, I must know the first forefather of the clan where all of them belong.' Malukha, answer me. Do you think all his remarks like these are reasonable?"

"They are not reasonable, Blessed One. I feel heavy on my chest and cannot stand any further, because he, while talking like this, is dying moment by moment."

Saying this, Malukha made a long face, and the Buddha said, "Malukha, all sentient beings are already pierced by the poisoned arrows of sufferings—physically, the sufferings of birth, aging, illness, and death, and mentally, the sufferings of being troubled by all sorts of afflictions. Therefore, the questions sentient beings require are not such metaphysical and unrealistic questions you asked the Tathagata, but such practical and realistic questions like how to cure the sufferings of life that they are facing. For this reason, Malukha, the Tathagata did not answer the metaphysical and unrealistic questions you asked and remained silent."

At such utterance of the Buddha, Malukha closed his eyes and was immersed in thought. After some time, tears streamed down his cheeks, and this was because he has fully understood the parable of the poisoned arrow.

The Buddha smiled and said, "My son Malukha, don't you cry. I explained the truths not to make you cry but to make you happy."

Still weeping, Malukha grinned and said, "The Blessed One called me his son and referred to himself as I, and this makes me extremely happy."

"A little while ago, you called me coldhearted and now you say I am warmhearted," said the Buddha, smiling again.

After making a prostration toward his noble master, Malukha joined his palms and said, "Blessed One, as I now clearly understand the fundamentals of the Buddhist teachings, I will give up all metaphysical and unrealistic questions and only ask, learn, and practice the way how to remove the poisoned arrow and extinguish sufferings."

"Then are you retracting the words you said a while ago that you wanted to go back to your secular home?"

"Yes, Blessed One, I will continue to remain in the Sangha and practice hard until all sufferings are extinguished."

"Sadhu! Sadhu! Sadhu!"

The Buddha praised his disciple and asked, "According to the law of the Tathagata, what is the state where all sufferings are extinguished called?"

"Blessed One, it is called enlightenment, nirvana, and liberation."

"That is right. Now, you better meet a disciple of the Tathagata who is proceeding well in that direction."

"Blessed One, please tell me who he is."

"Bhikkhu Bhaddiya is he, and now you go to him and hear his Dhamma discourse."

In response, Malukha said to the master, "That I will happily do, Blessed One."

CHAPTER 10
Bhaddiya, Abdicating the Throne to Be a Bhikkhu

(RETURNING BACK TO BHADDIYA'S DWELLING)

Malukha said to Bhaddiya, "So, for these reasons I came to see you elder."

"Well, even so," said Bhaddiya, "I'm not sure if I could help you in your practice, brother."

But Malukha replied, "I think for the Blessed One to send me to you means that you possess more than sufficient ability to help me. That is because he would not, in any circumstances, make a wrong judgment."

"That's right. His judgment is like an arrow that hits the bull's-eye in every circumstance." Having said that, Bhaddiya thought deeply and continued, "In my opinion, the Blessed One sent you to me because I made progress in my practice through loving-kindness meditation."

"Well, then please share with me your great advices, including the loving-kindness meditation."

Bhaddiya nodded his head and said, "I would be more than happy to. But dear brother, before I begin, I would like to share the experiences and beliefs I had before I became a monk. That is because my past experiences in the secular world may be beneficial for your practice."

With a happy expression Malukha responded, "To tell you the truth, I would love to hear your stories. Your karmic relations in the secular world are so amusing that they sometimes become a topic of interest even between the bhikkhus. I am quite curious about your experiences myself." Malukha continued, grinning, "Ah! Of course, I am aware that paying attention to such gossip is not appropriate for practitioners. But as suggested by the question I asked the Buddha, I am the type of person whose mind gets easily distracted by things not related to Buddhist practice."

Hearing Malukha speak so frankly, Bhikkhu Bhaddiya, with his cheerful expression, spoke with a smile, "Brother, I will tell you simply as you also speak so humbly. Part of the reason I share my secular experiences is to lay down that heavy burden of the past off my chest."

"I'd be happy to hear it," said Malukha.

Bhaddiya did not begin right away, but he gently closed his eyes for a while and calmed his mind. In the meantime, Malukha patiently waited for Bhaddiya to speak.

Just outside the hut, which was weaved with thick bamboo trunks, rustling sounds of dry foliage can be heard, carried by the gentle wind. After some time, Bhikkhu Bhaddiya opened his eyes and began to speak with a calm voice.

"Brother, I'm a descendent of Shakya Kingdom. My father was the younger brother of King Suddhodana, the father of the Blessed One. That makes me the first cousin of the Buddha. The Buddha was the only flesh and blood King Suddhodana ever had. With his one and only son becoming a monk, Suddhodana passed away, and my father Kaligodha succeeded the throne, and I became the crown prince as his only son. Soon my father too passed away, and I was enthroned as the next king."

Bhaddiya continued, "From then on, my life changed completely. I had a lot of power, fame, prestige, wealth, and women. Everyone paid respect and praised me. Basking in the joy of great abundance every day, I said, 'As such, the world is worth living. Look how everyone adores me!' But I realized soon enough that the world that I believe to be worth living wasn't really great at all, and the people were not all that kind. That is when my life took a different turn."

(A story of Bhikkhu Bhaddiya in the secular world before his renunciation)

The palace was burglarized nearly two months after Bhaddiya was enthroned. Around twenty thieves came and robbed the palace where treasures were stored, and they went further to invade the most private part of the palace, the king's chamber, where the king and his family resided. That was when the most awful thing Bhaddiya never wish to recall again happened—the thieves stabbed his mother to death.

King Bhaddiya ordered the royal guards to capture the thieves alive, and they did.

"How dare you! It wasn't enough to steal, but you went and took human life!" the king roared to the thieves. "It is only fair that darkness is paid back with darkness—execute them at once!"

At that moment, a voice spoke in his mind. *Killing them will not revive my mother! Is it really necessary to execute them?* Bhaddiya contemplated. The ministers and soldiers who were ready to carry out his order hesitated when they saw the king in reflection. The thieves seized this moment and begged him to spare their lives.

But the ministers came forth. They argued that other thieves may break into the palace if the king gave them pardon. Furthermore, once the law failed, it was difficult to set them back in place, and the king's responsibility in enforcing the law was not a private affair but a civic matter.

After a deep sigh, the man of power who held the fate of the thieves gave order, "The two leaders from the pack shall be sentenced to death, but the rest shall be punished appropriately as the judicial minister sees fit."

But ordering execution was a horrible experience for Bhaddiya, even if it was the punishment enforced by the state law. Any other king may have readily forgotten the incident. But not for Bhaddiya with his introverted tendencies. At the end, a great sense of guilt came over that he killed someone.

But this misfortune was not the only thing that troubled him. Being on the throne was too much of a burden in itself. As a king, Bhaddiya was responsible for making the final decision on various policies. But the problem was that his decision did not necessarily bring benefit to all. A small judgmental error by an individual brings a small effect, as its scope is limited. However, if a policy made by a king is unsuccessful, its adverse effect would bring suffering to everyone, which clearly became a burden on Bhaddiya's heart.

Another problem was that most kings found it difficult to accept their own policy failure. Bhaddiya was a noble and virtuous person by nature. Thus, he felt comfortable to accept his own mistake when something had gone wrong. But evidently such action would be very disadvantageous for maintaining his authority.

He thought to himself, *Even so, shouldn't I admit my failure honestly? Wouldn't it be better for me to apologize to the people who suffer because of my inadequacies?* But another thought appeared that whispered, *But the kingship will be weakened, and then I cannot realize great politics that I dream of.*

Moreover, there were other burdens of being a king. In particular, everybody wanted to take the throne, thus everyone was his potential enemy. In other words, there was always a possibility that someone could be lurking around, and this reality pushed Bhaddiya to the edge of restless apprehension.

Thus, Bhaddiya began to drink in order to forget his burden. In a way, alcohol shared his burden like a good friend would—it worked as his remedy. When he was drunk, he felt totally carefree, as if he had shaken all the burdens off of his shoulder. Thus, gradually he began to indulge in drinking.

Soon, the damaging effects of alcohol began to appear. His

digestion deteriorated and his mind became cloudy. He decided to refrain from alcohol and searched for other means of substituting his drinks—which was hunting. Hunting brought a renewed pleasure to Bhaddiya. When an arrow penetrated an animal, he felt elation like he had never felt before.

One day, he went hunting in the woods and hundreds of soldiers were mobilized to drive animals toward Bhaddiya. Chased by the soldiers and seized in terror, the animals ran toward the king. That was when Bhaddiya drew his bow toward the animals.

Thud, thud. His targets fell to the ground.

"Your majesty! That was a great hit!" howled the soldiers. Bhaddiya felt thrilled with a great joy. Leaving the fallen beasts behind, the king ran toward another target deep into the woods.

In the end, he somehow lost the soldiers and was left alone. That was the first time since he had become the king that no one was around to protect him. Suddenly, silence enclosed on him. He felt slight fear, but he was able to control his fear like any brave king should. In the next instant, he jumped with a surprise when a tiny wild rat suddenly appeared from the forest.

Am I such a weak person? He snorted at the thought.

He continued, *That's right, the stability I enjoy right now is only possible because I am protected by the soldiers. But what if there was no one else to protect me at this very moment?*

Bhaddiya dismounted from the horse and perched on the rock he found nearby. But a strange thing happened! The moment he sat on the rock, an unusual aura suddenly crept up around him. What a terrifying fear! What snuck up on him was the kind of fear he saw, heard, and felt as a child when thunderous lightning struck, the type of petrifying fear that left him trembling in despair, reaching out to his mother's bosom.

Although Bhaddiya was shaken by the strong force of fear that made him cringe, he realized soon enough that this fear was unavoidable, even if he tried his best. In order to set himself to face the fear that threatened him, he straightened the backbone of his mind.

Fear becomes a threat in the mind that tries to flee, but it ducks its tail and hides when faced head on. This can be described by the analogy of a dog on a bridge and its reflection on the surface of water.

When a dog on a bridge barks wildly, its reflection rushes in with ferocious defiance. But if the dog on the bridge decides to fight the reflection and jumps into the water, the reflection will vanish instantly. With such logic, when Bhaddiya decided to toughen up and face the fear, the fear rushed off as if a low tide flowing out.

But that did not completely solve his problem. Unlike ordinary people, he was a type of person who thought and explored the most subtle part of his mind. Such temperament led him inward even after his fear disappeared, but as a result he found a great void in his heart.

That was it. A void space, which is empty.

Little by little, this empty space began to eat away the rest of his mind. He simply couldn't deal with it anymore. He couldn't find the way to defend himself because it was an enemy without form.

Like ants that are bound to slip down when climbing an oily, vertical glass plate; like a bee trying to land on a flower sealed in a glass tube, he lifted and waved his hands of heart with no avail. But he knew fully well that such hand gestures were needless and in vain. Ultimately, his entire mind was swallowed up by this empty void.

"It's empty! I'm empty! I am simply a snake's cast skin! Just a shadow! And this is all for nothing!" Bhaddiya shook his head vigorously in order to get a hold of himself. He then got up and went to a nearby stream and washed his face.

He sat neatly on the grass nearby and contemplated on the dreadful fear he just experienced. After much consideration, he realized that this was not the first time he felt fear without any form. Ever since the time when his palace was burglarized, the fear constantly followed him like a shadow.

Then what is the nature of fear? he thought, *Why do people sense fear?*

After an extensive thought, he concluded: *The essence of fear stems from the fear of death. That is right, what people fear most* is that of death. And all life will end with death. Then . . . What? He continued his thought, *If that is right, isn't life itself fear?*

He thought about the empty feeling that accompanied fear. Then he finally understood. That was the result of the transient, uncertain life, and the nature of life that is finite and limited.

So he cried out, "Yes! I was just a peacock!"

Bhaddiya continued with his thought. *I shot, hunted, and captured various forms of animals until now. Out of them all, I have been particularly interested in hunting peacocks because of their attractive appearance.*

But now, I can see myself resembling a peacock. Its magnificence reminds me of the status of a king—just like my power, wealth, and women, which are envied by all, peacocks also have brilliant large feathers as if embroidered by hundreds of attractive jewels.

But the most important function of birds is their wings that allow them to fly away quickly, escaping their enemies or hunters. But peacocks' wings are too large, which makes it disadvantageous to fly. Additionally, their wings are so striking that they easily become a target of hunters. These splendorous wings in fact put them in grave danger.

Addressing Malukha, Bhaddiya said, "So I shouted, 'Beautiful appearance of a king is such a burden and dangerous. So, am I not same as just another peacock?'"

"Oh . . ." said Malukha.

Bhaddiya continued, "Then I thought about the feeble attitude of a peacock when faced with danger. It rushes away when chased by the enemy or hunter. But when it realizes that there is no escape, it takes cover with the closest thing it could find, perhaps under a pile of grass or behind a rock.

"Oh, those great and vibrant wings of a peacock at that moment! When its fate crosses between life and death, those dazzling-yet-massive wings are just unnecessary and impractical; they tell the hunter, 'I am here. So come and get me!'

"Imagine its head under a pile of grass, with its body fully exposed. So how could that be a suitable cover? Why would the enemy or hunter not detect it the way that it's hidden? What's more, there is no enemy or hunter that cares to give it a break.

"Mocking at its large, vibrant wings, the enemy or hunter approaches. Then without a moment of hesitation, the enemy gives a quick blow in its rear, or the hunter approaches and clutches its neck with smirk on his face. Then, while the peacock flutters making a gnawing sound, the hunter leisurely walks away holding the peacock."

"Oh . . ." exclaimed Malukha.

Bhaddiya continued, "Brother, my throne appeared to me like the peacock's wing. It was a realization that my powerful and mighty kingship drove me toward fear and danger rather than bringing me happiness.

"With such thought firmly engrained in my mind, I began to feel disillusioned and uncomfortable with the throne. Then I finally understood the reason behind my cousin Siddhattha's renunciation.

"In retrospect, I thought a lot about him even before my disillusionment. *Why did he leave the palace? He could have been a king! Why would he abandon the authority everyone in the world desires? No one would refuse because everyone desires it!* I thought.

"Then it finally dawned on me. The Buddha's decision to renounce the world stemmed from the same fear that I had. Even when the enemy and hunter stood behind lurking, the peacock hid its head under the pile of grass, as if that was a great solution. Just like that, while people tried to hide from the fundamental problems of life, the Buddha dealt with it head on.

"In other words, unlike the people who try hard to evade, the Buddha directly faced the problems of death, of the fact that he will eventually return to nothingness, that is, the emptiness, finitude, meaninglessness, and futility of life.

"But what could I do? While I was having these thoughts, the soldiers found me, and I had to act out my authority as a king.

"However, when I returned back to the palace, I realized that I was not the same man I once was. The fear and emptiness that I faced in hunting showed its real face and continued to haunt me right in front of my eyes."

Spinning the story up to this point, Bhaddiya took a deep breath and exhaled. Bhaddiya continued, "Since then, I stopped hunting and looked for something that could bring me greater joy, which could shield me better from the enemy named meaninglessness and futility. So instead I became fascinated with poetry and music. In fact, meeting a storyteller called Binggisa brought an opportunity for me to immerse myself in music and poetry. How about you, brother? Have you ever heard any stories about him?"

"I did hear some stories about him. Isn't he the world-renowned poet and musician?" asked Malukha.

Bhaddiya continued, "That's right. He was famous for wandering different villages, reciting poetry or quotes from classics at times while telling ancient stories or singing as he played string instruments at other times. I was aware of his reputation and around that time his feet led him to my kingdom of Shakya.

"I invited him to my court and requested him to play music and recite poetry. He was not only handsome, but his eyes were penetrative and his voice was crystal clear, and the poetries and songs he recited were absolutely beautiful. The art he had mastered reached the pinnacle of most subtle aesthetic accomplishment humanly possible, and he brought down the sky and clouds, along with the moon and the stars even to the ordinary men like us.

"When he recited poetry and played music, water sprang up around him and flowed in midair, birds sang in the sky, and legendary beasts appeared. All types of gods and heroes, good and evil, showed their meaning in his art, wishing to be recognized, all laughing and crying. As a result, he was always surrounded by masses of people that made it resemble a bazaar.

"Like all others, I also felt and realized the immensity of artistic poems and music, just by being acquainted with his genius talent. So I began to learn poetry and music from Binggisa. I not only built a new dwelling for Binggisa, but I dressed him in finest clothes and served him delicacies, making him my teacher of art. After a year of learning and enjoying the art, my sense of artistic appreciation matured greatly, but my wife Ayutha progressed much further than me . . . Oh, Ayutha! Brother, I feel such intolerable pain when her name is uttered through my lips, yet I also feel unbearable love toward her!"

"Oh, elder!"

"Ayutha not only possessed great physical beauty, but she had an inner attractiveness; she was great enough to be considered a rarity. I was mesmerized by these two qualities, and I made her my queen. She possessed a brave spirit—comparable to that of a warrior who had fought countless battles—and she also had bold determination, which was rare to find in most women.

"She also became his student after I was educated in poetry and music from Binggisa for a few months. I saw her falling for the art through the extraordinary teachings of Binggisa, and what new charm she developed as a result! Oh, can you imagine? She not only possessed great physical beauty, innocent heart, and brave soul, but a rich artistic talent as well!"

Reminiscing over his past, Bhaddiya's voice still whispered his love toward Ayutha, lingering attachment that remained even when he had become a monk. After a few moments, Bhaddiya pulled himself together and continued.

"Then one day, I noticed that Ayutha was very rarely seen. *What could she possibly be doing?* I thought to myself, but I tried not to let these thoughts progress further.

"But in the next moment, my suspicion toward her grew like a cumulus black smoke. When the doubt first appeared, I was absolutely stunned, so I shook my head feverously in order to shake it off. For me, doubting her was like a sin of doubting God for the religious, or a sin of tarnishing a pure sanctuary. I loved her with all my heart, trusted her without any reservation, and in no circumstance I should ever doubt this woman.

"But soon, a big arrow with its shaft thicker than a thumb and an arrowhead sharper than a dagger came flying toward me. The arrow pierced the dead center of my heart! That's right. Ayutha was having an affair with Binggisa, as a woman and a man do!"

Bhaddiya then stopped talking. Malukha remained silent, waiting for Bhaddiya to speak. Soon, Bhaddiya began again.

"I was furious. I shuddered with feelings of betrayal. Binggisa brought me great joy when he poured out beauty like a waterfall! Ayutha possessed great virtue that is humanly possible. And myself, I saw truth and beauty of life through these two! The relationship between the three of us turned greatly chaotic and disturbing at the end. It was something I couldn't even imagine and something that should have never happened.

"I was enraged. I lost equanimity that must be possessed by the king at all times. I brought them out and took one eye from Binggisa and made him blind for coveting someone else's wife. Then I poured poison into both of Ayutha's ears, for heeding to sweet whispering words of a strange man. Then they were vanished from the palace.

"I lost all meaning of life. I felt a great sense of futility that turned to fear. I was trembling like a helpless peacock that hid its head in a pile of grass, waiting for disposal by the heartless hunter that stood behind it.

"The name of the hunter is futility! Oh, my dear brother Malukha, life has no fundamental meaning because at the end there is only death. What is the point of being a king or a shepherd? Is being a king better than being a shepherd, when they are both so pitiful and tragic? No. In fact the king is worse off than the shepherd.

"The king has power, and shepherd has none. But death finds them without any distinction. Then, what is death? Death is none other than going back to nothingness. When faced with death, family turns to nothing, friends also become nothing, wealth goes to nothing, knowledge becomes nothing, and beauty also doesn't mean a thing. Authority and power turn to nothing, enemy means nothing, and honor also returns to nothing.

"Therefore, loss is small for someone who possesses a little, but it is great for those who possess too much. In that sense, a shepherd is much better off than a king, because a king has so much more to lose. Oh, just imagine how pathetic a king might feel when he realizes that no matter how much power or gold he possesses, he cannot bargain even a day when facing Yama, the King of Death!"

"Oh, elder!"

Bhaddiya went on after taking a deep breath, trying to calm his mind. "Dear brother, think how the Blessed One renounced the world even when he was guaranteed the throne. This means, before I even became the king, he already realized the order of things. He had the insight on the futility of life, thus he took out the sword called the truth, and went on the unprecedented long march to destroy the enemy that makes everything meaningless.

"Ultimately, the Buddha attained the supreme state no one else was able to reach, returned to his homeland, and led his father to enlightenment. That was not all. He accepted his stepmother, his wife, and his son before he renounced the world as a monastic disciple and led them all to the high level of enlightenment. There were many others from Shakya clan who became his disciples. Although I was moved by his sacredness, I was not ready to become a monk.

"Finally, a karmic association with Buddhadhamma came upon to me too. When the Buddha visited the Shakya Kingdom for the fourth time, I heard the following analogy that related to the very heart of the problems I faced in life:

> One day a traveler came upon a lion while walking through the field. He quickly turned his back and ran for his life. Fortunately, a well appeared before him, and he saw thick vines of wisteria outside the well, which was extended to inside. The traveler quickly grabbed hold of the vine and proceeded to lower himself into the well.
>
> But when the traveler looked down at his feet, he found hundreds of poisonous serpents waiting beneath. Thus, he

was suspended in mid-air, unable to move down nor move back up. What's worse, there were two mice, gnawing at the vine he was holding. But then—in the midst of all that danger—he sensed a sweet smell at the tip of his nose.

It was the smell of honey from honeycomb perched above the vine extending above his head. Enthralled by the delicious smell of honey, he completely forgot about his current predicament that placed him in grave danger. He opened his mouth to receive drops of honey that fell from the comb, smacking his lips.

"Upon hearing this parable from the Blessed One, my heart cried out *Yes!* The lion, serpent, and mice were the enemy that represented life, sickness, old age, and death as well as sorrow, distress, and afflictions of the mind. I was the traveler in the story who was being pushed toward death moment by moment, and who was being attacked by the enemy called impermanence. Despite of this fact, my heart and mind were still blinded by power, wealth, hunting, and art!

"The Buddha recognized that I was receptive to the 'Parable of the Wanderer in the Well' and then he recited the following verse:

> The man immersed in plucking flowers,
> His heart distracted
> Death sweeps him away—
> Like a mighty flood, when a village asleep.

> The man immersed in plucking flowers,
> His heart distracted
> Insatiable in sensual pleasures
> The Destroyer brings him under his sway

"Brother Malukha! That was how I abandoned the throne and became a bhikkhu."

CHAPTER 11
Happiness Spreads
Like a Fragrance

Bhaddiya ceased to talk for a while and then continued.

"Since I had been ordained as a bhikkhu, I followed the senior bhikkhus, like the wild geese that follow other wild geese flying ahead, and I took the example of what they did. I stood as they stood, walked as they walked, sat as they sat, and laid as they laid. Further, I went to bed when they went to bed, rose from bed when they rose from bed, and while awake, abided by the precepts the Buddha laid down for bhikkhus.

"While I observed the precepts, there was no time when I felt it exceptionally difficult to do so. Following the footsteps of senior bhikkhus, I did what they did and abstained from what they did not do, and before I knew it, observing the precepts became a part of me.

"Brother, as you are aware, practice of Buddhadhamma consists of threefold training, that is, ethics training that is moral discipline, concentration training that calms and brings happiness to mind, and wisdom training that develops insight. When I achieved certain progress in the ethics training, the Blessed One called me and asked, 'Bhaddiya, how long have you been a bhikkhu?' I answered,

'Blessed One, it is over five years since I renounced the secular life.'

"The Buddha asked, 'In the meantime, you should have heard a good deal of teachings from the senior bhikkhus. Bhaddiya, what do you think is the basic idea behind the teachings of the Tathagata?' I answered, 'Blessed One, I think they are the Four Noble Truths.'

"The Buddha said, 'So it is. The teachings of the Tathagata can all be placed in the big frame of the Four Noble Truths, which is like saying the footprint of any animal can be placed within that of an elephant. Then, what are the Four Noble Truths? They are the truth of suffering, the truth of the causes of suffering, the truth of the cessation of suffering, and the truth of the path leading to the cessation of suffering. The truth of suffering is a truth that you must understand, the truth of the causes of suffering is a truth that must be clarified, the truth of the cessation of suffering is a truth that must be attained, and the truth of the path to the cessation of suffering is a truth that must be cultivated,' said the Buddha. 'That is so, Blessed One,' I responded.

"The Buddha asked, 'Now the Tathagata will ask you a question to examine your understanding of the noble truth of suffering, which is the first truth of the Four Noble Truths. When you were in the secular world, you were the king of a kingdom and enjoyed all sorts of pleasure, which all sentient beings heartily hope for. Nevertheless, you have abandoned the enormous pleasures, renounced the secular life and became a man of non-possession. What is the reason behind all these?' the Buddha asked.

"'It was because the secular life was thought to be futile,' I responded.

"'Why did you think the secular life was futile?' asked the Buddha.

"In response to the question of the Blessed One, I addressed the motives that drove me to renunciation—that is, the fact that after being enthroned thieves broke in and killed my mother, that I sentenced the thieves to death, that the burden of the throne weighed upon me, that I was indulged in hunting, that I learned from Binggisa poetry and music, that my wife and Binggisa betrayed me, that when I knew it, I punished them, and that thereafter I spent the life drenched in a sense of futility, and so on."

(At that time, the Buddha and Bhaddiya thus conversed)

"The Buddha asked me, 'Bhaddiya, is life painful or pleasurable?'

"I responded, 'Blessed One, life is not pleasurable, but painful.'

"The Buddha responded, 'So it is, as a result the Dhamma of the Tathagata starts with the truth of suffering and ends with the truth of the cessation of suffering. The truth of suffering is followed by the truth of the causes of suffering, and the truth of the cessation of suffering is followed by the truth of the path to the cessation of suffering, thus resulting in the perfection of the Four Noble Truths.

"Bhaddiya, if the Tathagata had not realized this Four Noble Truths, the Tathagata should not have declared that 'I am the Buddha who, of all devas, Maras, Brahmas, brahmins, and humans, or the entire worlds where they reside in, has awakened to the supreme truth' However, as the Tathagata has seen the Four Noble Truths as they were and penetrated them without any residue, I declared that 'I am the Buddha who, of all devas, Maras, Brahmas, brahmins, and humans, or the entire worlds where they reside in, has awakened to the supreme truth,' the Buddha said.

"'Yes, Blessed One,' I responded.

"'Then, what is the truth of suffering?' the Buddha continued, 'Birth is suffering, aging is suffering, illness is suffering, and death is suffering. Association with what is displeasing is suffering, separation from what is pleasing is suffering, and being unable to get what one wants is suffering. In short, the mind and body subject to clinging, are suffering.

"'But you should know, when the Tathagata says life is suffering, he does not do so because he is a pessimist. Bhaddiya, how will you answer if someone asks you, "There are plenty of pleasures in life as well. Then, why does the Blessed One teach that life is suffering?"

"I answered, 'If someone asks like that, Blessed One, I will reply to him that it is because that, though there are three kinds of feelings, that is to say, the feeling of suffering, the feeling of pleasure, and the feeling in between, all these feelings will eventually return to the feeling of suffering.'

"'That is well said. Then Bhaddiya, what does the Four Noble Truths say the causes of the suffering of life are?' the Buddha asked.

"'The Four Noble Truths expound the causes of the suffering of life through twelve stages, namely, the twelve links of dependent arising.'

"'Then what is the last twelfth stage of the twelve links of dependent arising?' the Buddha asked.

"'It is aging and death. Aging and death mean aging, illness, and death of the body, and the distress, sorrow, and afflictions of the mind, and they are no other than the noble truth of suffering in the Four Noble Truths.'

"'Then again, what are the eleven stages, which precede the aging and death, related to the aging and death?'

"'They are eleven causes that make the aging and death possible.' I replied.

"'That is right. But the Tathagata will explain the eleven stages of the causes of suffering with only the first stage of ignorance and the eighth stage of craving. Of these two causes of suffering, the ignorance is the root cause and the craving is a cause derived therefrom. Therefore, if ignorance were the root, craving is like the stalk, and suffering is like the fruit.' explained the Buddha.

"He continued, 'Though, in resolving the sufferings of life, it would be better to resolve the problem at the root from the beginning, you are not yet prepared for that. So, the Tathagata will teach you, before taking out the root of the problem, one of the samatha meditations that control the stalk, namely the craving.

"'Then, what is the craving that is controlled through samatha meditation? Bhaddiya, craving is the three unwholesome minds, such as greed, hatred, and delusion, which lead sentient beings to sufferings.' explained the Buddha.

"'Yes, Blessed One,' I replied.

"'The Tathagata is about to look into the craving you have, so you shall answer my questions honestly. Bhaddiya, do you admit that there is hatred in your mind against Binggisa and Ayutha who have betrayed you?'

"'Yes, Blessed One, there is hatred against them in my mind,' I replied.

"As you are good at poetry, the Tathagata will compare your hatred with a poison. What do you think of this analogy of the Tathagata?'

"'I think it very appropriate to compare the hatred with a poison.'

"'Bhaddiya, there are three kinds of poison that sentient beings have in their mind, like the poison of greed, poison of hatred, and the poison of delusion. Then Bhaddiya, what do you think is at the opposites of the three poisons?'

"'As a poetic simile, at the opposites are the three fragrant minds.'

"'That is right. Then, how are the poisonous minds and the fragrant minds different from each other? Bhaddiya, you must know it correctly. The poisonous mind has the quality of contraction, and the fragrant mind has the quality of expansion. In other words, when three poisonous minds arise, the mind will be coagulated, and if it further worsens, it will be frozen as water freezes,' explained the Buddha.

"'On the other hand, if three fragrant minds arise, the coagulated and frozen mind will dissolve as a bundle of thread unravels or as the ice melts down, and in that place where the mind has dissolved, there will appear as much room as it has dissolved. Then, as the room grows bigger, fragrance arises in the mind, and if the fragrance gets thicker, it will first make one happy and then will spread to others nearby and make them happy as well.'

"'Oh . . .' I said.

"'Bhaddiya, you should know well. In the same context, a person who has three poisonous minds hurts himself first before he hurts others, like a person who suffers from a lung disease as evil things have invaded his lungs.

"'If a person is affected by lung disease, the doctor will send him to an isolated place away from others and let him stay there alone. That is not to cause any harm to other people nearby. Bhaddiya, what is your thought? Is the patient himself harmed first by the poison in his lungs or others will be harmed first?' asked the Buddha.

"'He will be harmed first.'

"'Now let's assume that there is a flower having a rich fragrance. Will the flower enjoy the benefit from the fragrance that it has first, or will bees and butterflies benefit first?'

"'The flower will enjoy the benefit first,' I said.

"'Then, does the flower have the fragrance for bees and butterflies, or for itself?'

"'The flower has the fragrance for itself.'

"'So it is. However, though the flower has the fragrance for itself, as the fragrance has the characteristic of spreading, it will, regardless of its intention, give benefit to bees and butterflies. Exactly as such, a person with the three fragrant minds will give benefit to others even when it was not intentional, not to mention when it was intentional.'

"I responded laughing, 'The Blessed One is now *intentionally* spreading the fragrance of wisdom toward me.'

"The Buddha also laughed saying, 'That is right. However, on the other hand, that is not right, because although the Tathagata makes intentions but no intention is actually made. The Tathagata makes intentions without any attachment in his mind, so he makes his mind just like this and like that, and acts just like this and just like that. Therefore, for Tathagata, there is no trace of mind like this, no abiding in action like that, no accumulation of mind like this, and no residue of action like that.'

"Being touched, I responded, 'Oh, Blessed One, so it is! I have looked up to the Blessed One as he does not act while he acts, and as he acts while he does not act, and thus, the Blessed One is not here while he is here, and he is wholly here while he is not here!'

"I praised like this, and the Buddha accepted such praise by remaining silent without uttering a word. At the next moment, from the noble master, the Buddha, the scent that can be felt by senses, such as the scent of sandalwood, the scent of the root of a carpe jasmine, the scent of a lotus flower, and the scent of a jasmine flower, started to exude.

"However, the scent was of a kind that can be felt by only those who have extreme respect toward the Buddha, namely, a fragrance as the power of the Dhamma. It was a fragrance and at the same time the sweetest taste of the Dhamma. It was something that was as fragrant as a flower and as sweet as honey," explained Bhaddiya to Malukha.

"As a result, a strong motive to attain a higher level of practice, where subtle fragrance and taste exude, occurred to me. I became adamantly hopeful that I would, as the Buddha did, reach the stage where he could make flowers blossom and honey produced.

"I addressed the Buddha, with eyes full of passion, 'Blessed One, an unbearably intense motivation to practice arises in me now! So, Blessed One, please teach me an appropriate method of practice!'

"'Excellent! Excellent! Excellent!' said the Buddha.

"Staring at me with a pleased look, the noble master said, 'Bhaddiya, to calm down the anger in you, you would better cultivate the mind of loving-kindness, being the first of the four immeasurable states of mind, and the mind of loving-kindness can be cultivated by way of practicing the loving-kindness meditation.'

"Having said this, the Buddha gave me a teaching on the four immeasurable states of mind as follows:

> Bhaddiya, there is a practitioner who fills one of the four directions of the world with the mind of loving-kindness toward others. And he fills all the second, third, and fourth directions of—and above and below the world—with the same mind. He is filling up all parts of the world evenly with the mind of loving-kindness that is rich, mature, and immeasurable without enmity and with no worry or concern.

> Bhaddiya, there is a practitioner who fills one of the four directions of the world with the mind of compassion that feels pain for the sufferings of others. And he fills all the second, third, and fourth directions of—and above and below the world—with the same mind. He is filling up all

parts of the world evenly with the mind of loving-kindness that is rich, mature, and immeasurable without enmity and with no worry or concern.

Bhaddiya, there is a practitioner who fills one of the four directions of the world with the mind of joy that feels happy with the joy of others. And he fills all the second, third, and fourth directions of—and above and below the world—with the same mind. He is filling up all parts of the world evenly with the mind of loving-kindness that is rich, mature, and immeasurable without enmity and with no worry or concern.

Bhaddiya, there is a practitioner who fills one of the four directions of the world with the mind of equanimity. And he fills all the second, third, and fourth directions of—and above and below the world—with the same mind. He is filling up all parts of the world evenly with the mind of loving-kindness that is rich, mature, and immeasurable without enmity and with no worry or concern.

"Having heard the teaching of the Buddha, I was soaked with the profound Dhamma-rain, and the Buddha, while observing the level of his disciple receiving the Dhamma, delivered a teaching on the loving-kindness:

For a bhikkhu well versed in precepts
To reach the state of tranquility
He shall thus cultivate the mind of loving-kindness.

Be capable, upright and undaunted
Be kind, decent and polite.
Learn to be satisfied and seek less
Unburdened from duties and live in freedom.

Calm sensory organs and control without any leak
Do not arouse greed when dealing with a secular person,
Never do the slightest thing
That the wise would later reprove

(Based on this foundation the practitioner wishes.)

May all beings be at ease and happy!
As they are alive and draw breath
Whoever they are, may they be happy!

Whether they are weak or strong
Big or small, long or short
Or in-between
Seen or unseen
Living near or far away
May all beings be happy!

(And the practitioner further wishes.)

May I do no harm
To anyone in the world!
May I never despise others in any event!
May I not wish ill for others!
May I not hold anger or a grudge!

Like a mother who is willing
To give up her life for her only son,
May I have the mind of limitless loving-kindness
Toward all living beings!
May the same spread up, down, and sideways
And fill up the whole world!

(Thus, the Tathagata spoke.)

A bhikkhu who develops loving-kindness
While standing, walking, sitting, and lying
Must hold firmly to the thought that,
Mindfulness of loving-kindness is where he shall abide in,
The path to becoming like Brahma,
The god of the heavenly world,
That has no enmity whatsoever.

But bhikkhus, you shall know.
The path to the truth lies in the threefold training,
After cultivating the loving-kindness based on precepts
You shall develop wisdom to gain insight into the true
reality,
Once attained the enlightenment as a result,
The practitioner shall transcend samsara
That keeps them to be drawn into a mother's womb.

Having taught a basic lesson, the Buddha sent Bhaddiya to one of his chief disciples, Sariputta. So, Bhaddiya went to Sariputta, and the latter taught the former in detail the method of loving-kindness meditation, along with the instruction to visit him often to report on the progress of the practice.

From then on, Bhaddiya practiced loving-kindness meditation under the guidance of Sariputta. During the first stage of the practice, his mind escaped from enmity, and during the next stage tranquility appeared, and at the following stage, the loving-kindness toward others arose.

Time flowed and it has been three years since Bhaddiya started loving-kindness meditation. One day, he was summoned by the Buddha. And, when he proceeded to the Buddha, another bhikkhu was also present.

The Buddha, pointing at that bhikkhu, said, "Bhaddiya, the Tathagata heard from this bhikkhu that you meditated, sitting alone in the woods away from your fellow bhikkhus, and during the meditation, often talked to yourself 'Oh, I am happy! I am really happy!' Bhaddiya, did such things happen to you?"

"Yes it happened indeed. While I meditated, I often talked to myself 'Oh, I am happy! I am really happy!'"

"Why did you say that?"

Being questioned by the Buddha, Bhaddiya addressed the master. "Blessed One, it is a verse of inspiration that flowed naturally from my mind. As happiness overflowed from my mind, I murmured to myself 'Oh, I am happy! I am really happy!'

"Blessed One, when I was a king in the secular world, thieves once broke into my palace. Therefore, I strengthened the security of the palace so that such a thing would never happen again. And I paid more attention to affairs of defense and tightened the border security. As a result, I could stay in the deepest part of the inner palace enclosed by layers of protective shields.

"Nevertheless, Blessed One, I was scared. It was because I thought it likely that someone might, taking advantage of certain unguarded spots that may exist, break in and take away my life, position, or property.

"My fear grew bigger day by day. Finally, doubt arose in me about life itself. Then the Blessed One honored me with his visit, and at that moment, I, a man like a child who owned everything but shuddered from fear, was standing before a noble one who owned nothing but was without any fear.

"Blessed One, you walk like the god of gods, abide as the god of gods, sit as the god of gods, and lie down as the god of gods. As if the Blessed One had the strength to lift the Mt. Himalaya with his hand, the Blessed One leads the life of a person who does not appear to have the slightest fear, worry, or concern.

"Blessed One, I am well aware. That Angulimala once jumped on the Blessed One wielding a sword. However, the Blessed One embraced the ferocious Angulimala with compassion and made him a monastic disciple.

"Being greatly touched at the sight of the Blessed One standing in front of me, I, without even realizing it, knelt down and gave a prostration to the Blessed One and volunteered to become a man who owns nothing, from a man who owned everything.

"Five years have passed since then, and, at the instruction of the Blessed One, I learned loving-kindness meditation under the guidance of Great Elder Sariputta. Since I began to practice the loving-kindness meditation, I found out that from day to day, my mind was getting warm, generous, rich, and happy.

"And, oh, Blessed One, my mind is now peacefully stabilized, and maintains the state of happiness well. As a result, like a young deer playing leisurely in wide and green grassland under the protection of a shepherd, I am living with a peaceful mind. For that reason, I spoke the verse of inspiration during meditation 'Oh, I am happy! I am really happy!' without even realizing it."

Having heard this from Bhaddiya, the Buddha, after praising him with various words, spoke a verse.

> Once a king who had everything but lived in fear
> Now a happy practitioner embracing loving-kindness
> Though he has nothing to be called his,
> Behold Bhaddiya, a prominent disciple of the Buddha!

(Again returning to Bhaddiya's abode)

Having shared up to this point in his story, Bhikkhu Bhaddiya ceased to talk.

Then, stillness settled. However, the stillness didn't mean that it was empty; there was something in the stillness. Between the two bhikkhus and in the small cottage of Bhaddiya, there was something like a cool and refreshing current of air that flows between the bushes in the early morning of an early winter. It is invisible by eyes but perceivable by mind, or like an atmosphere that drifts between two lovers when they do not dare to hold hands or embrace each other, because their lover is too endearing.

Therefore, the stillness was a stillness that was not stillness. But it was again stillness, a silence, and a silence that was not a silence.

The two bhikkhus, who were immersed in silence, looked beautiful.

The appearance of a person is more beautiful than the beauty of the nature, and the virtuous mind of a person is more beautiful than the appearance of a person. However, more beautiful than the virtuous mind is the beauty of practice—the beauty of ethics, the beauty of concentration, and the beauty of wisdom. And at that time, Bhikkhu Bhaddiya was harboring the beauty of practice and Malukha Bhikkhu saw the deepest part of the beauty.

The beauty of practice that the two bhikkhus harbored and saw was felt and seen by Raja and Sirima as well, who were watching them with their bodies hidden. It was a beauty that one could feel and see, and at the same time, a beauty that one would gain insight into by intuition as well. Therefore, though it was small, it was a kind of enlightenment. Minds of Raja and Sirima, though they have not practiced personally, have achieved certain progress as if they had gone through practice by themselves.

The stillness between Bhaddiya and Malukha ended.

"Oh, elder!" Malukha said, "Hearing your excellent Dhamma talk today, I have gained an enormous benefit in my mind."

"It does not deserve to be called a Dhamma talk," Bhaddiya said, "You better call it a grumble by a dull practitioner."

"You are excessively modest," Malukha said, laughing.

"Brother," Bhaddiya said, "You should be aware of that the Blessed One allowed us monastics only two kinds of talk, that is, the talk that is indispensable for daily life and the Dhamma exchange, and forbade us from telling anything other than that."

"So it is. I know well that bhikkhus shall be silent on all occasions, except those two," said Malukha.

"And the Blessed One commended not to talk too much of even the indispensable talk and the Dhamma exchange, and viewing from this perspective, I am concerned that I have talked way too much."

"I don't think so," said Malukha. "You gave me a big benefit of the Dhamma through your Dhamma talk, which is a sufficient proof that you spoke excellent discourse. What has particularly impressed me was, as well as the Dhamma talk themselves, the friendly and warm feeling that came from you when you delivered the Dhamma talk."

"Anyway, it seems better for us to stop our dialogue here," said Bhaddiya.

"Elder, I want to hear more of your Dhamma talk. Particularly, I am very curious about what Binggisa and Ayutha have become thereafter."

Saying this, Malukha laughed, but Bhaddiya did not answer the question; Bhaddiya changed the subject and asked, "Brother, I want to ask you a question. You can probably travel for about a month from now?"

"For what reason, are you asking the question to me?"

Bhaddiya responded, "Brother, even though I have tasted a little of the transmundane happiness through meditation, I have not yet attained enlightenment. What I am trying to say is that though I could have managed to provide a Dhamma talk for you today, you need a higher level of Dhamma talk.

"Incidentally, it so happened that Great Elder Sariputta asked me to come over to his place. So, in response to his request, I am about to leave here after three days heading for the place where he resides.

"He is now engaged in propagating the Buddhadhamma in Sunnitha. So, brother, will you please go with me to the place where the Marshall of Dhamma resides? There, together with him, let us propagate the Dhamma of truth and the Dhamma of sweet nectar that we have tasted, to those who have not yet experienced the fundamentals of the Buddhadhamma."

Malukha said, "Elder, I am still nothing more than a trivial ordinary bhikkhu. As such, I have no wisdom to teach on the Dhamma of truth, nor any power of practice to show them the Dhamma of sweet nectar."

"That may be true, brother, but if you go to the place, you will be able to hear plenty of excellent Dhamma discourses from a great master whose wisdom is second to none, except the Buddha. And who knows if you could attain enlightenment, if you hear his Dhamma discourses and practice under his guidance?"

Malukha's face radiated with joy and said, "That is entirely possible! Then, elder, I will go with you to Sunnitha!"

CHAPTER 12

Betrayal of the Son, Betrayal of the Wife

Three days later, Bhaddiya and Malukha departed for Sunnitha to meet with Elder Sariputta, while Raja and Sirima hid themselves and followed. Nearly a month later, the two bhikkhus stayed overnight in a forest near Sunnitha.

The next morning at dawn, the two bhikkhus got up from their bed, washed their faces, and sat neatly in meditation on the grass near a grave. Then, the two bhikkhus came out of meditation in time to beg for alms. Malukha told Bhaddiya, "Dear elder, I feel like something special is going to happen today."

"Is that right?" said Bhaddiya while laughing. "But brother, there is nothing particularly special for bhikkhus like us. Actually, I should not say that such a thing never happens, as I am not enlightened yet. So, let's just say that bhikkhus like us shouldn't take things to be too special or exceptional, as that's not proper thing to do for the monastics."

Malukha responded, "Don't take anything to be special? Elder, that doesn't sound like much fun to me. If nothing is special, wouldn't life be too insipid?"

Smiling again, Bhaddiya said, "Dhamma, in fact, is insipid indeed."

Malukha said while laughing together, "I heard from the Buddha a while back that you were a detached person, but today I hear from you that Dhamma is insipid. It seems like the path we bhikkhus follow is the exact reverse of the worldly pursuits. There will be no one who wants to be detached or insipid in this world."

"But brother, the Buddha, who calls himself to be detached, is in fact a very kind person as well," Bhaddiya said.

"That's right. I also felt that the last time when I was listening to the teachings of the Blessed One. In other words, the Buddha's detachment is beyond detachment and kindness. In the same vein, I think the insipidness you referred to is beyond insipidness and fun."

Breaking a smile, Bhaddiya said, "Brother, what you are telling me sounds a lot like a praise."

Smiling along, Malukha said, "But that's a fact."

"I will accept that as a compliment. Well, shall we then go out for alms?"

After exchanging these words, the two bhikkhus got up from their seats and walked out of the forest toward the village. They received enough food from the first village and went into a forest outside the village to eat. But then, they came across a special situation, at least so considered according to the bhikkhu Malukha's standard. The two found an elderly man trying to hang himself on a tree.

"No! Stop!" cried out Malukha, who rushed toward the elderly man. The man gazed toward Malukha who cried out, but with a blank stare as if he had given up all hope. Soon, when the elderly man came conscious of his situation, he said to flustered Malukha, "Don't come any closer."

In a meek, dark, and low voice that seemed to reverberate from the depth of the ground, he said, "Don't interfere; you do what you have to do—and let me do what I have to do . . ."

Bhaddiya remained calm, though any other person could have been alarmed in such a situation.

"The problem is," said Bhaddiya to the elderly man, "what is it that we should do now? I happen to think that stopping whatever you are trying to do right now is what I am supposed to do."

"What on earth?" said Malukha, rolling his eyes with an expression that said Bhaddiya was being absurd. "How can you be joking at a time like this?"

Smiling, Bhaddiya said, "Then should we be crying?" Bhaddiya said to the elderly man, "Sir, wouldn't you talk to us for a while? From what I can see, you look like you lived decently your whole life, but what strange fate has led you to this?" He removed the rope from the neck of the elderly man and helped the man down, beckoning for Malukha. "What are you doing? Come and help me."

"Oh, right," said Malukha.

Thus, the bhikkhus laid the elderly man down on the grass. When they gently massaged him, the man fell asleep, breathing heavily and looking rather exhausted.

Bhaddiya said to Malukha with a low tone of voice, "He probably didn't have breakfast. Let's make some porridge for him with food we received."

"That's a great idea," said Malukha with a sense of relief.

"They say talk of the devil and he appears, but isn't this exactly the kind of 'special situation' we were talking about? In any case, it was really impressive to see how calm you were just now."

"Brother, your face looks fairly relaxed too, though it seems little too late."

"I shouldn't be the only one so anxious in front of you, who remains so calm, right?" said Malukha, "When I saw you so composed in such a disastrous situation, I was able to confirm that a well-trained mind would cope with imminent situations with ease, while any ordinary person would have made a big fuss. By the way, we need a pot to make porridge, do you want me to go and get a pot from the village?"

"That would be great. I will take care of him in the meantime."

"Sure," replied Malukha, then he left to get a pot in the village. He returned back with some utensils, and the two bhikkhus managed to feed the man, who woke up after some time. However, the man stayed as stiff as a board and didn't speak a word when being cared for by the bhikkhus. He simply received the food offered and ate silently. Neither of the bhikkhus tried to make conversation with the man.

It was past noon. This meant the two bhikkhus missed their opportunity for their meal. Instead, the bhikkhus practiced walking meditation on the grass, waiting for the elderly man to recover his body and mind. In the meantime, the man dozed off once again.

It was near dusk. The two bhikkhus gave the leftovers from lunch to the elderly man, not eating it themselves as their precept states. The elderly man sat gazing at the bhikkhus for some time, then he quietly finished his dinner. He then washed his face and brushed his teeth, straightening his clothes in a casual manner, which demonstrated his refined culture. However, his clothes were not in any state that could be improved by smoothing them down.

The old man approached the two bhikkhus and bowed in a respectful manner.

"Elders, I thank you," said the old man, "Although I attempted to end my life, I think I should be grateful now that I'm alive, thanks to both of you." His eyes were filled with tears and brimful tears rolled down his cheeks shortly after.

Wiping away his tears, the elderly man said in a more tranquil voice, "Dear elders, you must be wondering why I tried to hang myself. And I wish to share with you what I have been through thus far. Because without it, there is no way I could let go of the knotted rage I feel inside my heart."

Malukha then asked the elderly man, "But sir, may I first ask you what your name is?"

"Sure. My name is Uggata," replied the elderly man.

Uggata was a millionaire who accumulated a great wealth through his business in Sunnitha. His wife passed away early, but he had a son and a daughter. When his son was grown, Uggata gave 100,000 rupees for him to get married and live out independently. Soon after, his daughter was married off as well with 50,000 rupees. Since he had had 800,000 rupees to begin with, he still had plenty of money in his possession, amounting to 650,000 rupees.

The problem was that his son, Koku, was a very greedy man. Koku never earned a penny with his own effort, but instead he spent all his time scheming and coveting after the rest of his father's fortune. He thought that was much easier than trying to earn money with his own effort.

Koku employed all kinds of clever schemes to deceive Uggata, and Uggata eventually lost all his possessions to his son and ended up wandering the streets aimlessly. Life became empty and meaningless when he lost faith in mankind. This ultimately led him to try to hang himself. After telling the story of his son's betrayal, Uggata sighed deeply and laid on the ground, utterly exhausted.

While Bhaddiya stayed close and took care of Uggata, Malukha remained a few steps away from them to soothe his own stifled mind from listening to the story of Uggata's heartless son.

Some time had passed, and Uggata got up from where he had was. When Uggata sat himself up, a faint smile seemed to appear, which on one hand appeared carefree, but on the other hand bore profound emotion that encompassed futility.

Bhaddiya enquired, "So, what are your plans, sir? Is the problem resolved now that the heavy burden has been lifted off your shoulders?"

"That's not the case," Uggata replied. The next moment, he roared in a husky voice, filled up with sudden fury that boiled up within his heart, "Oh, dear elders! What I need is justice! Revenge! My son must pay for his evil deed. That is all I ask!"

"But sir, this is not the time to think of revenge, but to arouse a generous heart."

"Elders, there is no place in my heart where such generosity can grow."

"But you do realize that the man you detest so much is your own son?"

"My son? Absolutely not! He is my arch enemy! A traitor! A thief! A ghost that sucks blood and eats flesh off people! He is more appalling than a serpent!" Uggata had eyes that flashed as sharp as a sword.

The three didn't say a word for a while. Uggata turned bright red and panted with rage, and Malukha tried to calm himself after Uggata's frenzied temper. Then, Malukha saw it. Bhaddiya revealed his confusion through the expression as complex as tangled up threads.

That's right, when Uggata declared his son to be an arch enemy, Bhaddiya recalled Binggisa and Ayutha. But Bhaddiya was not Uggata. Bhaddiya was a practitioner who basked in the bliss of meditation. Although shaken up for a moment, Bhaddiya restored his composure as a bhikkhu, who accepts everything as it is.

Bhaddiya's expression was simple and joyful again. Malukha, who had been eyeing his senior monk until then, allowed his mind to rest and turned his gaze toward the elderly man. The facial expression of the man had also been somewhat subdued a moment ago.

"Sir," said Bhaddiya with a sincere, yet poised and refreshing voice, "You said your son was the enemy."

"That's right, although I'm ashamed to admit it," Uggata responded with a voice slightly more composed than earlier. But in fact, his voice still remained harsh to a certain degree. In realizing this, Bhaddiya taught Uggata how to observe slowly the in-breath and out-breath with his eyes closed.

Uggata followed Bhaddiya's instruction. His body relaxed and as a result, Uggata's mind also became much more stable than before.

"Sir," said Bhaddiya. "You harbor great resentment toward your son right now, which means you are suffering from 'sickness of the mind.'"

"That's right."

"Therefore, in order to heal your mind afflicted by such illness, you must seek out an exceptional doctor who heals the mind," said Bhaddiya.

Lost in thought, the elderly man said, "A doctor that heals sickness of the mind—is there such a doctor?"

Bhaddiya said with a laugh, "Yes sir, we are the disciples of the Buddha who is respected by people around the world. Why is he respected by all these people around the world? That's because the Buddha realized the unsurpassed supreme truth. What is the supreme truth the Buddha realized? It's what heals the mind afflicted by sickness—it's the truth, that's all."

Bhaddiya continued, "This means all sentient beings are suffering from various illnesses of the mind, whether big or small. This also means bhikkhus (bhikkhunis) and countless lay Buddhists are ones who receive instructions from the Buddha to treat their sickness of mind. Sir, wouldn't you also like to treat your illness of mind under the guidance of the Buddha, the doctor?"

The elderly man said, "Yes, I definitely wish to be treated. But the Buddha is not with me at the moment. Should I go and see him?"

"Sir, I was also afflicted with the same kind of illness a long time ago. However, I think I've healed about half of my illness. So, I think I just might be able to help you on behalf of the Buddha."

The elderly man said "Oh!" with a delight.

"The problem is that in order to treat you, I have to recall the sickness I once had. That painful experience I never wish to dredge up again." As Bhaddiya was saying this, a mix of complex emotions he had felt just a moment ago reappeared across his face like a shadow, but then they disappeared.

Finally, Bhaddiya began the story of his painful past for Uggata:

"Sir, I once was a king who ruled the nation when I was still a lay man. I had a beautiful wife and a brilliant friend who led me to art. I truly loved my wife Ayutha and my friend Binggisa. At the time I thought, *We are one in body and soul. I am Ayutha, and Ayutha is me. I am Binggisa and Binggisa is me.* So I thought back then . . ."

Bhaddiya continued, "Still, they betrayed me with their adultery. Our unanimity was shattered as a result. Our oneness in soul was divided into two, and oneness in body was separated into two in discord. Consequently, I fell to the pit of suffering, and that pit was an absolute gutter. It was hell that was dark, filthy, humid, and crawling with maggots."

Bhaddiya spoke on, "I struggled and cried out from this hell. 'I want justice! Their treacherous act shall be paid back with a price!' So, I exercised my authority as a king and took revenge. As a punishment, poison was poured into Ayutha's ears, while Binggisa had one of his eyes taken."

"Oh!" exclaimed the elderly man.

Bhaddiya said, "But thinking back, it was such a great misfortune to have had authority as a king. Oh, only if I didn't have the power back then! Just like you, without any power to reprimand your son. If then, I wouldn't have committed such evil act of damaging others' flesh, and I could have avoided the karma of great confusion and disorder that followed me for so long."

"But dear elder, I myself am in a state of confusion and disorder, as I have no way of punishing my son."

"Sir, I would like to tell you how I controlled my own rage for your benefit."

"Elder, I shall listen closely, as you are revealing your past for my benefit, despite your own pain," said Uggata, who placed his palms together politely. Bhaddiya's face expressed a sincere desire for a sentient being in distress to find peace.

CHAPTER 13
Buddhadhamma Refers to Meditation

With a face teeming with affection, Bhaddiya said to Uggata, "At first, like you, I thought that the cause of the pain I was suffering was from the outside world—namely Ayutha and Binggisa who had betrayed me. However, while I was learning the Buddhadhamma, I realized that my thought was wrong. I learned that the Buddhadhamma sought the cause of the pain from inside, not from outside, that is, from oneself but not from others, and that the monastics and those lay practitioners, who had the same goals as the monastics, were doing so."

Having said this, Bhaddiya briefly expounded on the Four Noble Truths to Uggata. After that, Bhaddiya picked up a small stick from the ground. With it he drew a small circle on the ground and thereafter drew a big circle surrounding the small one. Though it was late at night, the moonlight was bright enough for the circles to be seen clearly.

Bhaddiya said, pointing at the circles, "Of these two circles, the inner circle means the world of 'I,' an existence distinguished from others, and the outer circle the world of 'others,' people or things, that surrounds me. The first thing to note is that the two circles are completely separated, which implicates that crossing back and forth between the two worlds is not possible. In this sense, the inner circle may be called an individual differentiated from the world. Yes, it is impossible to cross back and forth between I and others. Even a mother who loves her son dearly and is ready to sacrifice her whole life for him, is unable to eat or to be ill on behalf of her son. Of course, she could provide food and medicine for her son. However, her love is up to this limit, and it is the son who has to eat and digest the food and the medicine.

"And she cannot suffer in place of her son. She can certainly console her son with all sorts of words and give this and that advice. But if her son does not accept such consolation or advice, there will be nothing more for her to do to help him.

"The rule of life being as such, at the moment when her son meets death, how can she die on behalf of her son? Like this, no matter how much two people love each other, crossing back and forth in between is not possible.

"In this context, although the world is one when viewed objectively, it is two existentially: the world of I, and the world of all others excluding I.

"When viewed from the existential standpoint, the world is born when I am born. And the world perishes when I die. Some people dread the end of the world when all die together, but those who take the existentialist position do not fear the end of the world of that kind. What they fear is not the end of the world when a million people die together with him, but the end of the world when he alone dies."

Having said this, Bhaddiya divided the outer circle into five layers of concentric circles. And he continued, "Sir, as you see, I divided the outer circle into five concentric circles. It is because, I, being the individual, am surrounded by five distinct groups of others.

"What you have to note is that I drew the lines dividing the five concentric circles in dotted lines, and the five groups of others are differentiated but not separated or isolated, and therefore they can move from a circle where they belong to another circle. Then what kind of people are there in each concentric circle? In the first concentric circle are those whom I love. In the second concentric circle are those whom I like. In the third concentric circle are the neutrals that arouse neither love nor hatred in me. In the fourth concentric circle are competitors who contend with me for profits in accordance with fair rules. In the fifth concentric circle are enemies who take away my profits through unfair means."

Bhaddiya continued, "In the beginning, your son belonged to the first circle, among the five kinds of others. However, unnoticed by you, your son moved to the fourth circle, namely a competitor. And eventually he moved to the fifth circle, namely an enemy, but such change you failed to notice. If you think about it, a person in the first circle frequently moves to other concentric circles. What is worse, such phenomenon may happen several times even in a single day.

"For example, if I have a son I love, he is a person in my first concentric circle. However, my son will not always remain in the first circle. At some point in time, I may realize that my love for my son has loosened, that is, the love toward him weakened to the level of liking, and this means that the son has moved to the second concentric circle.

"Further on, there are times when I treat my son with a mind that does not particularly like or hate him, namely a neutral mind. This means that my son has moved through the second concentric circle to the third one. Of course, this phenomenon is just temporary, and thus I will soon recover the love for my son. However, there are times when the mind changes in the opposite direction, in the more unfavorable direction.

"My son and I may disagree on certain issues. I want my son to be more diligent, but my son thinks otherwise, and therefore I do not like what my son does.

"Then I give my son advice. And my son resents it. This means my son became my competitor, that is, my son who was in the first concentric circle has moved to the fourth one. If things get worse and I begin to hate my son, it means that my son has moved to the fifth concentric circle."

"Oh, elder, it is truly so, if I reflect on my experience!"

"Nevertheless, many people in the world regard those in the first concentric circle as one in body and soul with themselves, and they do not know or forget that they are most likely to move around frequently in the concentric circles at any given time. As was my case with Ayutha and Binggisa and yours with your son."

"Oh!"

"Sir, as I told you, people are bound to think of themselves ahead of others. I am a distinct individual, different in body and soul from others. Humans' love for others comes secondary to their first love called self-love, and the same is true of others' love for me. However, people long for someone who cherishes them dearly, as they love themselves, no, even more than they love themselves!"

"That is right. We all want it."

"Then suddenly, that beautiful miracle happens. A love with the opposite sex begins, who is, even among those in the first concentric circle, nearest to me, as a line closely adjoining me.

"They and I, who meet on the line that differentiates I and the others, adjoining together! And the love with them! When this love happens, them and I are one! Heartbreakingly, however, the love being one in body and soul is temporary and inconstant. It is true that love unites the hearts (bodies) of the two people. But though we do not know when it will happen, the two lines that have been overlapped are bound to be split and return to their original place.

"So, love is something like a three-legged race, where the left leg of a person is tied with the right leg of another person. When viewed from the two tied legs, they are one in body and soul. However, when viewed from the other untied legs, they are two bodies and two hearts.

"Of these two states, the former is temporary and variable, while the latter is permanent and constant. Even though there is a person who loves me as much as their own life, someday they will undo the line that ties the two legs and return to their own self.

"I do not just mean that their love for me may change. Even if their love for me does not change, them and I will be separated by death, by the dark-faced Yama who separates each and every person. At the time of death, however solid the 'one mind–one body' might be, it is bound to be dissolved into 'two minds–two bodies,' and this means that no one can carry the burden of life on my behalf that I am shouldering."

"Oh . . ." reacted the elderly man.

"However, many people who are unaware of this cruel law presume that my mind and the mind of my lover will maintain the same state of oneness tomorrow as they do today. This way, people believe that I and my lover are one in body and soul, load enormous expectations upon the belief, and on the strength of such expectations, walk on a grueling journey of life," Bhaddiya continued.

"However, the belief does not coincide with reality. The belief is what people wish to be true, but in reality, life does not develop in accordance with such wish. The most ruthless law of individuality strictly divides I and the others, lets others move back and forth between my five concentric circles, and at the same time lets myself also move back and forth the five concentric circles of the others," Bhaddiya said.

"Oh, how merciless is such change!" said the elderly man.

"That is right. The law of individuality is merciless. However, since it is merciless, it is rather fair. This law transfers people in the first circle to the fifth circle, but on the contrary, it moves people in the fifth circle to the first circle as well.

"We must not blame this law; we must understand it. There is no use of blaming the law, since however much we blame it, it will never change. Therefore, by way of understanding this law well, we shall not fall victim to the mercilessness of this law, but shall make good use of the fairness of the law. Therefore, the Buddha taught, 'Make yourself your own refuge,' and 'How can you rely on others?'"

Having said this, Bhaddiya recited a verse.

> Be your own refuge,
> For who else could be?
> Do practice and clear your mind.
> That is how to be your own refuge.

Having recited the verse, Bhaddiya stopped talking.

Uggata sat with his eyes closed, savoring the contents of the Dhamma talk of Bhaddiya, and the two monks waited silently for Uggata to take the next move. At last, Uggata opened his eyes, stood up, and made three prostrations to Bhaddiya.

"Dear elder," said Uggata, "I take refuge in the Three Jewels, so please allow me to learn under your tutelage."

"Excellent! Excellent! Excellent!"

Bhaddiya praised the man for becoming a Buddhist and asked, "What do you think? Do you have a hobby you are very much fond of, in which you can engage yourself fully and forget all other things except for it?"

"When it comes to that kind of hobby, I have music. I love to listen to music and I can play musical instruments," shared the elderly man.

"What about singing songs?"

"I think I am not far behind others."

"All right. Then, what do you think music is?"

The elderly man thought for a moment, then said, "I think music is what enters the mind, and thus brings one to the state of non-self. Dear elder, when I was young, whenever afflictions arose in my mind, I used to play music alone. Then, before I knew it, afflictions drifted far away and finally disappeared."

"Had the afflictions really disappeared?"

"Of course not," the elderly man said, laughing. "Being entranced with music does not mean the problems that caused the afflictions have vanished."

"That is right. So, at that time, you did not enter the state of non-self where you realized that there was no self, but you entered the state of self-absorption where the self is absorbed in the object. And this is similar to the state of mind of the Buddhists when they are in meditative absorption," said Bhaddiya.

"Another name of the meditative absorption is samadhi. Samadhi can be achieved through practicing Buddhadhamma or various other worldly methods. Samadhi—which means the state where the mind abides one pointedly and is absorbed in the object—can be achieved not only through the practice of Buddhadhamma, but also through enjoying hobbies, being absorbed in works, falling in love, and being deeply touched by arts, etc.

"However, they are not genuine samadhi in its literal sense. They can be called semi-samadhi or worldly samadhi, and the genuine Buddhadhamma samadhi means only the state of mind complete with the five elements that have been obtained through the methods of meditation set forth by the Buddha.

"When you are in samadhi, the mind is happy and calm. This means that samadhi provides rest to the mind of sentient beings. Therefore, it is necessary for us to find out the most suitable method of samadhi practice, according to the spiritual capacity of each one. As we live being weighed upon by numerous sufferings in our daily life, we need some preparations to be able to enter the ultimate state of enlightenment.

"In the case of myself, the Buddha thought that I was not yet prepared to proceed to the ultimate state of enlightenment, and he instructed me to practice various meditation methods, especially the loving-kindness meditation. Even though I could not root out the afflictions through the loving-kindness meditation, I was able to taste certain happiness in my own way. So, I would like to suggest you to practice one of the meditations leading to samadhi."

"Do you think I can practice meditation well?"

"If it is a meditation leading not to the Buddhadhamma samadhi, but to the worldly samadhi, I think you can do it sufficiently. And when you begin to feel that your mind has improved to a certain degree through worldly meditation, then you may practice the lovingkindness meditation, one of the Buddhadhamma meditation practices."

"Then please teach me the most appropriate meditation that leads to worldly samadhi."

"As you are talented in music, you better practice samadhi utilizing music."

"That I will do."

Having confirmed that the old man accepted his advice acquiescently, Bhaddiya closed his eyes and sat quietly for a while.

After a while, Bhaddiya put improvised tunes to the Buddha's verses well known among monks and started to sing.

> Should you have a wise, cooperative companion,
> You go happily with him.
> Should you not have a wise, cooperative companion,
> You go alone, like the horn of a rhinoceros,
> Like a king who lives in solitude
> Having abandoned the kingdom he conquered.
>
> Abandon wife and children, parents, friends,
> Relatives, properties, and honors.
> They are like thick rattans that twine around a tree.
> So, you go alone like the horn of a rhinoceros,
> Like a man who cuts off the vines in a single stroke
> And smiles contently.
>
> Be aware that this is ignorance, and that is desire.
> They are a huge net that locks you up.
> So, you go alone, like the horn of a rhinoceros,
> Like a fish that tears off the net confining it
> And swims leisurely onto a vast open ocean.
>
> Deep in meditative absorption, enjoy tranquility.
> With awakened mind, practice compassion.

These are what practitioners should attain and practice.

So, you go alone like the horn of a rhinoceros,

Become a free person of non-possession,

And sit with closed eyes in the forest or by graves.

Like a lion that is not frightened by thunder,

Like the wind that is not caught by a net,

Like a lotus that is not stained by muddy water,

You go alone like the horn of a rhinoceros,

Far away from the world of suffering

And along the path of the supra-mundane.

"Singing this song, you appreciate the meaning of the verses on the one hand, and feel the mood of the tunes on the other hand. Then, your mind will be gradually put at ease," said Bhaddiya.

"I understand," Uggata replied with a bright face.

Bhaddiya helped Uggata remember and practice the lyrics and the melody. Being distinctly intelligent and talented in music, Uggata soon mastered the lyrics and the melody. He sang in a cool voice, and the sound of the song, together with the moonlight that fell lighting the darkness, filled the entire forest.

The two monks noticed that, while he was practicing the song, his voice became clearer and carried more and more power. It meant that, while he appreciated the verses and sang the song, his pain was being cured little by little.

"Elders," having completely mastered the song, Uggata said to the two monks, "Now my mind is light and at the same time full of emotions. So, it seems that I cannot sleep tonight, and as it is already too late into the night, you two elders better go to sleep now."

"Will it be all right if you do not sleep?" asked Bhaddiya.

"Now I feel that the so-called body can be changed drastically by way of a small change in the mind. Dear elder, now my body is overflowing with energy as it was when I was young. So, elder, you do not have to worry about me. Even if I am not seen tomorrow morning, please do not be worried. In that event, I may, in a renewed spirit and full of vigor, have left this place." Having said this, Uggata stood up and walked toward a tomb several tens of steps away from the two monks.

After some time, the two monks could hear the song of Uggata. Strolling around the tomb, Uggata was singing in a loud voice, the "Go alone like the horn of a rhinoceros" that he had learned from Bhaddiya.

The two monks, with their faces full of smiles, began to look for a place to sleep.

CHAPTER 14

The Dimension Where the Law of Cause and Effect Is Overcome

The next day, at daybreak the two monks woke up, and Uggata was nowhere to be seen. They recalled Uggata having said not to be worried if he was not seen. For that reason, just like practitioners who do not keep in mind what have happened in the past, they did not talk anymore about Uggata.

The two monks, as any other day, washed their faces, ate the porridge that Uggata left, and quietly repeated sitting meditation and walking meditation. Then in time for an alms round, they left the forest, and after the alms round, they embarked on a journey and arrived late in the afternoon at the Vimaratta Monastery where Elder Sariputta resided.

The man who greeted them was Elder Sariputta's attendant, Bhikkhu Cunda. "Welcome, brothers!" he said.

Cunda said with joined palms, "The Great Elder said that Elder Bhaddiya would come today or tomorrow, and he was right. Well, please step in. The Great Elder went to the village with other monks on the invitation of a layman."

"Oh, I see!" said Bhaddiya.

After such dialogue, three monks entered Cunda's abode. As Cunda was the oldest, Bhaddiya and Malukha expressed respect by making three prostrations to Cunda.

After the greetings, Bhaddiya asked Cunda, "By the way, how is the propagation in this region going?"

"As you are well aware, the teaching of the Great Elder is quite excellent. Therefore, propagation here is going smooth as flowing water," explained Cunda.

"As a matter of fact, the lay believer who invited the Elder Sariputta was a man who gave extreme difficulty to many edification efforts. However, he was moved by the noble personality and teaching of Elder Sariputta, repented the wrong life he had lived in the past, and was reborn as a new man. So, in order to express his gratitude, he has invited and offered food to not only Elder Sariputta and the monks but also to a large number of village people."

Malukha said, "Ah, that's why all bhikkhus are out. By the way, what kind of a man was the lay believer and how did Elder Sariputta edify him?"

"He was exceedingly vulgar, and most of all, an unfilial son of very evil nature. In a tricky way, he made his father's money his, and after that, drove his father out of the house," explained Cunda.

"Yes?" Malukha's eyes popped out. "Isn't the man the son of Uggata, by any chance?"

"Who is Uggata?"

"Oh," laughed Bhaddiya, "Ironically, yesterday we also met an old man abandoned by his son, and his name was Uggata." Bhaddiya told the story of Uggata to Cunda.

Having listened to the story till the end, Cunda said, "Incidentally, two men have committed the same undutiful acts. However, the unfilial son edified by Elder Sariputta is not the son of the old man you two met. His name is Surya and his father's name is Subbatana."

"I see. Well, unfilial sons are not a few in this world." When they were having such talks, a bustling noise of people's presence was heard from outside. The three monks went out. One hundred or more monks were returning from the village after the meal.

Like the leader of a flock of wild geese, Elder Sariputta was walking at the front of the monks, and having found the three monks, stopped about five steps apart from them. Then other monks who were following in a line also halted one by one.

The three monks paid their respect by making three prostrations at the feet of Sariputta. After a while, Sariputta, having washed his hands, feet, and face, straightened his robe and received Bhaddiya and Malukha.

Sariputta simply watched the monks silently for some time without saying a word. Being full of compassion on the one hand and shining with clearheaded wisdom on the other, Sariputta looked at them with eyes filled with the elegance and nobleness of an arhat who has transcended the realm of a sentient being.

"You have taken so much trouble to come," Sariputta opened his mouth and said at last, and his voice carried a solemn dignity as the Marshall of Dhamma. "Has anything unusual happened on your trip?"

Laughing, Bhaddiya said, "For renunciant monks like us, there is nothing unusual in the world, but a little odd thing actually happened on the trip."

"Would you tell me what this unusual thing was?"

"Master, we met an old man abandoned by an undutiful son."

"Oh, did you?"

"When we saw him, he was about to hang himself. So, we saved him and explained a little on the teaching of the Buddhadhamma."

Bhaddiya told briefly on what happened between them and Uggata. "By the way, master," said Bhaddiya, "we heard from Cunda that you have restored the filial affection of a man who used to be an impious son."

"That is right. Surya now changed his mind and became a good man."

"However . . ." Bhaddiya was about to say something, but stopped. There was a puzzled look on his face.

Elder Sariputta said, "Brothers, do not hesitate to speak out if you have something on your mind."

"Master, a doubt suddenly arose in me that the man might not have really restored his filial affection," said Bhaddiya.

"Brother, I find in your tone that there is something unfavorable in your mind toward Surya."

"That is true. For some reason or other, I do not feel I can trust him."

"But you have never met him."

"That is true. But strangely enough, I feel that we must not trust him."

"Aren't you identifying Surya with the son of Uggata?"

"Probably."

"And brother, aren't you by any chance identifying the two men with Binggisa?"

At such question of Sariputta, a look of surprise crossed Bhaddiya's face. His thought had not reached that far. The chief disciple of the Buddha said, "Brother, the mind is extremely delicate. It means that a mind that was evil yesterday may suddenly turn virtuous today, and that on some occasion, such change takes place so drastically as to leap from the bottom of the hell to the highest sphere of the heaven, in a split second.

"So, please you must not judge Surya by common sense. Common sense is in most cases efficient, but not always correct. Further, you have to remove the dark shadow in your mind against the son of Uggata. It seems now that you judge him as an unreliable villain and tie him tight with the dark rope of your mind. But there is no rule that he shall not be reborn as a good man from a bad one, like Surya."

"It is not impossible, but . . ." Bhaddiya was still a little stubborn, "as far as the son of Uggata is concerned, I think it quite difficult for him to recover his noble heart."

At that moment, hostility toward Binggisa sprang violently from his mind. In no time, Bhaddiya's face turned grey as if it was plastered with ashes. He condemned Surya, instead of Binggisa who was the actual target, in a voice filled with agitation.

"Elder Sariputta, I should be happy too if Uggata's son will recover the filial affection in the future or the man by the name of Surya has really recovered his filial affection. However, I would like to tell you what I think. It is only right that an appropriate reward be given to a son for having recovered his filial affection to his father, but for the unfilial actions he had committed in the past, an appropriate and painful retribution shall also be given."

Having heard this thought of Bhaddiya, Elder Sariputta shook his head, "Oh, brother, I do not agree with you in that respect. It goes without saying that they must receive retribution for their evil action committed in the past, and they certainly will. It is because the world is operated by the great law of cause and effect. However, brother, from a different perspective, I would like to state that the law of causality can be transcended, and it must be transcended.

"I will speak from that uncommon perspective that all evildoers must be eventually forgiven and will definitely be forgiven! That at that time, their evil actions, howsoever big they might be, shall disappear like dust! Because, they are very miserable people! Because, they are the most wretched people!"

Bhaddiya was greatly astonished, with a wide open mouth. He said, "Elder, the law of causality is the Buddhadhamma. Being the chief gatekeeper of protecting the Buddhadhamma, and the vanguard of propagating the Buddhadhamma, how could you make such remarks that deny the law of causality?"

"As you just mentioned, the law of causality is the Buddhadhamma, and the Buddhadhamma is the law of causality. Our Buddhadhamma declares the law of causality that is as strict as the fundamental arithmetic operations—in other words, a universal rule that for ten evil actions, ten painful retributions will surely follow, and for a hundred good actions, a hundred blissful retributions will ensue without fail."

"That is right. So I became a monk to learn the Buddhadhamma built on the unbiased law of cause and effect, not a biased religion that teaches the evil karma committed by sentient beings can be forgiven by free pardon of the god."

"Brother, I would like to accommodate the free pardon of the religion, that you criticize, in the Buddhadhamma, without causing any damage to the integrity of Buddhadhamma. By doing so, your narrow mind can be broadened, and through which you can achieve an enlightenment much more expansive and greater than that which you imagine of."

"However, venerable elder, rather than attaining broader and greater enlightenment through other religions, I hope to achieve a narrower and lesser enlightenment within the Buddhadhamma. The reason is that I can by no means understand or accept what they are claiming."

"Then, please tell me the reason why you cannot accept or understand what they are arguing."

"I will try to rebuke their arguments by taking an incident that occurred to Your Reverence as an example."

An incident occurred to Elder Sariputta a few years back.

One day, Sariputta was entering a village to beg for food. At that time, some men from the village, looking at Sariputta from far away, praised him saying, "Elder Sariputta has a really noble character. That elder, in no event, is surprised or reveals negative emotion."

Then a man raised a question.

"Can there really be that kind of a man?"

He doubted, but the villagers again praised the noble personality of Sariputta. Then the man said, "If he is so, it means that he has never encountered a man like me." Having said this, he dashed to Sariputta like an arrow.

With the villagers having no time to restrain him, he approached Sariputta and slapped him strongly on the back of his shoulder.

However, though Sariputta just bent his back a little due to the blow, he was not surprised or agitated. What is more, he did not even look back and just kept moving in the same direction. Then the man once again attacked Sariputta, but the reaction shown by the latter was identical with the first one.

Like a big swan gliding on the surface of a lake, the gait of Sariputta was elegant, and Arhat Sariputta's gait was stately like the king of elephants wandering alone on the field.

The man was surprised. This is the first time for him to meet a person who made no reaction even when he was attacked without reasons. With a vacant expression, he simply watched Sariputta's back for some time. Then, the village men rushed out toward the man, with clubs and other weapons in their hands. Running closer, they shouted at him.

"Such a villain!" one shouted. "He must be punished heavily so that he cannot commit this kind of act anymore!" another cried.

Stunned by the turn of events, the man quickly approached Sariputta, knelt down, and pleaded, "Your Reverence, please forgive me! It is only you who can save me now!"

Sariputta said in a composed manner, "I forgive you. And I will do as you wish." Having said this, Sariputta gave his alms bowl to the man, who had just stood up from the ground, and had him follow behind him.

For this reason, villagers could not attack the man. They said to Sariputta, "Your Reverence, please take your alms bowl back."

Sariputta halted, turned back and asked them, "Everyone, did this man attack you or me?"

"He attacked you."

"That's right. This man attacked me, not you. And I forgave this man. So please go back and mind your business." Having saved the man from the crisis, Sariputta went to the man's house and was offered a lunch.

CHAPTER 15
The Mind-Path of an Enlightened One Has No Trace

haddiya asked Elder Sariputta, "Then master, that is what is being told among us bhikkhus, so did that really occur?"

"Yes. That's right."

"Then let me return to the example for a moment and ask you again. The man did you wrong and asked you for forgiveness. But what if this man went and asked for forgiveness from some unrelated person, for example if he came to me instead of you. Master, do you think his action is logical?"

"I think that would be illogical."

"But such irrational doctrines are exactly what these non-Buddhists are teaching people. They say, 'God can purify the sins of man. No matter how deep or heavy, no matter how big or dark they may be.' But Your Reverence, let me ask you this. How could their god forgive the sins his devotee committed against another, though it may be possible to pardon the sins committed against god himself? Dear elder, if we are to apply their teachings to the son of Uggata, the millionaire I spoke about a moment ago, this would mean that the god could forgive his son if asked for pardon, even if he leaves his father to suffer and let him wander like a beggar.

"As such, their doctrine that teaches that all is well only if people show devotion to their god—I see in the doctrine a probability that it will become unnecessary to purify one's mind, and that the good and bad deeds of mankind may be trifled. So, how could I not state such doctrine is wrong?"

Strangely, Bhaddiya was becoming more and more agitated while talking. Seeing otherwise very gentle and polite Bhaddiya become unusually agitated, Malukha thought, *Perhaps the elder's agitation is due to Binggisa and Ayutha.*

It was proven soon enough that his guess was right. After collecting his breath for a moment, Bhaddiya confessed the following on why he was agitated: "But master," Bhaddiya said quietly while calming himself, "I now realize that certain aspects of my mind are impure. It's quite embarrassing that although I seem to be criticizing non-Buddhists outwardly, I am in fact criticizing Binggisa, a devotee of God Huruva and my friend, before I became a monk. Before he went and asked his god for pardon, he should have come to me first and asked for forgiveness. He will never be forgiven by his god unless I forgive him! No, he must never be forgiven!" said Bhaddiya.

Calming his newly arising agitation by taking slower breaths, he spoke quietly and with sadness in his voice, "But master, I believed that I had forgiven him within my heart long ago. You taught me how to practice loving-kindness meditation, and my mind became filled with joy, and these feelings of joy and happiness allowed me to forgive him.

I told myself while feeling this great joy, *People who are happy are generous. Those who are generous can forgive even his enemy.* But oh master! Although I fooled myself to believe that I had forgiven him, I now see that I had not truly forgiven him! I once saw him in my dream. In my dream he had fallen into hell where boiling water bubbled and seethed, while I was looking down at him from above. He shouted while waving his two hands, 'Oh! King Bhaddiya, please forgive me!'

"So I answered, 'I forgive you! I had forgiven you long ago!'

"After I said this, I requested to the guardians of hell, 'Deliverers of justice! Please save my friend from hell.' But the hell guardians shook their heads and refused my request. Thus I asked them why he could not be rescued from hell. Then, one of the guardians answered, 'That is because you have not truly forgiven him.'

"I responded, 'But I forgave him.'

"The hell guardian then laughed and said, 'Is that right? Then let's carry out a test.'

"Upon saying this, he gave me a strange magical thread that could unwind endlessly. I released the thread and threw it down to hell.

"When the thread reached hell, Binggisa caught the thread and clung on to it. I brought him up very carefully. I felt my heartbeat rise with the thought that the thread could be cut off.

"Then, when I pulled him up and his body was about halfway out of the boiling pit of hell, other hell beings near him began to grab hold of his limbs and dragged him down. Despite it all, the thread was still intact, thus I paid greater attention in pulling up the thread. Sweat ran down my body like rain, with the thought that this will all be in vain with even a moment of distraction. And then I was exposed to the most amazing sight. I saw Binggisa reaching out his arm toward other beings in hell. Binggisa reached out to them in clamor, 'Grab hold of my hand! Come on, quickly! Hold on to my hand!'

"When those who had been holding onto the thread heard this, they shouted in anger with their eyes about to bulge out, 'There are enough people holding on to the thread even now!' they said. In the meantime, they kicked away other beings who were reaching out their arms toward Binggisa. Some even tried to get rid of Binggisa, who was the rightful owner of the thread.

"Then Binggisa said, while grabbing hold of the thread tightly with his hand, 'I will never let go of this thread. Oh brothers, it is not for me that I do not let go of this thread. But because not letting go of the thread is the only way to deliver more beings out of this hell. When all of you arise to heaven, I will let go of this thread and fall down to hell once again. Because I am a sinner! I am the lowest of the low!'

"I knew intuitively that he was not lying. Once again my heart was touched and tears rolled down endlessly from my eyes. And then! In that very instant a small gap was created in my mind, and a thought crept into my mind, *How beautiful is his consideration! But why did he cause such a great wound in my heart when he could be so kind and caring?*

"Master, and as soon as this impure thought penetrated my mind, I lost hold of the thread I was pulling the hell beings out of hell. Thus, Binggisa and all other hell beings that were holding onto the thread fell right back to the boiling pit of hell.

"Devastated, I sat with my head down. Then the guardian of hell came and said with a grin. 'Are you going to admit it now? That you did not forgive him sincerely.'"

Having said this, Bhaddiya stopped for a moment to calm his emotions. Elder Sariputta, with an expression of great compassion, and Bhikkhu Malukha also emotional and in tears, looked onto Bhikkhu Bhaddiya.

"Just like this, master," continued Bhaddiya, "Although I say that I have forgiven him, it is only at a superficial level even until now, not the complete forgiveness arising deep within my heart. Honestly master, from the depth of my mind there still remains a kind of subtle rivalry. I am always competing with him somehow in my mind.

"Although I have renounced the world I sometimes hear news of Binggisa. And every time, I compare myself to him from within. Sometimes I think, *I knew it! How could such a betrayer do well?* or *He had really advanced up to that level?* and I push myself with a whip to do better.

"Even about the dream I had, I kept thinking, *Even in my dreams he showed concern for other sentient beings before himself. On the other hand, I happen to think that I must practice first and then help other beings later. Between these two paths, am I the one who is correct or is he?*

"After these self-inquiries I told myself, *I am right*! But master, I doubt myself right away after I say this. I keep thinking, *Could he really be wrong?*

"Thus, I would like to ask your views on this matter. Dear master, please offer me teachings on this subject in order to resolve my doubt."

Smiling, Sariputta said, "Brother, I fully understand the feelings of competitiveness you have toward Binggisa. There is nothing wrong with you thinking that you must practice first and save sentient beings later. But your friend is also right, and all this you will come to realize the moment you are enlightened."

"Teacher, I don't understand how you could say both mine and his points of view are correct."

With a firm tone, as if stepping on the ground firmly, Sariputta said, "Brother, you should understand this. Dhamma accepts this and that perspective, and says things that at a glance don't seem to play out logically.

"Therefore, I will say this in order to help you open up your heart toward the boundless, open space. I can say that the great sinner Binggisa is in fact without any sins; if I see it from the highest dimension of Dhamma and if I limit the boundary to you who cannot forgive Binggisa wholeheartedly. Because sins are darkness, and darkness is simply an absence of light, which does not truly exist, like a mirage. If darkness truly exists, darkness should be able to shade the light, but that is impossible! But opposite is possible, darkness disappears without a trace the moment light shines forth! Burnt out firewood leaves ashes, but the place where darkness and shadow once resided leaves no trace with shining of light, not the smallest bit of darkness will be left!"

What Sariputta spoke of was a great shock for Bhaddiya. His chin dropped with his eyes wide open, and he couldn't dare question or refute what was being said.

Sariputta, the "father of Dhamma" and the holder of transcendental wisdom, continued while facing Bhaddiya, "Brother, you should understand that all truth of secular life is established on the basis of reason and logic, but what lies above it all is the transmundane wisdom. In other words, seemingly irrational wisdom may in fact be higher than rational wisdom. This transrational wisdom remains as a contradiction but yet is not a contradiction, it exists although it cannot exist, and is possible because it is impossible, that is the 'truth of transrational wisdom.'"

Bhaddiya, who was already in shock, once again was astonished immensely. Not only because what Sariputta said appeared to be very unreasonable but more so because his words were related to his competitor and enemy Binggisa. In the past, Bhaddiya heard from one of the bhikkhus that Binggisa insisted on the concept of transrationalism. At that time, Bhaddiya laughed at Binggisa while saying the story of transrationalism was pure nonsense.

However, when the words of Binggisa, the words that he laughed and scorned at, came out of his master's mouth exactly the same without a single difference, uncontrollable envy took over within the heart of Bhaddiya. With this, he felt extreme pain as if struck in the head with a blunt weapon and he collapsed to the ground with his two hands wrapped around his head.

Bhaddiya shouted while rolling on the ground, "Oh master! My head is about to burst with pain!"

Sariputta paid attention to Bhaddiya's mind, not his body. Then, the most discerning bodhisattva on heaven and earth next to the Buddha, was able to see through the inner state of Bhaddiya instantly. Sariputta, with the help of Malukha, laid Bhaddiya straight on the ground and put one hand on Bhaddiya's head.

The pain subsided significantly, and Sariputta said to Bhaddiya in a firm voice with full conviction, "Brother, put your mind together and listen carefully to what I have to say. The past is already gone and it no longer exists in this moment. Just like shadows cannot exist when light appears! Brother, completely erase all memories you have of Binggisa, like a clear sky after the rain. What he does is his own business. What you have to do, my brother, is to bring your mind back to here and now, and see your mind and body just as they are in awareness.

"Just like a person looking at white clouds that float through the clear sky, with no projection of desire to that looking, stay calm, but be mindful of your body and mind just as they are. Be aware of your body. Be aware of your feelings. Be aware of your mind. Be aware of Dhamma. Do not allow the notions of ideals or preconceptions get in the way of that awareness. Discard all knowledges. Throw away even the notions of Dhamma. Only allow pure awareness to be present.

"In that state, look into your body and mind and become aware. No, forget about even being aware. Just keep your mind in awakened state. Then your body and mind will become the object of knowing, just like the reflection of the moon on a pure, calm lake. This means your body and mind will become like the body and mind of someone else, brother. Therefore there is neither me nor mine."

Sariputta taught Bhaddiya this way, allowing time to pass while seeing how Bhaddiya reacted. In the meantime, Bhaddiya felt his pain subside and he turned his mind to the teachings of his teacher, returning back to his original self.

Next, Bhaddiya got himself up and sat properly with his eyes closed to practice vipassana meditation. Like a vulture descending from the sky toward the ground to seize the prey, or like a tightly woven bamboo shade without even the slightest gaps, he caught onto the object of meditation in a tranquil, fast manner.

After a while, in a state of deep concentration and full awareness, he entered into the state of the first jhana (meditative absorption). Then into the state of the second jhana, and then the third and fourth jhana in sequence; he remained in that state of absorption of universal equanimity for some time.

In time, Bhaddiya attained great awakening in the state of the fourth jhana and finally reached the state of seeing all worldly phenomena as impermanent, as suffering or dissatisfaction, and as having non-self, ultimately attaining the fruit of arhatship.

Bhikkhu Bhaddiya's facial expression brightened like a full moon. As if the world had been his—no, actually it should be the opposite. Not as if he had owned the world but as if he renounced the world, not as if he "renounced the world," but he, in fact, renounced the world, and his facial expression was pure beyond description.

Bhaddiya rose quietly and offered three prostrations to his teacher Sariputta to express his appreciation. Seeing this, Malukha said to Sariputta, "Elder, it seems that Bhaddiya has attained very high state of awakening."

"Yes, he has."

"Then, what level did Bhaddiya attain?"

"Brother, except for the Buddha, there is no one who can say what level a practitioner has reached, or we should not even tell. As such, this matter should be dealt very carefully. This is because there could be a great cause of confusion for the Sangha if not dealt appropriately.

"Therefore, I am not going to speak about the level of attainment he has reached. However, I just heard the sound of Dhamma proclaimed by the Buddha, the seer beyond time and space, that Bhaddiya has attained arhatship. Additionally, Brother Bhaddiya has acquired five sagely powers.

"Oh . . ." Malukha exclaimed, shivering with overwhelming joy.

Soon, he got up from his seat and recited a few verses of the Buddha in a clear, ringing voice.

> The journey of birth and death is over for an arhat.
> Liberated from the sorrow of the five aggregates,[36]
> Released from all worldly entanglements
> There is no more suffering for him.

---

36 Five aggregates (panca khandha): Buddhism analyzes human body and mind into five constituents of elements. Five aggregates are composed of qualities or elements that include form or matter (rupa khandha), sensations or feelings (vedana khandha), ideas or perceptions (sanna khandha), mental activity or formations (sankhara khandha), and consciousness (vinnana khandha).

For an arhat the mind is calm and peaceful.
So are his language and action.
Ah, the mind-path of arhat has no trace
Just as birds flying through the air leave no trace.

CHAPTER 16

Ecstatic Splendor, a Day under a Bodhi Tree

After recitation of the verses, Malukha made three prostrations to Bhaddiya, and said, "Oh, elder! I know how hard you have tried to accept Binggisa and Ayutha with a generous mind. Today the efforts became merits and as a result you have attained enlightenment in an instant, and in my thought, there is nothing nobler than a generous forgiving."

Arhat Bhaddiya accepted the praise of the junior bhikkhu with a deep silence. It was at that moment that delicate, unidentifiable scents began to spread and fill up the room. Sariputta, Chunda, and Bhaddiya had sagely powers, and the heavenly beings Raja and Sirima knew that they were heavenly scents. That was right. They were heavenly scents emanating from the bodies of the countless heavenly beings coming down from the three levels of heaven in the first meditation heaven.

Not only scents but, moments later, lights of various colors were emanating from the heavenly beings, filling the entire room. Further, beautiful music of the gandhabbas escorting the heavenly beings began to boom, and by that time, even bhikkhus without sagely powers noticed that something very special was happening.

Malukha looked at Sariputta in amazement. Sariputta, the noblest sage throughout heaven and earth, except the Buddha, joined two hands and made a mudra in the shape of a circle. Then came an amazing event. In a small room that could fit only six to seven persons, countless heavenly beings began to storm like clouds and take seats.

It was a smaller space but limitlessly wide at the same time! And the heavenly beings that had entered the room were not hindered by the walls and stood in orderly lines!

The number of the heavenly beings in the room of Sariputta was as many as several tens of thousands. Upon their arrival, Raja and Sirima retreated to the rearmost part of the room. It was because the status of the heavenly beings from the Brahma Heaven was higher than theirs.

Countless heavenly beings who enjoyed the bliss of meditative absorption in the Brahma Heaven took their positions and then the leader Sahampati,[37] the King of the Mahabrahma Heaven, who was standing at the forefront, raised his hand to stop the music performance of the gandhabbas. And he, together with all other heavenly beings, showed respect to Sariputta by making three prostrations, and before that, by the sagely powers of Sahampati, a lotus seat made of seven jewels had been placed at the spot where Sariputta had been sitting.

When the heavenly beings finished three prostrations and took their seats, Sariputta, by his sagely power, began to emit lights from his body. That was to show the greatness of the Buddhadhamma to the heavenly beings.

---

37 Sahampati : A heavenly being often appearing in the scriptures. In Buddhism, he is thought to be Mahabrahma worshiped by Indians at the time of the Buddha. When the Buddha, after attaining enlightenment, hesitated whether or not to preach to sentient beings, he recommended to preach, and when the Buddha entered parinirvana, he recited a verse commemorating the Buddha. There is no heavenly king in meditation heavens, but it is considered to be existent in this work.

The light emanated from the body of Elder Sariputta suppressed and extinguished the light of the heavenly beings at first, and thenfilled the room, and soon penetrated the wall to reach outside and illuminated the entire three realms. All beings in the room, owing to the sagely power of Sariputta, could see how far the light had reached. They could see the worlds beyond the limit of their own worlds—for Raja and Sirima, the heavens higher than the Tavatimsa Heaven, and for other heavenly beings, the heavens higher than the first meditation heaven.

The supernatural light emitted by Sariputta leaped over the Desire Realm, such as Hell, Hungry Ghost, Asura, Animal, and Human, and it illuminated the Form Realm directly.

The light illuminated the Heaven of Brahma Followers (*Brahma-parisadya*) in the first meditation heaven.

The light illuminated the Heaven of Brahma's Ministers (*Brahma-purohita*) in the first meditation heaven.

The light illuminated the Mahabrahma Heaven (*Mahabrahma*) in the first meditation heaven.

The light illuminated the Heaven of Lesser Light (*Parittabha*) in the second meditation heaven.

The light illuminated the Heaven of Immeasurable Light (*Apramanabha*) in the second meditation heaven.

The light illuminated the Heaven of Ultimate Light (*Abhasvara*) in the second meditation heaven.

The light illuminated the Heaven of Lesser Purity (*Paritta subha*) in the third meditation heaven.

The light illuminated the Heaven of Infinite Purity (*Apramana-subha*) in the third meditation heaven.

The light illuminated the Heaven of Universal Purity (*Subha-krtsna*) in the third meditation heaven.

The light illuminated the two heavens in the fourth meditation heaven, the Heaven of Extensive Fruition (*Bthatphala*) and the Non-conceptual Heaven (*Asamjnika*) in the fourth meditation heaven.

The light illuminated the Heaven of Pure Abode (*Suddhavasa*),[38] in the fourth meditation heaven.

At the next stage, the light emitted by Sariputta illuminated from the fifth to eighth meditation heavens in the Formless Realm. The Formless Realm consists of four heavens, but it does not have a predefined space. It is because the sentient beings born in those meditation heavens do not have physical bodies but only minds.

Sariputta removed the light and returned to his usual self. Then, lights revived at the bodies of the heavenly beings.

Sahampati, the King of the Mahabrahma Heaven, joined his palms and said, "The foremost disciple of the Buddha, now you have emitted light by sagely powers and illuminated the three realms. The Desire Realm and the Form Realm that we saw were enormous and magnificent beyond expression in words!"

"King of Mahabrahma Heaven! Even though I illuminated the three realms with a small supernatural light, it is nothing more than the light emitted by a small firefly under a full moon, when compared to that of the Buddha."

"That is right! I do know well how unprecedented, rare, and inconceivable the supernatural light of the Buddha is!" said Sahampati.

He continued, "Elder Sariputta! Being a resident of the Mahabrahma Heaven, with the lifespan of an incalculably long eon, I have seen in the present eon innumerable number of humans born and die on the earth. However, no Buddhadhamma existed in the past several hundreds of millions of years, and it was because there was no enlightened Buddha in that period to teach the truth.

"And at last, our Shakyamuni Buddha attained the unsurpassed complete enlightenment, and the Buddhadhamma thus first appeared in this world. I take refuge in the Buddha. I take refuge in the Dhamma. I take refuge in the Sangha. "Elder, our Shakyamuni

---

38 Heaven of Pure Abode (Suddhavasa): A special heaven where a Buddhist, who has attained the third level of awakening through Buddhist practice, will be reborn. Practitioners born in this heaven will not be given a next life, such as a life in this world, and complete enlightenment there.

Buddha became a bodhisattva one hundred thousand great eons ago, by receiving an honorable prediction from Dipankara Buddha that he would become a Buddha, and at that time his name was Sumedha.

"Since then up until the present day, the Buddhadhamma repeated disappearing and reappearing twenty-four times. Bodhisattva Sumedha, during this long period, lived as a bhikkhu, a renounced practitioner, or a wealthy Brahmin, and at other times was born as a dragon king, a yakkha, a lion king, or a heavenly king or a heavenly being, and practiced ten perfections, and also received predictions repeatedly from the then Buddhas of the time that he would become a Buddha.

"Then Bodhisattva Sumedha lived his previous life as Prince Vessantara in the Human Realm, and thereby accomplished all the merits to be a Buddha in the future. Immediately thereafter, he was born as a heavenly being in the Tusita Heaven, and the name of the bodhisattva at that time was Satyaketu.

"At long last, the time has come. The four heavenly kings and other heavenly kings that rule many different heavens, along with numerous heavenly beings of the Brahma Heaven, proceeded to the Bodhisattva Satyaketu and implored that he would go down to the Human Realm and widely teach the sentient beings ignorant in darkness.

"Having accepted their request with gentle words, the Buddha, before going down to the earth, pondered on the appropriate time, continent, region, and clan as well as an appropriate woman to be the mother.

"And in that great year (624 BCE), on the fifteenth day of the sixth lunar month, when the day was about to dawn, the bodhisattva entered the womb of the Queen Consort Mahamaya of the Shakya Kingdom in the northeastern region of the continent. And ten lunar months after entering the womb, on the fifteenth day of the fourth lunar month (Vesak), the bodhisattva was born in the Lumbini

Grove when Lady Mahayana was on her way to her parents' home.[39]

"Though venerable elder is well aware of what has happened to the bodhisattva ever since, what I want to tell, for all heavenly beings gathered here, is about what happened when he attained enlightenment.

"Oh, elder, I still remember clearly. The solemn scene when the bodhisattva attained the unsurpassed, complete enlightenment along with the ten powers, the four types of fearlessness and the six exclusive wisdoms of a Buddha.

"When the bodhisattva attained enlightenment and became the Buddha, the ten thousand worlds roared sonorously thirty-three times. The vibration was so tremendous that even devas like us shrunk and shuddered from fear. But not long after, myriad devas and heavenly beings, who had learned that it was not to be feared but to be delighted and praised, thronged to the side of the Buddha like clouds.

"At that time, the Buddha emitted light toward the whole Dhama Realm as Elder Sariputta has done a while ago. But the splendor, colorfulness, beauty, nobleness, and gloriousness of the light was beyond expression by words and unfathomable and unthinkable by sentient beings, and thus the best and the highest one in the world!

"And at that time the Buddha showed a special supernatural powers emitting two objects of opposite quality—water and fire—at the same time. It was due to the fact that there were heavenly beings that were still harboring doubts about the Buddha's enlightenment.

"To show this sagely power, the Buddha first decided that he would meditate fire kasina,[40] enter the fourth meditative absorption, come

---

39 In the northern tradition of Buddhism such as in China, Korea, and Japan, the Buddha is thought to have come on the eighth day of the fourth lunar month. But in the southern tradition of Buddhism, the Buddha is thought to have been born on the fifteenth day of the fourth lunar month, and his enlightenment and parinirvana are also considered to have occurred on this day.

40 Kasina: Objects of meditation used in the cultivation of meditative absorption. For example, when water is used as kasina, one will pour water in a basin, watching it with his eyes open, and thus obtain a sign (nimitta). Afterwards, one closes his eyes and watches the obtained sign, so that the sign will not be dispersed and will be maintained well. And again one expands the sign little by little and fills the whole universe.

out of it, and have fire spew from the upper part of the body, and then decided that he would meditate water kasina, enter the fourth meditative absorption, come out of it, and have water spurt out from the lower part of the body.

"The next moment, fire appeared at the upper part of his body, and water flew from the lower part of his body like a fountain. And instantly, the role of the upper part and the lower part was switched, thus fire appeared at the lower part of his body, and water flew from the upper part like a fountain. However as the switch took place in an instant, it appeared in the eyes of human beings as if both water and fire came out at the same time from his entire body.

"Next moment, fire appeared in the front part of the body and water flew from the rear part. Then it shifted instantly and fire appeared at the rear part of his body and water flew from the front part.

"Next moment, fire appeared at the right eye and water flew from the left eye. Then it shifted instantly and fire appeared at the left eye and water flew from the right eye.

"Next moment, fire appeared at the right ear and water flew from the left ear. Then it shifted instantly and fire appeared at the left ear and water flew from the right ear.

"Next moment, fire appeared at the right shoulder and water flew from the left shoulder. Then it shifted instantly and fire appeared at the left shoulder and water flew from the right shoulder.

"Next moment, fire appeared at the right side of his body and water flew from the left side. Then it shifted instantly and fire appeared at the left side and water flew from the right side.

"Next moment, fire appeared at the right leg and water flew from the left leg. Then it shifted instantly and fire appeared at the left leg and water flew from the right leg.

"Next moment, fire appeared at the ten fingers and toes and water flew from between the fingers and toes. Then it shifted instantly and fire appeared from between the fingers and toes and water flew from the ten fingers and toes.

"Next moment, fire appeared at all hairs in the left side of his body and water flew from all hairs in the right side. Then it shifted instantly and fire appeared at all hairs in the right side and water flew from all hairs in the left side of the body.

"Next moment, fire appeared at all pores in the left side of his body and water flew from the pores in the right side. Then it shifted instantly and fire appeared at all pores in the right side and water flew from all pores in the left side of the body.

"At the same time, lights of six colors emanated from all parts of the body. Lights of blue, yellow, red, white, and pink color, and a light of pure brightness emanated together.

"Blue color spewed from the hair and the beard.

"Yellow color spewed from the skin.

"Red color spewed from the flesh and the blood.

"White color spewed from the bones and teeth.

"Pink color spewed from the palms and the soles.

"The brightness spewed from the forehead and the nails of the hands and the feet.

"Six colors formed a melting pot of lights, and like molten gold, covered the entire Circular Iron Mountain Range. Thus, the great sagely power exercised by the Buddha made a great symphony of lights played by several hundreds of millions of musicians and resonated vividly to the end of the universe!"

Upon hearing the King of the Mahabrahma Heaven, Sahampati's old story of what he had seen, over eighty thousand heavenly beings praised the sagely power of the Buddha exclaiming, "Excellent! Excellent! Excellent!"

Having waited until the sound of praises subsided, Sariputta asked Sahampati, "Dear Heavenly King, what is the reason for your visit?"

"Elder Sariputta," said Sahampati, "Since a while go, the devas of the first to the eighth meditation heavens and the six heavenly kings of the Desire Realm were curious about why the World-Honored One was having a long journey to the south where he had never been to. So, the kings of the Brahma Heaven and the Desire

Realm gathered at the grand convention room of the Mahabrahma Heaven and discussed this matter.

"At the end of a long discussion, the devas and heavenly kings decided to dispatch a representative and ask the Buddha why he was traveling to such a remote area. And I was selected as the representative, and learning that I was going down to the earth to have an audience with the Buddha, eighty thousand or more of the heavenly beings in the first meditation heaven wanted to accompany me."

"Then, why you didn't go to the Buddha and came to me instead?"

"As a matter of fact, at first, I wanted to go to the Buddha, but when I was about to depart, I learned that you were guiding Elder Bhaddiya to the state of enlightenment. Because I learned that Elder Bhaddiya attained arhatship, we came here to meet the newly born great sage."

Having said this, Sahampati made three prostrations toward Bhaddiya and said, "Holy man, please give us your blessings."

Bhaddiya answered in a solemn voice, "I hereby do bless you, so you'd be happy, be happy, and be happy!"

"We thank you for your words of blessings," said Sahampati and looked at Sariputta.

Then, the foremost disciple of the Buddha asked Sahampati, "So what will you do from now on?"

"Elder, I want to leave for the place where the World-Honored One is heading, together with my family."

Sariputta said, "You are curious about the reason why the Buddha is heading to the south where he has never been to, but I am aware of the reason. Dear King of Mahabrahma Heaven, the reason for the Buddha going there is to meet Binggisa, whom Brother Bhaddiya just mentioned."

"Elder, he is a sentient being who has committed a grave offense. Then, why the World-Honored One, the teacher of humans and devas, makes such a long journey to meet with a mean sentient being?"

"As you said, Binggisa is a sinful sentient being. However, you must be aware of the profound reason why the Buddha is making such a long journey to meet a sinful sentient being.

"But even if the Buddha explains the meaning for you, you may not fully understand it now. Even if you understand it, your merit will fall far behind the merit of even watching the Buddha from far away when he meets Binggisa.

"And you should be aware as well that being the foremost disciple of the Buddha, I plan to leave here for Subbaraka tomorrow to witness the very particular and rare event of the Buddha meeting with Binggisa. Therefore, rather than going to the Buddha right away, you and your retinue should go along with me, because even now the place where the Buddha is full and teeming with countless heavenly beings gathered from the vast universe."

Upon hearing Sariputta's explanation, Sahampati said, "We are grateful to you for telling us all the details. If that is the case, Elder, I will now return to the Mahabrahma Heaven to report to the heavenly kings, who are waiting for me on what I have heard from you, and then come back together with the heavenly kings and their numerous followers."

"Please do as you said. But Heavenly King, I now see a heavenly being standing in the back of your followers and looking at me with pleading eyes."

"Is there such a heavenly being?" Sahampati said and looked back. In response to that, a heavenly being put his hands together and revealed himself for being the one that Elder Sariputta had mentioned.

"Wouldn't you please step forward," said Sahampati, and the heavenly being came forward.

Sahampati asked the heavenly being, "Why are you looking at the elder with pleading eyes?"

"Heavenly King, I had karmic ties with Elder Sariputta in my life before the previous. That is the reason why I was looking at the elder with admiring eyes."

"It is exactly as he said," Sariputta said to Sahampati. "And

Heavenly King, at the back of your retinue two heavenly beings from the Tavatimsa Heaven are standing with joined palms. Some time ago, they became special disciples of the Buddha and are learning the Buddhadhamma, and Raja of the two had deep karmic ties with the heavenly being standing in front of us."

Raja was surprised at the words of Sariputta and looked closely at the heavenly being whom, Sariputta said, had had special ties with him, also turning his head toward him with a curious look. Raja instantly noticed that the heavenly being is the old man named Chuchu whom he met in his previous life.

"Heavenly Being Raja, please come forward," said Elder Sariputta, so Raja stepped forward and said to Chuchu, "I would like to offer my heart felt congratulations to you, Heavenly Being!"

Chuchu, with a look full of gratitude on his face, said, "Oh, I received great assistance from you in my life before the previous. First of all, I would like to thank you for that. In addition, I congratulate you on having been born in the Tavatimsa Heaven."

"Yes, I could hear the Buddha's verses recited by you at the last moment of my previous life, and owing to such merits I was able to be born in the Tavatimsa Heaven. More fortunate is that I and my wife became special disciples of the Buddha."

Upon hearing Raja's words, Chuchu asked Sariputta, "Elder, what is the status of special disciples this couple has obtained?"

"Heavenly Being Chuchu, heavenly beings cannot be bhikkhus or bhikkhunis. However, the World-Honored One exceptionally accepted them as disciples equivalent to bhikkhus and bhikkhunis."

"Then elder, could you allow me a status similar to this husband and wife. If you would allow me, I want to be a special disciple like these two heavenly beings and learn the Buddhadhamma."

Sariputta said, "As you had karmic ties with me in the previous life, it wouldn't be unreasonable to accept you as my special disciple."

At Sariputta's words, Chuchu joined his palms and requested Sariputta, "Elder, please accept me as your special disciple!"

"Come forth, Heavenly Being, I consent to your request," Sariputta said and accepted his request. Chuchu made three prostrations with expression of gratitude.

After receiving Chuchu as a special disciple, the Great Marshall of Dhamma said to Sahampati, "Well, now you can go back to the Mahabrahma Heaven with your retinue and come back to me again with all the sentient beings that are waiting for you there."

To this, Sahampati, the King of the Mahabrahma Heaven, replied, "I will follow your instruction right away, elder," and he left the place together with more than eighty thousand heavenly beings.

CHAPTER 17
Heavenly Being Chuchu

After the departure of the heavenly beings from the Mahabrahma Heaven, Sariputta said to Chuchu and Raja, "As two of you had deep karmic ties in your previous lives, you better talk for some time and catch up."

Then Chuchu said to Raja, "Once again, I thank you for what you have done for me in my previous life. However, Heavenly Being Raja, though we encountered death at the same place and time, the retributions we attained were divided into light and darkness. I mean, my good friend, while you received good retribution of being reborn in the Tavatimsa Heaven upon death, I received evil retribution of falling into the pit of hell."

"Really?" Raja opened his eyes wide in surprise and cried, "However, aren't you now in the Brahma Heaven?"

Chuchu said, "I first fell into hell, but I could finish my evil retribution in a short period of time. Then I was immediately reborn on the Heaven of Brahma Followers, thanks to the good retribution from the virtuous deeds performed in my life before the previous. The reason for this is that in that previous life I received instruction on meditation from Elder Sariputta, and I attained the lowest level of the first meditative absorption.

"My friend! Some sentient beings receive good retribution first, and others receive evil retribution first. Which retribution to be received depends first on what you remember at the last moment of death. Being aware of this, I tried hard to keep good intentions even when I was suffering the pain of death.

"However, as you are well aware, mind does not always move as you wish. So, I, with insufficient performance in practice, wavered at the last moment of death and recalled the evil deeds committed in the previous life for a short while, and as a result I received an evil retribution to fall into hell," finished Chuchu.

"Deva of the Brahma Heaven! If it will not be painful for you to recall the evil karmas of the past, please tell me what was the evil karma that you recalled at the time of death," asked Raja.

"It will be painful for anyone to recall evil karmas of the past. But for me, who thinks one must look squarely at evil karmas to break through and overcome them, rather than avoiding them, I think it is something I have to do, no matter how painful it may feel.

"My friend, Raja! What I recalled at the time of death was Binggisa—things related to him whom the World-Honored One is now traveling to visit and my master will also embark on a long journey tomorrow to meet with. That's right. In my previous life, I was the archbishop of a religion that believed in the absolute God named Huruva, and Binggisa was a theology student of mine.

"Then, what a horrendous thing indeed! Full of good intentions, and for his spiritual salvation, and further, with an expectation that he would enhance the happiness of the people, I taught theology to him. But my good intentions, upon reaching him, turned evil. Thus, spiritual salvation was changed to spiritual destruction, and happiness turned to misery of people.

"What I realized through that experience was that good intentions would not always bring about good results. Evils that result from good intentions! Oh, actions without right view sometimes generate such evils, but I didn't realize it at that time.

"My friend, you have to be aware. That the most horrible evils in

178

the world are evils armed with good intentions. However, I planted the probability in Binggisa that such horrible and vicious evils could arise."

"Then, do you mean that due to the evil deeds committed by Binggisa, you fell into hell?"

"No, that is not true. Naturally, I fell into hell because of the evil deeds that I committed."

"Then what were the evil deeds that caused you to fall into hell?"

"What pushed me into hell were my evil deeds, which were committed with noble intentions but from a mistaken view. However, as my evil actions were not so grave as to kill people, I was able to finish the retribution for my evil actions in a short period of time.

"Then what kind of evil actions have I committed? Heavenly Being Raja, I was filled with good intentions to be loyal to God. Therefore, I once took advantage of my mother for the sake of God.

"However, how can a human take advantage of other humans? Moreover, she was my own mother! But when I was committing the evil, I did not realize it was an evil action. I even thought that it was a sacred deed, rather than an evil one."

"Oh . . ." reacted Raja.

"Heavenly Being Raja, at that time when I was filled with loyalty toward God, I thought that all other values of the world were, when compared to the absolute value called the loyalty to God, no more than trivial. It means that I regarded loyalty to God as the first commandment and all virtues between human beings, such as filial duty to parents, devotion to family, consideration for neighbors etc., as the second commandment, which could be disregarded when they conflicted with the first commandment.

"I knew, as a theologian and the religious leader, the importance of love between humans. However, for me, the love between humans was, rather than being the second amendment after the first one, nothing more than an addendum attached to the main rule.

"As to this subject, my ordinary disciples did not argue whether the two commandments are of same or different in value, and I didn't bother to distinguish and underline that point. But one day

Binggisa raised doubt about that issue and asked me, 'Master, you preached on the loyalty to God, and on the love between humans. If these two values conflict each other, in other words, if love between humans must be sacrificed for the sake of loyalty to God or loyalty to God must be sacrificed for love between humans, which one of the two we have to choose?'

"To this question, I replied, 'In that case, you have to choose loyalty to God, because God is the beginning and the end of everything. Binggisa, there is only single truth—God created all things. So, in the beginning before God created anything, things were not only non-existent, but improbable to be existent, in other words, there was no non-existence, let alone existence.

"'Then as God made all things, that were improbable to exist, exist, and made all things, that were not even nothingness, into something, so only then all things came into existence and became something. Therefore, humans are only a piece of what came into exist, in other words, a creature like a tiny speck of dust.

"'Then what does it mean that human beings are a piece of all things—in other words a creature like a tiny speck of dust? It means, going back to the beginning, that humans were not only non-existent but were of no probability of existence, in other words, an existence having the nature of 'nothingness of the nothingness.'

"'Then again, what does it mean that humans have the nature of being nothing of the nothingness? Binggisa, do not be surprised. All actions that humans dare to commit to advance themselves, before God who has the nature of 'existence of the existence,' are useless, in other words, no more than an effort exercised by a shadow or a phantom. Such kinds of human actions are of no value. Taking a step back, if they were of some value, they only have meaning at the lower level of the relations between humans, but are meaningless at the higher level of the relations between humans and God.

"'Therefore, you must understand. The two commandments, loyalty to God and love between humans, are different in their levels. In other words, the former is a strong and firm commandment that will not change at all from the beginning to the eternity, while the latter is a weak and small commandment attached to the great former commandment like bits of straw.

"'Binggisa, there is no substance in the dream, that is, it is nothingness. Accordingly, one who wakes up from a dream will soon forget everything that appeared in the dream. Likewise, viewing from the standpoint of the God Huruva, who is the only substance, only one that exists, self-existent, and manifests himself in all things, human beings are phantoms that appear in the dream of God. Thus, humans exist only by the will of God, so if God does not evoke will, they are similar to a shadow that will be forgotten like one awaken from a dream forgets the dream.

"'Therefore, Binggisa, when the loyalty to the God and love between humans clash, you have to choose the former without hesitation.'"

Having told this, Chuchu stopped talking and looked back at Elder Sariputta, and it was because he thought he was talking too much in front of the master.

Elder Sariputta guessed his mind and said, laughing, "My special disciple, do not worry about anything and continue your speech, as it will be valuable to the two heavenly beings."

"Thank you, master."

Having expressed thanks, Heavenly Being Chuchu continued his talk to Raja.

"Friend, before I tell you on the evil deeds in my previous life that pushed me into hell, I will tell you on the history of the Huruva Order."

CHAPTER 18
Chuchu and Binggisa

(THE STORY OF HEAVENLY BEING CHUCHU)

The Huruva Order, with more than two hundred years of history, began with a prophet named Sahamma, who received revelations from the God Huruva. Sahamma was the leader of 1,300 camel merchants before he received his revelations. At one time, he led the merchants through a vast desert toward a neighboring country. Only fifteen days into the voyage, a plague hit and his camels and people began to die. Sahamma did everything he could to fight off the plague, but the situation did not improve. Thus, within five days he lost nearly 200 camels and 330 people, including his most beloved brother Abrahma.

Utterly devastated, Sahamma sat in his tent all day, totally dumbfounded. Then, with his palms joined together he began to pray. But since he had not yet known God Huruva, he simply prayed blindly to that absolute being, which he believed existed somewhere up in heaven.

Perhaps owing to his prayers, the plague began to subside the next day. Then, those who still remained also joined Sahamma in prayers.

Ardor of prayers ablaze, Sahamma and his fellowship immersed themselves in prayers without eating or sleeping. After some time, many rushed out of the tent when they thought even that was not enough. They looked up to heaven and cried out, "Come on, let's carry out a test! Let's see which is hotter, our prayers or the sun blaze!"

They went up to a desert hill despite scorching midday sun, ardently praying their hearts out, crying and writhing in desperation. But it was impossible to win over the sweltering sun just with prayers alone. One after another, people began to drop down from exhaustion, and Sahamma had to order people into the tent. However, he himself remained at prayers at the top of the hill.

One day, two days, and three days had passed. The exact duration of the dates differs according to historical records, but it was certain that at least fifteen days had passed. On the last day in the middle of the night, Sahamma faced God under starlight.

According to what Sahamma stated on a later date, God descended toward him "under the starlight" in a most majestic form. Once God descended gloriously, he declared to Sahamma, "I am self-existent, the creator of all things, I am the God Huruva!"

Sahamma threw himself down before God with overwhelming fear, but in extremely uplifted spiritual excitement. God Huruva comforted Sahamma gently and said, "My beloved, I have chosen you, and you will be best among all creations."

Sahamma listened to God while trembling. God Huruva said again, "From now on, go out to the world and exalt me amongst them all. Proclaim widely of who I am."

"God, but I know little while lacking courage and wisdom. How could I take up such a heavy responsibility?"

"You need not worry, nothing is impossible for Huruva."

As soon as Huruva finished his sentence, Sahamma fell to the ground cringing in spasm, and he lost his consciousness on the very spot. After a while, when his consciousness was restored, he knew he had been reborn completely anew.

He rose boldly and said, "God, I dare to bear your holy work with my life!"

God Huruva then ordered, "Sahamma, firstly you must get out to the world and proclaim that Huruva is self-existent, and that he is the creator of all things."

"I will follow your commandment with my life."

"Secondly, get out to the world and teach people to love their neighbors far and wide."

"I will follow your commandment with my life."

Having received these two commandments from the God Huruva, Sahamma returned to the tent. The people in the tent were surprised to see how Sahamma had changed. Sahamma's face shone with nobility as never seen before, and his eyes sparkled with courage, signs of intelligence flowing with dignified spiritual presence, displaying an aura one dares not approach."

(Epilogue of Chuchu)

"A new order that worships God Huruva was founded by the prophet Sahamma. The Huruva Order expanded their congregation steadily and around one hundred years later, their number reached close to fifty thousand.

"In addition, study of its doctrine was actively carried out in the meantime. The scholars summarized multitudinous doctrines, amounting to over seventy volumes, into two commandments: 'loyalty to god' and 'brotherly love for our neighbors.'

"However, 150 years after the Huruva Order had been established, a new group of followers came forth from within, raising objections for the doctrine to be re-examined. The big question was whether these two commandments, loyalty to God and love for our neighbors were equally important in their classification.

"Concerning this issue, the Gariya School, more orthodox Huruvas, took a position that these two commandments should be regarded differently, while the new group, Suriya School, raised an objection to that view. Suriyas argued that love for neighbors is equally important, but it became a second commandment simply due to sequential order.

"These two schools had fierce debates. As time went on, the debate turned into controversy, controversy turned into blame, blame turned into grudge, and grudge turned into hatred. At the end, the two schools were engaged in a battle. Consequently, thirty-two people were killed and over eight hundred injured after a disastrous battle of swords, with the victory ultimately given to Gariya School.

"Ten years had passed, then I was born. I encountered the Huruva Order at a young age. But I waited until adulthood and became a junior priest. I was recognized to be a possessor of pure heart with relatively high intelligence and good ability to preach. And I later became the Archbishop of the Huruva Order at age fifty, which made me the head of all bishops and the highest agent of God Huruva who carried out the God's will on earth.

"Some time had passed and when I turned sixty, I had no choice but to seriously consider finding a successor. According to the rule of the Order, the successor must be chosen from one of the bishops. However, there were many bishops who did not fully accept the orthodox doctrine of Gariya School, and for this reason I was worried if my successor could faithfully carry on the doctrine of Gariya.

"I, a most ardent devotee of Gariya School, wished to select a successor who would fully engross himself in Gariya doctrine. But that alone was not enough.

"Generally, those who strictly abide in Gariya doctrine tend to be rigid in their endowment. They may be respected highly within the school for their faithful devotion to the denomination. However, their rigid temperament appeared to people outside of congregation much too incompliant and austere, showing little human emotion.

"For this reason, I wished for a successor with warm human nature, but at the same time faithful to the doctrine of Gariya School. It would be even better if that person possessed sharp intelligence, emotional sensitivity, and superior language skills. Soon enough, such person appeared before my eyes.

"The person I had my eyes on as my successor was Binggisa. Binggisa came to me after losing one of his eyes due to a negative karmic fate with Elder Bhaddiya, who is present here with us. Binggisa said he had been a devotee of Huruva from a young age. However, after years of his dedicated effort to art rather than religion, he finally came to me to engross himself once again in religious pursuit.

"It could have seemed unsightly if any other person appeared with an eye patch covering one eye. But on Binggisa, it appeared to have a deeper significance. To have only one eye signifies that he will not be distracted chasing after frivolous pursuits, only one remaining eye looking straight toward one God only.

"What's more! Just as I expected, he gave up his worldly values one by one and came before God. Therefore, day by day and month after month, his soul developed closer to God.

"While I taught him theology on one hand and observed his soul on the other, I came to realize that he was not ordinary, but possessed something profound that no ordinary man possessed.

"However, I tried not to let him notice my heart that I thought highly of him. That's because if he discovered, there was a risk of Binggisa becoming too proud and other bishops becoming envious.

"After some time had passed, Binggisa became the most highly regarded out of nearly a hundred of my other disciples. In my heart, I already had him as my next successor. He possessed all the qualities deserving to become my successor.

"However, there was just one disconcerting matter of him not fully accepting the doctrine of Gariya School. He wished to restore the doctrine of Suriya School, which lost its battle with Gariya School, and he considered devotion to God and loving neighbors equally important. Originally, people of Suriya, in comparison to Gariya School, tended to emphasize the profound and noble nature of man and this also seemed true for Binggisa.

"Though Binggisa became a man of religion, he had strong artistic temperament, possessing both theistic worldviews and humanistic spirit that praise the noble and beautiful nature of man. It only seemed natural for him to restore the doctrine of Suriya School.

In other words, the nature of profoundness that I had seen in him may have been religious, but he also possessed artistic and humanistic profoundness.

"But I believed that he would change, that I could lead him from the world of art to the world of religion. He was a true artist deep down to his bones. However, deep inside the bone you will find bone marrows, and deep down in our hearts there is religion. I wanted to lead this poet and musician much deeper, closer to the very heart of religion in order for him to be reborn into a divine being who transcended beyond man; a man of God and an apostle of God."

Speaking up to this point, Chuchu gently closed his eyes. He could not continue with his next sentence for some time. Raja waited silently until Chuchu was ready to speak, while Sirima also held her breath and glanced alternately between Chuchu and Raja.

After a long time, Chuchu began to speak again, but his voice was filled with bitterness, "My dear friend! A blessed man on a correct path of truth! When I look back, I was not walking the path of truth. Nevertheless, I never doubted that I could possibly be walking on the wrong path. So I finally came up with a devious plan. After much doubt and consideration, I decided to use my mother as bait. All this for Binggisa to accept the Gariya doctrine! My sacred heart said, God Huruva will be glorified forever more through Binggisa!

"Of course, I loved and respected my mother. But as I said before, in my view of religion, love, and respect exist simply within the boundaries of God's dream. It was only love and respect founded upon nothingness.

"Therefore, if I deny such dream and nothingness, it would not be a sin. I thought that by employing my mother, that is, by using a dream like phantom, we could glorify the truly awakened one even more; if we treat nothingness as nothingness and if we could correctly reveal God as the true existence, then that will be the greatest, rightful, and holy work of God.

"One day, I made a firm decision and called Binggisa into the archbishop's office.

"When Binggisa arrived, I said to the assistant bishop, 'Brother, go and stand outside the office and tell anyone who wishes to see me that I am not available today.'

"'Yes, I will do so, Your Grace,' answered the assistant bishop as he stepped out of the office and only Chuchu and Binggisa remained.

"I walked toward the wall where a number of sacred items were displayed and gently pushed the wall to the side. Then the wall slid open and another room appeared beyond the wall. I entered the room while Binggisa followed, and I slid the door shut behind him once Binggisa was inside.

"The secret room the we entered was filled with brilliant, mysterious energy. Binggisa quickly discovered the secret to that energy. He realized with his keen sense of insight that this special aura came from numerous mirrors placed in the room that manipulate the light entering from the outside, reflecting double or triple times, while the mirrors themselves rendered invisible.

"This did not mean Binggisa felt repulsed toward such artificial manipulation. On the contrary, his extraordinary artistic sensibility worked in favor and allowed him to accept this aura in awe, since it aligned beautifully with his inner heart. Binggisa looked at the wall in front, trying to calm his elation like he was standing in front of the entrance to heaven.

"The front wall Binggisa was facing consisted of a niche with a rectangular lower and semicircular upper section. Inside the niche, there was a five-pointed star, signifying God Huruva—among the five points, the central point on the top was exceptionally high up, and the star glowed brilliantly because it was studded throughout with numerous rubies and red jades.

"First, I placed my palms together toward the star and Binggisa followed.

"'Sit here,' I instructed, after he sat himself down first on a large chair. Binggisa sat down and looked at the agent of God Huruva.

"With most loving and gentle eyes filled with grace, I looked at my disciple, whom I loved very much. Some time passed while bright light of emotion deepened in Binggisa's only remaining eye, which already sparkled with great inspiration.

"Then I added in a lively tone, 'Glory to God Huruva!'

"'Glory to God Huruva!' said Binggisa.

"'And let you be filled with blessings under protection of God!' I said.

"'And also with you, Your Grace!' said Binggisa.

"Having exchanged these greetings of Huruva devotees, I continued, 'You, my beloved disciple, you are like the tongue in my mouth, and marrows in my bone, you are the spiritual son of mine.'

"'I feel honored beyond words that you refer to me as your son,' said Binggisa.

"'I called you here because I wish to lead you deeper into the heart of God. Binggisa, you told me for quite a long time, 'It is difficult for me to accept the doctrine of Gariya that states loyalty toward God differs in class from that of loving our neighbors. Yet, Your Grace, I am eager to accept the doctrine. On the one hand, I have doubts but on the other hand I feel desperate to want to accept it. Thus I harbor double standards regarding Gariya doctrine.'

"'That is right,' said Binggisa.

"'You also mentioned, As you already know, I am a great sinner. When I look back, I feel ashamed! I am a sinner that betrayed King Bhaddiya who trusted me infinitely, leading him to suffer as if he had fallen to hell.

"'Not only that, I committed a grave sin toward Ayutha, the most stunning, graceful, and noble woman. My heart tightens with sadness just thinking about her. I tempted this modest woman subtly and then I beat her once she was kicked out of the palace.

"'Now, I re-entered the Huruva Order to rid myself of my sins. Looking back, I've entered the Huruva faith at a young age, but I was never religiously devoted as I am now. Then, through the incidence that occurred with King Bhaddiya and Ayutha, I've decided to devote myself fully to Huruva Order.

"'Now, my soul has gained considerable degree of stability all thanks to your great knowledge and excellent character. But that is not enough. I am still unable to grasp fully the Gariya doctrine which states loyalty of God is the highest and only worthy virtue. This is the reason why my soul has not been healed completely.

"'Master, I see the possibility of all my sins being forgiven through Gariya doctrine. I see from its belief, that God alone is the highest of all commandments, the higher value to be able to move beyond the problem between humans—the problem with Bhaddiya and Ayutha. Isn't this what you said?' I asked.

"'Yes. That's what I said.'

"'If so, Binggisa, what would you say if someone came and asked you, "Why wouldn't you go and ask for forgiveness from King Bhaddiya and Ayutha?"'

"'In that case, master, I'd answer, "That may appear to be the obvious choice at first glance, but after another contemplation, I wouldn't go to them"'

"'What conclusion have you come up with after another contemplation?'

"'Your Grace, man cannot forgive the sins of another man. Of course, man can forgive another on a superficial level. But at a much deeper level, man cannot forgive the sins of another because the one who forgives surely also committed sins. Thus the only one who can forgive the sins of men is one without any sins, which is only God.

"'Master, I can of course go and ask for forgiveness from those two people just like the rest. And I most definitely will later. However, it is not yet time since they are imperfect and also have committed sins to others, like I have done to them.

"'That is why I would first like to receive complete forgiveness from God Huruva. Thus, I will purify my corrupted soul as clear as a snow-capped mountain of Hindu Kush. Then I can go and seek their forgiveness with pure heart.

"'Oh, they will see, feel, and realize my purity because they are just amazing creatures beyond ordinary. Then, they will forgive me and perhaps even accept my faith.

"'Thus, in the same faith, they will become my brother and sister. Moreover, they will, also forgive my sins at a human level, the sins already forgiven by God Huruva

"'Therefore, the three of us will hold the key to the kingdom of heaven. Your Grace! That's the reason why I do not go to them now, and it is my reason for rejoining the Huruva Order.'

"Having heard Binggisa speak, I said to him, 'This makes it clear what you expect from our truth, Binggisa. I will present you to the path of pure white, the path of pristine snow, for your own sake.'

"'If master could show me the path, I will walk that path with all my strength and determination, ready to face death if I have to.' said Binggisa.

"'Then, you must do as I tell you from this point on. That's the way you will be able to accept the doctrine of Gariya. Through it all, your soul will be purified at the highest level. Then you will see, through purified spiritual eyes, formless God as he is, and arrive in heaven that you have not arrived, just the way you are.'

"When I finished, Binggisa's only remaining eye sparkled like the ruby he saw on the five-pointed star a little while ago.

"Binggisa responded, 'Noble agent of God! My deepest desire is to be able to see the formless God as he truly is, and to enter the kingdom of heaven just the way I am!'

"When Binggisa spoke with pleading eye, I, who had been leading countless people to my faith, discarded the gentle and comforting tone of speech I had employed so far, and spoke with a strong authoritative tone: 'Binggisa, are you ready to accept all orders I give without hesitation?'

"'Any order you give, my teacher, I will follow without any hesitation.'

"'Then, go to the temple and confess your decision and return to me.'

"'I will do as you say.'

"Binggisa went to the Huruva temple and vowed to follow whatever order I gave faithfully.

"'From now on, you must go and wait on my mother closely.'

"'Yes, I will follow your order.'"

CHAPTER 19
Sacred Robes Become Armor

Thus, Binggisa began to attend to Chuchu's mother, Mahama, who had performed countless virtuous deeds all her life for the Order, which made her highly respected by the followers of the Order.

Originally called by the name Sumana, Mahama lost her husband when she was young and raised her only son Chuchu by herself. A woman of beautiful appearance, she was continuously courted by all sorts of men almost every day, despite being a widow who raised a son alone.

However, she responded to her suitors with a soft smile and only mentioned the name of her deceased husband or of her son Chuchu, who was growing well as a smart and brave boy. She never refused to do whatever chores available and educated Chuchu well, and such chastity and polite demeanor were renowned in the Order.

While Chuchu was gradually building his reputation in the Order, Sumana never hesitated to do further services and sacrifices. Now in her seventies, she was easily seen offering a helping hand at the cafeteria of the Order or taking care of sick people.

There was an elegant refinement and noble dignity in her, which might only be exuded by those who have cultivated high virtues.

Thus, many people felt happy just seeing her, and even greater number of people entered the Huruva Order arousing faith upon seeing her outstanding moral quality.

Therefore, the episcopal convention, which was the highest decision-making body of the Order, decided to give her an honorific title of Mahama, meaning *great mother*. She was the first one in the history of the Order who has received such an honorific title.

Five years have passed since then. In the meantime, some changes occurred in the Huruva Order: the religious power of the Order grew bigger, several of the bishops began to believe in the doctrines of the Suriya School, and Mahama became too old and feeble to move her body with ease.

So the episcopal convention decided to provide her with an attendant. However, as Mahama refused the good will of the episcopal convention, the issue of giving her an attendant languished slowly.

But several months later, Mahama's health deteriorated rapidly. So the episcopal convention again decided to give her an attendant, and at that time it occurred to Chuchu that Binggisa was the right person to wait upon Mahama.

Chuchu recommended Binggisa as Mahama's attendant and after obtaining an approval thereupon, informed his mother of the decision. Then, Mahama, who became blind was under great mobility impairment, finally gave in and allowed Binggisa to wait upon her.

From then on, Binggisa stayed by Mahama all day and nursed her with all his heart. Not long thereafter, Mahama's condition began to improve little by little. After a month of Binggisa's devoted care, she was able to walk in the room by herself, and after three months, she reappeared at the cafeteria.

However, as she was blind, she could not help with chores. Nevertheless, the simple fact that she was at the cafeteria made the believers think that it was nothing less than her actually working there.

Around that time, Chuchu called Binggisa and instructed, "From now on, you massage the body of my mother with the utmost sincerity."

"Yes, Your Reverence, I will do that."

From then on, Binggisa massaged Mahama's body four times a day. At first, Mahama felt it awkward for a man to touch her body, but finally accepted the action of a young man begrudgingly.

A few days elapsed. Chuchu summoned Binggisa and asked, "Did you do as I told you?"

"Yes, Your Grace."

"So what did my mother say about that?"

"She said that she was always thankful for that."

"Then from now on, you wash the hands and feet of my mother every day."

"Yes, Your Grace, I will do so."

After another several days had passed, Chuchu summoned Binggisa and asked, "Did you do as I told you?"

"Yes, Your Grace."

"So what did my mother say about that?"

"She said that she was always very grateful for that."

"Then from now on, while you wash the hands and feet of my mother, you tell her, 'How lovely your hands and feet are!'"

"Yes, Your Grace, I will do that."

Again, several days passed. Chuchu summoned Binggisa and asked, "Did you do as I told you?"

"Yes, Your Grace."

"So what did my mother say about that?"

"When I said so, Mahama exclaimed, 'What words of flattery you are speaking!'"

"Then from now on, if my mother says so, you tell her, 'No. I am serious. Swear to God, your skin is as fine as that of a maiden. Not only that! You still maintain the beauty that you had when you were young. Your beauty is enough to enthrall all men in the world. As I stay beside you, I realize every day that how attractive and lovely you are.'"

"Yes, Your Grace, I will do that."

Again, several days passed. Chuchu summoned Binggisa and asked, "Did you do as I told you?"

"Yes, Your Grace."

"So how did my mother react to that?"

"When I said so, Mahama showed utmost modesty of decline. Then, yesterday she told me, 'It could not be entirely true that I am still pretty enough to enthrall all men in the world. But I want to ask you, putting all men in the world aside, whether I am attractive enough to enthrall a man?'"

"From now on, if my mother so asks, you will tell her, 'That's true. You are attractive enough to enthrall a man.'"

"Yes, Your Grace, I will do that."

Again several days passed. Chuchu summoned Binggisa and asked, "Did you do as I told you?"

"Yes, Your Grace."

"So how did my mother react to that?"

"As soon as I said so, Mahama, after some hesitation, said, 'Young man, based on my trust in you who have devoted yourself to take care of me, may I ask you a question?' So, I replied, 'Mahama, please ask me whatever you wish.' Mahama stayed silent for some time with a look of hesitation and then asked, 'Do you think that it is possible for me, at this age, to love a man, or for a man to love me? This is a question that I ask you as a woman.'"

"From now on, if my mother asks so, you will tell her, 'Of course it is possible. As a matter of fact, I feel deeply attracted to you as a man.'"

"Yes, Your Grace, I will do that."

Again several days had passed. Chuchu summoned Binggisa and asked, "Did you do as I told you?"

"Yes, Your Grace."

"So how did my mother react to that?"

"Upon my remarks, she was surprised and asked, 'Is it true? Do you really like me as a woman?'"

"From now on, if my mother asks so, you will answer, 'I like Mahama as a woman. To tell the truth, I love you very much.'"

"Yes, Your Grace, I will do that."

Again several days had passed. Chuchu summoned Binggisa and asked, "Did you do as I told you?"

"Yes, Your Grace."

"So how did my mother react to that?"

"Upon my remarks, Mahama was greatly astonished and looked deeply touched."

"Everything is ripening well as I planned. From now on, you will do anything you can to express your affection to my mother."

"Yes, Your Grace, I will do that."

Again several days had passed. Chuchu summoned Binggisa and asked, "Did you do as I told you?"

"Yes, Your Grace."

"So how did my mother react to that?"

"Mahama confirmed my love again and again. Then finally she trusted and accepted my love. And at last, Mahama fell in love with me. Your Grace, now the love of Mahama toward me is very strong. Mahama feels very happy just to look at me with a reddish face like a maid fallen in love for the first time," said Binggisa.

Smiling, Chuchu responded, "Then from now on, you will accept 'wholly' the love of my mother, just as she wants it. I will not elaborate on the meaning of 'wholly,' but you should know, as a man, what you will have to do from now."

At such words of Chuchu, Binggisa, who had just followed the instructions of Chuchu obediently till then, showed a look of hesitation. Having noticed a look of hesitation on Binggisa's face, Archbishop Chuchu told Binggisa in a stern voice, "Binggisa, you shall recall the oath you made before God."

"However, master, this time I cannot bear to follow your instruction. It is because to follow your instruction means that I must embrace her in my arms or kiss her."

"What does it matter?"

"Master!" responded Binggisa.

"Binggisa you shall not be worried. You must not hesitate, if my mother so wishes, even to have sexual relations with her."

Binggisa was so astonished that he just looked at the master's face with his eyes wide open. However, unlike Binggisa who was surprised, no sign of wavering appeared on Chuchu's face.

Chuchu's face, which was like a mass of iron of unfathomable weight and a cliff of unfathomable depth, was solemnly filled with graveness and determination. Binggisa stood absentmindedly for some time, looking at the face of the master. And the next moment, he heard a strong voice resonating from the heart of his soul, "Execute, execute, and execute! You shall execute without hesitation and without fear. Divinity has no compunction, and the spirit has no fear."

Before he knew it, Binggisa looked straight on to the master and said, "Master, I will do that!"

Again several days had passed. Chuchu, the Archbishop of the Huruva Order and the head of the Gariya School, summoned Binggisa and asked, "Did you do as I told you?"

"Yes, Your Grace."

"What has happened between my mother and you in the meantime?"

"Master, as Mahama wanted, I slid into her bed and lied just next to her."

"Then?"

"Mahama caressed my face and neck. Then she caressed my hands, arms, shoulders, toes, feet, calves, thighs, and hips one by one. And then, she caressed my chest, and the passion she showed me during the time was so enormous that I could not believe it was from an old woman."

"Then?"

"Having caressed all my body, Mahama, panting from extreme excitement, snuggled into my chest and whispered, 'My man, please have me! To your heart's content, thoroughly, to the deepest abyss where the soul blacks out!' So I caressed her all over her body. Receiving my caress, she first groaned, and next she screamed, and then she burst into tears, and then she passed out. So I laid her down comfortably and waited beside her until she woke up."

"Did you merge with her in sexual union or not?"

"As she fainted, I could not merge with her in sexual union."

"I see. From now on, you show a hesitant attitude and do not respond at all to her expression of affection."

"Master, I will do that!"

Again several days had passed. Chuchu summoned Binggisa and asked, "Did you do as I told you?"

"Yes, Your Grace."

"When you showed a hesitant attitude and refused her love, what kind of reaction did she make?"

"Mahama held my hands and asked, 'Why have you changed so? Oh, my dear, please tell me.' However I behaved as if there was something in my mind that held me back, and did not give any answer."

"Then next time, if my mother says so, you will tell her, 'Oh my dear woman, my mind tells me to go as close to you as possible. However, my other mind whispers that to go close to you is not right. The reason is that, my dear woman who gives me happiness, while you are my lover, you are the mother of my master at the same time.' You should have no love affairs with her at all."

"Master, I will do that!"

Again several days had passed. Chuchu summoned Binggisa and asked, "Did you do as I told you?"

"Yes, Your Grace."

"How did she react upon hearing what you've said?"

"As I said what you had told me to do, Mahama closed her eyes tight and did not say a word. Since then she has been passing time mulling over something."

"I understand. You will continue to do what you have been doing."

"Master, I will do that."

Again several days had passed. Binggisa, before Chuchu called him, visited Chuchu and confessed, "Master, I am awfully sorry that, I disobeyed your instruction today."

"What do you mean? Tell me honestly."

"This morning Mahama said to me, 'My dear, there is one thing

I want to ask you.' So I replied, 'My dear, you ask me whatever you want to ask.' Then Mahama, after a pause, asked, 'If my son were not your master, could you still love me as before?' So I replied, 'However, such assumption is meaningless, because the archbishop is my master at present and will be my master forever.' After a long pause, Mahama asked again, 'Then, my dear, what would happen if . . . if . . . if . . . if my son wasn't there, if he did not exist in the world? What if he went beside the God, where his existence, which was nothing originally, became something that will exist forever, therefore if his death became something that is not death, if death became blessing? Then won't it be possible that our love, which is no other than nothingness of nothingness, becomes something of nothingness, if not something of somethingness?'

"I was surprised but as if nothing had happened, I held her hands and stroked them with lots of love. Then she threw herself into my arms, and for unknown reasons, it occurred to me at that moment that I should do something to fulfill her ardent desire.

"In that way, a love for Mahama swelled in me and I started to caress Mahama with true affection, not an assumed one. Then Mahama accepted my caress like a pure-hearted girl, and in that acceptance there was no air of ugliness of an old woman.

"Then, moments later, I came back to myself and said determinedly, while shaking my head. 'Oh Mahama, I was out of my mind for some time. Today will be the last day for this kind of love affair! It should be the last!'"

Having heard Binggisa's confession, Chuchu was lost in thought for some moments.

"Though your action deviated from the scope of my instruction, God's wisdom transforms even faults into a beginning of good results. Binggisa, you will meet my mother and tell her, 'If there were no master, if he would proceed to God and became something of somethingness, our love would go beyond something of nothingness, and become something of somethingness in another dimension.'"

"Yes, Your Grace, I will do that."

Again several days had passed. Chuchu called Binggisa and asked, "Did you do as I told you?"

"Yes, Your Grace."

"Having heard your remarks, how did my mother react?"

Binggisa replied, "I told Mahama as I had been told by you, master. I stopped any and every act of affection and treated her crudely. Then she began to ponder over something. This morning, I said to Mahama, 'If there weren't the master, if he proceeded to God and became something of somethingness, our love might, beyond something of nothingness, become something of somethingness in another dimension.'

"Since then Mahama began to pore upon something. And this morning Mahama said to me, 'My dear, who I love to death, you shall prepare for me and for our love a spool of thread. And when it reaches deep in the night, you will tie one end of the thread to my hand and the other end to the door knob of the room where my son sleeps.'

"Master, I think I know for what purpose she asked me to do such a thing. It is clear that Mahama must have set up a horrible scheme to hurt you master."

Chuchu nodded his head and said, "I foresaw from long time ago that my mother would scheme this kind of thing. My disciple, you do not need to be worried, just do as she instructed and watch secretly from her side how she behaves."

"Then what do you intend to do?

"I will lie down on the bed in my room."

"But . . ." started Binggisa.

"You don't have to worry about me and just do as I told you."

"Yes, master."

Binggisa, as Mahama asked, prepared a spool of thread and tied one end to the wrist of Mahama and the other to the door knob of the room where Chuchu sleeps.

Then, as Chuchu had instructed, Binggisa stayed stealthily in Mahama's room and watched how she behaved. However, Mahama, who was blind, did not notice that Binggisa, aided by the moonlight coming through the window, was watching her.

After some time, Mahama, who had been lying motionless, raised herself. Guided by the thread tied to her wrist, she carefully opened the door and stepped out to the corridor.

The steps of an eighty-year-old woman reached the front of her son's room. Taking care not to make any noise, she opened the door and stepped inside the room.

Once inside, Mahama felt the floor with her hands to find the bed where her son was sleeping. She confirmed the face of her son with a hand and took out a durable rope from her breast. Having confirmed once again by stroking the face of her son, she swiftly wound up the rope around his neck and started to strangle with all her strength.

She closed her lips tight and tightened her grip. The face of an eighty-year-old woman turned bright red, and soon beads of sweat began to roll down from her forehead.

Moments later, she felt something was wrong and stopped strangling. Unlike her expectation, her son did not put up a fight nor gave a groan. It was because Chuchu had swiftly slipped from the bed and laid a doll made of cloth in his place.

Embarrassed, Mahama groped over the object that she was strangling. The next moment, noticing that it was not a human that she was strangling, she was immensely shocked and collapsed down onto the floor.

Chuchu came near to Mahama, held her hands softly, and said, "Mother, what brought you here at this late hour?"

To Mahama, these words were nothing other than the sinister voice of an angel of death from hell. The eighty-year-old woman lost her senses and collapsed. Chuchu held the "object" which had been intended to prove the glory of God in his arms and laid it on the bed. He offered a short prayer to Huruva God thanking that everything has been well accomplished.

Binggisa looked at Chuchu vacantly with surprised eyes. His heart was pounding. But the next moment, a strange compassion flared up in his heart like a flame. To his ears, Chuchu's passionate words filled with holiness were heard like waters falling in cascade.

"Oh, Binggisa, you should have learned by now! That self-discipline and virtuous conduct of humankind cannot bring it to the state of completeness! That man cannot redeem himself on his own! And that as a result what we humans have to do is to prostrate before God!

"Binggisa, what humans have to do is only one thing; to confess, 'My Lord, what am I? Am I not a speck of dust? Am I not a grain of sand? How heavy a virtuous conduct of a dust could be, and how big a virtuous conduct of a grain of sand could be?'

"Oh, my disciple! For salvation of humanity, the truth beyond the human dimension, the truth beyond the dimension of rationality, namely a transrational truth, is necessary. However, the transrational truth will be seen, to the eyes of humans or rationalists, as irrational. That is right. The truth that the Gariya School is maintaining is an irrational truth.

"If God created everything, he should have created disease as well as health. If God created everything, he should have created pain as well as joy. If God created everything, he should have created death as well as life. If God created everything, he should have created evil as well as good.

"But how could God—who is complete, always good, and loves his creatures dearly—have created disease, pain, death, or evil? The fact that God created this world does not make sense.

"That's right. The doctrines of the Gariya School do not make logical sense. In other words, they are irrational. Because of this, the Suriya School, which criticizes the Gariya School, was founded. The Suriya School wanted to supplement the shortcomings of the Gariya doctrines with disciplined personality and virtuous deeds performed between human beings.

"But as you have witnessed, human beings are incomplete creatures. This means that human beings cannot save themselves by actions such as self-discipline or love for neighbors. Therefore, our

Gariya School declares. That to humanity something surpassing rationality is required to save them!

"In other words, unless we go beyond rationality, or establish God who is transrational, there will be no salvation for humanity. Therefore, Binggisa, my dear friend, the truth of the Gariya School is a truth that is quite rational because it is irrational, and rather possible because it is impossible!

"Oh, according to our truth, those who are saved by God are not those who cultivate themselves earnestly. And according to our truth, those who are saved by God are not those who love their neighbors very much. Those who cultivate themselves in earnest and those who love their neighbors very much may be abandoned by God, and those who are less disciplined but lower themselves and prostrate, and those who love less but deeply acknowledge their pitiable condition are to be saved, our truth is a truth of such nature.

"Binggisa, my flesh, blood, bone, marrow, brain, and heart! Now I conclude. The commandment that determines salvation is loyalty to God only! The virtues that have been built through cultivation, and the values accomplished through love for neighbors have nothing to do with salvation!"

This sermon of Chuchu, like a chorus of one hundred thousand angels, resonated wondrously to every corner of Binggisa's soul. Binggisa, shuddering uncontrollably, knelt down before Chuchu and shut his mouth tightly. At last, with his one eye widened as if about to pop out, he confessed his solid faith that has been established anew.

"Master, I do believe! That no two words are necessary for the truth! Loyalty to God is the single essence of the truth!

I believe in the truth!

I believe in the truth!

I believe in the truth!"

CHAPTER 20
The Path of God,
the Path of Humans

hen Chuchu spoke up to this point, Bhikkhu Malukha asked Elder Sariputta, "Elder, a few questions arose for me while hearing the story of Chuchu. Would it be okay for me to ask?"

"Yes, go ahead."

"How should we understand God Huruva Chuchu speaks about?"

Elder Sariputta replied, "That was the first question Chuchu came to ask me two lifetimes ago. Brother, when Binggisa committed a great sin as a result of immersing himself obsessively in Chuchu's teachings, Chuchu ended up leaving the denomination in shock and became a wanderer. However, in the end, Chuchu came to ask me that same question. After listening to my teachings on the subject, he was able to establish a right view.

"At that time, I pointed out to Chuchu that the idea he imparted to Binggisa, if not careful, could go as far as to make human the means to be utilized by God. The idea that human beings are creation of

God can lead to an understanding that humans are simply a possession of God. I pointed out that this could mean humans are seen as something to be utilized or exploited, as a means to an end called God.

"In addition, I pointed out many other wrongful views. After hearing my teachings, he realized that everything is caused by men and that human mind comes before God. He understood that for some people, God, just like all the rest, can't be established unless their human mind fully opens up.

"He thus ended up letting go of the idea that God is the principal of all things and accepted instead that mind is the principal of all things. In essence, evil he had committed was not the evil act of God, but of his own wicked doing, thus he had no choice but to repent his own sinful deeds from the depth of his heart.

"After a lengthy repentance, he took refuge in Buddhadhamma, and began to meditate on the subject I had given him. As a result, he finally attained first stage of meditative absorption. When he was heading toward Yaku village to thank and show his respect to the Buddha, he met Raja, a boy now reborn in the Tavatimsa Heaven, and fell from the cliff which ended his life as a human."

When Sariputta finished, Chuchu looked at Raja gratefully and Raja bowed his head in response.

Malukha made a request to Elder Sariputta, "Elder, please show me the difference between the path of God, as believed in the Huruva Order, and that of Buddhadhamma."

Sariputta said to Bhikkhu Malukha, "Brother, for your own understanding, I will now call the religion, which views the world maneuvered by an absolute personal (divine) God, as Religion of Divinity, and Buddhism, which views the world maneuvered by impersonal law, as Religion of Dhamma

"How does the Religion of Divinity and the Religion of Dhamma compare? Brother, the two religions differ in various aspects. But in relations to the topic being discussed, the Religion of Divinity begins with the belief that God has created and governed the world, while the Religion of Dhamma begins with the belief that mind perceives objects, in other words, the world.

"Therefore, we have to compare God with mind, and between God and mind I would assert that mind precedes God. The reason for my assertion is similar to an analogy of a house being built only when a firm foundation is established. Similarly, one who believes in God cannot build a home called faith without a proper foundation called mind.

"Brother, anyone will admit, irrespective of their faith, that the mind must exist first before having faith in God. This is not a religious doctrine, which may be deemed true for believers, but nothing more than a dogma for nonbelievers.

"This applies to all living beings throughout the world and is applicable even to God, because how could God make the dead, which has no mind, or those whose mind is sleeping or blacked out, recognize God or influence them in any way?

"I would like to enquire to the followers of the Religion of Divinity, whether God does possess a mind or does not. If they answer that God also possesses a mind, I'd say, 'Then God is also subject to the laws of mind and controlled by the laws of mind.' However, the very heart of the laws of mind is 'knowing[41] or awareness' and based on that the will or motivation arises. Therefore, if there is no knowing at the time of the mind first opening up, then how could God know himself to be God, and how could God confer and direct commandments, or exert his will through his creations?

"For such reasons, Buddhism explores the mind before debating whether God exists or not; otherwise we'd have no debates at all. There is much we must familiarize ourselves with before contemplating on the mind. But let me mention here that the mind of sentient beings are tinged or stained in numerous colors.

"Figuratively speaking, the minds of sentient beings are tinted

---

41 What is referred to by "knowing" here is not the type of everyday knowledge that recognizes things but is knowledge as consciousness as stated in Buddhism.

by rainbow colors that view things positively, or in black color that sees things negatively. This means sentient beings coat the external information with different colors before accepting them in. The information they favor is sugar-coated in rainbow colors, whereas disliked information is accepted in gloomy black color.

"As such, the flaws of mistaken views are present from the beginning stage when we first receive information from external phenomena. Then, more errors are created in subsequent steps of understanding, analyzing, and judging such information. Therefore, wrong motivations lead to wrong actions, and it is obvious what kind of wrong results would follow wrongful actions.

"Brother, there are numerous religious and philosophical views in the world, other than Buddhism. However, all religious and philosophical thoughts, except Buddhism, are established merely to maintain their own preconceptions, their own feelings, their own experiences, and their own stances, without recognizing how mind receives the information wrongly and how it processes the received information wrongly once it is received.

"There are now sixty-two philosophical or religious theories being claimed in the world, including creationism, determinism, nihilism, and skepticism. All of these are created without proper consideration on the concept of mind, which means they are theories being argued without proper foundation."

"Oh . . ." stuttered Malukha.

"Brother, there are two types of men: those like a dog and those like a lion. If someone throws a stone, the dog rushes toward the stone, but the lion rushes toward the man who threw the stone. As such, listeners can be divided into people who simply follow the spoken words and those who observe the mind or hearts of one who speaks.

"Let us say, for example, that a man comes and asserts his opinion on you. No matter what his views may be, even if he based his opinion on illegitimate grounds, brother, you must not follow his opinion. Rather, like a lion that straight away attacks the man who threw the rock, you should first observe the source or the mind who speaks."

"Oh . . ."

"In this aspect, I can admit that a man of certain opinion, for example, a man named Sahamma truly existed. However, I highly doubt whether there is a corresponding reality on existence of God Huruva, which Sahamma claims to have seen. Dwelling on the erroneous understanding and emotion, or wrong apprehension, analysis, and judgment of his experiences, that is, a mind tainted in rainbow colors, Sahamma could have aroused or projected a God image.

"This can be supported by the fact that there are many other Sahammas in the world who each claim to have seen God as Sahamma did. As a result, there are a number of self-proclaimed prophets in the world who claim to have seen God. These self-proclaimed prophets or other-designated prophets are comparable to those who attempt to neatly display their belonging on a moving carriage. Brother, if a person wishes to display his belongings properly on a carriage, he must first stop and stabilize the carriage. In spite of such obvious logic, these prophets often leave the moving carriage as it is—in other words without understanding how the mind works, they put care and effort in displaying their philosophical knowledge, which is simply their collection being displayed on a moving carriage. In this regard, I would like to say that the order of priority is inverted in the pursuit of the truth."

"Oh, such foolishness of prioritizing that which could be delayed, and delaying that which must be prioritized!"

"Brother, we need to appreciate the following words of the Buddha, 'The Buddha sees the world arising and disappearing in his body of one-fathom depth that embraces his mind.' I think these words could be restated as: 'The gods seen by self-proclaimed or other-designated prophets are only images projected in their own mind.'

"Brother, sentient beings create images in their mind, and not realizing they are creation of their own mind, they become attached and obsessed. That is similar to a great artist who paints a beautiful woman and falls in love with his own painting with the belief that she is real."

With Elder Sariputta's teachings, Bhikkhu Malukha with an expression of great admiration on his face began to contemplate deeply. However, the look of admiration disappeared soon from his face, replaced by a look of suspicion.

He told Sariputta, "However, despite hearing your teachings, a doubt still remains on the possibility that the God Sahamma saw could truly exists. That is because when Sahamma saw God named Huruva, his character transformed completely and he was reborn as a new person. How can such a powerful transformation of character and appearance occur upon seeing an entity that does not exist?"

"Brother, projection of the mind can be quite remarkable. The mind can project subjective images toward an object, and recognize the images as the object. Some even hear what these projected images speak. In some cases, groups collectively see and hear subjective images in a collective communal possession or fanatic state of excitement. When God enters a person, it is called possession by others, and when a person creates God in his immersed mind, it is called possession by self. However, ultimately all possessions are possessions by self."

"Oh . . ."

"Then, while they are deluded and attached to these images, how does Buddhism handle these images? Brother Malukha, Buddhism at its lowest level uses these images to lead practitioners, but on a higher level, Buddhism helps practitioners to transcend beyond images.

"As you may already know, brother, practices taught by the Buddha are based on threefold training: moral precepts, meditation, and wisdom. In former two stages of training, Buddhism does not point out that images are nothing but images. In this respect, Buddhism at its lower levels is not much different from non-Buddhist teachings. At this stage, thoughts or concepts become the principals and lead all things.

"However, on the third stage—that is, when one reaches the stage of developing wisdom in vipassana meditation, which is a practice found only in Buddhism, conceptual images will reveal its nature, thus practitioners are liberated from objective and subjective worlds, which are objects of concepts."

As you may already know, vipassana is a meditation to be aware of all phenomena occurring in the body and mind. Therefore, vipassana meditators get to see and know that all images arising from the mind—not only God, but even that which is heard and learnt in Dhamma—are nothing but images.

"Therefore, defilements or afflictions have no place for great practitioners, because all defilements stem from not realizing that concepts and feelings are simply concepts and feelings, and becoming attached to them.

"Because of this reason, the Buddha said, 'The disciples of the Buddha who completed learning of Dhamma, must not be attached even to Dhamma. Just as a person who crossed a river must abandon the raft, Dhamma must also be discarded.' Oh . . . brother, no other founders of religious traditions are able to take in this great state of freedom shown by the Buddha, a state that can be compared to space as it is vast without limit, as it allows nothing to hold on to, as it can be never deteriorated, and as it transcends all."

Malukha then asked Elder Sariputta again, "Dear elder, I still have a doubt which hasn't been resolved."

"Brother, do not hesitate to ask."

"Just a while ago, you taught Elder Bhaddiya on the truth of transrationalism and you mentioned Chuchu also taught the truth of transrationalism to Binggisa. Then is the truth of transrationalism you just spoke of same or different from that spoken by Chuchu?"

"It is the same, yet different."

"Elder, please teach me in greater detail how they could be distinguished as same yet different."

In response to this question, Sariputta shared the following details: "First, let's look at what is same of these two truths of transrationalism. Brother, all master religions present transrational doctrines. Why? That's because the essence of religion is to give

211

answers to the ultimate questions or concerns. Ultimate concerns mean all thoughts on the ultimate questions arising from finitude of life, such as how to overcome death, how to deal with afflictions, and how to attain lofty happiness, etc.

"The ultimate concerns cannot be fully understood by secular studies based on rationality. For example, secular studies cannot answer questions on life after death. That is because to deal with death rationally, one must have experienced death. For one to have experienced death means he must not currently exist in this world. Therefore, how could one consider death reasonably?

"This means in inquiries on ultimate concerns one can neither move forward nor move back. Thus, one would ultimately give up rationality, either partly or wholly, because without giving up rationality there is no way of resolving the ultimate concerns.

"That is to say, every religion abandons rationality to answer the ultimate concerns, and presents transrational doctrine. In this regard the truth of transrationalism Chuchu spoke of and the truth of transrationalism I spoke of could be said to be the same."

"Then what is the difference between these two truths of transrationalism?" asked Malukha.

"Religions centered on God present a transrational doctrine from the beginning that 'God reigns over world' and propagate this doctrine till the end. While the latter—Buddhism based on Dhamma—starts with the rational doctrine, such as man are faced with birth, old age, sickness, and death as well as with sorrows, distress, and afflictions, but at the end, Buddhism presents the transrational doctrine that 'nirvana is a state which goes beyond rationality.'

"Brother, the truth of transrationalism can be the truth that transcends rationality for its proponents, but non-proponents see it merely as irrational and obstinate contention. In other words, truth of transrationalism is not confirmed by objective proof but established by relying on subjective faith. It is not the type of truth such as one plus one becomes two, but is what an individual decides to believe, in order to solve the ultimate concerns.

"Therefore, Buddhism, in the process of answering the ultimate concerns to fulfill the duty of religion, insists on transrational truth without any choice, but tries to minimize the scope of assertion as much as possible. In other words, while the Religion of Divinity could be said to assert transrational truth in the scope from one to one hundred, Buddhism is rational from one to ninety-nine in developing doctrines based on proof and knowledge, and only in the last hundredth asserts doctrine of transrational truth.

"This demonstrates that Buddhism bases more on rationality to answer the ultimate concerns and thus reveals less contradiction than Religion of Divinity, which answers ultimate concerns based on irrationality. Therefore, accepting the path of Buddhism is easier than accepting Religion of Divinity.

"Brother, as the heavenly being Chuchu articulated to Binggisa, one saved by Religion of Divinity is not necessarily a good man, nor could one who is abandoned by it be called evil. The deciding factor of salvation shown in Religion of Divinity is not through merit of goodness but through loyalty to God. Therefore on such a path a good man can still be abandoned unless he believes in God, and even an evildoer can still be saved if he believes in God. On the other hand, simply being loyal to Buddhism or Dhamma cannot lead to realization of highest happiness, but only when Buddhists themselves gain merit, achieve high virtue, and purify their minds can the level of his happiness be increased.

"In other words, despite of one's belief in Buddhism, painful consequence is inevitable as long as ignorance and cravings remain in one's mind. But happiness would result when ignorance and cravings are reduced or eliminated, even if one does not believe in Buddhism. Thus, Buddhism presents very rational doctrine.

"Religion of Divinity is truth that flows top (God) to bottom (man)—that is to say, it presents unreasonable revelation as a truth and commands human to believe it, while Buddhism is based on truth that moves bottom (man) to top (awakening)—which means it is a system of truth that persuades humans by presenting comprehensible truth.

"Therefore, Buddhadhamma is a path that allows Buddhists to be the subject to refine oneself, while in Religion of Divinity, the one who decides on salvation is God, which means it is a path where its believer cannot be the subject. In other words, the Religion of Divinity thinks man cannot save oneself, whereas Buddhism believes that man can complete or perfect oneself.

"Then, Religion of Divinity may ask Buddhism, 'How can a man with finite power save and perfect oneself?' In desperation of being unable to answer this question, Religion of Divinity came to be, relying on the power of superior god, but Buddhism, a self-reliant religion, argues that humans can perfect themselves through their own strength, despite their limited powers.

"Then how do Buddhists perfect themselves? Through skillful use of wisdom they perfect themselves. Brother, you must understand that wisdom is most powerful, beneficial, brilliant, and exalted strength of all.

"Brother, just like a skillful animal trainer who employs wisdom in defeating a powerful elephant with use of a tiny single needle, which otherwise is undefeatable by those who used all kinds of powerful weapons, Buddhists who utilize wisdom skillfully can resolve the challenge of the ultimate question—unresolved even by the wisest in the world.

"For example, let's say the first weakness of the elephant is on the head, the second weakness on the forehead, the third on the center of the forehead, and the fourth a tiny vital point the size of a needle on the center of the forehead. Then, one who wishes to knock down the elephant should first narrow down the area of attack from the entire body to the head, and then narrow down further to forehead, and then narrow it down further onto the vital point.

"In the same way, Buddhists must deal with the ultimate concerns, which at a first glance seems impossible to resolve by human power because of its extensiveness. On the first stage, one must return to self by discarding the external objects and external humans such as past and future, or here and there; on the second stage, one observes and becomes aware of one's own body; on the third stage, one realizes that the concept that arises is simply a concept; on the fourth stage, one understands that when mind and object exist, the object is naturally recognized by the mind; and on the fifth stage, one becomes aware of the mind that is aware of the object. By narrowing down the object of interest in this way, even a human of finite power can reach the level where he can finally be able to answer the ultimate question.

"During the progress of practice in this way, especially when one nearly reaches the final stage, Buddhists no longer require faith. The disciples of the Buddha only know Dhamma, that is, they see and know natural process of the mind seeing and knowing objects; see and know the mind that sees and knows; again only see and know the mind that sees and knows the mind that sees and knows. When such knowing of knowing reaches an extreme level, like water boils to become vapor, quantitative changes will cause qualitative changes, which we call *nirvana*.

"Therefore, nirvana, practiced and attained through power of mind that sees and knows, at the final stage of Buddhadhamma, is a truth that, to those who have not reached it, must be conjectured. But for sages who have reached this state, it is a self-evident and self-authenticating truth that they know because they saw. As such, the truth of transrationalism in Buddhism is the truth that is rational and transrational at the same time."

When Elder Sariputta taught as such, Malukha became deeply impressed. "Dear elder, I know now! That is right. What is similar doesn't mean it is the same. Although it may seem to be similar truth of transrationalism at a first glance, through your teachings I understood in what sense our Buddhadhamma is superior, and how clearly it presents the truth, and I clearly see why the Buddha said that Buddhadhamma is the truth that can say, 'the door is always wide open, so all you critics and detractors, come and see!'"

CHAPTER 21
Sage Bhaddiya, Heavenly Woman Ayutha

The next day, Sariputta embarked on a journey with three other monks, Chunda, Bhaddiya, and Malukha, toward the port city of Subbaraka. (Raja, Sirima, and Chuchu concealed themselves and followed them.) They traveled one yojana per day, and after four months could reach the Karuna cave near Uriya village.

The reason why Sariputta came to the Karuna cave was to guide the seventeen monks practicing in the cave, including Amarani and Bhikkhu Malukha who had accompanied him, to enlightenment.

Next day, Bhikkhu Amarani, who had been sufficiently prepared, attained the level of the stream-enterer, the first of the four levels of enlightenment. And the following day, Amarani attained the level of the once-returner, the second of the four levels of enlightenment, and Malukha and four other monks attained the level of the stream-enterer. The following day, Amarani attained the level of the non-returner, the third of the four levels of enlightenment, Malukha and four other monks attained the level of the once-returner, and the remaining twelve monks attained the level of the stream-enterer.

So it thus happened that twenty-one noble monks stayed together in the cave.

In the evening, it began to drizzle as if to celebrate the birth of a small noble community. However, it did not make any change in the daily routine of the monks. They waited until the rain stopped, went to the village to beg for food, returned to the cave, took lunch, and repeated sitting meditation and walking meditation.

After sometime, they sat around together at one place. A light sense of freedom flared out on the face of the monks who just came out of a deep meditation, and verses that sang the joy of the Dhamma started to flow from their mouths at the same time:

> Heaven sends rain through a fine tune.
> And the cave which I stay remains cool.
> And my mind too is well liberated.
> So Heaven, please send rain with joy.
>
> When thunder roars in the rain clouds
> And it rains in the sky where no birds fly
> The monk sits in the cave in meditative absorption.
> He knows nothing more joyful than this.
>
> Watching his body and mind calmly
> Thus severing the tenacious rope binding humans
> The monk sits in the cave in meditative absorption.
> He knows nothing more joyful than this.
>
> Attaining peace, having left defilement and worry,
> Opening the latch, pulling out the arrow without any desire
> The monk sits in the cave in meditative absorption.
> He knows nothing more joyful than this.

Twenty-one monks, taking turns, continued to recite hundreds of verses of inspiration. Eventually they reverted to silence, and the cave was brightened all of a sudden. A bright light shone into the cave, which had been dark because of the cloudy sky even though the rain had stopped.

The next moment, the light coming into the cave turned freshly green. And stepping through the green color, a nun walked into the cave; she was the female elder Uppalavanna.

Uppalavanna was an arhat regarded as the foremost in sagely powers among the Buddha's female disciples. And she was one of the two foremost female disciples, together with Khema. The Buddha thought Khema[42] and Uppalavanna as his foremost female disciples just like he considered Sariputta and Moggallana as his foremost male disciples.

Uppalavanna made prostrations to Elder Sariputta and sat next to him.

Sariputta asked her, "Sister, what brought you here?"

"I am here to witness a special event of causality to occur here in just a moment."

Sariputta said, smiling, "Sister, I know what you mean by the event of causality, and I am happy to welcome you here. By the way, sister, a while ago we monks enjoyed the joy of the Dhamma, reciting verses that came naturally from the heart. So, sister, who is always enjoying the joy of the Dhamma! How is it, before the event of causality starts, that you recite verses of inspiration as we did?"

"Elder, before that I would like to give a present to all the monks here."

"I know as well what your present is, and I will be pleased to accept it."

Upon Sariputta's approval, Uppalavanna, the first in sagely powers among nuns, produced lotus-shaped seats made of diamond for all monks in the cave. So, all monks sat on diamond lotus seats, and

---

42 Khema: A disciple of the Buddha who was the foremost in wisdom. The Buddha considered her as one of the two chief female disciples. Before renunciation, she was the queen consort of the King Bimbisara of the Magadha Kingdom.

having confirmed that all were seated, she produced a lotus seat made of sapphire and sat on it upright.

Old Bhikkhuni Uppalavanna sang about her life journey from the time when she was home as a lay person, to when she was ordained as a nun, to when she attained enlightenment, in ten more verses of inspiration. After that, she again exercised the sagely powers and made one more sapphire lotus seat beside her.

A monk asked Elder Uppalavanna, "It is well known among the monks how marvelous your sagely powers are. However, upon seeing it by my own eyes, great joy arose from within. I thank you for that, and, sister, please tell me who is supposed to sit on the beautiful seat you have made beside you."

"Elder," the foremost female disciple replied, "The one who will sit on it arrived here a while ago and waited for me to make the seat. Heavenly being, this is the right time, so please reveal yourself."

As Uppalavanna said this, a dim red light got tangled like a bundle of thread in the air where the nun stared into, which expanded little by little. After a while, the expanded light changed into myriad colors, and the colors rolled in like a fog in a deep valley that rose slowly riding on the air draft.

After some moments, from inside the lovely foggy light, a heavenly woman appeared.

Oh, the beauty of her! The heavenly woman, who looked existent but non-existent, and looked non-existent but existent, had an exceptional beauty, which it was not enough just to call beautiful, and not enough yet just to call magical.

The heavenly woman proceeded to Elder Sariputta and made three prostrations, and greeted Elder Uppalavanna with a bow with joined palms. In the meantime, the colorful, foggy lights that wrapped her up spread throughout the cave little by little, and as she sat down on her lotus seat, returned to her and started to wrap her up again.

Like a pastel painting, there was a feeling of coziness on and around her, due to the foggy light that coiled her. Moments later the foggy light that looked real and at the same time unreal slowly died out, and thus the figure of the heavenly woman was exposed again clearly.

The heavenly woman paid respect to Bhaddiya by joining her palms and looked at him calmly with her beautiful eyes. Bhaddiya also looked at her with noble eyes and responded by joining two hands in front of his chest.

A silence hung between them for a while. It was a silence that was light as a feather, deep as the ocean, clear like the heaven, but distant like a mirage and faraway like eternity. In the silence, there was a sound that was not a sound. The sound that was not a sound that carried no words, but at the same time contained in it a lot of words heard only to practitioners who had sagely powers.

Bhaddiya released his joined hands and put them on his lap neatly, and then the heavenly woman released her joined hands as well and put them on her lap neatly. At that time, Elder Sariputta looked at Bhaddiya. Sariputta's eyes appeared as if to say, *Brother, it would be better for you to talk to her first.*

Having noticed the master's eyes, Bhaddiya slightly nodded in recognition of the master's suggestion, and said toward the heavenly woman, "Oh, Ayutha, the flower of my karmic ties! May you be always happy! May you be always in happiness!"

"I thank you for your words of blessing," Ayutha said with a clear, ringing voice that could have been uttered if the sapphire on which she was sitting were changed into sound. "I am happy now. However, there were times in the past when I was not happy. And I know that the misfortunes I have experienced were due to the faults of my own. And as you were immensely tormented due to my faults, I would like to sincerely apologize again and again for that. Dear elder, Please generously forgive me who wounded your heart so ruthlessly." Having said that, Ayutha joined her palms again toward Bhaddiya.

Bhaddiya responded, "Now you are in the Heaven of Pure Abode. This means that you have attained the state of the non-returner. So how could there be forgiving or being forgiven between you and me?

"My karmic tie, which was once a love, once hatred, and thereafter a sorrow and a grudge! By now I have completely realized the great truth that empties everything out. Therefore, I now look at you with a light heart and declare, as a knotted skein is unraveled, the karmic tie between us, which has been stained with love, hatred, pain, and grudge has been wholly unraveled.

"It was because you and I have realized the truth of non-self. If there were no self, there will be no love or hatred, and without love or hatred, there will be no betrayal, and without betrayal, there will be no pain, and without pain, there will be no grudge. If there were no love, hatred, betrayal, pain, or grudge, isn't it the genuine unraveling of the karmic tie, and isn't that the most flawless pardon, wherein even the word *forgiveness* becomes unnecessary?"

As Bhaddiya said this, Ayutha, a being in the Heaven of Pure Abode, once again expressed gratitude by joining her palms. The twenty monks and Elder Uppalavanna who knew the past karmic ties of the two beings praised the karmic ties having been amicably completed by shouting, "Excellent! Excellent! Excellent!"

CHAPTER 22
Symposium

ut the words of admiration were not uttered by them only. As soon as their veneration was over, a loud exclamation of "Sadhu, Sadhu! Sadhu!" echoed through the cave, loud enough to tear down the cave.

At that moment, Elder Sariputta displayed a circular hand mudra. Then in the next moment, countless heavenly kings and beings along with their retinues such as gandhabbas, kumbhandas, nagas, and yakkhas, that were already present in the cave, slowly began to take their shape.

The size of the cave remained the same, as the residence of Sariputta did before. However, the tiny cave did not appear to be crowded at all, despite of innumerable celestial beings that were present. How many heavenly kings and beings were present in the cave? *There should be at least a couple of million,* Raja and Sirima thought, while heading toward the back of the heavenly beings.

By offering prostrations, the heavenly kings and beings paid their respect to Elder Sariputta. After receiving prostrations, Sariputta said, "Let you all be freed from suffering! Let you all be happy!" He thus blessed all the heavenly beings.

Several heavenly kings representing various heavens stood on the front row. Then, heavenly King Kammakammaya, the king reigning the highest heaven of the four heavens of the Formless Realm, came forth toward Sariputta on behalf of the heavenly kings and beings and said with gratitude, "Most grateful for your blessings."[43]

Elder Sariputta then said to Kammakammaya, "I know why you are all here. You are curious as to why the Buddha seeks Binggisa, the sinner. You are here because as I promised Sahampati, the King of the Mahabrahma Heaven, you wish to go with me to meet with Binggisa."

"That is right. But great elder, just a moment ago Elder Bhaddiya said to Ayutha from the Heaven of Pure Abode, 'It was because you and I have realized the truth of non-self. If there were no self, there will be no love or hatred, and without love or hatred, there will be no betrayal, and without betrayal, there will be no pain, and without pain, there will be no grudge. If there were no love, hatred, betrayal, pain, or grudge, isn't it the genuine unraveling of the karmic ties and isn't that the most flawless forgiveness, where even the word forgiveness becomes unnecessary?'"

"That is right."

"Elder, those words came straight to my heart. However, I, along with fifty billion beings who gathered here, cannot fully comprehend the meaning behind those words. Thus, could you please encourage Bhaddiya to explain what he said to Ayutha?"

"Brother, what do you think about the words this ruler of the Heavenly Realm just said?"

Bhaddiya said to Elder Sariputta, "Master, what I said to Ayutha a while ago was based on the truth of non-self, which is one of the ultimate truths of Dhamma. But how could I dare to give a discourse on this matter, while the great Marshall of Dhamma is solemnly present?

---

43 Although heavenly beings from the Form Realm have eyes and ears to hear Buddhist teachings by the Buddha and other teachers, beings from the Formless Realm have mind without five senses and cannot listen to teachings. However, in this book, the author depicts these beings as being able to hear teachings, and there are no heavenly kings in the heavens of Form Realm and Formless Realm, but the author depicted it as if there are.

Master, would you please clearly discern for them the truth of non-self?"

"But Brother, the truth of non-self cannot be described through language. Such truth stands high where no language can reach, nor can it be conveyed through letters."

Bhaddiya said smiling, "But how could that apply only to the truth of non-self? Master, no language or letters could possibly convey to a third person exactly what occurred or was experienced. For example, let's assume that I feel pain due to a scab under my nail. No matter how much or how skillfully I describe in words, the person hearing it will never experience what I experienced.

"But come to think of it, master, communication is impossible without language. Thus in summary, language in one hand could be a great communicative tool to improve understanding of one another, but on the other hand it could also be the cause of misunderstanding. Therefore, we must employ language while taking into account its ambivalence."

"Precisely, brother. Thus language is double-faceted communication tool. For that reason, when the Buddha utilized language as a tool that promotes understanding, he used it quite precisely in order to minimize any misunderstanding. He then kept noble silence in situations where language could become the cause for misunderstanding."

"Yes, master. However, with correct application of language, speaker's experience can be reproduced in the mind of listeners in relative closeness. Furthermore, language can create images[44] in the mind of listeners, far beyond what was intended or even not intended by the speaker, for example, which is the literary languages. In fact, language is a tool created for mutual exchange of thoughts between humans. However, language has a secondary purpose beyond its original function of communication. Literature uses the secondary

---

44 Image: ① in literature, phenomenon achieved through senses are regenerated in the mind ② in psychology, what has been experienced appears visually in the mind as imagery.

function—such as the use of metaphors, symbols, suggestions, circumventions, implications, omissions, paradoxes, jumps of logic, and rhymes—as a tool to reach listeners. Through these, literature provides poetic awareness or emotional impression in the mind of the listener, which can't be reached with mere concepts.

"Master, when I was still a layman, I learned literature, music, and art from Binggisa, the troubadour. At those times, I was impressed and utterly captivated by the grandness of art, and later was able to form my own opinion of art. And now that I have gained insight into the truth of non-self as a practitioner, I can appreciate art from a different perspective. Art generates 'background scene' in the mind of observers.[45] In doing so, it inspires and comforts their hearts, which means art could be a great guide that leads sentient beings to realize the truth of non-self."

Elder Sariputta waited until Bhaddiya finished expressing his opinion on art, then said to Kammakammaya, "Heavenly king, you are curious to know about the truth of non-self."

"Yes, I am."

"And brother Bhaddiya just stated that art can be a great guide that could lead one to the truth of non-self."

"That's right."

"Heavenly king, as Bhaddiya described, art is a human activity that leaves profound impressions in the hearts of sentient beings. But you must understand that such inspiration felt through art remains on the lower domain, when compared to realization of the truth of non-self through Dhamma. This means art is an activity humans perform to comfort their weary and hardened heart, in the middle of their journey that begins from the attachment to self and the world and toward the ultimate goal of realizing the truth, which is non-self.

"In other words, practitioners may experience what Brother Bhaddiya just described, not only from art but through philosophy, religion, and love. They may experience the truth of non-self but up

---

45 Reference to the aesthetic theory by N. Hartmann.

to the intermediate stage. Although philosophy, religion, and love surely have their limitation of not being able to take practitioners to experience the truth of non-self, not up to final nirvana, it should nevertheless be encouraged as it enables people to go up at least to the intermediate level."

"Then, Great Elder, please teach us how art, philosophy, religion, and love could bring one to intermediate level of experience in the truth of non-self."

After receiving the request from Kammakammaya, Elder Sariputta looked at Bhaddiya and said, "Brother, wouldn't you share your opinion on art and non-self for Kammakammaya as well as various other heavenly kings and beings that gathered here?"

Bhaddiya placed his palms together to demonstrate heeding of his master's advice.

Bhaddiya then laid his hands down and said, "Many of the heavenly kings and beings who have gathered here, I just said, 'art generates a background scene in the mind of observers. In doing so, it inspires and comforts their heart/mind, which means art could be a great guide that leads sentient beings to realize the truth of non-self.' Then, what is a background scene? Heavenly kings and beings, you must know that when you see paintings of mountains, some simply depict mountains that lead you simply to think 'that is a mountain.' But some paintings lead us to think 'this contains something more than just a mountain.' Furthermore, there are paintings in which seeing a mountain once is not enough, but makes us want to see more and more from all different angles to appreciate it. But sometimes even that doesn't seem enough. Some paintings are harder to grasp with intellect alone, but must be embraced through one's emotion and feeling.

"Such paintings lead viewers to immerse their mind in mountains within the painting. As such, paintings that lead one to immerse themselves in—hus if there is a painting that induces deep involvement as if one is in a dream and haze, and as a result it draws one to be truly inspired in their heart, then we call that a true work of art.

"Dear heavenly king, a painting that simply leads one to think *this is a mountain* could be said to have only a foreground scene, whereas I happen to think that the true work of art shows even background scenes. Do you have some other thoughts on that?"

"I agree with that thought," said Kammakammaya.

"However, there are various forms of art, such as fine art, which uses sight to visualize background scenes, music which uses hearing to make the background scenes come alive, and other forms of art such as utilizing senses of smell, taste, and touch to help visualize the background scenes.

"And there exists even another form of grand art, which is literature. Literature on the one hand is art, but on the other hand is philosophy. Literature is human activity that creates background scenes in the mind of viewers and this background scenes bring emotional inspiration to the viewers, thus it must be classified as art. However, literature also provides intellectual understanding, that is, philosophical awareness. In that sense, literature is a human activity that combines both art and philosophy.

"The reasons why literature came to possess such dual characteristics are because while music and art use material objects such as sound and color, literature uses a mental object called language. The sound, color, and form contain no conceptual meaning, but language used in literature implies meaning, thus literature possesses philosophical aspect of human activity that pursues meaning.

"But if you look little more closely, art and music can also be philosophical. However, it can be said that music and painting have more artistic characteristic in proportion to philosophical characteristic, while literature is relatively less artistic but fills its missing gap with philosophy.

"Moreover, when art creates background scenes in the mind of observers, it does not end in just one level. In other words, a great work of art brings second and third background scenes in the mind of observers.

"As an analogy, higher mountains can be seen behind smaller mountains in the front, and even higher mountains exist further behind . . . Then the farthest mountain becomes blurry until it is difficult to distinguish whether it is a mountain or sky."

"Oh . . ."

"In this way, dependent on its degree of excellence, work of art can lead observer's mind farther beyond. If an ordinary painting could lead the observer to the first level, an artistic painting can lead the observer further to the second, third, fourth, and other levels beyond.

"It means the true work of art can drive the hearts of observers much deeper, drowning them in that object of art, which leads the mind to forget the self. Thus, the appreciator of art, in this vague, elusive self-effacement, stops the pain and defilement they feel living a life as an individual. Then why do pain and defilement stop at the level of self-effacement? That is because pain and defilement rely on consciousness that distinguish self from others. That is why I said 'art can be a great guide that leads sentient beings to the truth of non-self.' Because they deny self, the states of self-oblivion and self-effacement are similar to the truth of non-self.

"But there is yet another path that could comfort the bleakness of life through the state of self-oblivion and self-effacement, which we call philosophy. But I think Brother Malukha is more adept to give a discourse on philosophy, as he gained deeper insight from his time spent in his secular life."

Saying this, Bhaddiya looked toward Malukha. Then Elder Sariputta, who is also the chairman of the assembly, told Malukha, "Brother, do not refuse but freely express your opinion on philosophy."

In response Malukha said, "As directed by the elder, I will now share my opinion on philosophy. Heavenly kings and heavenly beings who have gathered here, Elder Bhaddiya just stated art can be a great guide on the path of truth that realizes non-self. However, I would also like to say that philosophy could also be a guide to realizing the truth of non-self. This means philosophy can also lead a person's mind from the world and self, which are the object of his contemplation, to the second, third, and fourth level.

"Thus, in that state of self-effacement and self-oblivion, the philosopher can put a stop to suffering and defilements he is bound to feel living as an individual. However, philosophy is different than art, because the state of immersion is not an emotional territory but a rational one.

"Beyond what is just mentioned here, various aspects must be reviewed to know philosophy. However, I wouldn't speak further on this matter. Except, there is a path, other than art and philosophy, which brings comfort to the life of suffering, and I'd just mention that it is religion. But the great Marshall of Dhamma is seated here, thus I think it is only appropriate for him to speak on the subject of religion."

After finishing his speech, Malukha looked toward the direction of Elder Sariputta.

Elder Sariputta spoke as endorsed by Malukha, "Dear heavenly kings and beings! Brothers Bhaddiya and Malukha each expressed their own views on art and philosophy. So what about religion in relations to the truth of non-self? First of all, religion is an activity of man that maintains emotional aspect on an artistic sense, and philosophical aspect on a rational sense.

"In other words, in order to lead sentient beings to self-oblivion and self-effacement, religion utilizes emotional worship to the most holy and honorable object on the one hand, and use reason on the other hand. Thus, the pain and defilements religious people had felt while living as distinct individual can be alleviated in the state of feeling wistful and distant.

"Dear kings and beings of heaven, almost every religion in the world worships God, and they preach that one must offer their life to the most sacred, ultimate God to relieve the pain and defilements felt in life. And in reality, this path provides the states of self-oblivion and self-effacement that arouse the fifth and sixth background scenes, higher than art and philosophy, which helps alleviate their pain and defilements.

"However, dear heavenly kings and heavenly beings, just as an artist cannot be inspired every moment of his day without any disruption, just as a philosopher cannot engage in philosophical deliberation every moment of the month, the religious who dedicate themselves to God cannot retain states of self-oblivion and self-effacement without any moment of disruption for a year or ten years.

"Why? That is because the states of self-oblivion and self-effacement are obtained through union with another. That is, union between different individuals is bound to dissipate due to grand universal law of impermanence. There is no exception whether that object is artistic, philosophical, or even God as an object of worship in religion."

"Oh . . ." Kammakammaya said.

"In that regard, I would like to say that mind is comprised of a mind that knows and a mind that is being known—in other words object-mind. Dear king, let's say here is a mirror, and a snake is in front of the mirror, which reflects it. In this comparison, the mirror corresponds to the mind that knows, and the image of a snake reflected is the object-mind that is being known.

"However, the mind-mirror of sentient beings is different from the actual mirror in that it can fabricate something non-existent by combining existent objects. Therefore, you may already know that when you genuinely envision something, it sometimes appears to be real, and when that gets worse, it appears to truly exist outside of the mind.

"As such, the reason why the mind produces something that does not truly exist is because the mind is tainted with ignorance and desire. Ignorance and desire interfere with seeing things as they truly are. For example, seeing a rope as a serpent, seeing a yellow stone as a piece of gold, and combining characteristics of various animals to create a bizarre imaginary animals.

"That is, if a person's mind-mirror has a subconscious memory of having seen a snake or picked up a piece of gold, and if that memory is combined with ignorance and desire, then a rope can be mistaken as a snake and a stone can be mistaken to be a piece of gold. As such, a new entity that is a half-human and half-animal can be created by combining various animals we once saw, or by combining one's imagination and expectations, a heavenly being of half-human and half-god can be created. To conclude, the God those believers in the Religion of Divinity worship is nothing but an ideation of object-mind that is combined by sentient beings' ignorance and desire—in other words mental formations."[46]

"Oh . . ."

"For the most part, I think it is quite noble that many believers of the Religion of Divinity have religious mind toward God. But this mind could very well be shaken up and collapse. Why? It is due to the impermanence of mental formations—in other words all that is conditioned and combined is impermanent. The law of impermanence that 'what is formed is bound to disappear, and what arises is bound to collapse,' is the first of the three laws that applies to all living beings.

"Due to the law of impermanence, the self-oblivion and self-efface-ment that the God believers attained most sincerely is difficult to maintain and is shaken up frequently. Then they pray to God, 'God, lead us not into temptation, and deliver us from evil. Give us the power to resist temptations when the devil comes to tempt us.'

"Then, when Buddhists see such prayers by believers of the Religion of Divinity, they think, *The devil they are so afraid of is simply an image reflected off of mind-mirror. Such image has no inherent nature, and even if such delusional evil comes to tempt me, what could they pos-sibly do? And for what reason would I request another being (God) to control my mind instead? My mind can be controlled all on my own!*

"Based on these thoughts, Buddhists make a firm resolve: When I am tempted by evil, I will find ignorance and desire that tempta-tion tries to get hold of. Then, I will eliminate them with everything in my power.

---

46 Mental formations (sankhara): It means primarily one's will or intention, but in a deeper sense it means karma, which is a mind that maintains human body and mind.

"Dear heavenly king, improvements are made in human mind only through practicing toward a right direction. No God or the Buddha or any other external being can learn, practice, and improve on your behalf.

"Moreover, through prayers or praises, etc., one can manipulate and construct mind. Although this could create peace on the intermediate level, it cannot generate ultimate peace. When the mind simply sees object-mind as an object-mind, it can let go of attachment to it and return back to the mind that knows. Thus by understanding how the mind creates object-minds, and how the mind combines and fabricates things that are seen, heard, smelled, tasted, felt, and thought, one can recognize how ignorance and desire are added in that process, and furthermore deep insight is developed to see how essence of defilement is thoroughly penetrated till the end. And that is when we reach ultimate peace.

"Thus, the Buddha said:

> All conditioned things are transient and empty
> He who sees this with the eye of wisdom
> Will turn away from all suffering
> This is the only path to nirvana.

> All conditioned things are suffering
> He who sees this with the eye of wisdom
> Will turn away from all suffering
> This is the only path to nirvana.

> All things are free from permanent self
> He who sees this with the eye of wisdom
> Will turn away from all suffering
> This is the only path to nirvana.

CHAPTER 23
About Things to Say, "Come and Behold"

Elder Sariputta said to Kammakammaya, the king ruling the Heaven of Neither Perception nor Non-Perception, "Therefore, Buddhist practitioners must stop fabricating through manipulating the mind, and practice vipassana meditation that recognizes all phenomena of the mind as they are. When one reaches such a state, even the Buddha will be just one of other individuals. In other words, ultimately one must only depend on oneself and the practice. The Buddha described this as taking self as refuge and taking Dhamma as refuge."

After stating this, Sariputta recited another verse.

> Whether at a village or a forest,
> Or a valley or a hill,
> Ah, regardless of where it may be,
> The place where an arhat resides
> Is where happiness is found!

The Marshall of Dhamma then continued, "This verse teaches that happiness fills wherever an arhat resides. But then, why is it always so blissful and happy? That is because arhats attained enlightenment on their own accord, not through external objects or people.

"In other words, the believers of the Religion of Divinity and their heavens are two very distinct entities and spaces, but arhats and their state of nirvana cannot be separated, as they are one and the same. This means the state of nirvana that arhats enjoy, a Buddhist state corresponding to the heaven referred to by the Religion of Divinity, is actually a state akin to what snail house means to a snail. In regards to this simile, I will ask you a few questions to facilitate better understanding. You may now answer."

"Yes, elder."

"Heavenly king, where do lay people go—that is, after going through so much competition and hostility from people and the world, where do they lay their weary body and mind to rest?"

"They return to their home and family to relax their body and mind."

"In that case, I think these homes where people rest are a form of heaven, do you not agree?"

"I think so too."

"But heavenly king! These so called heavenly homes could be filled with dark clouds at times. That is, the members of the family don't always agree with each other, and this so called heaven could turn into something quite far from heaven."

"That's right."

"Then why does this heavenly home change as such? That is because the conditions that constitute this heaven, such as a wife and a husband, a father and a child, all exist as a distinct individual or entity. Just as you have seen from the relationship between God and his devotees, between art and its appreciators, and also between a philosopher and his topic of philosophy, happiness created by an individual, dependent on the conditional relations with other persons or other things, will ultimately disappear and collapse. That is because all creation is bound to disappear and everything that arises will fall in accordance with the law of impermanence. Therefore, Dhamma brings people back to their self, not to other person or other things, to establish happiness that does not vanish or break down. And vipassana meditation is what brings people to become aware of their self as they truly are.

"Let's say, for example, there is a pure devotee of Dhamma and he maintains a good relationship with his wife. But according to the law of individuality, the mind of these two distinct individuals would not always coincide and this couple is bound to argue at times. In such cases, he who does not understand true Dhamma will attempt to comfort his wife or try to persuade her. He may leave his wife at home and go out, go drinking, and even whine to others about his wife. Maybe he will try to be patient and press down his anger, or maybe he would just get angry if that doesn't work.

"But a disciple of the Buddha who knows true Dhamma would practice vipassana meditation and turn his mind, which was directed toward his wife, back to himself. As a result, negative emotions harbored in his mind are alleviated and resolved. Such happiness would not arise through external object or person, but it means he is on a path to find happiness which develops through relationship with his self.

"This could also mean that he is widening the scope of his mind, and in a while he will move one step closer to his wife with an open heart. Thus, he will be able to care for his wife truly and act thoughtfully. If his wife accepts his heart and actions, then this couple is able to restore their kingdom of heaven."

"That will be the case, elder."

"Heavenly king! Unfortunately, however, even that heaven will fall one day after some time, unless they reach the highest state of practice. Thus, they would practice vipassana meditation more diligently and through such process, their level of happiness will increase until they reach the state of arhatship, where they feel happy no matter where they are.

"The heaven established by the holy arhat is, first of all, built all on his own without depending on external objects, people, gods, and values. In other words, it is a heaven established through taking refuge in oneself. Secondly, it is a heaven created though vipassana meditation, which is built by taking refuge in Dhamma.

"Dear heavenly king, for a holy arhat who has realized taking refuge in the self and Dhamma to the highest level, a village is his heaven when he is in a village, a forest heaven when he is in a forest, a valley heaven when he is in a valley, and a hill heaven when he is on a hill. This means heaven becomes one with the holy arhat and accompanies him, thus I liken an arhat to a snail that carries the home on its back."

"Oh . . ."

"Dear heavenly king, but here you must bear in mind that the heaven constructed by arhats exist on this very earth. That is, arhats do not live somewhere in heaven after his death, but enjoy heaven here in this very moment. This means that the heaven arhats enjoy is not a heaven to believe in but one to see, not a heaven to be imagined but one to be experienced directly. On the contrary, the heaven explained by the Religion of Divinity is not a heaven to see directly but one to believe in, not a heaven to experience directly, but one to imagine indirectly. Such differences in two heavenly states occur because while the former is fulfilled based on a belief, the latter is fulfilled based on knowing."

Then, Elder Sariputta said to Kammakammaya, "Dear heavenly king, knowing is clear and certain, but faith is unclear and ambiguous. I will now ask you a few questions to make you understand better, and you may answer."

"Elder, please lay out your questions as you please."

"You are now looking at my palm," he said as he stretched out his hand.

"Yes, I am looking at your palm."

"Then you are aware that nothing is in my palm."

"Yes, I am aware that nothing is in your palm."

"Oh heavenly king, through this you recognize that knowing occurs through seeing."

"Elder, I recognize that knowing occurs through seeing."

"Now I will put a small stone in the palm of my hand. Do you see the stone in my palm?"

"Yes, I see the stone in the palm of your hand."

"Now, I will make a fist. Now, you tell me. Do I have a stone in my fist or not?"

Seeing the stone with a sagely power, he answered, "There is a stone in your fist."

"But oh heavenly king, I could have removed the stone that you have seen a little while ago with my sagely power, or created an illusory stone. You must answer while keeping that in mind. Do you know if I have a stone in my fist or not?"

"I cannot confirm for certain. But I am guessing there is probably a stone in your fist."

"Oh heavenly king, I think the faith we have been discussing is a perception on that which is unclear and uncertain—similar to what you are guessing right now. Do you have any other thought on that?"

"I think so too."

"Now, I will open my fist. Heavenly king, do you see the stone in my palm and know that it is there?"

"Yes, I see the stone, and thus know that it is in your palm."

"Do you believe that I have a stone in my palm or know that?"

"I do not believe, but I know there is a stone in your palm."

"How do you not believe but know that the stone is in my palm?"

"That is because I know by seeing that a stone is in your palm."

"So, heavenly king, if the believers of the Religion of Divinity see God they believed in, just as you saw the stone, do you think they would believe God or know him?"

"In that case, they will know God, rather than believe in God."

"But why do they believe in God?"

"That is because they do not see God."

"Therefore, heavenly king, if they see God, they should say, 'Look at the God,' rather than 'Believe in the God,' when they preach. And people would turn their head toward the direction to which the finger is pointing and thus see God.

"From this point on, they would never discuss amongst themselves on whether or not they should believe in God. This is like a math student that initially believes in the answer teacher provides, but later he learns to solve problems on his own and see for himself what the answer is.

"Dear heavenly king, you must know this: Dhamma seeks the truth in knowing, just like teachers and students who teach and learn mathematics. In other words, Buddhism also starts off in faith, just like the Religion of Divinity, but this faith, in a sense, is a student that believes in what the teacher tells them. That is, ultimately Buddhist disciples will know how to solve problems on his own, and see and know whether the answer is correct without asking the teacher.

"By this, oh heavenly king, you understand why the opinions of many holy arhats in regards to the truth always coincide. This is like having only one right answer to a math problem. There is no argument between arhats in discussing the doctrine, just as there is no argument between the keenest math students in regards to that one correct answer."

After speaking thus far, Elder Sariputta stopped. Kammakammaya looked at the great Marshall of Dhamma with sincere respect and said, "Oh, elder! I know now why the Buddha referred to Buddhadhamma as 'something that one could come and see for himself' and why Buddhist practice emphasizes clear seeing and clear knowing!"

"O heavenly king, based on the fact that knowing provides higher awareness than faith, and just as I have proved thus far, Buddhadhamma offers a path to knowing—that is the path to enlightenment in which knowing is the essence of enlightenment.

"However, enlightenment is a special knowing that is different from the general knowing. While general knowing is obtained outside the framework of the Four Noble Truths, enlightenment is a knowing obtained within the structure of the Four Noble Truths. Also, general knowing is gained through the pursuit of outer objects or outer persons. In contrast, enlightenment is a knowing acquired through the understanding of self. General knowing is an intellectual knowing gained rapidly, while enlightenment is an intuitive and specific knowing obtained more gradually. In summary, the truth revealed through enlightenment is self-evident, with no room for controversy."

CHAPTER 24
Great Symphony

"Then, elder, what does it mean to attain enlightenment? On what is one enlightened?"

"Heavenly king, one is enlightened on the three marks of existence, such as impermanence, suffering, and non-self—especially on the last mark of non-self, that is, the truth of there being no self."

"Elder, a doubt has arisen in me, so may I ask you a question?"

"You may ask whatever you wish."

"I understand that the Buddhadhamma starts from the law of particular, am I right here?"

"Yes, you are right."

"However, elder, a particular means an independent entity that does not mix with others, doesn't it? Viewing from this perspective, how is it possible that there is no self in a particular?"

"Heavenly king, let's assume there is a good vipassana practitioner. And let's assume that he enters the fourth level of meditative absorption where the mind is extremely calm and clear, and becomes aware of his body and mind as they are.[47]

_____

47 Enlightenment is attained at the fourth stage of meditative absorption. Then why is enlightenment attained at the fourth stage of meditative absorption, while there are higher

"At that time, he has no thought of the Buddha and no thought of the Buddhadhamma. He neither thinks he is practicing, nor expects the merits of his practice. There is no thought of distinguishing himself from others, either. In this incomparably pure state devoid of other thoughts, he perceives his body and mind as they are, which it is now inappropriate to call 'himself' but there is no other way but to call it 'himself.'

"Then he sees that his body and mind consist of aggregates of innumerable fine and tiny elements. In other words, he sees that the body consists of aggregates of material elements, and that the mind consists of aggregates of feeling, perception, intention, and consciousness elements. These elements may, under different conditions, stick together or be detached from each other, or appear or disappear. This is like, under certain conditions, innumerable soil particles gather and stick together to make a lump of earth, or a lump of earth is broken and dispersed in tiny soil particles.

"That a practitioner sees his body and mind in fine and tiny elements means that he sees his body and mind after breaking them up in tiny elements, and this can be compared to that a mathematician endlessly repeats dividing one in half. But howsoever many times he divides one in half, he cannot arrive at zero, and this is because that even the smallest fractional number is, even though it is near zero, not zero.

"However, you shall know that a practitioner may, through fierce practice, arrive at zero, which a mathematician cannot reach through endless repetition of fractionizing. Like water changes into vapors at critical point, a practitioner may, by observing his body in fine and tiny elements, go beyond the critical point and reach the stage of zero where even elements do not exist—in other words the stage of emptiness.

(cont.) stages? It is because if one advances to the fifth or higher stages of meditative absorption, their power of awareness gets weakened. In other words, to attain enlightenment, an excessive meditative absorption will pose as rather an obstacle.

"As the second analogy, that a practitioner observes his body and mind in fine and tiny elements, is like that an 'island-I' as a particular, which is separated from other 'island-others,' goes deeper and deeper into the inner part of itself. At the end of it, he will finally reach the continent where the island-I and the island-others resolve the isolation and become one, and realize that all islands are one under the water, and this means that he transcends the island-nature of a particular, in other words, he reaches the stage of non-self.

"As the third analogy, that a practitioner observes his body and mind in fine and tiny elements, is like that a man who sees ants moving in a line from afar and considers it as a line realizes upon seeing them up close that it is not a line but a succession of isolated ants.

"Heavenly king, the material body and non-material mind elements that constitute sentient beings are cut and separated from each other on the one hand, and connected and entangled one another on the other. Among the innumerable number of elements that are interdependent of one another, there is no element that deserves to be called the self, and no element is the self.

"Nevertheless, like a clown who, standing at the end of a bunch of festival-goers marching in lines and pointing to the people in front of him, shouts, 'I am the master of these guys!' sentient beings have blear eyes to look at themselves. In other words, like a person who watches the ants only from far away, they consider the continuance of the body, continuance of the feeling, continuance of the perception, continuance of the intention, or the continuance of the consciousness as objects, or they suppose a substantial entity that is presumed to create and maintain them behind the scene, and arouse the concept of 'self.'

"That is to say, by way of seeing themselves as the elements that are cut and separated from each other, or by way of seeing that there is no one who creates and maintains these elements behind the scene, or that there is no substantial entity, one who has broken the concept of the self is a sage, while those who see the elements as connected and lumped, or presume a substantial entity behind the elements that creates and maintains them, and thus to generate the concept of the self, are sentient beings.

"This means that the body of a sentient being as reflected in his eyes is one that is combined with the concept of the self, and thus an object to be cherished. However, the body reflected in the eyes of a sage who realized the non-self is something that is not combined with the concept of the self, so it is like the body of others, a piece of wood dropped on the roadside, and in the same context, the mind is also like the mind of others or a white cloud floating in the sky."

"Oh, how light it is! Just by imagining this state of attainment, I feel like flying into the sky like a feather," said Kammakammaya.

"However, you have to go one step further, because the Buddhadhamma does not end there. Heavenly king, just like no elements constituting the 'I' as a particular can be considered 'I,' likewise, no elements constituting other people and things can be considered 'not I.' In other words, like the particular-I, all the others or other things in the world consist of innumerable small elements, and such elements do not cease to interact with the particular-I. Heavenly king, Let's assume that a man named Khanda feels thirsty and is about to drink a cup of water. I think, to Khanda, the water placed before is not himself, but an object. What do you think about it?"

"I think so too, elder."

"Then if he drinks the water and the water enters his mouth, then to whom does the water belong?"

"It belongs to Khanda."

"Then, is the water Khanda now or an object?"

Here, Kammakammaya hesitated to answer for some moments.

So, Elder Sariputta said, "As you hesitate to answer, I will ask you one more question. Now, the water Khanda dank flowed through his stomach to the small intestine, and via the small intestine to the large intestine. During the time, a part of the water was changed into blood and flowed into the blood vessel, and another part gathered at the bladder.

"Thereafter, the blood that flowed into the blood vessel was intricately mixed with other things. And at the end, it reached a state where it became unable to distinguish whether it was water or blood. Further thereafter, what I called water at first permeated each and every part of his body, mixed with other things, continued to be transformed and finally began to affect the whole body. By now, is it Khanda or something other than Khanda?"

"In that case, it must be called Khanda," said Kammakammaya.

"However, after some time, it became sweat and was discharged outside of his body. Now, can it still be Khanda?"

"Elder, no, it cannot."

"So far, I gave you an example in which an external thing called water became Khanda, and then transformed again into an external thing called sweat. With respect to the mind as well, I take information from other people or things, or give the information inside me to other people or other things. So some idea which was not mine becomes mine in some instances, and some idea which was mine becomes others' idea. Like this, the particular-I continuously interacts with other people and thing, not only in material (physical) aspect but also in non-material (mental) one. And you should know as well that between the body and the mind of the particular-I, among each element of the body and each element of the mind, the interaction to give and take takes place ceaselessly."

"Oh!"

"By now, you should have understood that it is not clearly distinguishable between the body and the mind and between the particular-I and the world surrounding it–namely, I and the world surrounding me is not one and not two, not same and not different. And you should have understood that appearance and disappearance, existence and non-existence are not one and not two, not same and not different.

"Heavenly king, what I have just expounded is the consummation of the Buddhadhamma, the truth of the dependent arising and Middle Way.[48] What do they mean? A sage who has attained complete enlightenment will not, in all matters which are divided by two extremes of being and nonbeing, tilt to either side but to stay and live in the middle, like a clown walking on a high tightrope does not tilt either to the left or to the right.

"So the Buddha said, 'A sage sees that elements combine together and arise, and thus, does not tilt to the thought that there is neither self nor world. He also sees that elements release the combination and extinguish, and thus, does not tilt to the thought that there are self and the world.'

"In other words, a sage who has attained enlightenment, seeing the arising (being) on the one hand, lives a most sincere life, and seeing the disappearance (nonbeing), has attachment to nothing. In the same sense, with respect to events arising between the particular-I and others, a sage does not insist that they should be attributed to me or to you. It is because, as in the case of two bundles of straw that stand leaning on each other, we cannot say the bundles are standing because of this bundle or that bundle."

Kammakammaya asked, "Elder, now I understand the depth of the Buddhadhamma, though it is still vague. Then, compared to the profound Buddhadhamma, are the thoughts of the non-followers not worth our attention?"

The foremost disciple of the Buddha answered. "Kammakammaya, the non-believers are teaching, in various forms, the doctrine of self-negation. While their thoughts are in many aspects contradictory

---

48 Middle Way (majjhima magga): Excluding and harmonizing the two extremes, the Middle Way is a very important concept in the Buddhist philosophy. The Early Buddhism expounded the Middle Way between being and nonbeing, between I and not-I, between the thought that everything finishes when one dies and the thought that there is a self that exists permanently, between whether the cause and effect are same or different, between coming and going of the cause and effect, and between joy and suffering, etc. was taught. However, Mahayana Buddhism greatly emphasized the concept of the Middle Way to explain the true nature of existence.

to the Buddhadhamma, they are unknowingly heading toward the Dhamma of non-self, the culmination of the truth of the Buddhadhamma, through their doctrine of self-negation.

"They deny the self through various doctrines, such as establishing soul or greater-self in human kinds, or asserting that there is a true-self beyond the false-self that people are conscious of, and that there is universal-self in the universe, and once one realizes the true-self, the false-self will melt into the universal-self, etc.

"However, their self-negation is not thorough when compared to the Buddhadhamma, in that they try to perpetuate the existence of self through clever means. For example, though they deny the self, they assert it will live eternally in the world of God; or while they deny the bubble-like false-self, they assert it will become an unlimited and infinite existence as the ocean-like true-self or the universal-self.

"Nevertheless, it is true that, in that they negate the self, they are proceeding in the same direction as the Buddhadhamma. This means that their doctrines, which unknowingly guide people to the truth of non-self, are part of the Buddhadhamma in a broader sense. Heavenly king, now you should know that I criticize their thought on the one hand but I accommodate them on the other hand, and in this sense, the Buddhadhamma can be called a grand symphony of thoughts. In other words, all meaningful activities of humanity—the art and philosophy mentioned by Malukha, the religion I mentioned, the enthusiasm for work that makes one be immersed in the objects, the infatuation with hobbies, etc.—will each form groups of percussion, string, and wind instruments in a grand orchestra called the Buddhadhamma, and solemnly and beautifully play the world of humans, the world of sentient beings and this world that includes insentient objects."

To this solemn and grand discourse of the Marshall of Dhamma, Kammakammaya shouted loudly, "Oh the vastness of the Buddhadhamma!" and thereafter, over five billion heavenly kings and beings assembled there praised the harmoniousness of the Buddhadhamma crying, "Excellent! Excellent! Excellent!"

Soon, Kammakammaya changed the topic and asked about a different subject.

"Then, elder, where does an arhat who has attained such a noble state of enlightenment head for upon his complete nirvana (parinirvana)?"

"Even the King of Death, Yama, as well as all you heavenly beings do not know where an arhat goes after parinirvana. In other words, as if we cannot tell the specific place where a fire has gone after it was blown out, we cannot tell the specific place where the arhat has gone, and such going is not going nor non-going.

"Like this, parinirvana of an arhat is a delicate event that cannot be described in words of affirmation, but in words of negation.[49] However, again, even with all the words of negation, the situation cannot be described completely without leaving anything behind, oh, heavenly king, about the delicate event of the parinirvana of an arhat, I simply give my explanation, which is not an explanation, by way of a deep silence."

Having said this, Sariputta ceased to talk, closed his eyes, and kept silent.

At last, a small smile like a crescent appeared at the corner of Sariputta's mouth. A crescent moon! That's right. It was a smile like a thin and clear moon that has just arisen, or like a naïve curiosity hanging at the corner of the eyes of a baby.

"Oh!"

A cry came out of the mouth of Kammakammaya from the eighth meditation heaven; it echoed and spread far through several millions of heavenly kings and beings.

Kammakammaya, in a voice overwhelmed by emotion, said to the foremost disciple of the Buddha, "A detailed analyzer of the

---

49 The realm of nirvana cannot be fully explained with affirmative words, because while affirmative words contain the objects in the concept, the realm of nirvana is a level transcending (illimitable) concepts. Therefore, the transcendent stage is commonly described not with affirmative words such as "It is this and that," but with words that are not affirmative, such as "It is neither this nor that," or "We cannot say that it is this or that."

Dhamma! A great master of the truth who accommodates everything like the ocean and embraces everything like the void! I have just received your teachings and now I am able to grasp the deepest and highest aspects of the Buddhadhamma, even though only by the concepts, without experiencing it through realization!

"How valuable these karmic ties are! Because of the merits earned through these precious karmic ties of hearing your discourse today, I will be given, I believe, a next life of a more advanced level. Elder, due to the merits of the karmic ties of today, I will be born, in my next life, in a noble family as a man of outstanding quality. Upon reaching maturity, I will become a monk, and not long thereafter, I will attain enlightenment, oh, my heart is overwhelmed by emotion and rolling like waves!"

In a stately voice Sariputta said, "Therefore, an outstanding heavenly being, you go! And be born as a man of outstanding quality in a noble family! After that, you leave home and become a monk upon maturity, and not long thereafter, attain enlightenment and become an arhat! Afterwards, before you enter parinirvana, you will propagate the Buddhadhamma widely to numerous sentient beings. As one of the foremost disciples of the Buddha, I foresee your future life, and I give my blessing beforehand!"

Upon Sariputta's blessing to the future of Kammakammaya, over one thousand heavenly beings from the highest heaven to the lowest one, who had deep karmic ties with Kammakammaya in their past lives, stepped forward and said to Sariputta.

"Great master, in our past several hundred or several thousand lives we had good karmic ties with Kammakammaya, as a family, a friend, or a relative. We hope that, when Kammakammaya receives a life of a human, we will be born in the human world with him, assist him, and upon his attaining arhatship, attain certain level of enlightenment fit for each one's perseverance and effort."

The Marshall of the Dhamma blessed them in a noble voice, "All heavenly beings, you go! Go and be born in the human world as sentient beings having karmic ties with future Kammakammaya! Then, assist Kammakammaya and upon Kammakammaya attaining the arhatship, and attain a certain level of enlightenment commensurate with each one's perseverance and effort. As one of the foremost disciples of the Buddha, I look into your future lives and give my blessing beforehand!"

As Sariputta encouraged and blessed Kammakammaya and the over one thousand heavenly beings, various signs appeared, such as, the heavenly clothes they were wearing got messy and the mind enjoying the heavenly world they were abiding in disappeared, etc. The next moment, Kammakammaya and the one thousand other heavenly beings suddenly vanished on the spot.

CHAPTER 25
Ayutha, Singing of Love

As Kammakammaya and one thousand heavenly beings disappeared, other heavenly kings and beings envied their future lives, or lamented on their leaving the heavenly world and being born in the human world full of afflictions, or worried about whether they themselves will be able to have good karmic ties with the Buddhadhamma in their future lives and attain enlightenment, or considered themselves as fortunate to still remain in the heavenly world.

As the remaining heavenly kings and beings showed signs of agitation, Sariputta raised his hands quietly, showing his palms. Then the eyes of the heavenly kings and beings that had been scattered here and there were attracted to Sariputta again and thus their minds were soon stabilized.

Sariputta turned his head toward Bhikkhuni Uppalavanna and said, "Sister, a while ago Heavenly King Kammakammaya asked me where a sage who has attained arhatship will go after his parinirvana."

"Yes he did."

"And I know that there is one who will achieve great parinirvana in front of us."

"That's right, elder." Having said this, Uppalavanna looked back at Ayutha, a heavenly being from the Heaven of Pure Abode.

In response, Ayutha looked at Uppalavanna and said, "My master, who has taught and guided me to the stage of a non-returner! As Sariputta mentioned, I would like to enter parinirvana here today. So master, please guide me to the stage of an arhat so that I can enter parinirvana. As soon as I attain arhatship, I will enter parinirvana."

"However, my lovely disciple, there is still a piece of mind that you have to let go of before entering parinirvana."

"I think I know what you are talking about. I will take your words as meaning that I shall release all the attachment to love lingering in my mind."

"That is right. Only after you have released the attachment for love remaining in you, howsoever slight it might be, you will be able to attain the arhatship and enter parinirvana. The reason is that, Ayutha, at the stage of an arhat, even love that overcomes hatred is no more than a subtle working of a craving that makes a sentient being a sentient being. So, here and now, you have to release all attachment related to love in your past lives."

"Oh, master! How cruel it is to sentient beings that love is merely the working of a craving! However, how sublime the Buddhadhamma is when we consider the fact that it will be complete only when such cruelty is transcended!"

Having said this, Ayutha quietly closed her eyes. As she has already reached the stage of a non-returner, she soon recovered a calm state of mind, and said, "That is right. Without transcending love, arhatship cannot be attained, so to arhat love is just a remote affair of sentient beings. In other words, master, for Bhaddiya who has already attained arhatship, the love he had for me in the past is like clouds sailing across the sky. No, it is like the reflection on the water of the clouds flying by in the sky.

"However, on the other hand, although he has long left the secular love, a love of an arhat sage, that is, a love without attachment to the objects, not a private love for a particular person, but a universal love toward sentient beings, must be springing from his heart. Such love is a love but it's not a love, and it is not a love but it is a love, that is, loving-kindness and compassion.

"Then what is the nature of the love in my heart? It is also a love but it is not a love, and it is not a love but it is a love. However, master, my love is not wholly identical with such love, because, being a non-returner who has yet to attain the last stage of enlightenment, I have transcended love but still have an extremely small fraction of mind that regards the love as beautiful and thus is attached to it.

"Looking back, master, there were times when I regarded the love as another form of art, philosophy or religion. In my two previous lives, I had a mind wishing, through love, to lead me to a faraway place, and thus to have my mind lapse into an obscure and far-off state, that is, a state where I lose the sense of self. Oh, master, at that time I used to sing like this."

Having said up to here, Ayutha stopped talking. From somewhere, music began to flow out. The music without musician softly filled the entire cave. At last, with the music as an accompaniment, Ayutha began to sing in a voice that shines like dew-washed grass leaves, which is pure and clear as if coming from a distant star.

> When I am compressed endlessly,
> When life presses down on my shoulders
> With limitless weight,
>
> When I am deaf from foolishness,
> When I am blind with recklessness,
> When I sob alone in the back alleys of life,
>
> Love,
> Because it is love,
> As a love,

Lends attentive ears,
To the warm, gentle winds of early spring
Running under the ice of heavy silence,
To its silent music.

Yes,
Love,
Because it is humanity,
As humanity,

With my eyes closed I see,
The pain of life, more brilliant than fireworks,
The sorrow of life, more dazzling than joy . . .

Ayutha's refined and graceful sound of song—which was soft sometimes, loaded with power some other times, and still some other times flowed out in between the silence when the beats and tunes halted—resonated to every nook and corner of the cave, from the water drops at the ceiling, to each and every tiny sand grains on the floor, and to the deepest and the most delicate part of the minds of all people in the cave.

Thus, the sages who have attained low level of enlightenment and all sentient beings in the cave who have not attained enlightenment were deeply touched by the song. It was an emotion like a dream, a haze, and a phantasm that spread little by little, spread and then shrank back, and gave the feeling that one was being melted into it.

The song ended. However, no human or no heavenly being in the cave praised Ayutha's song even though they were greatly impressed. It was because, as they were gripped by such a big emotion, they could not let out any words of praise out of mouth.

A silence fell for a while. At last Uppalavanna opened her mouth and said, "Ayutha, a deva from the Heaven of Pure Abode, you have deeply impressed many people here with an extremely beautiful song."

Upon Uppalavanna's such remarks, all sentient beings, awoken from the deep emotion, clapped thunderously and shouted, "Excellent! Excellent! Excellent!"

"Ayutha, a deva from the Heaven of Pure Abode," said Uppalavanna, "I know that a touched mind is joyful on the one hand and sad on the other. And I know as well that people who remain in the realm of sentient beings are most strongly touched when they are lost in love.

"So, being a woman who has experienced extreme and desperate loves in the last and before the last lives, you please give a discourse, with your deep insight, to the sentient beings assembled here on love, on how love touches the heart of people, and on why sadness is included in the heart of people who was so touched. Your discourse will certainly give those in the realm of sentient beings a great assistance, and this is the reason why I think that you better give them a discourse on love."

Ayutha, a deva from the Heaven of Pure Abode, who was so instructed by her master, answered, "As you just mentioned, I fell in extreme and desperate loves in my last and before the last lives. Based on such experience, and following your instruction, I will talk about my thought on love."

Upon saying this, an indescribable sensation of remorse flashed momentarily across Ayutha's face. However, as it was so short and faint, only sages who have attained enlightenment could notice it, while other sentient beings couldn't. In their eyes, Ayutha was reflected only as a noble sage who has left all emotions of a sentient being, including remorse.

"Heavenly kings and heavenly beings!" said Ayutha in a voice as soft as a light shining indirectly. "A while ago, Elder Bhaddiya said that art could be a good guide leading sentient beings to the truth of non-self. And Bhikkhu Malukha spoke of philosophy, and Elder Sariputta spoke of religion as a good guide leading sentient beings to the truth of non-self. But I would like to tell that, in addition to them, love too can be a good guide leading sentient beings to the truth of non-self. It is because love as well, like art, philosophy, and religion, can lead the mind to the state of self-effacement and self-oblivion.

"However, in that love at its lower level gives unusual joy while at its higher level touches the mind and leads it to the state of self-effacement and self-oblivion, love is more like an art than philosophy or religion. Meanwhile, love has connections with religion in that it sacrifices oneself and supports others. However, in that love and art are emotional, while philosophy is pursued with reason, we have to say that the two have different 'territories.'

"Heavenly kings and beings, sentient beings want to love and want to be loved. Love, like vines, strongly binds sentient beings themselves as well as the objects they love. Then, oh, flowers bloom on these vines. Love, like vines, makes sentient beings attached to their lovers, but on the other hand makes themselves blossom, beautiful and fragrant, therefore it is an emotion with two sides. Then, why do sentient beings want to love and want to be loved? It is because all living beings are particulars.

"That a living being is a particular means a situation where he must continuously seek after something, in other words he has desire. Therefore, to fill the empty cup called desire sentient beings go out to the society called a well. Then, with what does a sentient being satisfy his desire? It is through the ability that he possesses. At first, he, with his ability, fetches water from the well and fills the cup. But once the cup is filled, the cup will soon grow bigger.

"Then he again goes out to the well to fetch water. However, his cup, which has been filled with every effort will soon grow bigger again. Thereafter, the phenomenon that the cup grows bigger once it is filled with water, and that the cup grows even bigger once it is again filled with water, in other words, the phenomenon that he returns back to the original unsatisfactory state will be repeated. In the meantime, the sentient being becomes tired. He gets tired from the life in which even though he runs hard he always returns to the original place, like a squirrel turning a treadmill.

"Oh, heavenly kings and heavenly beings, as a result, the efforts of a sentient being to satisfy the desire will return back to frustration and failure, sighs and lamentation, pains and tears, namely, the sufferings referred to by the Four Noble Truths. Oh, frustration, failure! This situation of frustration, failure, sighs, lamentation, pains, tears, etc. makes a sentient being stand at a two-way fork of a road. At that time, the sentient being will encounter two paths, one to resolve his frustration to tears with a rightful method, and the other one to resolve them with an unlawful method against his conscience, such as illegality and circumvention of the law.

"At that time, will there be any sentient being who will handle the problem with only rightful methods? It is difficult to imagine. Oh, what a clean life it would be if it is lived without hurting his conscience at any time, place and in any events. What a cool life it would be if, looking back at oneself, there is nothing to be ashamed of, if there is nothing inside to conceal from others, and if there is no secret at all both inside and outside. How refreshing, wonderful and beautiful life it would be!

"However, sentient beings cannot live such lives. In other words, that a living being is called a sentient being means that he has shameful thoughts inside and commits shameful acts outside. This state of affairs, that sometimes a sentient being cannot but commit some actions against his conscience, means that an additional burden is put on the existing burden of filling up the cup that he has already been carrying.

"As a result, the despair and tears of 'I' who have to carry an additional burden upon the existing burden are growing bigger and deeper. Holding the heaviness and desperateness of the bigger and deeper burden in the chest, I return to the well where I associate with others, or leave the square and come to a space where I have to deal with only myself, that is, a box room.

"And in that box room, I look at my real self that has committed shameful acts against conscience, and that hid from others wearing a mask when I was in the square. I scold myself, *You should not have done that! and then I swear, I will never do that again!*

"However! Not long thereafter, I again go to the well or square and commit shameful acts. And again I return to my box room and scold myself. I swear again, as I did before, that I will never do that again. But once again, the reprimand and swear go down the drain. And, I begin to think that I am really worthless. It means that my mind is broken, sinks down, and becomes servile.

"And, as time passes, pains arising from the dispiritedness, despair, and servility build up in my mind. And the pains will change into a sense of isolation. Because it is only the self, not anyone else, that has to cope with the pains. Oh, my feeling of loneliness is like a gust of sandstorm blowing harshly over a barren clay field that has not a single clump of grass. And the loneliness is like a wild goose fallen from the flock flying alone in the sky.

"I, in order to relieve the feeling of loneliness, come out from the box room, a space of my own. Then where do I head for from the box room? That's right. I go again to the place where people have gathered, that is, the square. It is because, as the loneliness is the feeling of being alone, it is thought to be resolved by mixing with others.

"I search among as many people as sand grains, the one who would understand my loneliness, who would fill my empty and desolate mind, who would listen to my despair, failure, sighs, lamentation, pains, and tears, who would understand me, and who would share my thought, in other words, who will love me.

"But such person would not appear so easily. It is because the people in the square have the same empty and lonely mind as I do. To understand others, to fill the empty and lonely mind of others, to sympathize with the despair, failure, sighs, lamentation, pains, and tears of others, are not something anyone can do. It can be carried out only by the broad-minded, but such person is uncommon. However, fortunately, love is still possible between narrow-minded people. No, we may rather say that as they are poor in spirit, love is necessary, love is possible, and love becomes more desperate.

"That's right. Love is an emotion of consideration that arises when the mind is generous, but on the other hand it's an emotion of demand that arises when the mind is poor. The former is a love that people want to give and the latter is a love that people want to receive. The mind of sentient beings frequently crosses over between the generous and poor states. Accordingly, the love of a sentient being too comes and goes between giving and receiving."

"Oh . . ." reacted the heavenly kings and beings.

"And at last, to me who has a poor mind that craves for love, someone appears to give love. Finally a man who understands and sympathizes with my frustration or tears has appeared before me. He holds my hands, embraces me in his arms, comforts me with all sorts of language, and sheds hot tears for me. Oh, such a joy!

"In the joy, I forget my despair, failure, sighs, lamentation, pains, and tears, etc. Further, I forget too that I am a particular. I absorb myself in him (her), and the absorption leads me to the state of self-oblivion. Then, my mind reaches before the gate of the heaven, as a human that I am now, and praises the life in a clear and high tone like a lark's."

Having said this, Ayutha, a deva from the Heaven of Pure Abode, recited a verse:

> When, in disgrace with fortune and men's eyes,
> I all alone beweep my outcast state,
> And trouble deaf heaven with my bootless cries,
> And look upon myself, and curse my fate,
> Wishing me like to one more rich in hope,
> Featured like him, like him with friends possessed,
> Desiring this man's art and that man's scope,
> With what I most enjoy contented least;
> Yet in these thoughts myself almost despising,
> Haply I think on thee, and then my state,
> Like to the lark at break of day arising
> From sullen earth, sings hymns at heaven's gate;
> For thy sweet love remembered such wealth brings
> That then I scorn to change my state with kings."[50]

---

50 Revised from William Shakespeare's "Sonnet No. 29."

Having recited the verse, Ayutha, after a pause, continued her talk:

"Like this, we feel the highest joy in love, comparable to the emperor. However, in the highest joy is nested a delicate sadness. Of course, some people feel only joy in love. However, some other people, who desperately love their lovers with everything at stake, feel delicate sorrow in their love.

"However, he also felt joy at the beginning. But in the process of love getting deeper, he sees that the joy changes into delight and the delight into a state of being deeply touched. If he reaches the state of being deeply touched, it means that he has arrived at sadness, it is because the state of being deeply touched is a feeling of happiness but at the same time a feeling of sadness. Then, why the joy that has risen to its height turns into sadness? It is because of the impermanent nature of things.

"The fact that everything changes, we know it unconsciously, and when love reaches its height we perceive the fact unwittingly. At that time we feel instinctively that love is not eternal, and the feeling that this love too is not permanent, that it will crumble down at some time even though we hope to hold it forever, will change the joy filled up in our mind into sorrow.

"Of course, love is not the only source through which we feel such 'joyful sadness.' When we see or hear something extremely beautiful, for example when we see an extremely beautiful evening glow or hear extremely beautiful music, we feel a sensation imbued with a deep-felt sadness. Our intellect at its deepest sees the impermanence, and our emotion at its deepest feels the sorrow.

> That everything changes and I am part of everything!
> That I am a finite existence, and will finally return to
> nothingness!
>
> But that I do not want to return to nothingness!
> That this beautiful scenery will not last even if I
> want it permanent!

That this touching music will not last even if I
want it eternal!
That this joy of love will not last even if I
want it everlasting!

"Encountered by this situation we hope to hold on to the transient
beauty, at least for some moments, as long as we are not one of the
advanced practitioners who accept ephemeral things as they are with
insight. More and more we cling to love. That which they are fading
away makes us feel sad, and this sadness makes us fall deeper and
deeper into the beautiful scenery, music, and love."

"Oh!"

"However, the scene disappears, the music ends, and the love
breaks up. Thus, my lover, who has been the most precious in the
world, changes into an ordinary man. No, it is rather fortunate if the
matter ends there. In certain cases, he will even become an enemy
of mine. There may be someone who wants to refute my words. He
may say, 'In this word there is a love that never breaks.'

"That's right. There is such a love. And such love not broken till
the end is beautiful. However, even for that kind of love, there is an
unavoidable arch enemy. Far in the distance, one with black face
who breaks up any and all loves, the death, is waiting for the lovers."

"Oh!"

She continued, "Then why do I point out the limit of love, which,
regardless of the limit, all sentient beings long for? It is because I
have such an experience. That's right. I have such an experience. I
loved two men, and the two loves were all broken.

"So I learned through the frustration of love. That to me, and to
all living beings, a higher love transcending the personal level is
needed. And such love was in the Buddhadhamma that the Buddha
realized and taught."

CHAPTER 26

In Her Previous Life, Asatha (Ayutha) Was with Jatu (Bhaddiya)

S tory of Ayutha's life before the previous.[51]

"In my life before the previous one, I was born as the only daughter of a poor widower and given the name Asatha in a country called Salaha, the most southern region of the continent.

"Since my mother died soon after giving birth, my father raised me all on my own. We lived off the wage he earned doing manual labor, but one day he injured his leg and ended up bed ridden when I was seven years old. Soon, poverty led us nearly to starvation. Thus, after about three days, I made up my mind to go out and beg for food around my neighborhood, not only for myself but also for my poor father who was bed ridden.

---

51 The following narratives of Asatha, Jatu, and Dhammadinna have been created by the author based on the *Samguk Sagi (The Chronicle of Korea's Three Kingdoms)*. The author assembled many ideas and episodes, including the stories of the woman named Seol, Ondal (the wife of Domi), and Geomgun.

My village consisted of twenty-two families, excluding my own. I began with a house closest to mine and went around many different houses, but ended up without any food.

"My body shook with great shame from the depth of my heart, as it was bad enough for me to become a beggar, but it was worse I could not get any food. *Aren't I better off dead than to live like this? Should I just kill myself?* these thoughts surged out of me suddenly. But I gathered my strength with the thought of my father's sunken eyes from starvation.

"I dragged myself down the street until I finally reached the last house in the village. With the thought that I'd rather die in this house if I don't get any food here as well, I pushed myself on and entered its courtyard. But the next moment my mind just went blank and I collapsed in the middle of the yard. Who knows how much time had passed. I woke up with the sparkling sunlight flashing down my eyes. I looked around and realized that I was lying under a plumeria tree. I tossed and turned with an attempt to sit up. But my body did not heed to my orders. At that moment, I heard the soothing voice of someone who comforted my body gently.

"'Asatha . . . just . . . lie still . . .'

"I knew immediately who that was. The owner of that voice was Jatu, the only son in the house. Jatu belonged to one of the richest families in our village. He was twelve years older than me, almost a full grown man of nineteen.

"The problem was his physical appearance. Almost twice the size of an average man, his eyes bulged out like a frog and his mouth was as stumpy as a hippo. Not only that, Jatu was considered to be a half-witted fool. For that reason, he was often referred to by many as 'Jatu the fool,' despite of having a proper name.

"Everyone, whether a child or an adult, teased him when he passed by. 'Jatu the fool, Jatu the fool,' they would holler. But he simply grinned in response. Never succumbing to rage and always filled with smile in all situations, Jatu was such a person.

"With such an ugly appearance and dim intelligence, Jatu was not able to marry even when he had turned nineteen. Even his family had given up all hope for him to marry, and Jatu himself knew that he could not possibly ask for a hand of marriage by someone's precious daughter. Despite it all, there was one thing he excelled in. He possessed great strength that could fight off four or five adult males. With such energy and force, he always took home a winning from the annual wrestling match.

"At the young age of sixteen, he took home a goat as a winning from the village wrestling game, and when he was only fourteen, he won a milking cow from a township match. From then on, he went out and won countless number of wrestling competitions.

"Jatu's parents saved all the wages their son had earned by working for others as well as the money received in exchange for the prizes from wrestling matches. Therefore, even after he had turned nineteen and was still being called 'Jatu the fool,' he saved enough money to be called 'Jatu the rich.'

"In fact, I owed him a favor a year before I saw him under that plumeria tree. It was a year of great draught in the entire nation. Although my father and I seem to have managed without much problem, before long we also found ourselves without any food.

"Two days had passed without a single grain to eat. Then a girl next door came to see me. She was three years older, and just like me she didn't eat anything for a few days. She asked me to join her in climbing the mountain in search of food. 'At least we might find wild berries,' she said.

"Due to fear of being scolded to expose ourselves to danger, we went up to the mountain without telling the adults. It was not an easy task to search for food in those treacherous mountains, especially for the young girls like us. Our bodies were covered in scratches and scabs in wandering the valley.

"Finding food could have brought great relief even in such hardship, but we only managed to pick a few tiny berries for the entire day. We had to admit our failure and finally decided to descend the mountain.

"But my steps seemed to hover in air without much strength to go on and hallucinating yellow mirages floated before my eyes. After sitting repeatedly to rest and rising again to walk, I could hear ringing in my ears. Then, I just collapsed right there and then.

"I heard later that the girl I was with tried everything to wake me up. But it wasn't so easy to bring me around. Deep in the woods with her friend collapsed on the ground, I bet it wasn't easy for a nine-year-old girl to manage. As there was no one to help her in the woods, she was overcome with fear. Then the next moment the girl next door also collapsed beside me.

"Soon, I regained consciousness with the feeling of my body being shaken. Then I remembered the state I was in before I fainted. Unlike before, however, I could feel warmth wrapping around my body, with the clear blue sky open widely in front of my eyes.

"Some cotton-candy clouds floated away quietly in a distance. But I felt these clouds being shaken in regular intervals. And beside the peacefully floating clouds, quite contrary to those clear white clouds, I saw a man's face, ugly enough to be referred to as stump of an old tree.

"That's right. I was coming down the hill held within Jatu's two arms. While surveying the situation, I also realized that the girl next door was piggy-backed on Jatu. Apparently, Jatu came up the mountain that day to check on his animal trap. While he was on his way up the mountain, he discovered us. He threw the basket to the side and took off his inner and outer layers of clothing to wrap around our bodies. Then, he massaged our body to bring back warmth.

"Soon, the other girl woke up. But it was not easy to bring me around. Jatu then began to climb down the mountain with one girl on his back and holding me in his arms. This is how our lives had been spared. After this incident, I obviously saw Jatu in a different light. I felt rage when village kids teased or insulted Jatu, someone much older than they were. I would scold at them, 'Don't you dare make fun of nice Jatu!'

"Then the kids would respond, 'What are you? His new bride?'

"They would snicker, giggle amongst themselves, then point their fingers and tease me, 'Jatu's bride, Jatu's bride!'

"Then, my face would burn up and blush bright red. I was only six years old, too young to even imagine getting married and becoming a bride. All flustered, I heard the kids teasing me in one voice: 'Asatha is Jatu's bride! Asatha is the bride of Jatu the fool!'

"Right then, under the plumeria tree at Jatu's house I heard the voice of Jatu, 'Asatha . . . Just . . . Lie still . . .'

"But since I was yet to fully regain my consciousness, his voice felt like some far off dreams. Then I heard Jatu say again, 'You alright? Are you really okay?'

"I regained my awareness while hearing his voice almost unconscious. Although still lying down, Jatu's face appeared clearly in front of my face. Almost three times the size of my own face, eyes like a frog and mouth like a hippo, the one who I owed my life, the very face appeared in front of my eyes once again that I had seen amidst the clear blue sky with floating white clouds before.

"I was startled. But while being startled, I was not really surprised at all. Looking back, I was such a daring, perky girl. I had much affection in me, but at the same time, I was able to turn as cold as ice and respond calm and collected. I was that kind of girl.

"Although I didn't have much strength left, I smiled while looking up at Jatu. Jatu's expression turned numb for a moment. But soon his surprise transformed into a great smile the next moment. Oh, what beauty! Even after being reborn twice, I still remember that beautiful, big smile that appeared across Jatu's face, resembling a bright full moon.

"Jatu placed his hand on my forehead. His hands, which never rested even a single day of his life, were covered in calluses, tough as a tree bark and hard as a rock, but I could feel warmth of his heart through his hand, with deepest affection toward me. I reached out and held his hand. Actually, there was no way for my tiny little hand to hold on to his hand, which was giant as a cauldron's lid, so I barely held on to one of his forefingers.

"Surprised, Jatu looked down toward me still lying down. Yet another expression appeared across his face! What a smile it was! As gentle as a babe but as holy as great sage, as clear as spring water yet as wide as great sea!

"But then, I saw his eyes get all cloudy. And those clouds spread into damp mist, which turned into little dews on his eyes. Then tears appeared—the painful fate and the worldly people that made him into a forsaken man, the kind of tears that only appears in most extreme cases and the type of tears if unshed could make anyone go mad.

"Jatu pulled off his hands from mine and wiped off his tears with the back of his hand. At that moment, while he was trying to wipe off his tears, a tiny tear drop fell on the pupil of my eye. Thus, his tears were tangled up with my own, which had already welled up in my eyes. Just as he did, I also wiped off my tears with the back of my hand. At that moment, filled with great emotion, I heard my heart speak.

"Here is a human! And here I am!

"Soon, I moved onto the wooden floor and ate porridge Jatu brought out. While I had porridge, Jatu watched me with gentle admiration, as if he was happy to just see me, as if he was in heaven.

"When I was done with the porridge, Jatu went off to a storage where grains were stored and returned with grains filled in a large gourd dipper. I showed gratitude with my palms together and after accepting his offer, returned home.

"While all these incidences played out, Jatu didn't say a word and neither did I. Instead, I made a firm resolve, not externally but from the depth of my heart without words.

"I am going to be his bride when I grow up! I thought.

"Then, in the midst of such great poverty—with nothing in my hands and nothing left in my heart, my love began under a plumeria tree. With the sparkling sun shining down this plumeria tree, with creamy yellow flower petals showering down softly, my love began to blossom. And then, under that same tree, love also began to grow in a man who was forsaken by fate and the world."

CHAPTER 27
Jatu the General

'Five years had passed and I turned twelve while Jatu turned twenty-four. That year, a neighboring country invaded our state, and an exigent countermeasure had been declared to protect us from over 100,000 enemy forces.

"According to the plan, every household was required to send one man, between the ages of sixteen and fifty, to the battlefield—or they must supply twenty rolls of cloth, thirty sheets of animal hides, or five hundred rupees to support the war. However, practically no house in our village could afford such things. Thus, every household had to choose one man—for some it was their older fathers and for others it was their young sons—to be dragged off to be enlisted.

"Sounds of wailing gusted off of every home. Not only were there no guarantees for these men to return home safely, but people left behind were reduced to live off grass roots once these men left their homes. The grief and sorrow did not steer clear of my home. My father, who had turned forty-seven that year, was also marked to be enlisted.

"The day before the drafting date approached, my father and I went to the conscription officer and explained in every possible way about the unfortunate circumstance our family faced of being deathly poor. But that was all to no avail.

"'Who doesn't have a sad story to tell?' retorted the officer. 'Be here early tomorrow morning!'

"My father returned home and started packing. He kept his mouth firmly shut without speaking a word. I also watched him quietly with my tiny little mouth sealed firmly. Having turned twelve and having grown up too fast, knowing life's pain and agony at a young age, I knew fully well that it was all too painful for my father, and that there was no other way but to endure this circumstances silently.

"I assisted him with all his needs. I went to town with my father to purchase clothes, shoes, and a bit of meat jerky in case of emergency. These items were practically impossible to find, therefore their calling price rose to nearly five times the usual. But I purchased them all without hesitation.

"That evening, I prepared his meal with utmost sincerity and my father ate the food I made in silence. Then he smiled while looking at me and said, 'Now, little princess you must eat too.'

"'Yes, I will,' I said. But I did not take any food. I saved it so my father could have something to eat tomorrow at dawn. I put aside the leftovers in a cool shaft, burrowed under the floor of our kitchen for a time like this. Then, I came out of the kitchen. Suddenly, I saw someone stood tall in front of my eyes. It was Jatu.

"'I . . . I started.

"He began . . . 'I paid thirty sheets of fox hide for your father. So he doesn't have to be enlisted anymore.'

"With a lack of expression, Jatu said it in a vague voice as if that meant nothing special. Perhaps that was why it sounded quite natural to me. But in the next moment, when my heart realized little too late what he really meant, I was enthralled and deeply moved by his sincerity. I turned my head quickly, trying desperately to prevent him from seeing me blush with deep emotion. I quickly went inside the room, while he followed without words. The three of us sat quietly facing each other, in a dark room that was too poor to be lit.

"At that time, Jatu had lost both his parents and was living alone, having lost all the money he had when he was still called 'Jatu the rich.' After his parents died, one of his relatives deceived Jatu, who lacked intelligence, taking all his savings.

"That day, when he realized all his possessions were gone, Jatu sat all day in his room. Then the next day, he came out of his room as if nothing had happened and began to work and save money.

"The money he saved was nearly enough to buy thirty fox hides, just enough to keep himself from being enlisted. But in fact, he wanted to join the army at this opportunity. The only thing that distinguished him from others was his strength, and he thought this could be used to his advantage.

"Then what would I do with my money? he thought. In that moment, the thought of my father came across his mind. He went straight to the market and bought thirty fox hides, then asked the officer to waive my father's enlistment.

"That night, Jatu explained all this to us in slurred and awkward speech.

"'Young man!' My father cried out. 'You really saved this old man's life! You realize that you saved this old man and also my precious Asatha!'

"'Well then . . .' Jatu said, while trying to get up. But my father sat him down and said,

"'I wouldn't let you go that easy.'

"'Come on now! Say what's on your mind? What do you want from me instead?'

"But Jatu did not respond.

"'Are you perhaps . . .' My father continued, 'Do you by any chance have my daughter in mind? Are you going to come back from the war and ask for my Asatha's hand in marriage . . . Is that what you are thinking?'

"Jatu remained silent even when these questions were raised.

"After a moment of silence my father said, 'I am not that naive and I know what you must be thinking. But what's important in a marriage is the will of the persons involved.'

"Then my father turned around and looked at me.

"I replied without a moment of hesitation, 'Even if we search the end of the world, there is no one better than Jatu!'"

'Do you mean to say you wish to wed Jatu?'

"I nodded with my face flushed bright red.

"After Jatu enlisted, our army was defeated in the first battle. Everyone in the country was in a panic. We could be destined to become slaves to our enemies—my father and I went to the Shiva[52] temple just like the rest of the villagers, and joined the seven day prayer, which pleaded for our soldiers to bring home victory.

"Perhaps due to our efforts, our troops won the next battle and all the following battles thereafter. We were then able to drive the enemies out of our territory within the next six months.

"The cheers of joy echoed through the village. I was also very excited. Soon, Jatu would return and we would be engaged. Joy, happiness, and delight—my days were filled with these. Getting married at such ripe age, I will be able to live with Jatu for the rest of my life and take care of my father who had gone through hardship all his life.

"That day finally came. At last, Jatu returned home in glory, and from then on my life had been enchanted with blissful light of joy and happiness. When he returned from the war, he was not the same man he used to be. Distinguishing himself in nine different small and large battles, Jatu was promoted to be a raider general that led one thousand solders. And his eyes, often teased in the past for being a fool, now contained great dignity and self-esteem.

"He sold all his property when he returned home. Then he took me and my father on a carriage to the capital. An impeccable home waited for us upon arrival, and a prize was given to Jatu for defending our country.

"Since then, Jatu faithfully carried out his responsibilities as a soldier. He also worked hard to develop his intelligence and provided

---

52 Shiva, worshiped as a god of creation and destruction by modern Indians. Shiva was also seen as a god of wealth, happiness, and auspiciousness in ancient India.

me with good teachers. His efforts were always great, never lacking; his intelligence improved noticeably day by day, and my studies also evolved as well.

CHAPTER 28
Along with Asatha, Dhammadinna . . .

The years went on and the couple married in the year Jatu turned twenty-eight and Asatha turned sixteen. Asatha's father had already passed away by then. Some high-ranking officials from the royal court, along with commanding officers and Asatha's newfound friends, came to the wedding to congratulate them.

However, the couple remained virgins even after their first night. On the night of the wedding, Jatu and Asatha stayed up all night without words, simply snuggling up against each other in their embrace. For Jatu, it was unfathomable to possess Asatha's beautiful body, while for Asatha, Jatu was not simply a man but a great noble soul who reached the highest state of the truth.

Then five years flew by.

By this time, Asatha's unparalleled beauty was famed throughout the state. People often gossiped about the ugly Jatu winning the heart of beautiful Asatha and having her as his lawful wife. People were envious and jealous of the loving couple.

In that same year, Jatu was recognized for mollifying thousands of notorious bandits in the northern part of the border. He was thus promoted as a commander in charge of ten thousand soldiers. After a few days, an invitation was sent out to Jatu to enter the royal court as a couple, along with three other commanders and a chief commanding officer.

Jatu was teeming with excitement for a chance to enter the palace accompanied by his wife. He believed this to be the greatest honor of a lifetime, which he can present to his beloved. However, Asatha felt quite differently. She didn't feel at peace with the invitation. She knew fully well of the danger that lurked around a woman of beauty.

When her husband told her about the invitation, she had her doubts about the king's true intentions. Having heard of many bad rumors about inappropriate conducts of the king, Asatha suspected that the king had his eyes on her. She asked Jatu whether they could decline the invitation or whether Jatu could go alone without her. But Asatha already knew that would never be.

Thus, the only option left for her was to make herself look as shabby as possible, in order for the king not to take any notice of her beauty. But despite of her efforts to dress up in shambles, the king became infatuated with her the moment he laid his eyes on her. Of course, Jatu was too naïve to take notice, but on their first meeting, Asatha knew what the king had in store for her.

Every time the king cast a covert glance at her at the banquet, Asatha stared boldly and daringly back at him. Without neglecting to be courteous as a spouse of the king's subject, she firmly rejected his unspoken advances with her firm, imposing eyes.

Unfortunately, her actions only instigated the king's fervent lust for her. The king had never seen a woman so bold and valiant in his presence. Asatha's unwavering valor, combined with her striking beauty, fascinated him, which prompted him to want to possess her.

After the couple went home, the king thought deeply of a scheme to make Asatha his own. One of the king's closest eunuch, who perceived the king's intent, came up to him. Having had the chance to wait on the king for the past twenty years, the eunuch could easily recognize the king's every intent. Thus, the eunuch bid the king to wait a few days until he could come up with a plan.

In the meantime, Asatha returned home with overwhelming fear, nearly ten times worse than before she met the king. With numerous near-death experiences she had encountered since as child, Asatha rarely felt any fear. But Asatha was now afraid, mainly because of Jatu. She understood well that the problem she faced wouldn't end just with her being sacrificed. She knew too well that her husband was also at stake.

That night, concerned over being violated by the king when the situation worsened, Asatha made advances toward her husband, who was at times as naïve as a child.

"Oh my love, it's the moment for you to ravish me, and take every fiber of my body! That is all I desire, I will be forever yours and you'd be mine!"

Despite of it all, the same as ever, Jatu refused to take his wife that night. Feeling contented, Jatu simply embraced Asatha in his valiant arms, while Asatha bored deeper into his embrace. A few days later, as recommended by a treacherous eunuch and as discussed by the council, Jatu was appointed as a commander of Urui, the most southern coast of the continent approximately five days away by horse. But yet another order given with Jatu's promotion was of particular importance. The king made sure that Jatu was not to be accompanied by his family where he would be stationed.

The king provided various excuses, but his intention was clear and almost all eunuchs knew it. *Yet another woman will be disgraced,* they thought to themselves. This was not the first time the king took advantage of his subject's wives in a similar fashion. But to keep their own standing or to save their own lives, they had no choice but to endure what came to them. None of the subjects or their wives ever objected or protested these matters in public.

Three days later, Jatu left for his new post. And within a few days, the closest royal eunuch to the king came to visit Asatha. To be prepared for all eventualities, Asatha greeted him having wrapped her head with a white cloth.

The eunuch notified the king's visit that afternoon and told Asatha to dress up formally to greet the king with proper decorum. He gave excuses that the king would patrol her neighborhood and make a short visit to commander Jatu's home to make sure that everything was all right, but it's not as if Asatha had no clue of what the king had in mind.

Asatha therefore responded, "I'm a little under the weather today. With all due respect, would it be possible for the king to visit me tomorrow?"

The eunuch asked the maid waiting on Asatha, "Is what your mistress is saying really true?"

The maid responded politely, "Yes, that's right. Last night she was running high fever with horrible flu. Fortunately, she began to recover at dawn, but . . ."

The maid responded as Asatha had instructed her earlier on. The eunuch frowned, and then muttered softly, "Well, there is no other choice then . . ."

Eunuch then ordered a senior retainer that accompanied him, "Return back to the king and convey what you have just seen and heard. You could also make a report that I will spend a night here and welcome the great king here tomorrow."

"Yes, sir," said the retainer, and he left.

Then eunuch told Asatha, "As you have heard, I would like to spend a night at your place tonight. Would that be okay with you?"

"That wouldn't be possible, as the master of the house is not present at this time."

"You are right. But I need to stay overnight in my concern that you might go out. What I am trying to say is that I am just a king's humble servant, worried over whether your flu may worsen and you may not be ready to welcome the king, whether physically and mentally, when he arrives tomorrow."

Although it was pretty obvious what the eunuch had in mind, Asatha could not decline his request. "Well, if you insist," Asatha turned to face her servant in waiting. "Please escort him to our guest room."

"Yes, ma'am."

Thus, the eunuch followed the servant to the guest room, while Asatha took her maid to the master bedroom.

Once Asatha entered the master bedroom, she said to her maid Sachina, "This is an absolute disaster. Pay attention and listen to me carefully."

"Yes, ma'am."

"You will have to pretend to be me from this point on. Go on and lie here in my place." Asatha placed her own clothes on her servant Sachina and then laid her down in her own room. She then called yet another servant and explained what was happening and then told her, "You are going to decoct some medicinal herbs outside the room. If anyone comes asking for me, tell them I am on my sick bed. Both of you must deal with what's coming in this household, just as I told you before."

"But . . . then," started Sachina, "Ma'am . . . what are you planning to do?"

"I will go to be with my beloved," said Asatha.

"What do you mean?" questioned Sachina, wide-eyed.

Asatha then said, "I know, perhaps what I am about to do is impossible and it may all be futile or even aggravate the situation. But that doesn't matter. What's important is that I will go to be with my love. From the way the eunuch was behaving, it dawned on me the situation is quite more serious than I thought. I am quite certain my general is in grave danger as we speak. So I must leave here at once to be with him. Whatever the future brings I will leave it up to God Shiva, I know there is nothing more I can do."

"Oh, mistress! But what must we do now that we have no one else that we can depend on? It worries us greatly that by following your orders we may put ourselves in danger and we may need to beg the king for mercy to spare our lives."

"Try endure it up until tomorrow morning. Any time after that, you are free to tell the king that I escaped during the night to be with my general. You may say anything to save yourselves. You could blame or denounce me all you want or keep me in contempt. You may curse me and call me a demon or a tramp. Lastly, I saved up some rewards for you all. When all this is over, go and dig up under the mango tree in the back yard and you will find three gold nuggets the size of a fist. You may keep one nugget each, and give the last one to the servant Gurana."

"Yes, ma'am, we will follow your orders."

Upon giving these orders Asatha prepared to set off immediately. It didn't take much time since she had her bags ready in case something came up. She packed some food, clothes, and took five thousand rupees in her bag. Leaving her room behind, Asatha made sure the eunuch was asleep with the help of her servant Gurana, then she hopped the fence quietly with his help and straddled the horse in waiting at the darkest night of the hour. At first, the horse moved on silently, but it then sped up soon after. The next morning when the king arrived at Jatu's house, Asatha had escaped as far as thirty yojana away.

She could not afford any delays, as a tracker would clearly come chasing after her as ordered by the king. After a quick bite at an inn and feeding the horse, she took a short nap. Then, she rushed to Urui again where her husband stayed. But when she finally arrived at Urui after a diligent ride, Asatha realized that Jatu was nowhere to be found. With much enquiry, she discovered that her husband had been framed and punished by the king, just as she had imagined.

This certainly was not the first time the king estranged husbands from their wives and created false allegations to take their wives. But that was the extent of how far the king went, and no one had ever been sentenced to death before. That's because the king could see through the cowardice of those men and didn't feel the need to execute them.

But for the king, Jatu was quite different than any of these men. The king tried to visualize Jatu's reaction once he found out his wife had been raped. He then concluded that Jatu would take revenge in any means necessary.

The king discussed with his most favored eunuch on how best to deal with his dilemma. In response, the eunuch informed him that they must create a scheme to frame Jatu. He then reassured the king that he knew exactly how to deal with it, so the king needed not worry at all. The eunuch then fabricated a story that Jatu didn't return all the treasures that he confiscated from the bandits back to the state.

The king immediately raised these matters to the governing council. Two witnesses who received bribes from the eunuch came forward, fabricating different evidences and slandering deceptive accusations of Jatu. Then the king promptly sentenced Jatu to death.

The king's command was sent to Jatu through the newly appointed commander who was to take Jatu's place. Fortunately, Jatu did not have to face a grueling death. Jatu's life was spared by the officer who was to execute him. This officer by the name of Dhammadinna was widely known in the army for his noble character.

(The story of Dhammadinna)

A few years before Jatu arrived in Urui, there was a great famine that devastated the entire nation. The officers who could not stand to watch their family starve have gathered and discussed to pilfer the military provisions to distribute them among themselves. Dhammadinna, who was also present at the meeting, indicated that he would not take part in pilfering the food, but he neither objected nor favored their decision to take the food.

The officers then told him, "You are certainly aware that we are doing this as our last resort."

Then Dhammadinna responded, "I was educated for a long time on how a man must live and act. According to that, this doesn't seem right!"

On that day, Dhammadinna's response to the situation was extremely neutral but bold and audacious. He treated it as calmly as he did any other day when he attended the meeting and spoke his opinion decisively.

This troubled all the officers and they awkwardly pretended to give up the idea of pilfering the food. But that was simply under pretense and just a scheme to exclude Dhammadinna in order to keep the food only for themselves.

A few days later, they snatched away the food without Dhammadinna taking notice and then called for a meeting again. "We must get rid of that Dhammadinna. He will surely betray us to the higher up."

An officer who secretly overheard their discussion, came and told Dhammadinna of their decision. On the following day, Dhammadinna received a message from their colleagues to join them at midnight on the next day where the meeting last took place.

Dhammadinna of course knew why they were calling him up. But he acted neither surprised nor anxious. He went immediately to the teacher he had held in high esteem for a long time, and talked to him calmly.

He told the teacher, "I'm afraid we will not get a chance to see each other after today."

Taken by surprise, the teacher asked him why. Dhammadinna then described the incident that had taken place and said, "That's the reason why they are trying to kill me, and why I told you that I wouldn't be able to see you anymore."

The teacher, looking puzzled, asked, "Why wouldn't you report this to the top?"

"Well, perhaps I could save my own life, but they are sure to be punished, and I don't think I could possibly bring myself to do that."

"Well, fine. Let's leave it at that, but why wouldn't you at least try to save yourself?"

"The other side is crooked and this side is straight. Why should I hide myself when I am straight? That's not something a real man should do," said Dhammadinna.

Then on the following day in the middle of the night, Dhammad-inna headed toward the spot where the commanders were ready to take ambush. But Dhammadinna's steps were strong, dignified, and mature.

However, when he arrived on the spot where the commanders summoned him to, none of them could be found. One of the soldiers had blown the whistle for their dishonesty, and all those who pilfered the foods were arrested and sent away under escort.

When Dhammadinna was known for his morality and integrity, the state government wished to reward him, but he shook his head and said, "I only did what I was supposed to."

Since Dhammadinna was such a person, he could not possibly accept the respectable yet simple commander Jatu, with his naively resplendent character that was similar to himself, to fall under a ridiculous scheme and be punished.

Dhammadinna decided to rescue Jatu and requested the new commander, who took Jatu's place, for the permission to execute Jatu himself. With the permission given, Dhammadinna led Jatu to the sea.

Jatu did not say anything or resist his unexplained persecution. He knew too well that the blind god of fate sometimes struck arrows randomly to any directions he pleased. Thus, Jatu silently accepted his own fate and took on the arrows silently like a great rock that accepts torrential storm at the sea.

After reading through the king's order to Jatu, Dhammadinna commanded the soldiers to bring Jatu on the raft. Jatu was then tied to a pillar on the center of the raft. While the soldiers were pushing the raft away toward the sea, Dhammadinna alone got on board and pretended to check if Jatu was tied up well. Then, without his subordinates noticing, Dhammadinna cut off the rope with a sharp knife and whispered the fact into Jatu's ears.

Then, Dhammadinna said, "I entrust your life on fate, dear general."

Dhammadinna then came off the raft where Jatu was and commanded the soldiers to push the raft away into the sea.

Dhammadinna then shouted toward Jatu, "Somewhere beyond the sea . . ." he cried out. "Somewhere beyond the sea there may be a paradise! A paradise where happiness awaits for the noble, and great men never get punished!"

But Jatu remained in silence as before. In a few moments, the raft carrying Jatu floated away to the sea by the low tide. The soldiers, who had their legs dipped in water halfway up to their knees and stood there staring onto the raft, began to back away toward the shore. The soldiers shed their tears for Jatu, who had been a respected commander just a day before, but was now tied up on a raft and about to float around in the desolate sea, perhaps toward his ultimate death.

The raft that carried Jatu began to float away, carried by the waves. After staring briefly onto the sea, Dhammadinna eventually led his men back to the central quarters. However, he didn't report the final outcome to his commander. To make a report, he needed to offer Jatu's head as evidence, but Dhammadinna didn't have such evidence.

Moreover, there was bound to be a great problem if it became known that Jatu was left on a raft with his straps cut off. But Dhammadinna already made arrangements ahead of time. He left his unit and rode a horse toward the village, where Jatu was sent away to the sea. Dhammadinna then searched for the man named Sahuma when he arrived at the village. Dhammadinna had made prior arrangements for Sahuma to go and rescue Jatu when Dhammadinna and his men left the scene.

But Sahuma was nowhere to be found. Sahuma needed several men who could help him save Jatu. But this meant he had to share a thousand rupees he received from Dhammadinna, which he was reluctant to do. Thus, Sahuma took the money and ran.

Dhammadinna, as his last resort, bought a fishing boat with all the money he had. Then, he went back to the village to find anyone who was willing to help him, but no one was willing to stick their neck out for him. Without much choice, Dhammadinna went to the sea shore to rescue Jatu even if he had to do it alone.

When he arrived, there stood a beautiful woman staring out onto the ocean with her lips tightly closed. Dhammadinna immediately knew that was Jatu's wife.

They greeted each other and Dhammadinna briefly explained what happened thus far, in which Asatha thanked him in response. But more important than these formalities, they needed to get the boat afloat as soon as possible. They joined forces to sail the boat and hopped on board.

They searched the nearby coast all over, but they couldn't find Jatu's raft. Their search continued for several days. The weather kept changing unexpectedly. There were days when the wind began to blow swiftly and there were times when they were enveloped in thick veil of fog all day. As time went by, the two became exhausted.

On the fourth day of the search, they laid their weary bodies on the boat and closed their eyes. When they opened their eyes, however, the boat had already carried them afloat to the middle of the open sea. They had fallen asleep exhausted and didn't notice that the sun had gone down.

Unfortunately, there was no way for them to tell the direction because the sky was covered in clouds and no stars could be seen.

"Madam, there is nothing we can do right now," Dhammadinna told Asatha, "except to leave our future to the fate."

"Sure," said Asatha, "I am ready for whatever the future brings."

Asatha answered and tightening her lips in determination, thought to herself, *That's right. I will let the water carry me, just like it carried away my beloved. I will leave myself to fate. But at least the path I am about to face is not as lonely as it was for my beloved. Oh, look how loyal and faithful that man is who stands before me!*

A new day had dawned. Fortunately, the fog had cleared overnight. Leaving the continent behind, the two people decided to head toward Ceylon Island. It was obvious what the king would do when they returned. Thus, Dhammadinna lifted the sail toward the south.

Five days later, they finally reached Ceylon with a great hardship. A man found them lying on a beach, utterly exhausted. The villagers took them in and help them to restore their fatigued bodies. They listened to the story of how the two ended up there and practically no one could keep their tears from falling.

Moved by the ardent love and fortitude the two had displayed, the villagers provided a small dwelling where they could settle themselves down. As a token of her appreciation, Asatha then gave them four thousands out of her five thousand rupees she had brought with her.

CHAPTER 29
Along with Asatha (Ayutha), Dhammadinna (Binggisa) . . .

While residing at the house, the two continued to search for Jatu, wandering around the seaside villages in case Jatu he had drifted into Ceylon. For several days, Dhammadinna and Asatha looked for Jatu in different villages, but they found nothing. They trudged home dispirited.

But one day while searching, Asatha did not return until late at night. Feeling concerned, Dhammadinna went to the village where Asatha supposed to have visited for information. There, he heard a shocking news. They said Asatha had been abducted by the bandits when the village had been raided. There was no knowing in which part of the woods the bandits were hiding, and even if he knew, it was obvious that he could not fight them alone. He returned home and was absorbed in thought. In the end, he volunteered to join the army with the hope that it might help him discover Asatha's whereabouts or find Jatu.

Three years had passed since then. A massive rebellion occurred in Ceylon and the army to which Dhammadinna belonged took charge of the suppression of the rebellion. The commander of the state forces was Duvada, who was renowned as a clever, tactical general.

The rebel forces and the state forces fought the battle at a field in front of the Maguna Castle, where a stronghold of the rebel forces stood. The battle could not be decided easily. It was partly because the size of the rebel forces was as big as the state forces, and partly because the ringleader of the rebel forces commanded the army skillfully.

Duvada, who failed to win the first battle, was furious. His fury was a genuine one but at the same time a directed one. He knew that his fury encouraged his generals.

His generals were anxious and worried about the penalties to be imposed on them for having failed to win the first battle. But Duvada calmed down, soon after showing a bout of storming fury. The silence gave rise to even greater fear in his general. As they were well aware of Duvada's character in doing whatever without any hesitation for the sake of victory, the quietude felt more like a lull before the storm.

That night, Duvada invited his generals to a feast of encouragement. At the place, his four generals took a vow in one voice that they should completely destroy the rebel forces without fail or they would give up their positions.

"Generals!" Duvada jumped up from the chair and said, "I don't want to hear anything like that at all!" The commander's demeanor and his tone of voice was firm and strong. The blazing flame of anger in his eyes could swallow his generals at any time.

Duvada said, "You must be well aware of my burning desire for victory, yet these words are best you can do? What? Just a position? You're implying that the positions you all hold is of great importance! However, generals, if you fail to win the next battle, my reprimand to you will not cease at the level of removing you from your positions! I say, I cannot guarantee your lives!"

The generals waited, with a strained expression, for the next remarks of the commander who had the power to decide their life and death.

Duvada gave an order to the aide-de-camp standing next to him: "Bring them over before the soldiers."

Having said this, Duvada strode toward the area where the soldiers were assembled. The generals and staff followed him, and when they arrived there, the soldiers had been assembled around a big blazing bonfire.

A moment later, a burly man in old and shabby clothes and a well-dressed woman were dragged on a wagon in front. Duvada ordered the officer who brought them.

"Let the soldiers see the chap and the tramp properly."

The officer drove the carriage back and forth in front of the army. When the carriage came back, Duvada stepped onto a high platform set up for his speech.

"My dear soldiers! My love for you is like the love of a father for his children!"

The soldiers roared. They knew it was a courtesy to the commander.

Duvada began to speak eloquently: "Dear soldiers, the rebels are my enemies and your father's enemies. Therefore, the rebels are also enemies of yours, and we came here to defeat them. My sons! Stab them! Crush them! And kill them! Then what is next?

"Then we will enter their castle. Within their castle, there are five areas, the central area where the rebel ringleader's command is located, and the areas surrounding each of the four cardinal directions. Do not even touch the area of the ringleader's command. That is because I, your father, will take possession of that area. Then, what with the remaining four areas? Yes, they are all for you, my sons!"

"Wah! Wah!" The soldiers roared and waved their spears and swords wildly. Duvada raised his voice and continued his speech: "Soldiers! You can do anything in your own area. In other words, you are the king and the god in the area. That's right. You are the king and the god with great powers, and you can do anything, without reserve, with the rebels. What does this mean? It means I allow you all those chaps and tramps and everything they own. From the love of the father, I am giving all that away to my sons.

"First, I give you their lives. So you have the right to kill at your will those old and young men who were not recruited as soldiers. If you don't want to kill them, you can force them to submission, to your heart's content. Let them kneel in front of you and lick your feet! Let them beg for their lives! Make them your slaves! Also, I give you all the properties they have. So, soldiers, take all that they have. Take their houses! Take golds and silvers! Take their furniture! Be sure to take possession of all they have, as much as you like!

"Furthermore, oh, I give you the right to take all the women in the castle. My soldiers, all females, whether they are married, single, old or young, are all yours. Make them your wife or mistress! Your maid! Your plaything!"

After this, Duvada pointed at the man and woman who had been brought in front of him. "This guy is an agent of the rebels, who snuck in our area and was arrested by my loyal soldiers. And this woman was captured while cooperating with the rebel forces. These two were caught when they snuck in our area with disguise to steal information," he said, although it was untrue.

"Dear soldiers, look at this woman. Oh, how beautiful this woman is! How pretty her eyebrows are, how clear her eyes, and how straight and shapely her nose is! And behold, her slender hand and the feminine figure of this woman! And her lovely breasts! And I know. This woman smells like jasmine, especially around her breasts. Oh, soldiers, when I knew it, I had a strong erection and had an irresistible desire to own this woman. But I suppressed my desire! With all my strength!

"I didn't take this woman even though I could do it whenever I wanted. Instead, I bathed her with clean water and adorned her with the best cosmetics. Then I dressed her up in gorgeous clothes. Then, a refreshed desire to own this woman arose in me again. Then why? For what reason? Why didn't I take this woman?"

Duvada shouted in excitement and the soldiers became excited too. He suddenly lowered his voice. "Why did I not take this woman?"

Then, he suddenly raised his voice and spoke in a rapid and

forceful tone. "Yes, it is because of you! I did not take this woman to give her to you!"

"Wahhh! Wahhh! Wahhhh!" The roar of the soldiers shook the heaven and the earth.

Duvada then said, "Anyone can come out and take this woman! But the soldier who wants to take possession of this woman must first compete with the agent of the rebels."

As soon as the words were over, a soldier came forward. A duel between him and the rebel began. The two men faced each other with daggers.

The duel ended quickly with the victory going out to the man from the rebel army, who quickly found and took advantage of the other soldier's weak spot.

"I'm mortified, but I can't help it!"

After saying this, Duvada asked the rebel, "What is your name?"

"Sir, my name is Majji."

"Majji, this woman belongs to you. So now you can have this woman, here in front of me."

These words of Duvada were a surprise to Majji. He hesitated momentarily with a puzzled look at the unexpected order from the commander. Then Duvada's decision was immediately revised.

"Soldiers, as you have seen, Majji did not reap the fruits of his victory. So, the second challenger, come forward!"

Another soldier stepped forward and fought with Majji. Again, the victory was Majji's. This time Majji did not hesitate. He walked up to the woman and took the sari and underwear off of her and pushed her down. Then he began to caress her breasts wildly.

Men groaned here and there. There were men who panted for breath, moaned, and even bit their lips. It was then. There was an officer who upon seeing Majji and the woman, felt shocked as if he had been hit on the back of his head with a blunt weapon, and he was Dhammadinna, a veteran officer who joined the riot force as an intermediate officer. He ran madly toward the woman, Asatha, whom he had been desperately searching for.

Asatha opened her eyes wide and stared at Dhammadinna who was looking down at her. A shadow of deep pain flitted by across the eyes of the woman who had been the play thing of lots of bandits and was now being trampled on in public.

But soon a bright light glittered through the dark cloud of pain. A man! A man of dignity! Seeing such a man! For her, it was the strength that helped her endure the hardships throughout her life, particularly for the past several years when she was succumbed to hellish pains, and when she saw Dhammadinna standing in front of her, she cried out in her heart, *Now everything is fine! As long as I am with this man!*

Dhammadinna yelled at Majji, "I'll deal with you!"

Surprised, Majji hurried on his cloths and stood up. The two men stood facing each other with a dagger. The match was not easily decided. Both men had equal skills.

"Fight with swords!" Duvada said and threw two swords to the two men. Majji caught the sword in the air, and Dhammadinna stooped to grab the sword that landed on the ground. Majji rushed toward Dhammadinna like a flash of lightning.

Whoosh!

The next moment, a dark curtain fell before the eyes of Dhammadinna. His left arm, which was slashed deep by more than half, was dangling. There were screams from the mouths of the soldiers. However, the next moment Majji, with the sword stuck in his heart, fell at the feet of Dhammadinna who swayed and found it difficult to stand. After realizing the victory, then he looked at his left arm. And he collapsed abruptly, feeling the strong tremble of pain that shook the whole world.

"Take care of his injured arm quickly!" Duvada shouted at an officer, and the officer soon commanded the medics to move Dhammadinna beside a bonfire nearby. Majji was still alive. Blood gushed from his heart emitting spurting sound. That excited the soldiers. The soldiers hurled their fists into the air and shouted with one voice.

"Kill him! Finish him off now!"

The cunning commander, having confirmed that the soldiers had transformed into evil spirits as he intended, smiled contentedly. He drew the sword that he wore at his waist. Soldiers waited, with bated breath, for the commander's next move.

Duvada strode toward Majji. He cut the neck of Majji with a single a stroke, picked up Majji's head covered with blood, and shouted at the soldiers, "This guy must die! It is because he is a soldier of the rebel forces who stabbed your friends, slashed them, and killed them!"

The soldiers shouted and roared. Then twelve soldiers carried a body of an unknown soldier on their shoulders and laid it before the commander. The corpse was covered with pure white cloth, and numerous flowers were scattered over the cloth. When the soldiers put the body beside Majji, Duvada approached the body and knelt down to kiss it.

Duvada stood up and shouted, "Look, our fellow soldiers! Look, our great hero! Soldiers, this is my real son, Khaddika!"

But what he said was not true. The body was not the son of Duvada's. But for Duvada, to whom victory over somebody is the sole virtue and meaning, truth was not necessary. What he needed was the madness of the soldiers, being fearless of death.

The ingenious tactician shouted, "Look! Look! Here my son is dead!"

Tears dropped from the eyes of Duvada. He wiped the tears off his cheeks with a flourish, straightened his shoulders and said again. "Then, who? Who on earth killed him? Who took him away from me?" He shook Majji's head in his hands and said, "Right! It is the rebels!"

The soldiers' excitement reached its climax. Orders fell from the lips of the commander of the state forces who saw through the mental development of the soldiers.

"Go, soldiers! Go and defeat those rebels!"

Then he jumped on his horse. He hurled Majji's head onto the ground and cried out again, "Let's go! As I will stand in front of you, you will follow behind me!"

The horse carrying Duvada began to gallop fiercely. The generals followed him, and then the officers and the soldiers followed thereafter.

The troops moved out like a falling tide. So only Dhammadinna and Asatha were left in the place from which tens of thousands of demon-soldiers had just left.

The woman walked toward the man who had become entangled with her like a cruel wisteria vine of fate. One arm of Dhammadinna, who was lying unconscious in a pool of blood, the arm that had been cut deep by more than half and had to be severed, seemed to have been properly treated.

The groan of Dhammadinna rang in the ears of Asatha painfully. A few moments later, he suddenly grabbed the wounded arm with the other hand and rolled on the ground. "Ouch! Ouch!" Cries of pain reverberated far into the air where there was no one to help.

"What shall I do?! What shall I do?!" But there was nothing Asatha could do to help. She wished she could have taken over the pain from him, but she could not feel the pain on his behalf. Only if the severed arm could return back in its place, she would feel happy even if both of her arms were to be cut off! However, that was not possible.

She quickly looked around. Nearby, she noticed that fragments of peyote cactus were scattered over the ground, that were the leftovers from the medics' treatment of Dhammadinna.

During the time of Asatha's stay with the bandits, she learned that the juice of the peyote cactus had an anesthetic effect, and attentively watched how it was to be used. She picked up the cactus pieces and crushed them with stones to make juice and fed it to Dhammadinna. Then she cautiously unwrapped the cloth covering the butt of the severed arm. Her head was rather clear. In extreme situations, the mind became rather calm, which seemed to be nature of the mind of human beings.

With composure, but with nimble fingers, Asatha applied the juice of the peyote cactus over the wound. Dhammadinna's groan subsided slowly. He soon drifted into a deep sleep, and woke up after a long while, and owing to the anesthetic effect of the cactus juice, his face looked distant and hazy.

The two sat side by side in front of the embers of the bonfire. For quite a while, the two silently watched the fire as it burned with snapping sounds. Sounds of neighing horses and hoofbeats, crashing of spears and swords, and cries of people in the throes of death were heard from afar like a hallucination.

The woman extended her hand toward the man, but the man did not hold her hand. Still, she gently placed her hand on the back of the man's hand, without shyness or hesitation, but like a butterfly perching on a flower. The man did not refuse it this time, and the woman softly stroked the back of his hand.

Then the man heard. Silent words from the hand of the woman. The hand was speaking.

"The truthful person should be given a deserved reward! Oh, Dhammadinna, I do hope you be surely, surely happy!"

Then, after a while, "Oh . . ." Yelling this, the man who was sitting with his back to the woman turned around and took the woman's hand. With sorrowful eyes, he stared at the eyes of Asatha, and in that sorrowfulness was still lingering some haziness.

Asatha gazed onto the eyes of the man who held her hand, and in those eyes, sorrow and haziness were oddly mixed in. Dhammadinna dissolved into her eyes. Yes, her eyes were of a woman's. But yet again, they could be of a sister's and a mother's.

The hand of a woman, a sister, and a mother reached toward the cheek of a man, a brother, and a son. Asatha slowly stroked Dhammadinna's cheek. During that time, Dhammadinna obediently left his face with Asatha, as an innocent child did with its mother.

At last, Asatha's hand that fell down from Dhammadinna's face, the hand that had flailed in the air in search of someone who could save her, whenever she was raped by the bandits, reached out and landed softly on the single, remaining wrist of the man who came to her as a savior on behalf of Shiva.

Asatha, with the other hand, opened her sari. Her clothes, which had been ripped off forcibly by innumerable unwanted men while she had been kept by the bandits, were undressed on her own will.

She drew the hand of the man and laid it softly on her chest. There, there were two small mounds of breasts. There, there was the most feminine part of a woman's body, the most secretive one that seduced countless men, and that countless men longed for. That was the flower, food, spring, and paradise that fed and raised countless men and women.

The woman stroked tenderly the back of the man's hand resting on her breasts. *Oh* . . . with a silent shout in his heart, his eyes were closed softly. *Oh, breasts of a woman! But at the same time breasts of a mother!*

The man caressed the woman's breasts. The woman's hand still smoothly stroked that hand of the man. At that moment, the man was not a man to the woman. And to the man, the woman was not a woman either. The man was a man of integrity, but ended up in misery. The woman too pursued the truth, but suffered a series of misfortunes. As a result, the two were a man and a woman on the one hand, but on the other hand were same human beings transcending the distinction of a man and a woman.

After a while, Dhammadinna fell into a deep sleep like he was dead, with his head laid in the bosom of Asatha. He dreamed in the sleep of the dead. At first, a dream of various hungry ghosts swarming in and out, and next consecutive dreams of paradise after paradise and paradise . . .

After the incident, Dhammadinna left the army. First of all, being a man who had lost an arm, he could no longer remain in the army. But the biggest reason why he came out of the army was because he had found Asatha.

Asatha decided to share her fate with Dhammadinna. Thus, Dhammadinna became the second lover of Asatha. However, her second lover, like her first one, did not take her body. He did not want or demand anything from Asatha, and Asatha also would not give herself away again.

The reason why Jatu did not take her body was because he loved her too much, and it was same with Asatha. The reason why Dhammadinna did not take her body was because he was concerned about the fact that Asatha was Jatu's wife, and it was same with Asatha.

The two made their living through farming. However, since Jatu had lost an arm, and further he was getting weaker and weaker and thus suffered from illness frequently, he was not much of help in farming. Because of that, their income depended heavily on the labor of Asatha.

The years rolled by.

Meanwhile, because of the painful past and of the toil that forced her to overwork herself, Asatha's body became noticeably depleted. Then a decade later, her appearance had changed so much that the captivating beauty of her youth could not be found anymore.

So, Dhammadinna felt sad. It was a lament for the fate of Asatha, but it was also a sorrow arising from the regret for his own destiny. Furthermore, it was a sorrow from the regret for the fate of Jatu, so it was a sorrow for the root of life or life itself.

Before he knew it, teardrops of sorrow that were shed one by one filled the jar of his mind. And at last the teardrops soaked his body, down to each and every one of its cells.

So he composed poems and sang songs. Poems and songs with heartbreakingly woeful tone and depth of philosophical contemplation.

> Where is paradise?
> I know,
> That paradise is here.
>
> Paradise is her,
> A longing for her.
> A woman that can never be mine,
> Near but far away,
> My paradise is her.
> But, oh!

What is this sorrow?
Why, in this paradise,
Do I cry like a baby?

Where is paradise?
Where is paradise for me?
For her, for all of us
Where is paradise?

Paradise—the land of no sorrow,
Where is the land of no tears?

After some time, both Asatha, who wanted to live in paradise with Jatu, and Dhammadinna, who did not want to send Jatu to Paradise Lost, but found the possibility of a paradise in Asatha, died. Dhammadinna first, and Asatha soon thereafter.

CHAPTER 30
Is There a Land of No Tears?

Asatha, Dhammadinna, and Jatu received their next lives in a different place called *Jambudvipa*—the continent around India. Asatha became Ayutha, Dhammadinna became Binggisa, and Jatu became Bhaddiya.

The relations of the three people resumed when Bhaddiya and Ayutha met. When the two first met, Bhaddiya was the crown prince of the Shakya Kingdom who would succeed to the throne, and Ayutha was a maid of a rich brahmin with a great fortune.

One day, Prince Bhaddiya went hunting in the woods. After some time, Bhaddiya, who was left alone away from the company while he was chasing a deer on a horseback shooting arrows, suddenly felt thirsty. He pulled up the horse and looked around in search of a place where water could be found.

He caught sight of a girl who was drawing water at a well a short distance away, and urged his horse toward her and asked.

"I'm very thirsty, please give me a gourd of water."

"Yes, Your Honor," the girl replied.

But the girl was not in any hurry. Slowly, in a descent manner, the girl drew water in the gourd and gave it to Bhaddiya, but two leaves were floating on the water.

After drinking the water, Bhaddiya returned the gourd and asked her, "Did you know that leaves were floating on the water I drank?"

"Yes sir, I washed the leaves and floated them on the water."

"Why did you float the leaves on the water?"

"Your Honor," said Ayutha, "it was because you were rushing in such a hurry. So I thought that if I float the leaves, you will drink it slowly."

"Oh, you mean to say that as you were concerned that I might choke while drinking the water, so you left the leaves afloat?"

"Yes, Your Honor." The way she replied was so calm to the extent of appearing arrogant. However, as she her head was in lowered position due to her lowly status, Bhaddiya could not see her face.

Bhaddiya, who had noticed something particular in the way she talked, smiled and asked, "Are you trying to teach me a lesson now?"

"Being a woman of low status, how could I ever teach a man of such high status? But I simply mentioned one thing I have learned while I grew up to be seventeen. But upon hearing your words of reproach, I realize that I have to cultivate more modesty. I am grateful to Your Honor for teaching me the virtues of modesty, and now please allow me to go back to where I belong."

"Wait!" said the prince of the Shakya Kingdom. "You hold on just a minute, and look up to my face."

This was because suddenly a strong curiosity about the girl arose in Bhaddiya. At last, when the girl, as he instructed, looked up at him, who was still on the horse, he could hardly hold back his surprise. First of all, her appearance was so stunning. Her facial features were as sleek as a piece of marble, her skin was crystal clear, and the light around the greyish pupils of her eyes were bright and deep at the same time. Hence, his heart was strongly attracted to Ayutha.

But his attraction could be attributed more to the strength of the karmic ties in their past life, than to her beauty. In his previous life, Bhaddiya (Jatu) was, with the help of Dhammadinna, placed on a raft and drifted endlessly into the sea. First, his raft drifted toward the sea along with the waves. Then, after some time, the raft started to change its course little by little and reached a village named Mauka, about twenty miles away from where he had first left.

Jatu, who alighted from the raft, picked up his tired body and spirit for two days and left for his own home. He concealed his identity and after a long journey of over a month arrived at his house. Everything was almost the same as he had expected. His house was confiscated by the state and hence the ownership had changed. Fortunately, Gurana was still working as a servant at the house. He secretly approached Gurana and could hear in detail what had happened here in the meantime.

Everything else felt unimportant. The most important thing to Jatu was the whereabouts of Asatha. Gurana said Asatha had left home to share her fate with her husband. So, Jatu left and went back to the shore where he had been put on the raft. It took another month again to get there. He asked the villagers what had happened there-after. The village people knew what had happened to Asatha and Dhammadinna relatively well in detail.

The villagers told Jatu that, to save him, Dhammadinna had gone out into the middle of the sea with a beautiful woman on a sailboat, and that the boat had been pushed endlessly into the sea. *Then, are the two still alive?* he thought.

In the heart of Jatu, arose a groundless confidence that they must be still alive. It was rather a desperate wish than a confidence, which was as firm as a confidence. Yes, they had to be still alive. If not, it would be too absurd for such good people to end their lives in pain.

"Oh, Lord Shiva!" Jatu exclaimed and knelt down on the sand. "Shiva Almighty, please help them! They shouldn't die like this! Oh, Holy God! I do not wish that deserving pain shall be given to those who inflicted pain on me. So, Lord Shiva, you will decide whether to destroy them or to throw them into the fire of hell. But please reward the good people! Make sure to do so!

"Lord Shiva, commander of the world and king of the universe! If my beloved wife Asatha does not live a happy life, and if Dham-madinna is not rewarded for his righteousness, I will dare to curse you! I will defy you and fight against you for a thousand years, no, ten thousand years!"

Crying like that, he wandered the surrounding villages and looked for Asatha and Dhammadinna, thinking that they might have drifted back ashore. In this way ten years passed. Finally Jatu returned to the shore where Asatha and Dhammadinna had first left in search of him. Jatu then collapsed and died on that shore.

So, when he met Asatha (Ayutha), whom he had been searching for so desperately in his past life, the time and the space stopped in Bhaddiya's mind. It was also the same with Ayutha. Drawn by the strong power of karma in their past life, Bhaddiya and Ayutha fell in love with each other instantly.

After a while, Bhaddiya, who began to see the girl from a completely different light, asked her name and identity. She replied that her name was Ayutha, a maid of Saraka, a Brahmin who owned all the land in the area.

"Come along, maiden!" Bhaddiya cried out. "I am the Prince Bhaddiya of this state. I want to have you as my lady. So let's go, to my palace! Be my lady!"

As such, the two became husband and wife once again. After becoming the crowned princess, she assisted and took care of her husband with utmost care. Bhaddiya's numerous concubines also competed to show their dedication to Bhaddiya. However, Ayutha's devotion was different from the others' in that there was no servility in her devotion.

Bhaddiya has never seen a woman who, being as beautiful as Ayutha, was so devotional to others like Ayutha. So the love of the couple began to take on an aura uncharacteristic of young ones, which was as deep and solid as only elderly couples who had lived together for thirty years could possess.

However, Bhaddiya still did not offer her all his heart. Bhaddiya had heard several times from his father, the king, warnings about the danger of the beauty of a woman, but he was clever enough to recognize it even if he hadn't heard such warnings from his father.

So he was careful that his love for Ayutha would not progress to the extent of giving all his heart to her.

Not long after he married Ayutha, his father, the king, passed away, and Bhaddiya ascended to the throne. The problem was that the burden he had to bear grew ten times or hundred times bigger. As his power grew stronger, Bhaddiya was more careful about women than when he was just a prince, especially of beautiful women, including his wife. Furthermore, he was also cautious and wary of men. Everyone surrounding him was thought to be an enemy, who approached him in disguise of a friend.

However, as a human being before anything else, including being a king, he also had his share of frustration, despair, sigh, groan, pain, and tears. They demanded him to find a human to say, "I am suffering now, almost unbearably!" But he had not yet found a reliable person to whom he could tell such words, which, upon reaching the ears of others, could have been changed to such words as, "I am such a fool!"

The mindset and behavior of Bhaddiya that would not give his heart to others, even to Ayutha whom he loved more than anyone else, might be an indispensable attitude for a king who governs a country. But on the other hand, it meant that as a human, not a king, he had no place to take the load off his mind and rest against.

Thus, Bhaddiya's mind became barren as a sand field, and the only person with the distinct possibility of saving him was just Ayutha.

And the time when this possibility became reality had come. One day, after the second year of his enthronement, Bhaddiya took a walk in the palace alone, and suddenly an idea came across his mind: *Most people love themselves more than others. This is undoubtedly a self-evident truth. Therefore, it is impossible for a person to love others more than oneself.*

He continued thinking, *But Ayutha may be an exception. Her devotion to me! Looking at her makes me think she may love me more than herself.*

Bhaddiya soon called his wife and told her the thought he had just come across and asked, "Tell me what is your thought on this."

Being questioned by her husband, Ayutha was lost in thought for a while. At last, looking calmly at her husband, she said quietly, "After observing my mind quietly, I realize that I have the same inclination as anyone else. My Lord, I love myself more than you, just like everyone else."

Ayutha's words were not the answer that Bhaddiya wanted to hear. So he was disappointed, but soon he took note of the honesty nesting in the words. If she had been one of the other women, she would have answered, "I love you more than myself." Or, she could have given an evasive answer with her charm to escape the awkward situation or turn the subject of the conversation to avoid an answer—but Ayutha did not do that.

After the incident, Bhaddiya watched and tested her honesty whenever he had an opportunity. Finally, the door of his mind, which had been half-open yet half-closed, opened up completely. He saw the honesty springing from the deepest part of her heart, and the sincerity that enabled her honesty.

To trust someone totally, to be a friend of someone with such deep sincerity, and to have someone with deep sincerity as his wife, the closest friend of friends, is a great happiness to Bhaddiya. No, it was rather a religious sanctuary more than happiness.

Bhaddiya went to the sanctum by the name of Ayutha, and confessed all his shame, without exception, that had been sitting in his mind as a heavy burden, and she listened attentively to all his confession without a single rejection. That's right. It was an attentive listening with the utmost sincerity, hence, it was a profound acceptance.

Ayutha's acceptance was like water. Water does not leave any gap between an object and itself. Like this, Bhaddiya felt as if there were no gap between him and Ayutha, who came to him like water. Ayutha appeared to him as a person who would retreat as much as he drew near, and who would take a step closer as much as he stepped back.

In that space where the borderline of the two particulars met and became one, Ayutha simply sympathized when Bhaddiya confessed his shame, without revealing any blame. Even when he showed pride, she just gladly echoed such pride and did not add a small bit of encouragement. Thus, again, Ayutha was the sea. The sea that embraced everything whether it was clean or dirty. Bhaddiya, who was a low-minded sentient being even though he was a king, found great peace by discarding all his pollution, and his cleanness as well, into the sea. Ayutha was a holy sanctuary to Bhaddiya, and in that sanctuary he felt so relieved like a religious man who was forgiven all the sins he had committed.

But it was to elevate his dependence on Ayutha to the maximum, which meant that the consequences, when the object of the dependence tumbles down, would be just as big. Eventually, such an unfortunate event occurred. A few years later, not long after Binggisa became a court poet, Ayutha's mind leaned uncontrollably toward Binggisa, and Bhaddiya's sanctuary, that had been believed to be noble forever, turned into a lowly and shabby one.

CHAPTER 31
Ayutha (Asatha) and Bhaddiya (Jatu) in This Life

Driven by the power of karma from their previous lives, Binggisa and Ayutha fell in love the moment they laid eyes on each other.

Previous life! In that painful life, Asatha loved Jatu, and Dhammadinna tried to keep their love alive until the very end, but due to some cruel twist of fate, Asatha and Dhammadinna ended up with each other, and he fell in love with her as a result.

Asatha also felt a very strong attraction toward Dhammadinna. However, despite of his strong integrity and noble character, Dhammadinna had to lead a very painful life. Moreover, Asatha knew that all the pain he went through was a struggle for her sake. So this made her heart ache, the kind of pain that bore deep into her heart, so very sore that it throbbed. In the beginning, whatever feelings Asatha developed for Dhammadinna could have been just a sentimental sympathy, but it ultimately transformed into love.

However, these two never expressed their love toward each other, even until their death. Therefore, the shower of love stored in their hearts grew and grew, until a reservoir formed out of hundreds and thousands of pails of water. Then, a day finally arrived in this very life. Binggisa felt the lake of his mind being swallowed up by the storm, with uncontrollable waves that kept the surface rough. Then, the great overflow of water broke down the dam and at the end swallowed up the whole island that stood in the center of the lake. An island as beautiful as a paradise, one as ecstatic as arts and mystical as in dreams—an island called Ayutha.

The water from the lake and the island soon mixed together in a jumble. By the power of love that could never be in their previous lives or through the very force of craving that leads sentient beings through the cycles of life and death. Then, eventually their relation became known to Bhaddiya.

When Bhaddiya discovered that the two people that he loved so dearly fell in love with each other, he was greatly shocked as if the sky would split into two. Then absolute devastation took over. It was beyond the kind of despair a man feels when he discovers his woman had been taken by another man, or that he was betrayed by his trusted wife and friend. It encompassed his disappointment on men in general, and the shattering of his belief that men are truthful.

The persons who he loved truly with all his heart! The very two people that he found through betting on the existence itself, that he believed were the sparkling silver of honesty and truth among all the sands of people who pretended to be true and honest. When these trusted two betrayed him, he could not contain himself any longer, because the faith he had of the truth and honesty in mankind crumbled down before him.

Like a scarecrow without a soul, Bhaddiya wandered through the palace. The chancellor stood by with his hands together, waiting for the king's final decision on how the two sinners shall be punished.

"Oh, the evil that blinds others' eyes, in the disguise of the truth!" Bhaddiya shouted. "That is abominable felony. Decorating themselves with most flamboyant colors, they are like serpents that hide their poisonous venoms between their teeth. Therefore, they deserve to be expelled while being beaten with stones and sticks!" shouted Bhaddiya with his bloodshot eyes.

He then cried out to the chancellor, "With the eyes to appreciate the beauty of art, he coveted the beauty of another's wife. Thus Binggisa's eyes shall be struck and blinded. Also, with the ears to listen to my words only, Ayutha followed the sweet tempting words of another man. Thus, the sentence is to pour poison in her ears and make them deaf. Then, kick both of them out of this palace at once!"

In this way, Binggisa and Ayutha were vanished from the palace. Fortunately for Binggisa, the chancellor who valued his artistic talent convinced the king to strike only one of his eyes, salvaging at least one of his sights. When Binggisa lost his one eye, he felt deeper pain in his heart than of a physical pain. The kind of pain that burrowed deep into his bones, as if his whole being was denied from within. Praised and glorified by the people until then, and secretly believing himself to be worthiest of all, Binggisa couldn't stand the thought of being humiliated.

Therefore, the lively spirit he had in the love toward life, which used to spring forth at all time and in all places, the very essence of his spirit from deep within, that which praised all that was beautiful, was now cut off. The problem was, from that spot that was now closed off, steamy contaminated lava of fury, rather than a pure crystal spring, began to boil over. The angry lava quickly closed the spot where the spring once flowed and slowly moved downwards.

Clack! Clack! The fiery lava exploded with sparks. At first, that spark was pointing toward Bhaddiya. However, Binggisa soon realized that he wasn't directing his anger in a proper way. That's right. It didn't seem right that the very cause of misfortune that came upon him should be pointed toward Bhaddiya. Although he was knowledgeable in art and of secular world, he knew nothing of the path that directed inward, thus his mind went out and searched for external objects that he could vent his anger. Thus, his mind discovered destiny and fate to blame, rather than toward Bhaddiya.

That's right. It was all because of destiny! That which gave him the ingenious talent, leading him to become a great minstrel, and then leading him to the Shakya Kingdom, captivating the King Bhaddiya with his art, and for the king to possess a beautiful wife called Ayutha, preparing her to be so seductive in a way that Binggisa had no way to take control over his own mental power. It was destiny and fate that prepared all this.

"Oh, dear fate!" Binggisa cried out. "Oh, fate! You played me for a fool with your unseen, conniving play of hands! You came to me while bearing honey in your bosom with the appearance of a flower, but in truth you were neither beautiful nor fragrant, but just a master of great disguise. What do you want from me? What cunning tricks have you prepared on my path ahead?" So he cried out, staring into the empty space with his bloodshot eye, filled with determination to find that dark play of hands in destiny.

Then, there was Ayutha on his side. What was more important, she was the one who practically plummeted from heaven to hell, yet she viewed everything in a different light unlike Binggisa. Banished from the palace, Binggisa and Ayutha suddenly became beggars overnight. They begged for food, slept on the street, a kind of life that was extremely humiliating, disgusting, and shameful. Although the one who should have felt more disgusted and disgraced, should have been Ayutha who was once a queen of the state, and not the wandering minstrel Binggisa, the reality was quite the opposite.

Although they both turned into beggars, Ayutha was different than Binggisa. Ayutha never blamed her misfortune on Bhaddiya or toward destiny.

I lost my hearing because of my own wrongdoing. Everything is due to the consequences of my own action, she thought to herself.

In this way, while Binggisa blurted his anger outward, Ayutha withdrew inward without anger. In fact, Ayutha's withdrawal had deepened by her loss of hearing. While Binggisa displayed his anger toward others through his only remaining eye, Ayutha opened her hearing toward her heart and soul, in substitute for her loss of physical hearing.

Binggisa may have experienced discomfort in losing an eye, but at least he didn't lose his entire sight. On the contrary, Ayutha lost both sides of her hearing, thus she completely lost any ability to hear. Paradoxically, the loss of the entire physical faculty of a sense organ, rather than a partial faculty, induced her to withdraw further, a cause for some crucial changes thereafter. Without the ability to hear, the world turned into desolate stillness for Ayutha. The heaven and earth were covered with snow. Not a single bird flew by, nor a mouse moved about. Everything stood still. Even all that which moved remained still while in moving.

At first, she felt afraid of such desolate stillness. However, the usual fortitude in her character gave her an order at some point to "throw yourself into the stillness!" Throwing self to the stillness meant to demolish the ignorance and desire, which also meant to reject the activity tinged with ignorance and desire. This meant embracing everything with a passive mind.

Ayutha gradually widened the extent of this passive mind. All her senses, for example of seeing, hearing, smelling, tasting, and touching became passive. In other words, she did not search out for any sensory stimulation. She simply accepted the state of her sensory experiences.

These two people were different. To pursue a sensory stimulation meant that desire still remained in the mind or that it intensified desires. On the contrary, simply accepting without searching out for the object of sensory experiences meant that her desire has stopped or weakened. After a month, Ayutha became a totally different person. A passive figure, who had given up all her desires and she appeared like a battered vegetable or a remnant hollow skin from cicada.

In such a way, Ayutha often tried to hear something. She would suddenly stop and stand still while walking or she would stop her busy hands while eating, in trying to hear something while totally dumbfounded.

Binggisa, who watched all this by her side, was driven into a strange psychological state. In watching Ayutha, questions arose inside him, *What is she doing? What is she listening to?* He would then ask her questions by writing on the ground, but Ayutha didn't write anything back. She simply stared into her lover's eyes.

While Ayutha's mind sank deeper and deeper into herself, Binggisa's fury was set ablaze. At the next stage, the outraged fury from Binggisa changed its course and pointed toward himself. He would punch himself or bang his head against the wall. He didn't freshen himself up nor brush his hair.

Soon enough, his lips that used to carry beautiful words like flow of river, now poured out the most vulgar words. Then, he began to throw those vulgar words at others and people immediately took revenge back at him, but he never stopped cursing at others, and as a result people continued to beat him up with vengeance.

Even while he was getting beaten up, he snickered and snorted sarcastically, the kind of snicker that was quite offensive to the onlookers. He in fact looked as if he had lost his mind. In response to Binggisa's eerie snort, people became more furious and pounded on him that much harder.

Then one day, Binggisa quarreled with four young men. While Binggisa was getting beaten, Ayutha squatted about twelve feet away and stared blankly at Binggisa and the four men.

At first, these overexcited men were not aware that a woman was staring at them in a close proximity, but they suddenly noticed her when it became clear that Binggisa could not resist them anymore. Only then did they realize that a beggar woman was nearby, and she possessed a very mysterious aura that was really difficult to explain in words.

These men retreated hesitantly, and Ayutha helped Binggisa up and moved him to a safe place where she began nursing him. Binggisa, who was beaten up nearly to death, fainted a few times in between and then came back around. When he finally came back around, he saw it all. Beyond Ayutha's grey eyes wavered something so stunning and sadly beautiful, which made him unable to hold back hot tears that swelled up deep from the root of his existence.

Binggisa, with tears streaming down his face, embraced Ayutha in his arms. In the arms of her lover, Ayutha gently closed her eyes. A few teardrops also rolled down her face. But just with that, she stopped crying. After some time had passed, Ayutha pulled herself away and looked onto her lover with a faint smile. From that time on, she never shed another tear.

A month had passed like that. What was noticeable was that Binggisa began to vent his anger toward Ayutha. Of course, he felt extremely sorry for Ayutha, since he regarded himself as a highly cultured person. However, his heart and mind had been distorted beyond redemption after he left the palace and the feelings of remorse he had toward Ayutha began to express itself in a distorted way.

"That's right! This is all because of you!" Binggisa screamed toward Ayutha. "If you weren't so inspirational, beautiful, and elegant, how could I dare to take the king's woman?"

Unfortunately, or very fortunately on the other hand, Ayutha was deaf. Therefore, the abusive profanity that poured out of her lover in a great storm, turned into a tranquil lake on reaching Ayutha. Despite of Binggisa's frenzied outrage, Ayutha's expressions and attitude remained forever calm and still. Just like this, she responded with the calmness of a lake. A very strange lake that never wavered, even to a rough wind.

But it only exacerbated Binggisa's fury, and he began to beat her in a near frantic rampage. If Ayutha had resisted him, perhaps his sanity could have been restored. He could have embraced her in his arms, or maybe knelt before her and cried, confessing his own stupidity.

But she never resisted his brutality. When Binggisa beat her, she quietly received his assault. With every punch he threw, her eyes seem to ask, *Why is he doing this? Have I done something wrong?* then the eyes said, *There must be a reason why he is doing this . . .*

Her receptive attitude only set Binggisa's fury ablaze. Binggisa lifted his feet and kicked her while screaming, "You fool! You don't even know how to fight back! Why don't you writhe and spit out curse after curse?"

Ayutha fell to the ground, while crouching her body into a ball. Even then, Binggisa didn't stop his cruelty until Ayutha finally lost consciousness, her body soaked in blood.

He finally snapped out of what he was doing. "Oh, what have I done?"

But even repenting seemed too much at the time. Like the time when he had been beaten up and was soaked in blood, Binggisa raised Ayutha from the ground and carefully nursed her. Finally, Ayutha's complexion came back to normal again.

Binggisa wept while holding the hands of his lover. After watching Binggisa cry for a long time, Ayutha extended her hands and grabbed hold of his. He was quite taken aback. Having passively accepted everything until then, this was the first time Ayutha actually moved proactively.

"Oh my dear love . . ." said Ayutha, "Please do not obsess over others . . . Don't fight against the destiny. Please return back to who you really are . . ." She spoke very slowly and then Ayutha squeezed Binggisa's hands that she was holding on to. "Love, discover love for yourself. Oh, my beloved!"

An outstanding artist that he was—he felt it then. In that warm join of hands held just once contained much deeper compassion and consolation than the hands of hundreds or perhaps thousands that may have tried to console him. So he broke down into crying. He wept and wept in Ayutha's embrace. His lamenting continued for a long time.

Ayutha comforted Binggisa, who rested in her arms obediently like an innocent child, stroking his back with her gentle touch. While being soothed by her affectionate hands, he then thought to himself, *Oh, this is the soothing touch of an angel!*

And then, on the third day after this incident, Ayutha left him without a word or any indication as to where she was going. When Binggisa woke up that same day at dawn, Ayutha was nowhere to be seen. As soon as he saw the spot next to him was empty, he instinctively knew that Ayutha had left him, and she left him for good. He knew that he would never find her even if he tried.

He sat idly, reminiscing about the person who was more precious than his own life, and trying to remember the face of his lover, the very person that brought him absolute pure bliss. Maybe others could have viewed them as having an affair, but it was nearly a pure religious bliss, quite unconventional in their own terrain, far from the fenced in social customs.

He then thought of her comforting touch that embraced his pain—a small yet warm and quiescent, but with such great consolation. "But that comforting touch is gone now!" he told himself, "My heart remains just as frozen! She is the only one who could melt away this frozen heart!"

Indescribable pain stabbed his heart like a blazing sword. From then on, Binggisa's heart became a prisoner to the void and meaninglessness. All that is worthwhile has crumbled down! All that is meaningful has disappeared!

Binggisa was exposed to a powerful enemy called void and futility; an enemy that he was unable to fight even if he wanted to and too difficult to grab hold of even if he tried.

Binggisa then let out a deep sigh. With a heartbreaking regret, he wept again and again. He ripped up his shirt in agony, writhed his body, hit his head against the tree, and threw his body against the rock. Then at the end, he climbed up to the cliff and threw himself down to deep river.

But his karma wouldn't allow him to die. In receiving help from a farmer, Binggisa was able to save his own life. But he no longer tried to kill himself nor abused himself from that point on.

"What's the meaning of life?" he asked himself. "Binggisa, you have a duty to find the meaning of life!" He said again, with a greater strength "Binggisa, you must not die until you find that meaning! You do not have the right to take your own life without it!"

After this declaration, Binggisa drifted from one house to another, begging for alms. Then one day, he heard most divine sound while passing through a village, the sound of a bell ringing from a temple devoted to God Shiva. Suddenly, his mind was at peace. Oh, such peace! That's right, something that he had not felt for a long time. The kind of peace he had never experienced before. Not even when he was at his greatest, being an artist. It was the music from heaven, beyond any music found in this world. He sat on the side of the road and listened to the sound. Although, the actual sound of the bell ringing had stopped long ago, the ringing echoed in his ears without stopping.

They were simple tones, but something much more holy than any of his music he used to adorn with complicated technicality. Then he mumbled to himself, "My music brought intoxicating bliss to myself and to its listeners, but the melody I just heard presented me with such sublime peace!"

Then he said again, "That's right! From this day forward, I will strive toward the peace that dwells in the sound of that bell! I will explore the sublime world of religion, which could never be reached through art!"

He stood up from where he was sitting. Suddenly a powerful strength rose from the center of his heart. That source of power was from what he had seen and experienced from his childhood, which was from the karma of this life.

Binggisa grew up in a wealthy Brahmin family as a child, with a father who believed in the Huruva faith. During that time, not a day passed by without hearing the sound of a bell, similar to that which he just heard from the Shiva temple. Thus, on that very day when the ringing of the bell from the Shiva temple echoed through his heart, he called to his mind the religion he believed as a child. Then, he found himself up already and moving about.

"The age of fine art is over for me now," he said to himself while walking briskly in lively steps. "From now on, I will be touched by the heavenly angels rather than human angels. I will take refuge in God Huruva. From the God I will find love which Ayutha spoke about!"

In this way, to return back to his past religious faith, Binggisa went to the headquarters of Huruva, and there he met Archbishop Chuchu. However, the love Ayutha referred to was not the kind Binggisa believed to be on the "path of God." What she truly meant was love one finds on the opposite of what he sought, the kind of love found on the "human path."

CHAPTER 32
Karmic Ties Diverging

Three days after being beaten by Binggisa, Ayutha woke up alone at early dawn. She stayed lying down, looking up to the showering of stars, and the vibrant sparkles looked as though they were about to plummet at any minute. As her heart opened up and her mind became clear, she completely forgot about the aching pain she had from her lover's beating.

She suddenly thought of the word *uppalavanna* (blue lotus flower) and for some unknown reason a thought came across her mind that she must go and search for the Bhikkhuni Uppalavanna straight away. The thought struck her so strongly that she had no choice but to go and find the nun, and that was the utmost priority at this very moment.

Her thought was still just a thought, but it was no ordinary thought. It consisted of unwavering determination, like a final resolution she could never turn her back to. Therefore, the very moment a doubt arose on whether it was just a thought, it had already transformed into an action. In any normal situation, a decision is made after some thinking, and then the action is subsequently taken based on the decision. However, she got up the moment a thought appeared, and she left without saying a word to Binggisa in search of her future master.

Ayutha heard of Uppalavanna, when she was still a queen, through the exchanges taken place between the ladies of the court. At that time, the court ladies were gossiping about a bhikkhuni who was raped long time ago.

"You think the bhikkhu felt pleasure at that time?" one court lady questioned.

"Oh, don't be ridiculous! What pleasure at a time like that?" another lady responded and they all burst out laughing. Ayutha then asked the court ladies about Uppalavanna and what had happened to her.

The man who raped Uppalavanna was her cousin, the son of her own uncle. Even before Uppalavanna became a bhikkhuni, her cousin had been infatuated with Uppalavanna's outstanding beauty. However, Uppalavanna had absolutely no desire for a husband, nor to raise children, nor to lead a contented family life. Therefore, she renounced and became a bhikkhuni in the sangha of the Buddha, and that was when her cousin stole in to her solitary practice in the forest and forced himself on her.

However, Uppalavanna was an arhat, who was already enlightened. Thus, she didn't take the incident seriously and had already let go of the incident without too much difficulty. After the incident, however, the Buddha took measures for bhikkhunis not to practice alone in the forest, and to receive protections from the bhikkhu sangha as well.

But for those who could not comprehend the supreme transcendental state of arhatship, the incident of Uppalavanna's rape became a subject of great interest. The rumor spread until it reached the palace of Shakya Kingdom, and Ayutha eventually found out what had happened to the bhikkhuni.

Simply by listening to the stories of Uppalavanna, Ayutha realized the bhikkhuni had reached a very high spiritual state. As luminous as the moon cleared out of clouds, Uppalavanna's state was beyond what an average person could possibly comprehend. Pureness! Her purity could not be tarnished by any vulgarity, just like dark clouds could not possibly taint the luminous moon. Thus, Ayutha intuitively knew that the great bhikkhuni gained higher spiritual advancement and nothing could possibly make her impure.

Therefore, after parting with Binggisa, Ayutha begged for food, slept on streets, and enquired to various people on her way to find the Elder Uppalavanna. After traveling for half a month, Ayutha finally reached the temple where her future master resided. Ayutha laid down her past in front of the great bhikkhuni, unburdening everything that had happened to her.

Through a short practice but a very long vipassana meditation, in that she had put in all she had, not only in this life but in hundreds and thousands of her past lives, all the accumulated karma of her past that had been dragging her down, finally disintegrated before her. On the day she met Uppalavanna, Ayutha attained the third stage of enlightenment, also referred to as the "non-returner."

In addition, Ayutha's hearing was restored through her own accomplishments and by the great supernatural power of the great arhat Uppalavanna. Through her refreshed new ears, Ayutha heard the voice of the elder bhikkhuni.

"Dear Dhamma sister!" said Uppalavanna. "You now have two paths that you can choose from. The first choice is to renounce the world to become a bhikkhuni and attain arhatship after progressing through your practices. The second is for you to remain in this world as a non-returner, until you are reborn in the Heaven of Pure Abode, where you can then become an arhat."

Ayutha contemplated for a moment. "Master!" said Ayutha. "But I must go and visit King Bhaddiya first, as he is suffering greatly because of me. I would like to go and ask for his forgiveness and perhaps bring him on to the path of Dhamma if possible."

"Oh, my disciple!" said Elder Uppalavanna. "You do not need to go and find King Bhaddiya. He will renounce the world to become a bhikkhu in due time and a few years later he will attain enlightenment."

"Oh, how wonderful that is!"

"So set aside your worries and choose from the two paths I presented to you."

Ayutha thought for a moment again. Then, Ayutha spoke with a look of firm determination, "Master, I will follow the second path. From now on, I will go throughout the continent and live for the sake of all sentient beings. Master, I lost my hearing due to my own misconduct, but it was restored once again thanks to the great Buddhadhamma. Thus, my ears are not my own, but belong to the Buddha, the Dhamma, and the Sangha. On behalf of the Three Jewels I will now listen attentively to the sentient being's devastation, failures, sighs, lamentations, sufferings, and cries."

"Sadhu! Sadhu! Sadhu!" The great bhikkhuni praised her disciple's resolution and said, "I praise your decision with a great pleasure. I would like to tell you in addition that by completing this holy path, you will have a chance to assist a man who you have deep connection to."

"Oh, how great that would be!" saying that, Ayutha offered three prostrations to her master, Uppalavanna. From then on, Ayutha lived her life for the sake of sentient beings. She wandered through numerous towns in the continent. She spent one day at one town, next day a different town, off to another city the following day and then yet another city the day after.

As such, she wandered and shared the pains, failures, and frustrations of sentient beings, crying and suffering together with the people. However, her mind always remained calm inwardly. While maintaining her inner peace, she presented boundless compassion on the outside.

In the end, her final journey led her to a port city called Subbaraka. The place she settled in was a densely populated area with the people stricken with poverty. Here, she fulfilled her vow and concluded her life. After her death, she was born in the Heaven of Pure Abode, where practitioners who attained the fruit of non-returner are reborn.

(Returning to the cave where Elder Sariputta is the principal of the group)

Ayutha, the heavenly being, paused after finishing the story of her previous life. Some time had passed in total silence. Nobody, including the Elder Sariputta, twenty-one bhikkhus, Elder Uppalavanna, and nearly five billion heavenly kings and beings present opened their mouth to speak.

After some time had passed, Ayutha looked up at Elder Uppalavanna and said, "Master, you said to me a short while ago, 'I know the touching experience of deep emotion accompanies both feelings of joy and sorrow. I also know that this deep emotion is most strongly felt when in love. Therefore, since you experienced such great love in your previous life and in the life before the previous, please share your insight and teach us how love moves our heart, and how this deeply impressed emotion comprises of sorrow.' In response, I explained for the sake of heavenly kings and other beings present here that love can be an exceptional path to understanding the truth of selflessness, just as much as art, philosophy, and religion could.

"I then spoke about my previous life and the life before the previous. However, while I was speaking about my not-so-short tale, you, my great master, miraculously condensed the time required, as if making folds into a cloth. I would like to thank you, master, for reducing the time required for the heavenly kings and other beings to hear my story, which otherwise would have taken much longer."

"My lovely disciple," said Elder Uppalavanna, "Perhaps my supernatural power may have played a role, but everyone immersed themselves fully in your story because it was very intriguing. Of course, doesn't time pass quickly when our mind is completely immersed in something?"

"Master!" said Ayutha. "You told me just a moment ago, 'In order for you to attain arhatship and enter parinirvana, you must clear away all the lingering attachments you have to love. I will tell you why, heavenly being Ayutha! In the state of arhatship, even love that overcomes hate is nothing more than a subtle function of craving that makes a sentient being just a sentient being. Therefore, dear one, why wouldn't you resolve to let go of all attachments you have of the love from your past lives.'"

"That's right."

"Therefore, I would like to recite an inspirational poem that could bring to an end all attachments I had of love from my past lives—belief in love, facing toward love, cherishing love as something beautiful, and any clinging attachments to love."

"Well, this seems to be the perfect time to do so, so why don't you go ahead."

Ayutha remained silent after receiving the permission from her master.

Then finally she began.

". . . My home, Salaha, was beautiful . . ."

The words began to flow softly from her lips. The sound of her voice that came out of her lips was so crystal clear and serene that not even a glimpse of dark shadow could be perceived. However, the spiritual masters who reached higher than the state of non-returner could still sense slight shadow of reminiscence that remained in her verses.

"My home, Salaha, was beautiful.
Beautiful was the blue sky
I looked in the embrace of his arms
And the calm swaying of white clouds.

Beautiful was under the plumeria tree
Where the sun shone between leaves.
Beautiful was his love
And our love.

Beautiful was the Ceylon Island
And my love Dhammadinna.
Beautiful was his love,

And our love.
Meeting once again in another life
The three minds entangled in a net[53]
Were beautiful, yet so painful.
Hatred encroached upon love,
It was a floret and a vine.

Love is a vine, and a flower!
Love is a shackle, but happiness!

And now I become a strand of scent
And want to leave for a place
Where there is neither vines nor flowers,
Where it is more flowery than flowers,

Now I want go to a place
Where there is going but no going
Where there is vast emptiness."

Ayutha was silent again after reciting the verse. After a few moments, she said to her master, "Master, please lead me now to the state of arhatship. Then, I will merge into Parinirvana at the same time of attaining arhatship."

"But Ayutha," said Elder Uppalavanna. "You can surely enter into arhatship on your own, without any of my help."

---

53 The Indra's Net: According to the *Flower Garland Sutra (Avatamsaka Sutra)*, a great heavenly net called Indra's Net exists in the palace of Indra Heaven, ruled by the Heavenly King Sakka. The clear crystals dangle on each mesh of the net and all things of the universe are reflected on each of these crystals. This reflection is infinite and boundless. In other words, a crystal is reflected on another crystal, yet the other crystal is reflected on this crystal. The crystals of mind are reflected on the crystals of material, and vice versa. The crystals of human are reflected on the crystals of nature, and vice versa. The crystals of time are reflected on the crystals of space, and vice versa. The landscape reflected on the Indra's net is splendid, enchanting, mysterious, and strikingly beautiful. Therefore, the *Flower Garland Sutra* teaches that everything in this world is intricately related; "you are me and I am you, all in the one, and the one in all."

Upon hearing her master's words, Ayutha got up and descended from her throne. She then offered three prostrations to her master and sat back down on her throne.

"Master," continued Ayutha. "I would now like to say my final goodbye to you."

There was no response from Uppalavanna, except she simply glanced peacefully into Ayutha's eyes. The sentimental reminiscence, which beings in the higher state than non-returner had seen in the face of Ayutha just a moment ago, had now vanished completely. Instead, a bright and transparent shine like a morning sun spread throughout her face. Before long, her face became more divine and beautiful than the gods.

The heavenly being Ayutha closed her eyes. She immersed herself in meditation, which deepened in time. Finally, an exquisite splendor blossomed on her face, which surpassed the divine beauty that rested on her face just a moment ago.

Oh, what a beauty! The beauty that must be expressed in words, but words alone cannot describe the beauty so refine and exquisite! That beauty was pure and distant. A beaming pureness so stunning, yet wistful as it was too far away in the distance. But it was not just a personal sadness, but a sorrow of a universal. Thus, it was the sorrow of silver snow, the sorrow of white clouds, the sorrow of rainbows, and the sorrow of sky blue.

Before long, her sorrow gradually settled and a delicate light, beyond description, radiated mysteriously throughout her face. In that radiance, she penetrated into the emptiness, a true reality of existence, by concentrating on "a certain body and mind" that cannot be described as "hers."

Then the sadness of silver snow turned into silver radiance that was stripped away of all defilements, and the sadness of white clouds turned into a state of liberation in which all experiences became light as white clouds. The sadness of rainbow turned into compassion which reaches sentient beings in a most noble way, and the sky-blue sadness turned into manifestation of nirvana, which, like sky, cannot be destroyed in any way.

The ultimate state of human!
The profound depth of the mind!
The purified flower of the world!

Ayutha sat up straight and entered into the sublime parinirvana by ending her life—the most sublime state any living being could realize. All practitioners, heavenly kings, and heavenly beings, except for the bhikkhus who achieved the higher state than non-returner, trembled with overwhelmed amazement. For them, seeing right in front of their eyes a practitioner that moved on toward the non-conditioned state, and to see someone conquer and surpass death by killing the death itself, was a majestic experience that transcended space and time.

On the other hand, those who went beyond the state of non-returner peacefully observed the way Ayutha entered into parinirvana. They thought in their mind, *All things are impermanent. Here a practitioner has transcended all suffering that arises from that which is transient.*

A few moments later, Arhat Bhaddiya, who had been quietly watching Ayutha enter into parinirvana, rose silently from his throne. He slowly approached Ayutha. Bhaddiya stopped in front of the woman for a moment, the one who he once loved with all his heart.

Bhaddiya then lifted both of his hands and put them over Ayutha's ears. When he took his hands off and stepped away, something very amazing happened. Beginning with her two ears, Ayutha's upper body began to transform into ashes of light green color, while her lower body turned into light pink ashes. Thus, that once called Ayutha has now turned into colored ashes. Right before the eyes of all present, the ashes turned darker until the light green ashes turned green, and the light pink ashes turned pink. Then the ashes again turned light green and light pink, the colors became even lighter again and her ashes settled down onto the floor.

Moments later, as if a mirage, the ashes that settled on the floor disappeared into thin air . . .

CHAPTER 33
The Legend of the Port City

The day after Ayutha entered into parinirvana, Elder Sariputta, together with the bhikkhus including Cunda and numerous heavenly kings and beings, left Karuna Cave toward the port city of Subbaraka for which the Buddha was heading. After witnessing Ayutha's parinirvana, Elder Uppalavanna returned to her own place of practice.

Afterwards, when Sariputta and his group, at the end of a long trip, arrived at Satika village near Subbaraka. The Buddha and his disciple Ananda had arrived there two days before and just finished a Dhamma talk for the villagers that day.

Sariputta, with his group, made three prostrations to the Buddha and asked, "World-Honored One, were you comfortable while you traveled all the way here?" The Buddha replied, "I was comfortable in all respects, Sariputta, any practitioner who has attained enlightenment, just like you, is happy at any place where he stays and at any time that he spends."

After this, he briefly told the innumerable people who gathered there about what had happened before he arrived at Satika; it was as follows:

On the first day of his journey, the Buddha delivered a Dhamma talk at Mudu village for five hundred lay believers. The next day, by the Saribu River, he edified a merchant, Barijattha, and the next day, edified a female lay believer, Venani, at Sangita village. On the next day, the Buddha delivered a Dhamma talk for seven hundred bhikkhus at Buruvana Monastery, and the next day, delivered a Dhamma talk for a rich man, Baru, and his family who were on their hunting journey. On the following day, after begging food, he stayed in a small cave in Kokti wood together with Elder Ananda and enjoyed the pleasure of meditative absorption for the rest of the day.

Like this, the Buddha dropped by various villages, monasteries, and forests and crossed many rivers, edifying numerous people, and, besides the foregoing examples, the number of people edified by the Buddha was too many to count one by one.

On the day following the arrival of Sariputta and his group, the Buddha first went out to a village for alms, took his meal, and then said to his disciples, "Dear bhikkhus. Now, let us go to him."

Whereupon, Ananda said, "World-Honored One, you just said, 'Dear bhikkhus, now, let us go to him.'"

"That is correct."

"But we do not know who the World-Honored One refers to."

"Ananda, you know who he is, but you are asking the question for others, as if you did not know."

"Yes, World-Honored One, I do remember that when you left Jetavana Monastery six months ago you said that you would go to Subbaraka to meet Binggisa. However, World-Honored One, I still do not understand why you, being the teacher of human and heavenly beings, made such a long journey of six months to meet sinful Binggisa."

"Ananda, when you see or think about someone, you must forget what he was in the past, and just see or think about him as he is at present. It is because one morning a man can shake off everything in the past and be reborn as a new man. So, you be aware that Binggisa at present is not Binggisa in the past."

"World-Honored One, do you mean that Binggisa was reborn as a new man?"

"That's right, Ananda, a few years ago, he came out of the dark world into the bright one. But at first, even though he returned to the bright world, he didn't completely come within the Buddhadhamma. However, thanks to the merits of a woman who had past karmic ties with him as a vine and a flower, he is now walking a path to the truth in a small way at a place very close to the Buddhadhamma."

"Then, that's very fortunate. World-Honored One, please tell me and all who are assembled here about how he came out of the dark world and headed for the bright one."

"Now is the right time to tell, Ananda, so, the Tathagata will tell you and all others here about him."

Having said this, the Buddha told the following story in a very short time that a strong man would take to bend and stretch his arm once, by use of his supernatural powers.

The story was about Binggisa who appeared in the port city of Subbaraka.

There was a beautiful port city of Subbaraka.

There were dreamy blue sky; rolling dark blue waves; blazing sunlight; a stretch of picturesque beach; and white, blue, and redbrick houses with spiky roofs. There were men with well-nourished faces and well-dressed ladies.

However, the city did not only have a bright side. In the beautiful port city, there was the dark backward area standing in stark contrast with the bright side. Those who first came to the city used to gush out words of admiration at the sight of the beautiful façade. However, filth was hidden at the back of the beautiful city. Lining stand bars were filled with the smell of alcohol, and there was noisy vulgar language of the sailors, arguments and physical fights, seductions and tricks, vanities and humiliations, mingling of men and women, and trade of black money.

It was a curious city with two distinct sides, like night and day. Therefore, the people in the port city of Subbaraka were divided into the people of the forward area and those of the backward area. The people of the two regions were easily distinguishable from their appearance. They lived apart from each other and did not even greet each other. They seldom knew each other, but even though they knew, they didn't want their relationship known to others. Also, the laws of the city set forth various regulations to distinguish or discriminate between the two areas and the people. The lawmakers were from the forward area of the city. Having the power, they protected their wealth and honor by creating unfair laws and oppressing the people of the other side.

One day, on a street of the forward area of the city, a gentleman appeared. He was a man of medium height. His hair hung down to his shoulders, his stubble was shaggy, and his dress was so simple as to wind his body with a long cloth. He was wearing leather shoes exposing the top of the feet, and judging from his seriously tattered shoes, it could be guessed that he had landed in the city after a long trip.

A feature of his appearance that first caught the eyes of the people was the white eye patch covering one of his eyes. With only one eye, he gave an unfavorable impression to the people. But it was only for a moment, and people forgot all about his appearance as well as his single eye.

The part of his body that revealed his character the most, and people could not help but being absorbed in, was his remaining left eye. It was an indescribably mysterious eye. Upon looking at the eye that was so mystic, people would often be sucked into the pupil of the eye.

The eye was the eye of the water. It was the eye of the dew, of the well, and of the creek. It was also the eye of the lake and of the sea. It was the eye that reminded the horizon—an eye that was filled with faint dreams and eternal ideals, looking up far into the distance.

His behavior was also different from ordinary people. Most conspicuous of all was that his motion was very slow. Walking slowly, very slowly, he looked at people with the sad eye of a sheep, which was being dragged to the sacrificial rite as an offering, or with the pure eye of a deer, which returned alive away from the claws of a beast, and when he encountered an interesting object, he often stopped and quietly stared at it. Then, again, he resumed his slow walking.

Nobody knew where he came from. It was only widely known that on a fine morning he was first seen at the square before the city hall in the central part of the forward area of the city. Because it was a holiday, diligent citizens came out to the square. Some took a walk, others chatted, and still others enjoyed a light exercise.

At one point in time, hundreds of people who gathered there felt something unusual. It was a sacred power that pulled them at the clothes, the napes, the shoulders, and the legs. Their hearts were drawn with irresistible intensity to the epicenter of the power, and their bodies too followed their hearts toward the direction. The epicenter of the force was just "the gentleman."

Without even noticing it, people were pulled to him. When people gathered around him, he walked slowly to sit down at a corner of the square. Then, without saying a word, he gazed at the front with a clear, sad eye. His body refused to budge. He didn't even talk.

Over time, more and more people gathered around the gentleman. So when half a day had passed, nearly a thousand people gathered around him. The crowd too, like the gentleman, didn't move nor talk. They just stared fixedly at him. An air filled with spirituality shrouded them. If one looked at them from afar, they may have noticed that like a lunar halo there was a hazy mist around them.

At one point, people realized that they were having a very rare experience. At the same time, long forgotten memories began to rise slowly in their mind. Memories of childhood when they went before God and praised him with their hands held by their parents, and when they repented before God and shed tears after having committed big and small sins. They didn't know when, but pure faith disappeared from the people in the city. However, as they shared the silence with the gentleman, the long forgotten memories of the old faith recurred to their mind.

People began to stir. After a while, by ones and twos, people began to kneel down in front of the gentleman, even though they were not instructed or induced to do so. Some people shed tears. The tears that were shed by only a few people soon moved on to everyone else.

Everyone wept. People wept and wept, too immersed to mind their appearance, refinement or decency. Their neat clothes, well-groomed hair and the powdered face were all messed up. However, they didn't mind. It was because, the feeling of emptiness—which was coming from the intuitive realization of the fact that flowers bloom but would soon fade, that men are born but would die not long after, and that everything is transient, the fact not forgotten even though they tried hard to forget by covering it up with elegant refinement—was being washed away with the tears.

"Abandon everything . . ." finally the gentleman opened his mouth. "Abandon your parents, your children, your brothers, and your friends. Abandon your house, your property, your status, and your honor." It was a dreadful remark. It was more horrible than an epidemic. People were horrified.

Those who were listening to the gentleman were the people who lived in the forward area of the city. They had a lot of possessions. They had loving families. They had properties that maintained their dignity and the honor that looked splendid to others. They were their raison d'être. But the gentleman was saying that they had to abandon them, in an irresistibly authoritative tone of voice.

However, no one could disapprove his horrifying remarks. People had already been gripped by his unknown powers. So they had to wait for his next words, shaking from fear.

The gentleman continued his talk: "Like an adult who forgot the pure first love in his younger days, you have forgotten your mind or soul for a long time. Therefore, even though you live rich and splendid, you are as good as dead. Oh, you arise being unaware that you are dead, you eat being unaware that you are dead, you work being unaware that you are dead, and you talk without knowing that you are dead.

"Behold, the well-cleaned marble roads. Look at the city hall decorated with fine sculptures. And look at the beautiful houses that were built neatly. And again look at the numerous well-dressed, attractive people. Oh, but I don't say that this is a beautiful place. Because there is no true heart here! Because no pure soul can be found here!

"You, who are dancing at a masquerade! While outwardly you smile in the rowdy atmosphere, inwardly your soul is crying. It is because you are thirsty, you are parched with thirst, and your heart is dry and barren.

"You with barren hearts, you with thirsty souls! So I tell you, you shall walk along the path of truth, discarding everything you own! Don't possess three or four extra sets of clothes. Don't decorate your body or your clothes. Don't worry about what to eat and what to drink. Look at the lilies in the field. Look at the birds flying in the air. They don't spin yarns, nor do they sow seeds. But I say that the beauty of those dewy lilies is much greater than all the beauty accumulated in the city, and the prosperity of the birds flying in the air is bigger than all the riches accumulated in the city."

A wave of inspiration rose in the crowd, as if tens of thousands of lilies, bloomed all over the mountain slope, were swaying gently by the passing breeze. Then they joined their palms, shaking from fear on the one hand and feeling pure bliss on the other hand.

Soon, the gentleman began to walk again. His slender body moved slowly, drawing a forlorn line. Before they knew it, people knelt down before him as he walked by or kissed on his sleeves. Some people were sobbing. When the gentleman raised his right hand and opened it in a silent gesture, the crowd stepped away like the water being parted, and thus a path was created in the direction he was heading. The gentleman walked slowly through the crowd and looked at people with such an inexplicably sorrowful eye.

The gentleman cleared himself away from the crowd, but no one in the crowd followed him. In fact, there were some who wanted to follow him, but the problem was that he was telling them to abandon everything. Even if it was his instruction, it was not possible for them to abandon everything. Because to the gentleman, having a family, possessions, status, and honor might mean to live in a way that was as good as dead, but to the people, abandoning them meant as good as dying while being alive.

From that day on, the gentleman showed up in various parts of the city. One day, early in the morning, at the hill of one hundred mango trees, the next day, at the sunset, on the wooden bridge of lovers, and the day after that, early in the evening, on the silver sand beach that the waves licked.

Like this, the gentleman used to appear quietly at different parts of the city, and said something mysterious that one would never forget once they heard it. Then the people who met him and listened to him would stay up the whole night, recalling his tragically sad look and profound teaching.

What is life?

Where did I come from?

And in the end, where do I go?

For them, these questions have long been thrown away. They wallowed in gorgeous attire, joyful dance, and a moderately sophisticated but slightly promiscuous society. Among them, it was an implicit taboo to ask what life was, where one came from, and where one would go. To these people, the gentleman had evoked the question that had long been forgotten.

After some time, there emerged his followers. It was young men who started to follow him first. Soon after, however, a few women came, followed by seniors, and finally, some middle-aged men.

The number of followers increased day by day. Then, two months after the gentleman had first appeared, the number of disciples who followed him counted more than a hundred. The passion of his disciples toward their master grew hotter as days went by. At last, the disciples began to call him a prophet openly, but he never called himself a prophet.

The gentleman did not say anything about himself, but it was true that he preached in such a polite and elegant language that it didn't seem strange for him to be called a prophet. At last, the municipal authorities began to pay attention to the gentleman. Subbaraka was a city that adopted an oligarchy where many senior citizens governed by agreement, and the senior citizens of the city thought he might have a political goal.

They did not want to break the safety and prosperity of the beautiful port city of Subbaraka, which they had developed by carefully establishing laws and institutions. The mayor, who served as the chairman of the elders' council, convened the council.

Each of the participants expressed their opinion at the council meeting of the elders, which had established the laws and deliberated important issues of municipal policies. Half of the elders had friendly opinions about the gentleman and half had doubts.

The favorable side expressed their opinion that the gentleman was a true human being, a mysterious man, and maybe a saint. However, the elders in the opposite side felt differently. "It is highly likely that he has a political ambition. Though he is now hiding it, he may have an intention to start a revolution to overthrow the city," they argued.

Finally, an elder with an unfavorable opinion against the gentleman was given a voice. He expressed his disapproval of the gentleman in various words while making a false expression that he didn't hate the gentleman at all and that he was a fairly reasonable man. First of all, he said, "The teachings of truth must be preached in an orderly manner by a priest well dressed up with clean robes in the magnificently built holy temple." He also said, "After completion of the holy ceremony, important people who attended the ceremony should be introduced as guests. It is also prerequisite that there are polite exchange of greetings among participants, customary humors and light laughter, courteous offering of flowers, and a lavishing tea party after the sermon."

He continued, "But this man doesn't follow such routines. It means that he disturbs the culture of the city of Subbaraka, which emphasizes refinement above everything else," he criticized. The elder also criticized the way the gentleman talked, which was not entirely unfounded. There was no pretense or formality in his talk. There was no fixed prologue, or assumed modesty to earn the mind of the audience. It was a discourse on one hand, but on the other hand it was a conversation. Maybe it wasn't even a conversation. It was interrupted intermittently and then continued, it continued and again was interrupted, smiles broke out at some point, laughter burst, and suddenly, everything was reduced to a quiet stillness, which was a natural and integrated harmony of life, words, and minds. However, there was no evidence that the gentleman had a bad intention, even though there was a lot of criticism. Furthermore, even if he had a bad intention, they could not punish him at the present moment when no bad action has yet been committed. Because of this, the resolution that his critics had submitted to the council could not pass.

Soon the critics came up with another idea. It was to create and spread bad rumors about him. They began to spread words of slander together with their supporters. It was the gist of the rumor that he had a woman and that the woman had been a prostitute. According to the rumor, she used to live in the backward area of the city that they hated terribly, and very recently, came to the forward area. The rumor spread like wildfire. Finally, people began to whisper in a sly voice, and soon afterwards, there were people who, facing each other, pouted their lips or exchanged whispers, even right behind the place where the gentleman talked with his disciples in a gathering.

"He is hiding a dirty woman, they say!"

"Oh, is he! No wonder . . ."

But the rumor couldn't be true. The gentleman spent all day with his disciples, and his disciples had never seen his hidden lover. The gentleman had not explained any of the rumors. He quietly shook his head when a disciple requested him that they should clarity the falsity of the rumors more actively. From the shaking of his head, the disciples read his message, "The rumors must be soon forgotten." Also, from the shaking of his head, the disciples read the message, "Let them do their job. I will just do my job."

The problem was that as the gentleman made no explanation,

some disciples began to harbor doubt on him. So the disciples were divided into two groups, one that trusted the teacher and one that had misgivings about him. After a while, there arose a quarrel between them. The dispute grew worse, and finally the two groups conceived enmity against each other. Then the disciples who doubted him left him, and the odd thing was that the disciples who left him became the strongest enemies of him.

They hated the gentleman and his disciples more seriously than any other critics. Their hearts were full of hostility toward him and his disciples. Their hostility grew over time, and finally they decided to attack him and his disciples. At that time, the gentleman was staying at a hill, located at the back side of a village, a little away from the city. The antagonists carefully approached him and his disciples. Razor-sharp daggers were in their hands, and they held a twig between their teeth for fear that the revolt might fail if they made a noise.

When they arrived, the twelve disciples, who abandoned their families and left their homes to be with him all the time, were sleeping under a large boulder at one side of the hill. Attackers first searched for him, walking cautiously so that they would not make any footstep noise. However, no matter how closely they searched for him, he was nowhere to be seen. There were only twelve people at the place where there should have been thirteen.

Nonetheless, nothing changed about what the attackers were to carry out. Each of the attackers took on a disciple, as had been fixed among them beforehand. With the sickening sound of dagger strike, painful groans were continuously heard.

The next day, the city officials, having learned that a grave incident had occurred, visited the scene of the incident.

But there was nobody. Not a single body was seen. The visitors were terrified.

"It's unbelievable!" they shouted. "Where on earth did everyone go?"

However, despite all the efforts made, the city authorities could not find out where the gentleman and his disciples had disappeared.

So, some of the people who could not get over their curiosity—most of whom were those who had attacked the gentleman—decided to stay overnight on the scene of the incident, in the hope that they could figure out the reason why he and his disciples had disappeared.

Night deepened. On the last day of the lunar month when there was no moon, the stars in the sky were shining brightly. After a while, the sky suddenly went dark. It was because dark clouds had rushed in and covered the sky.

Boom! Boom! Dry thunder rumbled. The rolling thunders seemed to storm at the people, *I am Shiva, the lord of the heaven, you have killed my sons!*, or to ask, *Why did you kill my sons?*, or to condemn them, *Your sins can never be washed away!*

Suddenly a huge column of clouds fell from the heaven, and stood on the ground. Standing tall in front of the people, the column of clouds soon shrouded the people. Shady and cold energy! People were overwhelmed with fear. They embraced each other and shuddered uncontrollably.

Suddenly, a magical and odd wisp of wind blew into the column of clouds from outside. A wind hot like fire! The wind had a hot spiritual energy in it. Flames flared up. Several people fell unconscious with the foam in their mouth. After a while, all those who had collapsed woke up. And they found that, while they were lying unconscious, their companions, buoyed by an unknowable excitement, had been praising the gentleman's holiness loudly. They participated in the praise, adding their passion to the hot passion of their companions.

Through this process, they became the gentleman's enthusiastic admirers. For them, he was not a dead man. They believed that he was dead only physically. The gentleman was the man who, together with his disciples, rose from the dead, went to heaven, and returned to them as a blazing fire energy.

Thus, people's views on him divided into two categories: those who remembered him without interest as if to say, "Once there was such a man," and those others who were his admirers who had received him in the blazing fire energy.

The important thing was that the admirers' memories of him became more and more vivid day by day. They recalled his eyes, his gestures, and his words clearly. So to them, he became a comforter and a torturer at the same time. They received great encouragement thinking of him, but at the same time, they had to solve the homework that he had left behind—the question of who the gentleman was.

They had several meetings to solve the problem. They talked about him, and in the process, their memories of him were overglorified. They determined to commemorate the gentleman forever, to record his sayings and doings, and thus to continue to explore the meaning of his coming to them and going back. Finally, they honored him as a prophet, and then established a ritual to praise him.

However, not long after the admirers raised his status as a prophet, they heard a strange rumor that they could never accommodate. It was the core of the rumor that the gentleman, who was believed to be already in heaven, still remained on earth. Then exactly where would he be?

"Ouch!" the admirers screamed. According to the rumor, the place where he stayed was the backward area of the city, and the dirtiest spot of the dirty ones—in a brothel! Although ordinary citizens were also surprised, the rumor was a shock itself to those who served him as a prophet. How could the gentleman be in such a place that was smeared with prostitutes, hostesses, sensual pleasures, shameful conducts, and crimes and full of darkness!

To think of it, the gentleman was a transcendental being beyond human dimension to his followers. He was a man who was recorded in golden letters—who stamped on a devil under his foot, and who angels were dancing around. He was the personification of God, or at least one of the God's apostles, and the symbol of holiness, the hope of salvation, and the object of praise. Then, how come he was still on Earth? Even worse, in the filthy backward area of the city?

The admirers could not believe the rumor. No, they didn't want to believe it. But against their wishes, the rumor spread like wildfire. The number of people who said they had seen him increased. Thus, the issue eventually became the biggest concern for the citizens. Now the veil of the rumor had to be lifted. But it was not easy to put the matter in its true light. Though someone must go to the backward area of the city to find the truth, nobody wanted to go there. As such, no investigation was carried out, and only the rumor ramified rampantly.

After a while, a new rumor began to circulate. According to the rumor, he performed all kinds of miracles there. It was said that a crippled man stood up, a leper was healed, and a mute talked. It was said that repentance, tears, rebirth, salvation, and glory were pouring down like a cascade.

Finally, people were no longer able to tolerate it. Thus, several representatives were chosen at the elders' council. They were assigned a mission to go to the backward area of the city and find out whether the rumor was true or not.

The representatives stole into the backward area of the city. It was an alley of darkness, indeed. Those who suffered from various ailments, old men stricken by hunger, emaciated children who stumbled around, dead bodies with the eyes looking upward into the air, drunken men and women who were high on dope and kept smiling, finger-pointing, and gang fights . . .

In the stream where black rats wriggled, dirty excremental water flowed, and many people lined up in order to relieve themselves, no single line of song was heard. No word of appreciation or admiration for life was heard.

But there was a mission to accomplish. The representatives asked around and found out where he was. It seemed true that he was there, but a tinge of doubt remained. When they put together what they had heard, it occurred to them that the man that the people had claimed to meet might not be the gentleman they knew.

"It is true that he has a single, sad eye . . ." an old woman told them. She added, "But he is drunk all day. He is also wearing so many accessories . . ."

Is he drunk? The man who had such a deep and mystic eye? Again, does he wear accessories? The man who instructed us to abandon everything and not possess three or four sets of cloths? Could he really be the man who we are looking for?

However, everything would be brought to light when they checked it out. They hurried to the center of the backward area of the city, to the dirtiest spot in the dirty place. It was around evening. The sailors who disembarked from a boat that had just arrived were coming, spitting out vulgar language, and several prostitutes rushed toward them, shrieking.

Then they knew intuitively that the gentleman was there. They felt an undeniable holy atmosphere that they had never felt. Step by step, they approached the epicenter of the force. In the end, they arrived at the bar where he was supposed to be, opened the door and went inside.

But what is this all about? The gentleman was there, for sure, but he was not the man that they had known in the past. All over his cheeks that were reddish with alcohol, there were red spots from alcohol poisoning, together with blackish age spots. An eye as murky as a gutter, the bashed-in nose that was turned red as a rotten carrot, the disproportionately wide mouth, the teeth decaying black in that mouth, the neck with layers of wrinkles, and the long dirty fingernails that seemed never have been trimmed.

What surprised them more was the way he talked. He was speaking in vulgar language, not distinguishable from the rest of the people in the backward area of the city, from which not a modicum of refinement or dignity was perceived. And what a lowly shape of him who was giggling!

What was more embarrassing was his outfit. As the old woman had said, he wore accessories all over his body. There were seven pairs of earrings, twelve strings of necklaces, five pairs of bracelets, layers of rings worn on each finger, and in addition, a lot of stuff were hung on his body.

As if they were not enough, countless accessories were scattered around him. However, none of the ornaments looked expensive or were elaborately cut so that one could feel any artistic beauty. For the representatives familiar with sophisticated aesthetic refinement, it was an intolerable pain to see them.

Nonetheless, it was undeniable that the gentleman was still what he used to be in the past. The holy power that emanated from him, at least it was as strong as before, and the attitude toward him of the people in the backward area was as sincere as they themselves had been before.

There were old people and young people. There were women and men. They looked up at him with unwavering eyes, and listened intently to his words. While he was talking or holding their hands and rubbing them, people laughed at times and wept at other times, looking at his sorrowful eye.

"Oh, honorable master!" one of the most ardent representatives could not contain himself any longer and cried out loud, "What the hell is this? What the hell are you doing in this dirty place?"

Instantly, the gentleman's eye and the eyes of the people surrounding him were directed at him. The space stood still as if frozen—the people were trapped in a stifling silence for a moment.

The gentleman looked at the representatives quietly. Embarrassed, the representatives tucked in their well-ironed underwear with a haste, which was sticking out from under the old clothes worn as a disguise to infiltrate into the backward area.

At last, the gentleman opened his mouth and blessed them with his earlier refined language. "May you be always healthy! Also, may you be always blessed!"

The representative asked him almost wailingly, "Honorable master, please tell us! Why are you here like this?"

The gentleman mused for a moment. There was a silence. Everyone held their breaths waiting for his next remark.

At long last, the gentleman, Binggisa, opened his mouth and began to talk.

"A long time ago . . ."

CHAPTER 34
Binggisa, Ayutha, and Bhaddiya

(STORY OF BINGGISA'S PAST LIFE)

'A long time ago, when I was a wandering minstrel that sang and recited poems, my footsteps were led to the Shakya Kingdom. Since I was famous throughout the continent, my performance was also a great success at the Shakya kingdom.

"One day, the Shakya King Bhaddiya invited me to his palace. Enchanted by my genius spirit of art, the king requested me to remain at the court after the performance and I accepted his offer.

"From then on, I trained him on poetry and music. King Bhaddiya was bright and filled with artistic sensitivity, thus he deeply immersed himself in the beauty of art. Soon, the two of us were able to share heart to heart from the very depth of our being.

"'My dearest friend, Binggisa!' he said. 'I had my doubts of whether truth and beauty exist in men, but you convinced me that they do in fact exist. Thus, I express my deepest gratitude and acknowledge you as my true friend. Now I stand on the same ground of truth with you and look to the beauty together, the goal of our path.'

"'Yes, I do too . . .' I responded, 'I have never seen anyone who is so sincere in pursuit of the truth like you and who can sense beauty in such great depth.'

"The King Bhaddiya said, 'Oh, my dear friend, I can't be the only one taking delight in this profound happiness that I can reach through art, in the world of utmost beauty that I have learned through you! What I am saying . . . You, the great creator and elaborate performer of poetry and music! I wish to share this utmost beauty and profound happiness together with my wife, Queen Ayutha, whom I love with all my heart.'

"Then, Bhaddiya sent someone for the queen, requesting her to join us to the place where we stayed. In a few moment she appeared before us.

"Oh! The moment she appeared at the end of the corridor, a raging storm appeared in my heart, despite of the fact that I only saw her from a distance! After a while, she came and stood before me. She also seemed to be caught up in some kind of inexplicable emotional storm. The two of us stared at each other for a while as if bewitched. The King Bhaddiya must have also noticed that the two of us developed a particular impression toward one another.

"King Bhaddiya said something before presenting me to Ayutha, but for some peculiar reason I could not remember it. That's because my very soul went out for a moment, reaching out to Queen Ayutha. In that moment,

"'Isn't that right, my friend? Aren't you startled by my true companion, to whom you must bring infinite world of utmost beauty and profound joy from this point on?' I heard the king repeat his words. I then brought myself back to present, and quickly responded.

"'Yes, indeed I am astounded . . . to the extent that I seem to have lost my mind for a second. Oh my majesty the king! Your queen is already the world of utmost beauty. Thus what more could I possibly enhance her with? Your majesty! Adding flowers on top of the silk may add brilliance to what is already beautiful; however layering flowers with silk on top will only conceal the beauty of flower. The queen is already the exquisite flower and my art will simply be the silk that conceal her beauty.'"

As such, I complimented her of being the world of utmost beauty, but she was not only the exquisite beauty, but also my heavenly delight. In that moment, my mind was overflowing in elation and joy, so subtle and profound that it felt virtually indescribable. But I only described to the king that she was a world of utmost beauty, while concealing my thought on her being my profound happiness. Something told me that, this should be the extent of how much I should share with the king.

"King Bhaddiya smiled gently and said to Ayutha while pointing to me, 'He is the master of poetry and music. His arts make stars prick up their ears and awe the beasts in forest. My queen, I have been learning poetry and music from him until now. I did not introduce him to you till today, but I am quite convinced that it is about time that I introduce him to you.

"'You are my companion, but even before that you are my true friend. As he stated, you are already a world of utmost beauty and profound happiness in itself. However, I learned from him that there is no limit to beauty and happiness. What I'm trying to say is that, just as I did, I hope your studies will complement the utmost inner beauty to your utmost outer beauty, and the scent of happiness will freshly be added onto your present blossom of happiness.

"'Moreover, you will be led to the paradise just as I was, through the guidance of this angel from Earth. Then the three of us will hold our hands together to sing and take delight in the truth of the paradise, good of the paradise and the beauty of the paradise. I am truly pleased that I have invited you to come and join us in the artistic paradise.'

"Then, the King Bhaddiya introduced two of us and requested me to teach the queen well. After a while, the king left, and I was left privately with the Queen Ayutha in the room.

"The two of us were so enthralled by each other that we just sat and stared at each other blankly for a long time without saying much. It was probably I, out of the two, who displayed more vacant look.

"Oh, you dear ones. Could you imagine? The way she looked at that moment, the way she carried herself, the way she spoke, and just her ambience itself was beyond all the poems that I've ever exquisitely portrayed in different languages and the kind of mysterious harmony that I ever played up until then.

"I got deeply immersed in that poem and in that harmony. So, my mind disappeared into a strange, far off space, which was more like a paradise that was dreamy and rainbow-like.

"Before I knew it, I reached out and grasped her wrist. She carefully took my hands off. I suddenly recalled my own status, thus I bent down and showed my respect as her humble retainer. It was very awkward for a moment, but that was only for a short while until I began to give a talk on art. I realized at a certain point that she was becoming more and more immersed in my words. Just like me, she was drifting off to some far and remote place, as if walking through a dream or a rainbow-like paradise.

"Fortunately, or perhaps quite regrettably, we often had a chance to meet in seclusion, without the presence of the king. The King Bhaddiya trusted us in a most confiding manner, and on top of that he was very busy with his work. Thus, I often had opportunities to teach Queen Ayutha privately on poetry and music.

"However, I wouldn't go in detail about what happened next, but all I can say is that it didn't take long till I held her in my arms. While she was in my arms, I felt incredibly blissful and euphoric. I felt like time and space melt away, a state of self-oblivion, which was quite difficult to describe.

"Of course I had hesitated! I felt guilty and it went against my conscience. When I thought of King Bhaddiya, how could I possibly not feel sorry for him, who regarded me as his only friend in the whole world? I mean, how could that not break my heart also?

"Nonetheless, my love was much stronger than those hesitations and my conscience. Talk of ethics and morality didn't find a place to intrude in our love. These ethics and morality that lingered in my heart vanished at one point and the blazing passion between us turned us into two tiger moths spiraling toward the flames."

Listen, oh dear ones. After much time had passed, I repented my past actions, and I was reborn again. And looking back, I still had a chance to redeem myself at that time. I could have solved my painful dilemmas by confessing to the King Bhaddiya.

"If we confessed honestly about the emotional and mental love we felt toward each other, King Bhaddiya, who had deeper understanding of human nature compared to others, could have given us permission to the love that we felt in our hearts, or even of our physical love perhaps. I don't think that could have been totally impossible, because to him, truth was more important than love. Because the values truly paramount for him were not the truth or beauty, but the beauty of the truth.

"I believe he had the mental power to overcome the shock that the direction Ayutha's love had changed its course from him to me. So, if we had taken the risk and honestly confessed our love, he could have sacrificed that love in order to preserve the path of truth.

"But at the time I lacked understanding in profundity of human potential. I was confident to say I had some degree of understanding in art. But just because I understood art, doesn't mean that I understood the depth of human mind. Being a person of such meager understanding, I could not fathom the existence of a man who could give up his lover for the sake of the truth.

"But now—having experienced such horrific suffering and extended spiritual practice, I can now see beauty in all that looks deceitful and ugly. I can finally think that King Bhaddiya could have forgiven us, but at that time I didn't have such a high level of thought.

"Thus, at long last my deceitful cover was stripped off by King Bhaddiya. The king was in shock upon discovering the relationship I had with Ayutha. It was shock of his paradise being ripped apart, or actually the kind of shock of seeing the whole world collapse. Thus, we were banished from the court by King Bhaddiya after I lost my one eye and Ayutha lost her hearing.

"From that point on Ayutha changed. But just as I didn't take notice of the internal working of King Bhaddiya, I also neglected to see the inner changes Ayutha was going through. While she was being reborn into a new person, I remained still the old Binggisa or was becoming the worst of Binggisa. After a while Ayutha left, and I remained alone empty hearted. I lost the only person who truly understood me, and I had to face the terrifying fact that there was no one left in this world who could possibly understand me. This led me to an unbearable void. Thus, from here my life took a different turn, from art to religion."

CHAPTER 35
Binggisa, the Warrior of God

'With regard to religion, I was born and raised in a family that believed the Huruva Order. I decided to go back to the God to whom I had gone and praised as a child, held by the hands of my parents. So I visited Archbishop Chuchu, at the headquarters of the Huruva Order. Soon after, I became a close associate of Archbishop Chuchu. Chuchu, who had been eyeing me as his successor, put forth a lot of effort to pass his religious beliefs to me. He tried to instill loyalty to Huruva in me, even by sacrificing his own mother.

"So, as he wished, I became a warrior of God armed with strong religious beliefs. Clad in a red robe—but the robe was a suit of armor, wearing a priest hat—but the hat was a helmet, with a staff twice as tall as my height—but the staff was a spear, and holding a holy book—but the holy book was the law book to judge non-believers.

"As a holy general armed with firm conviction, my steps headed westward. I succeeded in propagating my religious beliefs to the chief of a tribe ruling a region in the Hindu Kush Mountains. The chief, by the name of Tajiski, inducted me as the religious teacher of his Mahala Tribe, and consulted me on all important issues of the tribe. He often knelt down in front of me and received my advice.

"Three years later, the whole of the Mahala Tribe became the follower of the Huruva Order. They pledged to discard their old gods that were as many as forty-six, and to give allegiance to one God Huruva until death. Idols were burned down, and temples enshrining Huruva were built one after another. Every day at sunrise and sunset, voices of the people shouting 'Huruva! Huruva!' rang in every village.

"As the next step, I dispatched thoroughly trained missionaries to the neighboring area where the Harama Tribe lived. But there arose a problem. The people of Harama persecuted our missionaries. It was also well known to the Mahala that the Harama worshipped one god, Avaru, for generations. However, the Harama didn't propagate their faith to neighboring tribes, because Avaru was a tribal god exclusively for them. Avaru was the god who protected and guided only the Harama Tribe of all tribes of the mankind.

"It meant that they stuck strongly together ethnically and had a very exclusive mind toward other tribes. So they violently rejected the missionaries I sent and severely oppressed them. However, the more they oppressed, the more the loyalty of our missionaries to Huruva grew strong. So they finally collided with the locals. In the end, our missionaries were brought to trial by the Harama. The court sentenced them to death, and they were executed immediately.

"A few days later, the news came to me.

"'Oh, you! Sacred is the blood you shed!' I wailed, and then swore, 'Oh, the wicked Avaru! The symbol of arrogance, the symbol of disloyalty, who was born as an angel by God's blessing but dared to stand up against God! It would have been better if you had not been born at all or if you had not been an angel. Now, I will destroy you completely and return you to your original state, the state of nothingness!'

"After this, I went into the temple, fasted, and prayed for fifteen days. On the fifteenth day, finally the God Huruva came down to me amid blue starlight. I came out of the temple. Outside of the temple, Tajiski, the chief of the Mahala, along with other lower chiefs, were waiting for me to come out to hear the words of God.

"Showing no sign of fatigue in spite of the fifteen-day long fasting, and shrouded by holy splendor, I delivered the order of the God Huruva to the ten chiefs including Tajiski, the order to thoroughly punish and exterminate His rival god, Avaru and his followers, and to return everything related to them to nothingness.

"The next day, ten chiefs, including Tajiski, proceeded to the temple and swore allegiance to God. They soon conscripted more than fifty thousand soldiers and sent a man to Harama and demanded them to apologize for the execution of our missionaries, punish those who were involved in the execution, and from then on not to interfere with our missionary works.

"But they replied, 'Our God Avaru does not approve of Huruva. Therefore, we cannot but decline your request.'

"Thus, a showdown between the two tribes became inevitable. Before going to war, our chiefs and I, each holding an eagle blindfolded with a piece of cloth, proceeded to the temple of Huruva, and pledged victory in the war, spraying on the altar the blood of five kinds of animals, such as camel, sheep, deer, pig, and bear. Our troops marched into the territory of Harama. When we arrived, the Harama people were waiting for us in a huge castle built in preparation for that kind of confrontation, and the murderous spirit spewing from them was so fierce as to make our soldiers shrink.

"The two armies shouted the name of their own god of worship who they believed without doubt would protect them, but in the end one of whom would become the loser and vanish. After the first confrontation, Tajiski and his chiefs called on me in the middle of the night. 'Your Excellency, our army will attack the castle tomorrow!' Tajiski told me on behalf of the chiefs, in a voice full of awe. 'And we will slaughter every single one of those insolent people who rebelled against Huruva!'

"'Oh, my dear chiefs, tomorrow's battle will be remembered forever until the end of the world as a sacred work to glorify Huruva! And your names will also be written in gold letters in the register of undying achievements in the name of Huruva, and will never be erased even if the angels' names are erased.'

"But there was a look of perplexity lingering on the face of Tajiski. He opened his mouth hesitantly. 'But Your Excellency, there is one problem.'

"'Don't hesitate to speak out.'

"'Your Excellency, in the castle, together with the non-believers, there are our brothers and sisters who believe the Huruva Order, although they are a small minority. So we have to distinguish them from the enemy, but battles cannot be successfully engaged if we have to take every minute detail into consideration. Your Excellency, if we have to save our believers in the castle, we can't win this battle. Rather than we slaughter them, we may face a situation where we will be slaughtered by them. Please tell us how we shall deal with this problem.'

"I thought for a moment. The next moment, I heard the voice of Huruva: 'You do not worry, life on earth, when compared to the life in heaven, is nothing more than that of a dayfly!'

"I jumped up and shouted, 'My dear chiefs, you do not hesitate, you do not scruple, because the hesitation and scruples are the trembling of the children born by weak faith. So I tell you in the name of God, kill them! Kill them! Kill them all! My dear chiefs, do not worry about you becoming guilty of killing your brothers or sisters, because He in heaven will select your brothers and sisters whom you worry about well among the dead and give them rewards for their loyalty to Him on earth, worth ten thousand times, one hundred million times of their loyalty!'

"So the next morning, the tribal chiefs, who were ebullient at my strong instructions, commanded the army and launched an attack on the castle of the Harama. The battle continued all morning. Finally, our army seized the opportunity to win a decisive victory. Our soldiers rushed into the castle of the Harama like a flood, and from then on judgment on those who rebelled against Huruva began.

"It was pandemonium! No distinction was made between adults and children, men and women, aristocrats and commoners, rich and poor ones. Those who were staying in the castle had to be all killed. At this and that house, in this and that alley, in this exposed and that hidden area, murders were committed. The cries of people in the throes of death rose high into the sky.

"Oh, but brothers and sisters! There was a very serious problem— the scene that should have been naturally the most evil and ugly one seemed to me as the most virtuous and the most beautiful one that no genius painter could depict!

"What a painful thing! What a shameful thing that I do not want to recall ever again! However, I must not run away from it! I cannot escape from it, even if I want to! Oh, at that time, I reveled in a sacred spiritual bliss in front of the hellish scene where tens of thousands were being slaughtered. In my heart I cried, *The Great God Huruva is working here now, so, behold! The great providence of God! The righteous punishment imposed on those who disobeyed God!*"

Having said all this, Binggisa ceased to talk for a while. He repeated to inhale deeply and exhale several times, and thus regained his composure.

At last, Binggisa resumed his talk in a low voice.

CHAPTER 36
Go Back to the Beginning

'Fifteen days later I was back in the castle of the Mahala with my troops. Later that evening, I held a prayer meeting with my faithful disciples and the chiefs of the Mahala in commemoration of the victory. As it was the last day of the fifteen-day prayer meeting, far more believers joined it than usual.

"At the front, I led the prayer, facing the five-pointed star that enshrined God Huruva. But when the prayers were well in progress, I heard a buzzing sound coming from behind. Without paying attention to the sound, I said my prayer of thanks to Huruva at the top of my voice, almost wailingly.

"But the noise grew bigger and bigger, and as it grew bigger, the voices of the congregation that was praising Huruva along with me became smaller. Finally, I stopped praying and turned back because the congregation almost did not follow my prayers.

"Weaving through the congregation, a man with a stick in one hand was walking toward me, limping with a splinted leg. Even though he did not have a sound body, due to his high spirits that ordinary people lacked, the congregation made way for him like water being parted.

"At last, his steps stopped about seven paces away from me. His eyes were bloodshot and his face was full of scars that were not yet healed. I just watched him without a word, and waited for him to speak, but he kept staring at me for a while, and said nothing.

"There was a silence. And silence again. The silence was like the calm before the storm. The believers were looking at us with a deeply interested look. At this moment there was no Huruva in their hearts. It was like two different kinds of drinks cannot be contained in one glass. In other words, pouring mango juice into a glass full of water meant the water that had first been there would disappear. Likewise, upon the believers becoming curious about the showdown between the two of us, Huruva was pushed out of their minds.

"That was the same with me. His sudden appearance before me was so unexpected that my mind was entirely absorbed in it and became unable to think of anything else, and thus Huruva was forgotten in my mind too.

"What remained between the man and me, and between the two of us and the congregation were—oh, although we were in a place called a shrine of God, there was no God there, but only human beings.

"'Oh, Binggisa!' Finally, the man opened his mouth. 'An angel, but a devil! Smart but stupid! A man who has a beautiful language but with that beautiful language charms people into an ugly place, a man who has a mysterious voice, but with that mysterious voice covers the eyes of the people and leads them to ignorance!'

"I didn't respond to him. It was because I felt a powerful spiritual force emanating from him that I could never ignore. So I couldn't but listen to him rather than retort. His voice was relatively calm compared to the content of his remarks. Even though he was attacking me, there was no hatred carried in his words, but his eyes were flaming as if he would burn me down any minute.

"He said again, 'Binggisa, you listen to me! Not as a priest of a religion, but as a human being! I saw you when you were young. I was invited to stay at your house by your father when I was wandering around as a minstrel. I remember seeing you as a young baby smiling in your father's arms. Oh! How innocent you were then! How pure you were! How cute and how cheerful you were! But! There is no such Binggisa in you now. The innocent infant, the pure child has left away from you. Now you are a demon! A murderer who killed tens of thousands of lives! You believe you are doing good, but in fact you are doing evil—the most foolish man in the world!'

"One moment, the calm in his voice disappeared. He raised his splinted leg up and shouted, 'Come on! Look, Binggisa! The evil actions that those, who entrusted their free wills to you, have committed! My body that they injured! It is not a big thing that I lost a leg! I could still save my life! However, my sons and daughters, my grandchildren, my friends and relatives, and all who were in the castle died! Oh! They were all brutally sacrificed as victims of your fanaticism.'

"He strode onto the altar limping. At that time, the priests, who were just listening to him, rushed in to grab him. I raised my right hand to hold them back and watched what he was doing. Once on the altar, he hobbled past me toward a place where the five-pointed star, the divinity itself to the believers of Huruva, was enshrined, and ripped it off at once.

"He came close to me holding the five-pointed star in his hands, pushed it toward my eyes, and said, 'Look, look! Here is your God!'

"I kept my mouth tightly closed and listened to what he said. In my mind, an uncontrollable whirlwind arose. He looked at me with a piercing gaze and said, 'But! As you saw it, your God showed no reaction, even though I blasphemed him. Then again, I will put the house where your God stays in contempt—at that time you will see how your God reacts!'

"Having said this, he raised the five-pointed star aloft and hurled it hard on the floor. The star was broken into pieces and scattered all over the place, and the priests winced in amazement and stepped back. He sneered at the priests, 'Why are you backing away from the God? For fear of injury? For fear of death? Oh! But isn't death the virtue that you hope for the most? To you, death means going to heaven, then why are you afraid of death? It is because there is no paradise in your eyes. Also, it is because God does not stay in what I've just smashed. Whatever you may say otherwise in public, you are well aware of it in your mind! So, you listen up! This five-pointed star is neither your God nor his house. Not only that, know it straight that nowhere in this world is your God! If there were.'

"Saying this, he turned his eyes from the priests and the congregation toward me. 'You the Bishop of the Huruva Order, one who mysteriously communicates with Huruva, one who listens to Him and realizes His will on earth! You do not know, but I do know. The God that you saw and heard is simply the God you yourself saw and heard, and not the God that everyone saw and heard! It is no more than that you just saw and heard the God in your delusion! If it's not, then you call your God before me, right away! I will deal with Him!'

"He pushed me hard. 'Call your God out! Now! Why are you hesitating? Why don't you call your God out? Or are you unable to call Him out?'

"I could not make any response and had to wait for his next remark. He continued his talk. 'Therefore! Therefore, your God is non-existent! The God exists only in your mind, in other words, he is no more than a mass of delusion! Nevertheless! Nevertheless, you inflicted pains that are more terrible than hell on numerous people, for the God that is not even existent! Oh! What a fool you are! You are a fool who, for the life in dream, has thrown away the real life!'

"As he said, all in the temple just watched him in amazement, and I too couldn't make any response, because his words, to my surprise, appeared to suit me precisely.

"I cried out in my heart, *Oh, if only I could call out Huruva! Then, I would be able to submit this man! But I cannot call Him out and show Him to this man! I continued to think, This being the case, isn't it that I cannot simply deny his argument that the God who only I can see or hear is no more than a mass of delusion?*

"As a result, my mind suddenly swerved from the man toward myself. I flopped down on the floor of the altar and was absorbed in thought. Even forgetting the fact that, being the leader of numerous followers, I was not in a position to do so, and also being unaware of the screams of the believers who were surprised at my behavior that looked as if I had been knocked down by the strong punches of the man. While I sat down on the floor and was locked in deep thought, the priests who just came to their senses rushed to the man with some young followers. I later learned that they had grabbed the man and dragged him out of the temple.

"He was beaten by the believers at the square outside of the temple. In an instant his body was covered with blood, and even when such thing was happening in front of the temple of Huruva who taught to love the neighbors, no word was heard from the high sky where God abode, and no divine power was displayed.

"After a while, I suddenly came back to my senses and hurriedly ran out of the temple. When I arrived at the square, the men who had beaten him moved away from him hesitantly. 'Oh! Brothers!' I shouted at the men. 'Did you forget the commandment God gave us? The commandment to love your neighbors!'

"I approached the man. The man was dying short of breath. I walked up to him and took his hand. My single eye was filled with scalding tears.

"'Oh! You!' I cried.

"'It's you who made me see what I've never seen before!'

"A faint smile crossed his face. With the eyes that were more bloodshot than a little while ago, he spoke to me brokenly, with a light smile instead of hostility on his face. 'Oh, Mr. Binggisa! I want to believe that you . . . are now changing . . . the direction of . . . your mind. How . . . fortunate . . . it is!'

"I added strength to my hands that were holding his hand. He said, 'Mr. Binggisa . . . please go back to yourself, to the innocence in your childhood . . .' Having said this, the man soon expired."

CHAPTER 37
A Prickly Pear

'I managed to collect and bury the man's corpse. Then I contemplated immediately on what this event entails. The first thought was how God Huruva did not subjugate the old man, despite of his contempt directed toward God himself. I also thought about the man's opinion on how the concept of God is simply an illusion. Step by step, I moved toward the belief that perhaps God does not truly exist at all.

God may not exist?

"That was such a ludicrous assumption for me at that time. I shook my head vigorously in denial, in order to cast away such presumptuous idea.

"However, once the thought entered my mind, it simply wouldn't leave me alone. Thus, I resolved to confront these devilish whispers head on. But as time passed, I had no choice but to admit the fact that these whispers were not from the devil but arising from the depth of my own mind.

"That is, those voices were the pure, innocent, charming, and cheerful voices from my own childhood. Those whispers were arising from within me, before God settled and when my mind wasn't engaged with other preconceptions.

"However, before I managed to organize these thoughts, my mind had already wandered toward the thought of Ayutha, as the dying words of the man, 'Please return to yourself . . .' were exactly what my love Ayutha said to me before she left.

"At that time, I entrusted all my religious work to the most senior priest and shut myself in a small room of my own. Of course, my devotees haven't got a clue of the transformation taking place in my mind. They thought I had cut off all contact with others and immersed myself in extended fasting prayers in order to move closer to God.

"But in fact, I sat in a small isolated room and thought about Ayutha over and over. As a result, I finally came to understand the meaning of her last words before she left me. 'Please don't get attached to other people . . . do not resist your fate . . . and please return back to yourself.'

"With that realization, I felt some profound changes began to occur, and then my mind suddenly felt more at ease. It was unlike the kind of peace I had ever experienced before. I understood intuitively that it was not the kind of rigid stability attained behind closed doors, or by building great barriers and fences. Rather, it was a smooth and relaxed feeling of liberation, appreciated in an open space through stripping away barriers and fences.

"I sprang up from my seat and ran out from my small isolated room. I rushed away the assisting priest with my hands, who tried to follow me out, and walked alone toward a place where no one could be found. When a meadow appeared, I lay myself down. Pure white clouds drifted away slowly on pristine blue sky. I thought of Ayutha's unconventional behavior, which was like pristine blue sky and pure white clouds I was staring up at that moment.

"*That's right!* I thought to myself. *She responded completely differently even when we were in exact same situation. What was our fundamental difference?*

"After being vanished from the palace, Ayutha exhibited a very receptive attitude. This placed me in a very awkward state, which even led me to beat her eventually. But despite of my brutishness, she maintained her very receptive behavior yet again—a real pathetic and weak manner that corresponds almost to 'no defense is my defense.'

"When I was lying on the ground and looking at those pure blissful whites clouds, I realized her receptive mind was a significant one, and what seemed like a weakness was not simply a weakness but strength within the weakness, which was much stronger than any great strength imaginable. I also knew that my brief experience of that peaceful mind was related to the receptive mind Ayutha exhibited before.

"With such thoughts, all vitality began to drain out of my body. At first, I was a little afraid of that experience. But I soon listened to the voices of my heart and those words said to me: *Just let it be. That is tension that dissipates from you right now; tension is poisonous and poison arises from the defilements of the mind. The tension escaping you means defilements of your mind is being released.*

"Therefore, I allowed the energy to drain out of my body, letting nature take its course in whatever it was supposed to do, and let happen what was supposed to happen. For the next stage, I also left my mind alone to take its course as I had done with my body. In that state of mind and my body being surrendered, I watched my mind silently.

"Could mind observe the mind? Perhaps this may sound like a contradiction to you all. But it is possible to see mind with the mind. Not only that, it is even possible to see the mind that observes the mind, which indicates that mind is really that subtle. While I was observing my own mind, I felt my body and mind sink further and further down abyss, and finally I felt my mind hit the rock bottom.

"The bottom! The very rock bottom! That solid rock bottom!

"My intuition told me that hitting rock bottom is the foundation for me to stand firmly. However, that was the extent of my advancement. My mind evidently was not ready to advance further at that time, as it maintained its state of peace for a little while but reverted back to my prior mental state, to my usual state of mind.

"Then, pure white clouds came to view once again.

"That's it! The mind! I thought to myself. *The mind like the sky and the mind like the clouds! That subtle mind, the mind that sees! The mind that again sees the mind that perceives!*

"Thus, I stood up after a few moments. As vigorous as possible, so even the crown of my head could pierce through the sky! That's right! My mind was grounded on the one hand, but reached out to the sky at the same time. My mind was planted firmly on the ground, which meant that I was not the same person I used to be a moment ago. It also meant that God was not my priority as it did before, but my mind became my top priority.

"I began to walk slowly. My feet were directed toward the location where the stack of corpses formed a mountain, blood stains colored the streams, and the scent of blood filled the air. No more than just a few days ago, my eyes flicked on this very spot as I relished the outcome of my divine triumph. But when I returned to the very spot, as a person whose mind was restored to the place where Huruva had remained, only then I finally began to perceive those corpses as people. That is right. Those were also people that possessed the mind! Just like the Mahala people! And just like me!

"From the very core of my being, I could hear the scream, 'No! This is all wrong!' Just like the loving lullaby my mother used to sing for me, or like the long-forgotten flute tunes that I once played as a boy, the words of conscience suddenly returned back to my mind.

"Suddenly, a great pain struck my whole body with a great blow. I searched for a weapon like a lunatic amongst those countless corpses, which was half buried and half still exposed. At last, I got a hold of a sword and almost stabbed my heart without a second thought. But in fact, the moment I tried to stab down at my heart, I collapsed on the very spot, deterred by an unknown force, perhaps protected by whatever little positive karma I gained from my past life. It was not until early the next morning that I woke up while puking my guts out. The sun peeped out its head on the ridges of the mountain, which was filled with misty haze. I got myself up somehow.

"All kinds of pests, including ants and flies, swarmed all over, while wolves, wild dogs, hyenas, and eagles flocked over to take their share of the bodies from which the souls had already left. Tears streamed down endlessly from my eyes, entrenched by the scent of gory blood bath that would make people clasp their nose with disgust.

"Clenching my teeth tight and wiping off the tears with the back of my hands, I began to stumble forward. I continued walking without much purpose. I had no idea toward which direction or how far I walked. After some time, however, I realized I was quite hungry. I looked toward every direction in search of food. But I could not find anything edible.

"At the time I was walking through a vast field. After wandering through the field for some time, I ended up in a sand field with black stones scattered randomly. Whirlwind blew past the empty space and murky sand dust was rising over. I kept walking without even covering my face. When the wind settled, the field view cleared up once again. I then saw a prickly pear that stood nearby. The cactus I saw was quite small and I squatted in front to take a closer look. I did it just like the time long ago, when I was around six years old.

"I often saw the same species of small prickly pear in my father's study when I was a child. My father showed particular fondness toward the flower of prickly pear cacti. Hence, he made sure that this particular flower was kept in the study at all times. Along with all the cacti my father kept separately in his den, there was a very small cactus often referred to as baby cactus. Those who visited my father were absolutely amazed by these cacti since its flowers were more stunning than any other cactus flowers they had seen. In that moment I saw the same family of the baby cactus in the desert, which I used to see in my father's study.

"At first, I thought about taking the prickly pear as my breakfast. I reached out and tried to grab hold of the cactus. However, my weak hands trembled and due to lack of energy I ended up pricking my finger deeply by its sharp thorn rather than grabbing the cactus. A fit of annoyance came, but in next instant, a mocking smile of self-contempt arose on my face. I took away tens of thousands of lives, yet I was irritated merely by a small prick on a finger. Disdained by such a self-destructive thought, I was seized by the great uncontrollable pain in an instant. I fainted with my two hands wrapped around my head.

"After a long struggle, I somehow regained my consciousness while still lying on the ground. The cactus caught my eyes again. A yellow flower had appeared somehow, which was not there just a moment ago and its attractive scent tickled my nose. I closed my eyes gently and appreciated its beautiful fragrance. Its scent got me drunk, just like the alcohol, poetry, and music could. After a while, when I gazed back to the flower while still intoxicated by its beautiful fragrance, the flower appeared to me as if it was the most lovely flower in the whole wide world. I sat up and asked this mysterious flower whether it was happy. I asked, 'Are you happy? Even when no one sees you or no one is here to praise your beauty?'

"The flower then answered, 'I am happy. Regardless of whether people admire my beauty, I still feel happy. That is because beauty is enough in being beauty itself.'

"Right at that moment, I understood: I must return back to myself! I thought about the cactus that I was looking at and the cacti from my father's study. When you think about it, the splendor of the two flowers were equally beautiful. However, these two cacti were different in that the cactus that I was looking at didn't have anyone to admire its beauty, whereas the cacti from my father's study had numerous people who admired them.

"Oh, but there is something you must all realize. The joy of basking in its own beauty, both for the case of the former and latter flowers is the same. The satisfaction of being beautiful does not depend on whether they received praise or not. That was because beauty is enough in just being beauty itself.

"That's right. The true value of good deeds lies in the good deeds themselves. It is unnecessary to try to gain admiration from others—it is enough of an assurance to know that I am good, and be confident that my heart remains fresh, pure, and graceful. Therefore, for those who are true and good, it doesn't matter whether they receive admiration or not, as those praises are nothing more than a sound of breeze that passes by lightly.

"My dear ones, the life's path branches off into a path of self-sufficiency and that of dependency on other people or objects. Between those two, the path of self-sufficiency or independence remains pure. This path does not expect any compensation or reward from anyone or anything. In comparison, however, the path which depends on other things or other people encompasses something impure, and goodness that arises from this path is not from the higher plane of goodness.

"That is precisely right. Performing good deeds 'without anyone noticing,' or as the saying goes, 'not letting the left hand know what the right hand is doing' is what is truly considered good deeds. If what the right hand does is truly genuine, then it should be rewarding and joyful in itself without the praise from the left hand.

"Thus, the value of self-sufficiency is a true value. This logic dawned on me when I was watching the flower of the prickly pear cactus, which contained meaning of my denial in doctrines that placed God before men. This also explicitly meant that we must discuss humanity before God and that one must know the self before all else. Therefore, even God became an external being in relations to the self, thus God is that which exists subsequent to the existence of self.

"To reflect on this further, to the prickly pear in my father's study, those who poured out myriad praises were external to itself. In other words, they were all strangers and simply the others. Moreover, to us humans, God also exists externally, thus he is an extrinsic being and a stranger. Therefore, God is ultimately an extension of other being in its extreme form.

"We are already aware that for the prickly pear cactus, the true value of its own beauty does not depend on whether or not it receives recognition from others. This also meant that our intrinsic value does not arise by the acceptance from an external God nor would our value depreciate simply by being denied by God.

"We don't feel happy by receiving praises from others or when being accepted by God in leading a good life, but when we find ourselves looking into our own inner self to discover purity within. That is, we will discover happiness by developing self-esteem and self-confidence, achieved through self-reflection and self-acknowledgement. Just like the lone flower of prickly pear cactus that blossoms, even if none is around.

"Therefore, based on the enlightening revelation that I just spoke of, I pondered for the next three days and nights and I have abandoned the God Huruva, and moreover I have forsaken all gods of this world. *Then, where must I go from here?*

"In answer to that question, Ayutha was the one who came to my mind in that moment. I realized that she had already gone forth toward the path of humanity and the path of the mind, well before I was able to. Thus, Ayutha was the only true teacher who could direct the path for those who had abandoned God, toward the path of humanity and path of our mind. She gained new significance as the only person who could direct me to the path which I must move forth."

CHAPTER 38
Oh, at the Place, Ayutha . . .

'Standing in the midst of the humane path I entered anew, I realized how far I have drifted off from being human and what great sins I have committed down to my bones. How could I wash away my sins?

"I then came up with the conclusion that there was no other way but be steadfast to walk the path of truth I found anew this very moment. Thus, I immediately left in search of Ayutha. However, in this great, wide continent, I had no idea where she could possibly be. So, I wandered about aimlessly. Having once been a minstrel, a life of drifting without much direction or purpose was a familiar one for me. But I did not recite any poems nor sang songs for people since I was no longer a poet. I only enquired on whereabouts of Ayutha.

"Even after some years have passed, I did not have any leads as to her whereabouts. Thus, my heart sank deeper in sorrow. What made me more sorrowful was that she could have died, in that case there was no way for me to be forgiven or gain redemption by her. Also, I would not be able to learn from her the path to humanity.

"Then one day, while I was walking through a parched desert road, I saw yet another prickly pear. I advanced toward the cactus and poured the water that I had. Then a flower blossomed on the

371

cactus and the flower transformed into Ayutha in my vision. In a few moments, the fantasy of Ayutha changed again into Sakka, the King of Tavatimsa Heaven, and he informed me with a joyful news that Ayutha was in fact alive after all.

"With this encouragement, I once again wandered all over the continent to search for Ayutha. Then finally I found a village where she had stayed just a few years back. Starting from that village, I went on to the next village and then the next. I kept on going and gained more news of her after she left each village. She left quite an impression on people as she passed through these villages.

"I heard repeatedly from the people of villages where she stayed, 'She was a noble being, who transcended dimension of Human Realm.'

"I requested them to tell me her demeanor as accurately as possible. As a result, I discovered that she took refuge in Buddhadhmma and she had accomplished a very high state of spirituality. But she must have known that the praise she received from the people had little to do with the high spiritual state she lived out; she surely knew the secret meaning behind the single prickly pear flower. She left her dwelling the moment people became attached to her, and from her action I saw that she did not wish to rely on other people even one bit. The only thing she relied on was the truth and trust in herself.

"Thus, the path she walked was as pure and empty as the bare sky after birds flew off without a trace. The path she walked was without desire, obsession, impurity, or defilements, and she strode forward, walking the walk that was not a walking on the path without a path.

"Therefore, when I followed the path she once had walked, each step turned to a practice eventually. I discovered a different side of Ayutha on each village that I passed through and received a new revelation as to what it meant to live truly. As such, I progressed further and further each day. And, my dear ones, this is how my steps, in search of Ayutha, eventually led me in this forward area of Subbaraka, where you all live.

"When I arrived at Subbaraka, some of you accepted me as your teacher. Thus, I taught you what I realized up to that point. But then, one day I discovered that Ayutha lived in the backward area of the city. I soon set off for the backward area. I did not tell anyone where I was going. I had more than a few disciples at that time, but I did not communicate with them of where I was headed. I knew for certain that they would not approve of me going to see a woman from the backward area.

"When I first heard the news, I left in a hurry in search of her. But again, I did not get to meet her. When I arrived in this degenerated and shabby backward area of the city, Ayutha was already long dead. *Then, what kind of life did Ayutha live here and how?* I wondered.

"Dear ones, she lived here as a bar maid. Yet, again she was not a woman who peddled drinks, but with everything she had she led people to peace and tranquility. Living in this filthy and jagged backward area, she embraced all men who came to her. Then she wept. She stared into their eyes, held their hands, listened to their moans, and went into the very core of their hearts and played the music of the heart, as delicate as stringed instruments yet as strong as the percussions.

"All men who came before her, most of whom were sailors, confessed to her of their pains and agonies. Their ill-fated existence, abandoned by destiny and the world, and the lewd filth that arose from such a life and sighs that arose from that filth, regrets, fears, and dismays—they came and released it all on her.

"That's right. Their lives were about fears and traumas all in itself. For they were ones who drifted off from one harbor to the next, relying only on a ship where hell waited just below a layer of plank.

"It was a rough journey where a father died today, a brother tomorrow, and a friend the day after. It was a dreadful life, being treated contemptuously here today, there tomorrow, and then a different place the day after. But there was no hope for escape from this misery, being tied up in a contract of near slavery with the forward city people. With big sighs, they came to her. Then, she embraced them again and comforted them every time.

"She did not try to be wise in giving answers to life's problems nor encouraged them to fight against those who forced them into unfair contracts. She simply watched them with a hollow expression as if she had given up everything. It was as if she was saying *I'll take the blow that you throw, and I'll die if you slay me*. Then, with extreme sadness in her eyes, she embraced them in her arms.

"Strangely enough, the people who came to her beamed with a great smile and gained their strength again to go out on a journey of new life. As such, she became their mother, sister, wife, and a lover. Thus, when they returned back from their sailing, the first place they found was the sanctuary called Ayutha. On each of those hands were offerings for an altar, but the offerings they prepared were not genuine ornaments but these imitations," he said, pointing to objects beside him.

"She cherished them, like a priest who delicately handles sacred offerings to present on God's altar. She polished and stroked them gently. Then, at some point or another she began to put on the ornaments they had offered. She clasped them on her wrists, ankles, and neck, and stuck them on her head and her clothes. Soon enough she was covered with myriad ornaments.

"Her appearance could not be said to be beautiful. However, not a single one of her sons, brothers, husbands, and lovers regarded her as dreadful or horrid; they were simply grateful that she treasured their gifts so kindly. When they returned and found their cheap trinkets just as they had left them in the holy sanctuary, they burst into tears enthralled with whirl of emotion.

"Years have passed since then. She had aged and turned into an old granny, a stark difference from the time when she first arrived looking beautiful as heavenly goddess. After exhausting all her physical strength, she once again lost her hearing. At first, her ears wouldn't pay attention to anything dishonest, but those ears lost their hearing when they paid attention to my sweet words. However, her hearing was restored again by the sacred Buddhadhamma, and later those ears listened to the pains of numerous others. At the end, however, her ears succumbed to quietude in the dark abyss.

"Oh but dear ones, I know. Just like she did when she was a frail beggar, she must have heard words that worldly people could not hear in this abyss of quietude. They were things that words could not express, but then again, they were words that could not be denied their function as words. At the end, however, she died in this quietude. And since then, these people have become the abandoned sons, abandoned husbands, and abandoned brothers. Oh, my dear ones. So you asked me why I am here and why in such a state. So this is my answer to you.

"Dear ones, I am merely substituting for Ayutha, the woman whom I loved most dearly and who loved me in return; I am to fill that empty space now that she is gone, because that is the least I could do."

Binggisa stopped after such an explanation.

There was silence.

No one opened their mouth.

No one moved.

After some time, someone began to weep while covering the face with his two hands. Then the sobbing spread to all, dispersed like the color of paint. In this putrid rotten back street, a lone candle brightly lit in the darkness—and a bright star plummeted toward it, making a lengthy streak across the night sky.

Ten days passed.

Fifty representatives from the forward area made a visit to Binggisa. After a few questions, they went with him on a tour around the backward area. They returned back to the forward area of the city and reported to the council of elders on what they had seen and heard.

Then, after approximately one month, the representatives from the forward and backward area of the city gathered in Binggisa's room. For the extent of three days and nights, they tried to find ways for both regions to prosper.

Binggisa did not actively intervene in their discussion. But since reconciliation could not have ensued smoothly without him, it could be insinuated that he carried on the meeting without words. A few months had passed again. The construction project began for the rebirth of the backward area into a brand new city, now renamed as the district of brotherhood. The project was to be allocated into seven districts, being spread out through an extent of ten years.

CHAPTER 39
Like the Moon Freed from the Clouds

(BACK TO THE BUDDHA AGAIN)

The Buddha said to Ananda and several bhikkhus, "Ananda, the Tathagata has described Binggisa up until he appeared in the port city of Subbaraka, and about what he has done there."

"Yes, World-Honored One."

"Now, bhikkhus, let us go to Binggisa."

"Yes, World-Honored One."

Having answered as such, Ananda and the bhikkhus rose from the seat with the Buddha. The Buddha walked toward Subbaraka along the way by the seashore, leading the bhikkhu disciples. When the Buddha and his company have walked about a half yojana, they found a caravan that the Subbaraka people had pitched to receive great guests. Beside the caravan, the mayor of Subbaraka city, together with ten elders and over one hundred citizens, was waiting for the Buddha.

The Buddha and the bhikkhus washed their hands and feet with the water prepared by the people of Subbaraka, and finished their meal. After a while, upon the Buddha sitting in the Dhamma seat under the caravan, the Subbaraka mayor and its citizens made three prostrations to the holy teacher to show respect. Although they made prostrations, they were not Buddhists. Nevertheless, as they had heard a lot about this noble teacher, and the Buddha's appearance that they saw personally was extremely sacred, a big faith in the Buddha and the Buddhadhamma arose in their minds. But the Buddha did not think that their faith was strong enough. In particular, the Buddha believed that they needed a higher and stronger faith to fully understand the rare and great causal event that they would witness after a while.

Therefore, the Buddha entered a meditative absorption to exercise the great spiritual power available only to those who have attained unsurpassed, perfect enlightenment. After a while, the Buddha emerged from the meditative absorption and made a circular hand mudra. Then, in a moment, in the small space in the caravan, the whole three realms of the Desire Realm, the Form Realm, and the Formless Realm, from the hell at the lowest to the Heaven of Neither Perception nor Non-Perception at the highest, were all contained. The Buddha made a circular hand mudra again. Then, this time, the great trichiliocosm, as myriad other worlds outside the three realms, were contained in the caravan.

It does not mean that the space inside the caravan was enlarged. The space remained unchanged from its original size. Also, it was not that the world outside of the caravan disappeared, and contained inside the caravan. The world remained unchanged from as it was before. However, the worlds inside and outside of the caravan are such that the inner one is the outer one and the outer one is the inner one, and this and that, and that and this are infinitely superimposed on each other.

The first three realms, called a small world, were contained.

The small chiliocosm, comprising a thousand small worlds, was contained.

The medium chiliocosm, comprising a thousand small chilio-cosms, was contained.

The great chiliocosm, comprising a thousand medium chiliocosms, was contained.

The great trichiliocosm, comprising three thousand great chilio-cosms, was contained.

The small world was filled with one kind of light.

The small chiliocosm was filled with a thousand kinds of lights.

The medium chiliocosm was filled with a million kinds of lights.

The great chiliocosm was filled with a billion kinds of lights.

The great trichiliocosm was filled with three trillion kinds of lights.

The inside and outside of the small world were infinitely super-imposed.

The inside and outside of the small chiliocosm were infinitely superimposed.

The inside and outside of the medium chiliocosm were infinitely superimposed.

The inside and outside of the great chiliocosm were infinitely superimposed.

The inside and outside of the great trichiliocosm were infinitely superimposed.

The lights inside and outside of the small world were infinitely superimposed. The lights inside and outside of the small chilio-cosm were infinitely superimposed. The lights inside and outside of the medium chiliocosm were infinitely superimposed.

The lights inside and outside of the great chiliocosm were infinitely superimposed.

The lights inside and outside of the great trichiliocosm were infinitely superimposed.

After a while, the Buddha once again made a circular hand mudra, and there appeared in the caravan an innumerable number of heavenly beings, and many non-human beings such as gandhabbas, kumbhandas, dragons, yakkhas, etc. from the great trichiliocosm, respectfully joining their palms and escorting the Buddha.

In unison, they recited the verses to express their respect to the Buddha and to take refuge in the Three Jewels.

> I take refuge in the most honorable one,
> In the most precious one,
> Who has attained the perfect enlightenment on his own.

They repeated this three times. Listening to the magnificent recitation that filled the sky, the mayor and the citizens of Subbaraka felt a great faith in the Buddhadhamma and a heart-thumping excitement from deep in their hearts.

"Oh, World-Honored One!" the mayor said in a thrilled voice, pulling himself from the overwhelming sensation, "We are deeply touched that you have come to this faraway place and showed us the great sagely powers."

The Buddha silently accepted his words. Once again the Buddha gathered his two hands and made a circular hand mudra. Then, the great trichiliocosm contained in the caravan returned to its original form, and the far-off and mysterious atmosphere was also changed to its usual state.

The mayor and the elders sat in front of the Buddha waiting for the discourse the Buddha was about to give.

The Buddha first blessed them, with a look full of joy, then said, "Citizens of Subbaraka, be always healthy! Be happy any time, any place!"

"Thank you for the words of blessing," said the mayor.

"Mayor, as the Tathagata sees it, this place is beautiful! This place is beautiful!"

"Yes. This area we live in is truly beautiful."

"Mayor, the beauty that the Tathagata sees in Subbaraka is not the beauty that you think it is. It is not the gentle waves rolling in, the picturesque stretch of beach, nor the clear and blue sky, nor the soft sunlight shining all over the place, nor the white, blue and red brick houses with spiky roofs, nor the men with well-nourished face, nor the well-clad ladies. Mayor, the beauty that the Tathagata sees is the beauty of the place where Binggisa is working with his companions. Now it is the place of truth, the place of goodness, the place of beauty, the place of will, the place of dynamics and the place of creation, where people forsaken by the destiny resist the destiny."

"World-Honored One," said the mayor, "You just mentioned destiny."

"Yes, I did."

"But we heard that you expounded not on destiny but on karmic causality," he said.

"That is right. Mayor, sentient beings become pure or contaminated not by the external cause of destiny, but by the internal cause of the law of karmic causality, and therefore the Tathagata teaches on karmic cause and effect. Then, what is destiny and what is karmic causality? Mayor and citizens of Subbaraka, the words destiny and karmic causality all mean, from the standpoint of an individual that is distinct from the world and others, a force applied by the world toward the self. And the word *destiny* is used to mean that the force is approaching regardless of the will or action of an individual, while the word *karmic causality* is used to mean that the force follows as a result of one's will or action.

"Between the two, the Tathagata expounds on the latter more often, and whenever there is a chance, the Tathagata teaches, 'There is the law of karma and causality. Sentient beings make good or evil karma, and the retribution comes to sentient beings as happiness or suffering.'

"It means that sentient beings can do virtuous deeds or evil deeds at their own will—namely this is a teaching based on the fact that sentient beings have the freedom to act on their own free will. However, the Tathagata also teaches that 'all dhammas[54] are rela-

---

54 All Dhammas (sabbe dhamma): The smallest unit of substance that forms the universe. But it cannot be called a substance or a non-substance, and it is a substance that is not a substance (emptiness). This is a Buddhist doctrine that corresponds to the natural science explaining that the smallest material unit is a particle on the one hand but a wave on the other hand, and the *Heart Sutra* explains this as "form is emptiness, and emptiness is form, and the same is true of all mental elements."

tive, and as they are relative, they are interdependent and mutually causative, and as they are interdependent and mutually causative, and therefore, any view biased toward one of the two relative sides must be thrown away, and we must achieve harmony on the Middle Way away from the two extremes.'

"Figuratively speaking, when a black cow and a white cow are tied to one rope, one can say either the black cow is tied to the white cow, or the white cow is tied to the black cow. Yet, sentient beings with lack of wisdom lean to one side of the two views. The view that to the black cow of I, self, the white cow of the world, other persons or other things, is tied is a view biased to this side of the relative two, and the view that to the white cow of the god presiding the world, the black cow of I is tied is a view biased to that side of the relative two.

"Mayor and citizens, the Tathagata critically explored and correctly practiced these two views, and finally arrived at the most outstanding wisdom of the Middle Way. With that wisdom, the Tathagata teaches that by either one of the two extreme views, arguments cannot be reconciled, nor sufferings resolved, nor afflictions annihilated.

"Therefore, everyone who wants to be wise must rationally understand the Middle Way that harmonizes the views of the two sides, and proceed toward it through practical practice. And in the process, one must select one of the two views according to the situation and condition—at times, from the standpoint of I, one must passionately proceed to other persons and other things to improve the situation, and at other times, from the standpoint of other persons and other things, one must understand them and accept one's situation.

"From the latter point of view, even though a practitioner attained enlightenment, it was because there was, together with his own effort, direct and indirect assistance of other persons and other things. And the reason why sentient beings have suffering is that there was insufficient support from other persons and other things. From this viewpoint, there is room for what the people call destiny to be acknowledged, even though restrictively.

"Therefore, a wise man leads others from two standpoints. On the one hand, he treats them with calm wisdom from a standpoint that emphasizes their individual nature and free will—namely, a standpoint that they are the actors of their actions and producers of karma, and on the other hand, he comforts and encourages them with a compassionate warm heart from a standpoint that they are the victims of destiny.

"This is why the Tathagata told you that 'The beauty the Tathagata sees here now is the beauty of the place where Binggisa works with his companions. That is the place where those who were forsaken by the destiny resist the destiny.' You have to see them not only from the standpoint that they are the actors and producers of karma, but also from the standpoint that they are the victims of destiny."

When the Buddha expounded like this, the mayor of Subbaraka and many of his followers joined palms politely implying their acceptance of the Buddha's teaching.

The Buddha said, "Citizens of Subbaraka, the wisdom and the compassion that the Tathagata just mentioned are the two wheels of the Buddhadhamma. Namely, as a wagon that cannot go forward with only a wheel, the Buddhadhamma also cannot be realized with the wisdom or the compassion only. Therefore, the path of the Buddhadhamma is divided into the path of arhats that centers on wisdom, and the path of bodhisattvas that centers on compassion."

"World-Honored One, please teach us on the path of arhats and that of bodhisattvas so that we can understand them clearly," the mayor requested.

"Dear ones! The path of arhats is a path where one achieves enlightenment first and then with the wisdom obtained thereby edifies sentient beings, and the path of bodhisattvas is a path where one conducts practice of compassion first and then with the merits earned thereby pursues his enlightenment. In other words, when we compare the beginning part of the two paths, the path of arhats is an easier path of learning the Four Noble Truths and practicing the Noble Eightfold Path, while the path of bodhisattvas is a more difficult path where one serves for others for a long period of time while repeating innumerable rebirths. So, by now you will understand that the path of arhats is to walk the lesser path to Buddhahood now, while the path of bodhisattvas is to attain the greater path to Buddhahood in the future."

Mayor, as a practitioner who will become a Buddha in a distant future world, a bodhisattva has to perform ten kinds of perfections over a long period of time. Ten perfections are generosity, morality, renunciation, insight, energy, patience, truthfulness, resolution, loving-kindness, and equanimity, and they are supreme virtues that cannot be fully achieved even by those who possess outstanding religious capacity, let alone those who have ordinary one.

"In other words, one who wants to become a Buddha by practicing ten perfections must cultivate and attain, together with a big compassion toward others, the quality to become a Buddha, without the assistance from teachers, such as the ten powers, the four types of fearlessness and the six exclusive wisdoms of a Buddha, and those who possess this level of religious capacity are very rare.

"Therefore, to his disciples, the Buddha does not recommend the path of bodhisattvas that he had walked in his previous lives, a path not everyone can walk; but recommends the path of arhats, a path everyone can walk. It is because if the Buddha recommends only the path of bodhisattvas, the Buddhist path will become a narrower one that only a minimum number of people can walk.

"Namely, the bodhisattva path is not one to be taken at the recommendation of others, but to be taken when a bodhisattva arouses a great compassion and great vow in themselves that they will help with the suffering of sentient beings. A bodhisattva feels the suffering of others and exerts a great compassion and great vow on his own, before any instructions given by the Buddha. Thus, the Buddha does not particularly teach this bodhisattva, who has the highest religious capacity, but just confirms, acknowledges, and praises the vows he has made.

"However, the Buddha teaches Dhamma to those who have lower religious capacity according to their respective capacity. As a result, those with the most outstanding religious capacity will attain the stage of an arhat, the next one a non-returner, the next one a once-returner, and the next one a stream enterer.

"The rest of the disciples also gain the benefit of the Dhamma attaining the appropriate stage of practice according to their capacity and effort. However, you should know that the reason why they are able to gain a great benefit of Dhamma is that they walked the path of a junior bodhisattva[55] during their numerous previous lives.

"A full bodhisattva accrues merits during his lives after lives. But rather than doing that alone, he more often guides innumerable people and accrues merits together with them. For example, when a full bodhisattva was accruing merits as the leader of a group of five hundred people, he needed to have ten midlevel leaders to assist him, and these were the junior bodhisattvas. These junior bodhisattvas will become disciples of the Buddha when the full bodhisattva attains Buddhahood, and they gain the benefits of the Dhamma based on the merits of the virtuous deeds in their previous lives.

"The ten chief disciples of the Tathagata had assisted him when he was a bodhisattva, in their numerous previous lives, and based on such merits they became the chief disciples of the Tathagata, and in their previous lives, when the bodhisattva was accruing merits with one thousand people, they each led one hundred people.

"And, the other arhat disciples of the Tathagata also accrued great merits assisting the Tathagata when he was a bodhisattva, in their numerous previous lives, and thereby became the arhat disciples of the Tathagata, and in their previous lives, when the bodhisattva was accruing merits with ten thousand people, they led one hundred people each.

"Also, many outstanding disciples of the Tathagata accrued big merits assisting the Tathagata when he was a bodhisattva in their numerous previous lives, thereby becoming the outstanding disciples of the Tathagata, and in their previous lives, when the bodhisattva

---

55 A junior bodhisattva is a new concept proposed by the author.

was accruing merits with a hundred thousand, or one million people, they led a small number of people each.

"Citizens of Subbaraka, the fact that the outstanding disciples of the Tathagata made great merits in their previous lives means that while they are walking the path of arhats in the present life, they walked the path of junior bodhisattvas in their previous lives. Like this, a Buddhist is bound to alternately walk the path of bodhisattvas and that of arhats.

"The two paths start apart at first, but sometimes converge in the middle, and are separated again at times and overlapped at other times, and this does not happen only to this case but this is the way how all things and events of the world arise and cease. In relation thereto, mayor elders! The Tathagata knows that you guided the people of the forward area of Subbaraka to reconcile with the people of the backward area, and your such virtuous deeds constitute on the one hand a part of the Noble Eightfold Path, being the path of arhats, and constitute on the other hand a perfection, being the path of junior bodhisattvas."

"World-Honored One, we did our best to make peace with the people in the backward area, though in a humble measure," shared the mayor.

"Beautiful are your acts of altruism! Great are your acts of altruism!" With this compliment, the Buddha continued to speak. "However, you better move one step further, because your acts of altruism are not exactly same as the perfections of a full bodhisattva, though comparable."

"World-Honored One, how different is our acts of altruism and the perfections of a full bodhisattva?" the mayor asked.

"Mayor and elders, with regards to your virtuous deeds, you are thinking in your heart that *I am now doing virtuous deeds*. But virtuous deeds with that kind of thought are not pure virtuous deeds and accordingly good retribution resulting therefrom is also limited, and you should know that a bodhisattva, when he does virtuous deeds, does not think that *I am now doing virtuous deeds*.

"A full bodhisattva, when he gives something to others, never thinks that he is the one who gives, that there is someone who receives it, nor that there is something that is exchanged between the two. Like this, a full bodhisattva does ten kinds of virtuous deeds, including alms giving, with pure heart, and hence virtuous deeds of a full bodhisattva become a good cause for him to attain enlightenment that extinguishes afflictions in the future world.

"Therefore, you shall think as follows in order to perform purer virtuous deeds:

> That I was born in the forward area of Subbaraka,
> That I was born as a son of a wealthy family,
> That I was born under a refined and loving parents,
> That I was born with a strong healthy body,
> That I was born with beautiful looks,
> That I was born with an extraordinary intelligence,
> That I was able to get a good education,
> That I was able to get the help of good friends,
>
> That I was able to seize a good opportunity,
> That I was able to succeed in business,
> That I was able to climb to a high position,
> That I was able to marry a wife whom I love,
> And that I was able to get good sons and daughters,
> Are all only coincidence.

"And you should further think, *The fact that I was able to rise to the position of a mayor or an elder, and that I could perform the duties well for the citizens are nothing more than I just adding one more flower to the bouquet of flowers that were bestowed to me by the goddess of chance, and therefore I will forget the meritorious deed that my right hand has done, when I am about perform with my left hand.*"

"World-Honored One, as you instructed, we will do our best to make our mind more pure."

The Buddha looked at the citizens with a smile for a moment and said, "Mayor and citizens, you shall go one step further again and think that the people born in the backward area of the city were just compelled to be born there, pushed by the force of blind abusers called coincidence or destiny, and that this is same with respect to all other aspects.

"You should appreciate the meaning of the life of Binggisa, the leader of the people of the backward area, with the same thought, and as you all know, Binggisa carried out big evil deeds that deserve countless hells. But by doing great virtuous deeds that deserve countless lives in heaven, he has, like a moon that escapes the clouds, escaped from the evil path, and by shining bright lights broadly, he is now covering his evil deeds of the past. The Tathagata reveals his virtuous deeds and highly praises them, but does not particularly mention publicly the evil deeds committed by him in the past.

"Mayor and citizens, and all different lives of the great trichiliocosm who are assembled here! The Tathagata again goes one step further from there to say that seeing from the broadest point of view, all evils are bound to turn their directions toward virtue eventually, and therefore it can be said that all evils will ultimately move toward virtues!

"To understand that point, you look how the ignorant evil deeds of Binggisa in the past are reborn as wise and virtuous deeds these days! The example of Binggisa suggests that all human wills are destined to head for virtues in the end, and it again means that all human wills go beyond relative good toward absolute good—in other words, pursue nirvana.

"This means that all wills of human beings, or all the processes up until attaining nirvana, or all living beings as the sum of all such processes, are distinguished from other beings when they play their own musical instruments, but that, when viewed as a whole, a grand symphony is played where all instruments supplement and harmonize with each other."

When the Buddha stated as such, all living beings assembled were deeply impressed, and exclaimed, "Oh, World-Honored One!"

The Buddha's discourse continued: "Mayor and elders, the reason why even evil will eventually head for good is because while the good mind is the unchanging root-mind, the evil mind is a branch-mind. This theory can be confirmed by anyone once who quietly listens to the words of his own mind, and those who have listened to their minds are obliged to learn that evil is wrong and good is right. When the mind dwells in the root-mind, it is peaceful, but when the mind is divided in two upon arising of the branch-mind, the mind will be enveloped by afflictions. To attain peace in our mind we should remove one out of the two divided minds, but while we can remove the branch-mind, we cannot remove the root-mind.

"In this respect, practice means to remove the changing branch-mind and retain the unchanging root-mind. Upon attaining this stage, even though we act as our mind directs, we will never go against the Dhamma.[56] Dear ones, this is our true mind that is originally as it is, and liberated mind. Therefore, with your aim at such sublime stage, you shall make meritorious deeds you are doing even more pure, and thereby improve them to untainted meritorious deeds."

Having said up to here, the Buddha fell into a silence.

---

56 From the chapter "Politics" in *The Analects of Confucius.*

CHAPTER 40
Buddha Speaks
of the Prodigal Son

The Buddha continued by extending his discourse to the heavenly beings.

"Innumerable beings that have gathered here! I will now offer a discourse on the parable of the bodhisattva and two sons.[57]

"In one of his previous lives, Shakyamuni Buddha was a bodhisattva named Maddiya, who led a life of a millionaire. Maddiya, the millionaire, had two sons and the elder son was Mahapanna and the younger son was Culasiddha. Mahapanna was well mannered with noble character, and he fulfilled his father's wish from a young age and diligently assisted his father's business when he grew up.

"Contrary to this, Culasiddha, the younger son, had been nothing but trouble from his youth, and when he grew up, he wanted to move away and start a business of his own. Maddiya therefore gave the younger son his share of the estate.

---

57 This story was recreated by the author based on the parable of the prodigal son (Luke 15: 11–32) and the concept of bodhisattva from Buddhist philosophy.

"With his portion of the inheritance, Culasiddha traveled to a distant country. He did not create his own business, however. With the character that gave in easily to temptation, Culasiddha was pulled further into a lifestyle of pleasure as soon as he distanced himself away from his father, who used to give him somewhat of control. Thus, he spent his years on drinking and gambling, squandering away all his inheritance.

"When he turned desperately poor, all those who came to him during the prime of his life, who called him brother or a friend, turned their back on him. With no one else to turn to, he hired himself out as a servant at a stranger's house.

"His body was tossed and turned in the pig feces, and his mind wandered in darkness and self-pity, sighing in lamentation and resentment, and shedding tears. Then, one day a thought came across Culasiddha's mind: *If I am bound to be a servant, then I'd rather return home to become my father's. At least I have fond memories of love my father had shown me. Even if I were wallowed up in grief and sorrow, I could think back to those great memories and summon up the courage to go on.*

"Filled with these ideas, Culasiddha left and set out toward his hometown. Maddiya received news from a random traveler that his son was returning home. Hearing the news, the father rushed out toward the path where his younger son was coming from.

"Soon enough, blood gushed out from the feet of Maddiya as he had left home barefooted in such a hurry. Delighted with the thought that his younger son, that he had been worried sick over, was returning home, Maddiya rushed out while forgetting to put on his shoes and forgetting that he could have used a wagon he had owned.

"The son then saw his father from far waving his hands and rushing toward to greet him. Moved deeply in his heart, Culasiddha fell to his knees and bowed down to his father.

"'Father, I am not worthy to be called your son. I will be honored just to become your lowermost subordinate. Please accept me as your hired servant!' He then began to wail while holding on to his father's two feet where blood was still gushing out, but the father grabbed his son's hands and raised him up from the ground.

"'How could I keep you as my servant? Son, you shall be comforted rather than scolded; I will invite the villagers and throw a great feast to celebrate your return!' At that moment, Maddiya's servants arrived at the scene while carrying myriad objects on a carriage. The father washed his son, dressed him good clothes, and fed him delightful food. Then, he headed back to his home, riding the carriage with his son.

"About this time, Mahapanna, the elder son, was in the field grazing the sheep. Someone relayed the news that his younger brother had returned and their father was throwing a great feast to celebrate. Greatly enraged, Mahapanna said, 'For the past ten years I have served father. Yet, he never threw a single feast for me. How could he hold a celebration for this son of his, who has done nothing for him?'

"After some time the elder son came home, and the father said to him, 'Dear son, your brother has returned! Let us invite the villagers and throw a great feast for him!'

"The elder son said in protest, 'Father, I willingly carried out all sorts of difficult work for you for the last decade. On the contrary, Culasiddha left home and we have heard only disconcerting news of him since then. Not even once you offered a feast for me, yet you want to invite and celebrate with the villagers for the sake of that son of yours, who returned home with shame and dishonor. Your actions are difficult for me to take in with delight.'

"The father then said to the elder son, 'It doesn't seem very fitting to compare you and your brother's situation side by side. You were alive and well all this time, yet your brother was considered dead but came back alive. So, how could I not be happy for that son of mine?'

"'I do not understand what you say. Father, the way you treat me and my brother is like leaving behind ninety-nine sheep in search of one that went astray. Father, you may go and search for that one sheep, but you will lose the other ninety-nine.'[58]

---

58 The story is a citation from the New Testament (Matthew 18).

"In response to these words from the elder son, the father embraced the younger son sitting on his left and said with joy, 'That is right, even if I lose the other ninety-nine sheep, I will do everything in my power to seek out that one lost sheep.'

"'Oh, Father! Your words are rather irrational, as ninety-nine is much greater in number, while one is so very trivial.'

"'That's right. My words may seem unreasonable.' The father loosened up his embrace from the younger son. He then gracefully gazed into the eyes of the elder son and said, 'Son, put aside your objective and rational perspective for a moment. What you need right now is to see your brother in more subjective and existential view.'

"After this brief introduction, the father told the elder son Mahapanna the following for him to better apprehend the situation: 'My Son, you suffered from severe fever just a few months back.'

"'Yes, father.'

"'I also suffered from that same fever last year.'

"'Yes, that's right.'

"'Now, look back to those two situations and answer me. Think about the fever and pain that I suffered last year and compare that to what you have suffered this year. Which felt more painful to you?'

"'Father, I'm sorry to say that those two are distinctively different, enough to be called incomparable, in fact. Seeing you in such a great pain was quite agonizing when I nursed you the year before. But it was not distressing enough for me not to be able to collect myself. However, everything changed when I became sick. During that time, I couldn't see nor hear anything, and it was impossible to keep my mind straight! Father! I never want to be reminded of that fever gain! Just the thought of it brings sweats on my forehead!'

"The father waited for a moment for his elder son to calm down and said, 'Son, you are a virtuous, earnest, and competent man.'

"'Yes, I am always striving to become a virtuous, earnest, and competent person.'

"'Then, with that virtuousness, earnestness, and competence, do you believe that you will be able to solve all life's problem that you may face in the future, or will there be times of discouragement and failure?'

"'The complexity of life is impossible for me to predict within my capacities, but I believe I will face frustrations and failures.'

"'If so, you will then experience the same bodily fever that you had this year within your heart.'

"'Father, but I do not wish to experience such heartache.'

"'But son, life will not allow you that wish, and someday you will suffer from the same kind of feverish sickness.'

"'Oh, Father! Why are you calling down such a curse on me?'

"'I am not calling down a curse, but explaining the true state of life. My son, I too was a virtuous, earnest, and competent man when I was young. But I made a great fortune of today through countless frustrations and failures. In fact, there is not a living soul who has not suffered from frustrations and failures.'

"'Then, father, how should I deal with this problem in the future?'

"'What you need is someone who could truly understand your frustrations and failures. Someone who feels your pain with sincerity, cries for you wholeheartedly and comforts you genuinely.'

"'Father, where and how could I find such a person?'

"'But son, if you are truly a virtuous, earnest, and competent person, before you try to find someone to console and comfort you, you must become that someone to help others first. You should cultivate your mind to become such a person.'

"'Father, how can I cultivate my mind to better understand others' frustrations and failures to feel their pain with sincerity, cry for them wholeheartedly, and comfort them genuinely?'

"'Emphasize with their heart and put yourself in their shoes. Remind yourself of your sickness from this year and see the person suffering from frustrations and failures with the same kind of pain. Hence, you should embrace him and cry your hearts out in pain. He will then become your friend and brother because you possess the mind that could put yourself in someone else's shoes. Having you as a friend and brother, who shares his pain and sorrow, will allow him to rest his weary body and mind on you.'

"'Yes, that may be right.'

"'My son, you must take a step further and reconsider. There may be many frustrations and failures coming in the future, but not all of them can be attributed to your own deeds. Success and failures can be the consequences of your own action. But on the other hand, things also occur by chance, and influenced by other external circumstances. In this case, many competent people often take credit for their success and believe that their own competence has led them to success while those less competent think their failure is due to chances and blames external forces. However, this is not the right way to think. It is better for the competent to attribute their success externally to other people and conditions, while the less competent accept failures internally as the result of their own deeds.

"'Now, son, let's say there is a man who has failed and this is solely due to his own deeds and without any coincidence. He has failed because he tread on the wrong path. Then, let's say that this man sits alone, crying on a filthy alleyway where people are scarce and repents his own mistake. Would he then want someone to scold him or approach him with an open arm filled with empathy, weep for his sake, and comfort him?'

"'He would hope somebody who understands him would come to empathize with him, weeps, and comforts him.'

"'Then could you reach out to such a person with empathy, and feel his pain, weep for him, and comfort him?'

"'It's not that I can't do that, but it would be difficult for me to be truly genuine.'

"'Why is that?'

"'That's because the consequences of his frustrations and failures are due to his own deeds.'

"'If so, let's say there was an earthquake and your house collapsed. Or perhaps you got injured in an accident or some unforeseen national crisis caused the value of currency to fall substantially. If such unexpected misfortune ensues, well beyond your ability to handle, you may feel devastated by these failures, which may lead you to have the same kind of feverish sickness you experienced this year. Then, could you say for certain that you will continue to walk on the right path? That you wouldn't become like the man on the alley who tread the wrong path?'

"The son then enquired back to his father, 'Father, a while ago you gave an example of a man who had failed, and that his failure was due solely to his own deeds. But now you give another example in which some extremely adverse situations hit me. However, those adverse situations were not instigated by me. In other words, you are applying the misfortune from external causes to me, which you did not apply to the man who had failed.'

"'Yes, that's right. But son, have I not told you already? A person who succeeded should attribute his success to external causes, while a person who failed should accept the results as his internal attributes. I am telling you this because I see you as a person who thinks success and failure are the result of your own deeds. For you are a man of great virtue, honor, and that much of a great being.'

"'Oh, Father, I don't know if I am such a great person now, but it's undeniable that I wish to become such a person.'

"'Then, my son, I will ask you once again. Son, let's say an adverse condition that exceeds your limitation occurred unexpectedly and you feel devastated by these failures, which leads you to the same kind of feverish sickness you experienced this year. Could you say for certain that you will continue to walk on the right path? That you wouldn't become like the man in the alley who tread on the wrong path?' When the father tossed the question once again, the elder son closed his eyes and turned into his heart. After a while, the elder son spoke to his father with a gloomy expression.

"'Father, I was confident I had been leading a proper and virtuous life, but there is no guarantee that I could direct my mind appropriately in such adverse conditions to lead a proper and virtuous life.'

"'Then, what have you learned from our conversations thus far"?'

Then the father allowed the elder son more time to reflect. The elder son closed his eyes again and contemplated further. After a moment, Mahapanna's eyes were filled with tears, which were streaming down his face. The father came up and embraced his son and said, 'My son, any men can fall into the wrong hands when faced with adverse conditions. In that respect, you or just about anyone except saints are not any different in essence from those who tread on the mistaken path. I treated your brother, who had gone astray, with this perspective, rather than blaming your brother for his faults and mistakes. I see the pain he experienced as a result of being a mortal who wishes to survive. All human are subject to frustrations and failures, thus he inevitably experiences sorrow and heartbreak. Son, oh my dear son, you must understand from that perspective. Just as I wouldn't hold him responsible for his mistakes and faults, I will not blame you no matter what wrong you may commit in the future. You will also be forgiven and be comforted by me, just like your brother. Therefore, you can swim freely like a fish in my ocean of forgiveness, and through my sky of condolences you can fly like a bird without any barrier. Through those dips and flights, you will mature into a person who can understand and accept people just like I do.'

"The son responded while weeping, 'Father, why haven't you told me of such a compassionate and wise words before?'

"'That is because time was not ripe yet. With your brother's return at last, the time has come to speak about father's boundless love for his son.'

"'Oh, Father!'

"'Son, my beloved son! The father's true mind as I described before, is the mind of the father that searches out for the one lost sheep while leaving behind the other ninety-nine sheep. When faced with the frustrated and failed, you must leave aside any objective and rational perspective for a while, and help those who feel frustrated, embrace those who feel failed, and console them with a subjective and existential perspective. That is the mind of a bodhisattva.'

"Saying this, the father smiled compassionately toward the elder son. The son then realized the depth of the father's heart in that moment. The son threw himself in his father's embrace and cried his hearts out. The father did not speak a word, but he embraced his son and stroked his back. A mixture of sorrowful sobbing and cry of joy continued for some time. After a while, the elder son felt a soft embrace from behind. Mahapanna wiped away his tears and turned around. The embrace came from his father's younger son and his younger brother.

"'Dear, brother!' His brother's voice was drenched in misery like that of a gutter. The young one wept and said in faltering voice, 'Brother . . . Please take me back . . . Please return as my dependable elder brother and show me sympathy.'

"The elder brother turned and looked at his younger brother. They hugged each other firmly and came as one again, 'Yes! Welcome back, my brother!' said the elder brother.

"A glimpse of relief came across the younger brother's face. Soon, the father sat them down and said to the elder son, 'Son, not a day passed by without worrying over your brother in distress. I was always troubled over when he would change his mind, waiting on him to gain healthier perspective if not tomorrow. Finally, I heard he was returning home with much regret. I was so happy to hear the news that I had lost the sight of all your great effort, and thought only of your younger brother. But now that I have regained proper discernment, I was reminded of all the hard work you have done for me for the past decade. Therefore, I will postpone the feast for your brother for the time being, but instead I will hold a big feast tomorrow in honor of you. I will present your great merits from the past decade and honor you in front of all the people.'

"Then, the elder son bowed before his father and said, 'Thank you for your thoughtful consideration.'

"Then the elder brother added with a big grin, 'Father, all those disappointment and anger are gone now, and my heart feels pure and fresh like the sky cleared out of clouds. Dear father, please throw a feast for me tomorrow, and a feast for the younger brother the day after. Then I would like to throw a great celebration on the third day for you and my younger brother. Dear father, please rejoice that we have restored our brotherhood!'

"Just as discussed, the father offered a feast for his elder son the next day, and also for the younger son on the day after. On the third day, the elder son also threw a great feast for his father and his younger brother."

CHAPTER 41
You Will Become a Buddha in the Future!

At that time, Binggisa was carrying out a housing project in the backward area of the city, but his facial expression, in which sadness had been the main tone, had been replaced by one full of will and purpose. Nevertheless, the highly artistic sad tone of a man who had once been a minstrel did not wholly disappear. Rather, it was revealing itself in a form even more elegantly and nobly refined than before.

Under Binggisa's direction, the faces of the people in the backward area reflected the healthy and energetic will of Binggisa. Their faces shone brightly with the joy that came from having a job that paid as they worked, and the expectation that they would soon have a nice house.

"My friends," said Binggisa, smiling, "You are shedding two drops of sweat while you get a drop of wages."

"No doubt!"

An old man stopped the shovel, smiled and said, "Mr. Binggisa, our friend and leader, our strength and hope, and thus our master! We do not receive a drop of wages for two drops of sweat, and even if we did, we would be just grateful for having a job to do with pride."

"But dear elderly, if you do not stop at this point, you will certainly be working overly hard."

At these remarks of Binggisa, the old man, with a big smile on his face, shouted to the people around him, "All right, folks! Since there is an advice of the master, let us take a break for a while!"

People stood up straightening their back, with their faces smeared with sweat. They gathered in the tents. There were snacks and drinks prepared by their wives and sisters for the hardworking men. After briefly washing their hands, the men filled their hungry stomachs, feeling the eyes of their wives and sisters watching them with happy faces. Then some of them lied down on the ground and fell for a short nap, and others sat together in twos and threes and chatted. Some people discussed with their wives of their domestic affairs, while others held their babies their wives brought in their arms and laughed.

It was then. Someone outside of the tents shouted, "The Buddha is coming! The Buddha is coming!"

At that moment, they got the feeling of their mind being brightened to its core, which they used to feel when someone cried out, "The sun is out, the sun is out," at the end of a long and boring rainy season. To them, the Buddha meant the bright sun that awakened a fundamental, good, joyful, and happy mind.

Everyone rushed out of the tents, and those who had fallen asleep were woken by the fuss and followed. After a while, the people from dozens of tents saw the Buddha and his group coming toward them from afar. The Buddha led the group at the very front in a stately manner like a great lion king, who reaches the top of Mount Sumeru with a single reap, followed by many bhikkhus, including Elder Sariputta, and by the mayor, elders and citizens of Subbaraka who had received the Buddha, and further by many citizens who had waited for the Buddha to arrive and joined the group, carrying various kinds of offerings such as flowers, incenses, etc. in their hands.

Also, those who came out of the tents saw an innumerable number of heavenly beings who tightly packed the air following the Buddha.

The heavenly beings in various white, red, blue, and yellow heavenly clothes, who wore jeweled crowns on their heads, hung necklaces around their necks, held Dhamma-wheels or jars of nectar, or wore jewels or flower ornaments around their waists, were slowly following the Buddha and his group. It was a magnificent scene that they could never see even if they lived tens of thousands lives.

People waited for the Buddha to come near them and made prostrations to show respect. Binggisa also saw the Buddha approaching from afar and threw himself on the ground. In the heart of Binggisa who first saw with his own eyes the noble appearance of the Buddha and, through his unique sensitivity, gained an insight into the profundity of the enlightenment and the depth of the Buddhadhamma contained in his appearance, a strong emotion rushed in like waves. He thought, *Oh, this is the honorable man! It is this one who has accomplished the highest stage of enlightenment throughout heaven and earth!*

He further thought: *Oh! If not the Buddha, who else can show the way to break the chain of endless reincarnation—the long chain of rebirths marked by frustrations, failures, lamentations, sighs, pains, and tears of sentient beings? Thus, the teachings taught by the Buddha are the beginning and the end of meaning, the beginning and the end of value, and the Buddhadhamma is the truth itself. Therefore, I will surrender all I have for the Buddha who teaches the highest perfect law, and for the Buddhadhamma! I will do everything I can!*

Thinking like this, Binggisa took off his shirt that was soaked with sweat and covered the uneven part of the ground that has not yet been finished. But the next moment, the horrible evil acts that he had committed in the past sprang to his mind. So his only eye was filled with tears. He closed his eye and mouth tight and held back his tears. At that time, the steps of the Buddha reached before Binggisa. Binggisa saw the two dirtied feet stopped side by side before him. He wiped the dirt on the two feet of the Buddha with his two hands.

"Dear, Binggisa!" the Buddha said to Binggisa. "You are wiping the dust on the Tathagata's feet, as if a practitioner wipes the dust on his mind."

At this point, Binggisa could not look up at the Buddha. It was because he knew that the sins committed by him in the past, out of his foolish thoughts were too thick and deep for him to look up straight at the most noble Buddha. There was silence. Human beings, heavenly beings were all watching the Buddha and Binggisa. And at last, the tears that had stopped for a while swelled again in the eye of Binggisa. They were the tears from his blinded eye—the eye that caused cravings as it had been covered by delusion, the eye that induced well-earned sufferings, and they were the water shed by the eye, which was flowing from the depth of the sea of karma.

The sea of karma!

The sea of delusion, the sea of cravings!

Therefore, the sea of suffering, the sea of afflictions!

Binggisa lifted his face at last. Tears flowed from both of his open and closed eyes! They were even more shameful tears to shed before the Buddha who is wholly truthful, wholly good, and wholly beautiful, because they were tears from the sons and daughters of evil karmas, and of the remorseful self-condemnation and shame that could make one pull one's hairs out.

"Oh! Honorable master who is the embodiment of perfect truth, goodness and beauty!" Binggisa said, looking up at the Buddha, "I cannot fully express in words, this aching heart of mine!"

The Buddha did not answer, but just watched him quietly. There was a silence again. Binggisa, who had fallen to the bottom of the realms of Hell, Hungry Ghost, Asura, and Animal, looked up, and the Buddha, who had ascended to the highest heaven and even transcended it, looked down quietly.

After a while, slowly, a bright light began to return to the face of Binggisa while he was looking up at the Buddha, and it was because Binggisa's long past karma has ceased, thanks to the meeting with the Buddha in person. The Buddha smiled gently. The smile flashed into the mind of Binggisa like a morning sunlight heralding the end of a rainy season, and Binggisa too smiled for a moment in the sunlight.

"World-Honored One!" said Binggisa. "The supreme master throughout heaven and earth! You know well how much sinful time I have spent!"

"Yes, I do."

"If so, World-Honored One, then, how can I open the dimly-lit dawn, and meet with it?"

At Binggisa's question, the Buddha said, with a happy look spreading slowly in his face like a rosy morning glow, "Dear Binggisa, the morning sun shines only on the eastern mountains, and the evening sun shines only on the western mountains, but the midday sun shines on all mountains. Binggisa, do you understand this metaphor?"

"Yes, I understand it, the morning and evening sun mean the arhat disciples of the Buddha, and the midday sun means the Buddha."

"There is a well that dries up once you draw a pot of water, while there is one that never dries up no matter how often you draw water. Binggisa, do you understand this metaphor?"

"Yes, I understand it. The well that dries up upon drawing a pot of water means the wisdom of the arhat disciples of the Buddha, and the well that never dries up no matter how often water is drawn means the wisdom of the Buddha."

"Binggisa, there are reasons for the two wisdoms being so different, do you guess what they are?"

"Yes, it is because the source of the former well is shallow and short, while that of the latter is deep and long, and the reason why the wisdoms of the arhats and the Buddha are so different is that while arhats made little merits in their previous lives, the Buddha made immeasurable merits in his previous lives."

"That's correct, Binggisa!" The Buddha said in a meaningful voice, "You shall appreciate for a while the words that the Tathagata has just uttered."

So Binggisa thought to himself: *Oh! I am a man of great sins, a man for whom one hundred thousand hells are waiting. Hence, I once lived with a grave sense of shame, sighed heavy sighs, wailed pounding the ground with the fist, plucked at the clothes and twisted, banged my*

head against a tree and threw my body against a rock, and climbed on
a cliff and threw myself into a deep river. Through those experiences,
I know now what I did not know before, because I have learned the
teachings of a noble wise woman named Ayutha that she showed me
by her actions. Yes, the thing which sinful sentient beings need the
most is comfort. They need a man who, as Ayutha did, approaches
them with an empty mind without any expectation or desire, who
listens to their pains, and embraces their foolishness and cries for
them, that is, considers them as the victim of destiny.

Binggisa thought further: *And now there are two roads before me.*
One is, like the Buddha's bhikkhu disciples, to renounce the world
to be a monk under the Buddha and become an arhat, and the other
is, to live through many lives as a bodhisattva who wipes the tears
of others, and then by the merits thereby earned become a Buddha!

As he thought this, a mind far bigger than Mount Sumeru arose
wildly in the midst of his heart, which was the mixture of a mind of
love for Ayutha who had to languish in agony because of him and a
mind of self-reproach for Bhaddiya who had been his good companion,
a mind that he should expiate for the innumerable deaths caused by
him, and a mind that he should attain a liberation free from love, hate,
attachment, or affliction, and so on. He gathered the minds into one
and firmly resolved.

"Oh! I will walk the path of bodhisattvas for numerous lives to come!
For the long period of time, my love for others will not be one for
reward, and further, I will love all sentient beings without any dis-
crimination! I will love the good one because he is good, love the
sinful one because he is sinful, love the clean one because he is clean,
and love the dirty one because he is dirty! Then at the end of it, in a
distant future world, I will become a Buddha possessing all the ten
powers, the four types of fearlessness and the six exclusive wisdoms
of a Buddha! Then, in the middle of the world of sentient beings, I
will build my Buddha Land, and in the Buddha Land, those who fail
will succeed at the end of the failure, those who are frustrated will
rise from such frustration, those who shed tears will laugh after the

tears, those who sigh will change the sigh into a song, those who are sick or old will have the strength to overcome such sickness or aging, and those who are worried or afflicted will be free from such worries or afflictions! So they will be freed from the yoke of the long and distant transmigration which it is rather insufficient to count by hundreds of millions of eons!"

After taking vows like this, he looked up at the Buddha and asked, "Once I fell in the pit of evil, and I was late realizing that my mind was covered with the dust of delusion. Then I rose high from the dust of delusion and came here with a mind that does not want life but loves life, a mind that loves life but does not want life. World-Honored One, you know well what kind of vows I have just taken."

"That is right, I know the vows you have taken."

"Then, World-Honored One," asked Binggisa, "shall the vows I have taken be realized in the end?"

The Buddha looked back at those who followed him, and said, "Dear ones, please look at this man."[59]

"Yes, World-Honored One, we are looking at him."

The Buddha gazed down at Binggisa with his two eyes that were clear and blue like opening a window made of jewels, and gave a prediction magnificently: "Dear ones, this man, Binggisa has vowed to take the pains of the sentient beings in his bosom for many lives to come. As the Tathagata sees with the unsurpassable wisdom possessed only by a Buddha, his vow will be finally realized, and after a hundred thousand great kalpas from now, he will become a Buddha who has attained the unsurpassed perfect enlightenment, and possesses the ten powers, the four types of fearlessness and the six exclusive wisdoms of a Buddha!

"Then, in the midst of the world of sentient beings, he will build his Buddha Land, and in the Buddha Land, those who fail will succeed at the end of the failure, those who are frustrated will rise from such frustration, those who shed tears will laugh after the tears, those

---

59 Chapter 19, Gospel of John, New Testament.

who sigh will change the sigh into a song, those who are sick or old will have the strength to overcome such sickness or aging, and those who are worried or afflicted will be free from such worries or afflictions! So they will be freed from the yoke of the long and distant transmigration, which it is rather insufficient to count by hundreds of millions of kalpas!"

When the Buddha gave this prediction, Binggisa's heart was filled with joyful spirits like a lake shining with tiny waves, or a diamond sparkling purely. For a moment, a silence that seemed to have stopped the time quietly fell, just like a sunshade coming down. In that silence the uncountable number of heavenly beings who had been escorting the Buddha noticed belatedly what was happening in front of them. So from their mouths, came an exclamation that resonated in the sky.

"Oh!" they all proclaimed. Even though the sound of the exclamation made by each deva or heavenly being was low and small, as it was made by too many of them, it became tremendous as if ten thousand thunders rumbled at the same time. And again, a sound like one million thunders resonated in the air, as all heavenly beings shouted out loud "Excellent! Excellent! Excellent!" The majestic sound spread all over the great trichiliocosm.

The sound of praise echoed repeatedly as if it was shouted toward inside of a large rocky cave. The king of Tavatimsa Heaven, Sakka, waited for the echoes to subdue as if the ripples on the surface of a lake settled down, and quietly sent a look to King Dhrtarastra in charge of the eastern quarter of the universe, being one of the Four Heavenly Kings surrounding the four corners and protecting the congregation. King Dhrtarastra began to play a heavenly sitar in his hand. A subtle heavenly music, which no one can hear in the human world, flowed from the sound box of the string instrument made of heavenly wood and thus having deep resonance. In response to the tune, one hundred thousand gandhabbas staying in the air surrounding King Dhrtarastra played various instruments and praised the Buddhadhamma by singing and dancing. They flew down like butterflies, fluttering their beautiful heavenly cloths.

Then, King Virudhaka, who is in charge of the south, led two hundred thousand kumbhandas, being his dependents and came down scattering splendidly various kinds of jewels available in the human world such as gold, silver, coral, pearl, ruby, diamond, etc., and other jewels which were available only in the heaven. The jewels rose up into the air, forming a huge fountain, and flew slowly down, like autumn leaves in a windless day. After a while, by the big hand signal of King Virudhaka, the jewels broke into pieces and turned into thirty-seven colored clouds and rose up into the sky.

Three hundred thousand dragons and forty thousand yakkhas descended from heaven and praised the greatness and truthfulness of the Buddhadhamma with their unique finesses. Under the direction of King Virupaksa, who was in charge of the west, the dragons spouting water out of their mouths and produced numerous large and small fountains colored with rainbows of different colors, and the forty thousand yakkhas, out of joy from attending the Dhamma assembly, under the direction of King Vaisravana, praised the greatness of the Buddhadhamma, by means of sprinkling flowers, dancing, singing, hugging one another, and doing summersaults, together with gandhabbas, kumbhandas, and dragons.

CHAPTER 42
Sadhu! Sadhu! Sadhu!

The Buddha waited quietly for the four heavenly kings and their retinues to complete their praise of Buddhadhamma. When they finally returned back to their respective places after their praise, the Buddha bent forward and held Binggisa's hands and raised him up. Thus, the great holy man of the present and the great holy man to be, stood side by side facing each other. Then, the present Buddha smiled and said to the future Buddha, "Dear bodhisattva, do you not agree with my prediction?"

"The World-Honored One, I think I know what you are referring to. The World-Honored One is indicating that I have my one eye closed."

"Thus, it is not appropriate for a bodhisattva to possess a physical imperfection."

In saying this, the Buddha turned and looked at Bhaddiya. The Elder Bhaddiya, who stood a short distance away from the Buddha, came forward. Binggisa took a couple of steps aside from the Buddha and welcomed Bhaddiya. The two stood at some distance apart and gazed into each other's eyes silently.

After a while Binggisa said, "The venerable who has reached the innermost level of Buddhadhamma! Thus, without a hint of distress, you can simply refer me as 'once my enemy.' In that long time past, my mind's eye was already blind before you stabbed it. When you gouged my physical eye, it was slaying in vain of what was already a lifeless eye. But I was very imprudent back then and I could not accept the outcome of such obvious karma owed to my own deeds. As a result, subsequent to losing my physical eye, my wisdom eye also closed. Thus, I put a forest of swords on numerous people, creating such grave karmic debt never to be repaid even after countless eons.

"And now, for the sake of embodying the Buddhadhamma, which may discontinue at times but never to disappear completely, I, Binggisa walked toward the brilliant light from darkness. So, I now stand in front of you under this very pure and noble supreme truth, without any love or grudge left in me. Thus, please dear sage, shone your light upon me through the brightness of sun, which does not discriminate what is pure from impure!"

"Venerable one who was once my greatest shining light, but swallowed me whole with the darkness of shadow," said Elder Bhaddiya. "But I know now that shadow means just an absence of light, and thus, shadow is simply an illusion without any substantial reality. By clearly realizing this now, I stand in the midst of this illuminating light, without even a glimpse of the shadow left in me. I am grateful to the Buddha and Dhamma for enabling me to express it to you in person. My dear friend Binggisa! The Buddha of future, who will become father of all sentient beings in the future! Now that you finished illumination with your wisdom eye in the mind, dear Bodhisattva, you should rightfully open your physical eye that was blind till now. Bodhisattva, with your eyes of mind and body, please see the immeasurable frustrations and failures, sighs and lamentations, and pains and tears of sentient beings . . . please see them all, recognize them all, understand them all, and comfort them thoroughly."

By saying this, Bhaddiya took a step closer to Binggisa the Bodhisattva. Then Binggisa took off the eye patch that covered his eye, and Elder Bhaddiya stroked Binggisa's closed eye. Then, through the mystical power of Elder Bhaddiya, the bodhisattva's sight was restored immediately back to its original state.

"Dear holy man!" said Bodhisattva Binggisa and smiled at Elder Bhaddiya with both of his double lid eyes, shining with intelligence. "I wouldn't try to thank you in particular. But rather, I'd like to make a beautiful avarice to ask for another blessing on top of the great blessing I already received in regaining my eye sight. Dear Holy One, who have already provided me with a new eye! Please add a flower on top of what you have presented me!"

"But dear Bodhisattva," laughed Elder Bhaddiya who added, "the Buddha stands beside me now, while holding flowers to congratulate you with. So, how could I dare to take the first position of glory in congratulating the future Buddha to be?"

And what the Elder Bhaddiya said was in fact true. The Buddha stood with flowers in his hands, waiting for them to finish their conversation. After waiting for Bhaddiya to take a step back, the Buddha handed flowers over to Binggisa to congratulate him in realizing the level of bodhisattva. Then in following succession, numerous bhikkhus including the great Elder Sariputta moved forward and offered flowers to congratulate the Bodhisattva. Then, all citizens, including the mayor of Subbaraka, gave various offerings and praises for the future attainment of the bodhisattva.

While everyone was presenting offerings and giving praises to the Bodhisattva Binggisa, seven thousand layers of rainbows appeared in the sky, eight hundred thousand garudas[60] flew up to the sky, and ten million udumbaras and one billion white, red, and blue lotus flowers blossomed.

The udumbaras and lotus flowers were not the only kind of flowers that blossomed up in the sky. Millions of different flowers seen in the Human Realm and ten billion flowers seen only in the heavenly world bloomed successively. Countless heavenly beings, who stood

---

60 Garuda is an Indian mythic bird with golden wings which spews fire from the mouth and feeds on dragons.

densely in the air, picked up a flower that blossomed up in the sky in front of them and tossed it toward the Bodhisattva Binggisa. Innumerable flowers, some in buds and others in petals, fluttered away through the sky and began to shower down. These flowers turned into red jades, or rubies, or sapphires, or jades, or pearls, or corals, or diamonds.

As they descended from the sky, they crumbled into fine powders, forming a great mist of clouds. Various fragrances scattered softly amongst these shower of flowers that were falling in the climax of extravagant luxury and grandeur and amongst the misty cloud of jewels. Then, in the next moment, blasting of sounds—heavenly music played by numerous gandhabbas, which stood guard for devas and heavenly beings, resumed, followed by praises from kumbhandas, dragons, and yakkhas. The sound of gandhabbas music echoed throughout the end of the three realms, and then returned back to Binggisa along with the scents of flowers.

"Sadhu! Sadhu! Sadhu!"

Then everyone gave praise to the future attainment of Bodhisattva Binggisa. A great earthquake that shook heaven and earth befell. It was not an earthquake triggered naturally, but earthquake originating from the sound that praised the eternity and infinity of Buddhadhamma, offered by countless heavenly beings, which reached the end of the great trichiliocosm and came back.

However, the location, where the real earthquake occurred, from which the kind of infinitesimal strength, which could shake up the great trichiliocosm, arose, was in fact within the heart of Bodhisattva Binggisa. This earthquake was an earthquake of great determination, the earthquake of greatest love that aspires for the happiness of all beings, and the earthquake of great compassion. It was the earthquake of Buddhadhamma, and the earthquake of great light.

EPILOGUE
Like the Reddening Eastern Sky at Dawn

After a while, the Buddha sent all his bhikkhu disciples, except for Ananda, back to their respective places. The Buddha then walked one third of a yojana away from where Binggisa stayed, and rested with Ananda beneath the shades of sandalwood, bursting with tagara and jasmine blossoms nearby.

At that moment Raja and Sirima appeared before the Buddha.

"World-Honored One. We are grateful for your guidance until now." Raja said to the Buddha. "But we must be on our way now."

"Tathagata's special disciples! Which path do you wish to go from now?"

"At this point . . ." said Raja, with his eyes glittering with tears. "At this point, we are reminded again of the fact that all beings exist as particulars. Therefore, we realized through the teachings received thus far, that we as a married couple would need to go separate ways in our future lives. For me, Raja, the arhatship would be an appropriate path, while for my wife Sirima, the path of bodhisattva would be right for her. Thus, when our lives in the Tavatimsa Heaven are over, I aspire to be reborn in the Human Realm where the Buddhadhamma is freely propagated to attain arhatship. As for Sirima, she wishes to be reborn wherever Bodhisattva Binggisa will reincarnate, in order for her to be the junior bodhisattva assisting him."

The Buddha asked Sirima, "Dear Sirima, have you decided to live as Raja suggests? As a junior bodhisattva, offering your countless future lives for the sake of others?"

Then, Sirima answered with a serious expression, "That is right, World-Honored One. As your special disciple, I have seen, heard, and thought of various things for the last six months. Therefore, Oh! Most honorable One in the whole universe! The resentment I felt toward my father of two lives ago, who had left me in a pit of despair, is quietly settling down now! Also, from the very core of my mind that had settled down, now arises compassion for all sentient beings that had been violated by the aggressor named fate. For that reason . . . my love toward Raja of Tavatimsa Heaven, the heaven of pleasure, is transforming from the shade of passion into that of compassionate love. But World-Honored One, that is also sad and heart-breaking for me. But I understand that is the only way to move toward the truth of life. Oh, World-Honored One, my love toward Raja is transforming from a private love into that of more open love. Moreover, it is sad and painful, but I accept our love to last only up to this life.

"World-Honored One! I will go to Bodhisattva Binggisa in my next life! Then, I will walk the path of junior bodhisattva with him in many more lives to come! Then, I will wait for him to ultimately become the Buddha and receive teachings from him to attain nirvana!"

With these vows, Sirima and Raja stood, with their backs straightened, facing the Buddha and placed their palms together in a prayer position. The Buddha got up from his seat and blessed the two heavenly beings: "Go, heavenly beings! Go and walk the noble path of your choices. Tathagata blesses your paths with profuse sandalwood scents of moral precepts, tagara scents of meditation, and jasmine scents of wisdom!"

After saying this, the Buddha recited a few verses, summarizing Buddhadhamma for these two heavenly beings:

When danger hits, people
Look up to the noble mountains,
Offer prayers to the far-off sky,
Or call the names of holy God.

However, all of these
Are not the true source of refuge—
You are the only source of refuge for yourselves,
Because your life belongs to you.

To anyone who comes to the Three Jewels
The Three Jewels will present the Four Noble Truths,
The Four Noble Truths will lead them skillfully
To let them save themselves on their own.

The truth of suffering.
The truth of the cause of suffering.
The truth of the cessation of suffering.
The truth of the path to the cessation of suffering.

This is the most sublime refuge,
This is the ultimate refuge,
This is the highest true refuge—
this is the eternal truth!

Walk the path following the Dhamma.
Then all suffering shall end.
Tathagata also followed the Dhamma
And crossed the desert of suffering.
Dear ones, make your own efforts.
Tathagata will only show you the path.

The Buddha is not your master,
But simply your guide to the path.

Arouse most courageous bravery.
Understand the preciousness of your life.
Understand the preciousness of others' lives
And develop compassion toward sentient beings.

Come! Come and be the friends of Tathagata!
Just like the eastern sky turning red at dawn
See the beautiful signs of liberation!
Follow the path that is good in the beginning and also the middle
Shine like the sun without a glimpse of a shadow!

After reciting these verses, the Buddha, a descendant of the Sun Clan, left the two heavenly beings behind and walked toward the Subbaraka Tribe, known as the Ocean Clan, where a great benefactor waits for the Buddha, having arranged a Dhamma seat. The Buddha slowly walked forward like the wind that never gets caught in the net, like lotus flower that never steeps with the dew, and like the lion that never gets startled by lurid sounds.

Acknowledgment of Gratitude

First of all, I offer my gratitude to my late grandfather who helped me cultivate a deep understanding of the spoken and written language of my mother tongue, and who also inspired me to learn the spirit of the holy saints and sacred sages; to my late good-hearted mother whom I strive to emulate; and to my elder sister, Guinam Kim and her husband Haeng-il Park, who supported me most generously in the publishing of my first book.

I am also grateful to all the superb writers who came before me and opened my eyes to the depth and beauty of literature. Of these, I must mention a few. In the East, Li Bai, Du Fu, and Rabindranath Tagore, and in the West, Dante Alighieri, William Shakespeare, Johann Wolfgang von Goethe, Fyodor Mikhailovich Dostoyevsky, and Antoine de Saint-Exupéry.

In addition, I convey my gratitude to the following: the late Chyun-Deuk Pi, an excellent essayist, renowned English literature scholar, and former professor at Seoul National University, for his guidance in unleashing my literary potential; to the late Seok-ghi Yeo, an expert in Shakespeare and former professor at Korea University; to the late Moo Han who had a profound knowledge of French literature and a former professor at Pai Chai University; to Prof. Byungjong Kim of Seoul National University who encouraged my studies in literature and art as a colleague in both; to the wonderful painter and sculptor Soonwoo Moon; to the two pure and honest poets Jeongchoon Seo & Sukjoo Chang; to the marvelous writer of children's stories Sangbae Lee; and lastly, to the talented essayist Taewon Jung.

I'd like to offer my gratitude to Ooghee Jin, who translated this book from Korean to English, and the editors of Mascot Books who worked hard to publish this book in America—including Jess Cohn, Brandon Coward, Rebecca Andersen, and CEO Naren Aryal.

I also express my gratitude to the artist Byeongyong Choi who created the cover picture for the book; to the late Inkyu Lim who published the first edition of this novel in Korean at his Literature of Literature Publishing Co.; to Keunbae Lee, president of the National Academy of Arts of the Republic of Korea who introduced me to Mr. Lim and guided and encouraged me for several years in my early literary career; to Dr. Chan-goo Lee who introduced me to Youn-suk Lee, president of Duck Ju Books, who published the second Korean edition of this novel together with its chief editor Hyang-geum Choi, to both of whom I also owe a debt of gratitude; to the late Kyunghee Cho, former president of the National Academy of Arts of the Republic of Korea who introduced me to Korea's literary circles; to the late Yeonhyun Cho, former Chairman of the Board, Korean Writers Association; and the late Wonsu Lee, president of Children's Literature Society.

I also extend my gratitude to Dohyun Gwon, Abbot of Muryangsa Temple in Hawaii; to Mr. Donald Choi and his wife Mrs. Bo Choi whom my wife and I met when we stayed at that beautiful temple in 2013. These two noble people deeply empathize with and understand the pain and sorrow of others, and they gave me great support, both material and emotional, in writing and publishing this book. I will keep and cherish them in my heart for as long as I live.

I also offer my gratitude to Dahn Master Taehun Gwon whose story was adapted by me into the novel *Dahn: Korean Yoga*, my first successful work, and to Soonhyun Song who published the novel at his Inner World Publishing Co. I also express my friendly gratitude and affection to Hyungkyun Kim who published many of my works at his Eastland Publishing Co.

I also give my gratitude to the late Ven. Daehaeng who helped me much in my journey of Buddhist practice; to Jeyol Lee, president of the Buddhist Scripture Research Institute who helped me in my Buddhist studies; to Ohyun Kwon, abbot of Goshimsa Buddhist Temple; to Sayadaw Ashin Janakabhivamsa at Chanmyay Meditation Center in Yangon, Myanmar, who taught me vipassana meditation; to Ven. Gerhae who cotranslated the Pāli version of *Dhammapada Stories* into Korean with me and helped me better understand the society and monastic community during the Buddha's time, in addition to introducing me to numerous Buddhist anecdotes; to Gunwoo Lee, Myungsoo Cha, Jooyung Jang, Miss Khema, and Younghee Kim, all of whom are my friends in Buddhism and meditation; to Dr. Jae-Seong Cheon and Ven. Bogeom (Dr. Chi-ran Lee), both of whom helped me broaden my understanding of the Pāli suttas; and to Jongmi Kang who meticulously reviewed the Pāli expressions in this novel.

In addition, I'd like to extend my gratitude to Hyongkyu Kim, President of the Buddhist newspaper *Beopbo Sinmun*, its Editor-in-Chief Jaehyong Yi, and its former President Baehyeon Nam.

I have not spent much time in regular schools, but studied many topics on my own without teachers. Still, I have published seventy books, and given special lectures on literature, philosophy, religion, and meditation via television, radio, meditation centers, public institutions, businesses, organizations, and YouTube. My achievements have been recognized by Key-chong Park, President of Mokpo Science University, who gave me the opportunity to teach as a professor there, and I offer him my gratitude too.

Lastly, I want to convey my love and gratitude to Ghain Chung, my kind and warmhearted wife who has stood by me; to her parents and siblings who have consistently supported my writing activities; to my two sons, Seungkyu and Taekyu who have grown to be adults of sound mind; and to Daun Song, my daughter-in-law who has recently joined my family and exudes gentleness and a good heart.

There are many more beautiful karmic associations in my life, and I cannot possibly name them all here. Like spider webs, karmic ties form and expand without end. With humility, I pray that sparkling drops of morning dew form on every intersection of these karmic ties so that their brilliance may radiate out to all people of the world.

About the Author

Born in 1952 in Jangsu-gun, Jeollabuk-do Province, South Korea, Jeong-bin Kim began to release literary works in 1980. In 1985, his novel *Dahn: Korean Yoga* was a #1 bestseller for a year. Since then, he has published seventy books spanning diverse fields such as literature, religion, philosophy, education, and meditation. His novel, *Dahn: Korean Yoga*, has been translated into Japanese, and his *Analects, the Teaching of Confucius* has been translated into Chinese in both China and Taiwan. He did not attend college and is primarily self-taught, but his achievements in writing and meditation are recognized. He also served as chair-professor for a class titled Self-Realization at Mokpo Science University.

Email: jeongbin22@hanmail.net (author) / raykim0422@naver.com (agent)